# My Refuge and Fortress

# My Refuge and Fortress

## Havoc in Wyoming, Part 7

### Millie Copper

Copyright © 2021 CU Publishing
ISBN-13: 978-1-7353101-4-5

Written by Millie Copper

Edited by Ameryn Tucker

Proofread by Light Hand Proofreading

Cover design by Dauntless Cover Design

Original cover design by Kesandra Adams

# Also by Millie Copper

## The Havoc in Wyoming Series

When a series of coordinated attacks devastate the United States, the people of Bakerville, Wyoming, must come together to survive. Unfortunately, not everyone has the town's best interest at heart. Some are striving for personal gain during the apocalypse.

## The Montana Mayhem Series

A group from Bakerville, Wyoming strikes out on their own while searching for the desires of their heart. Unfortunately, the road will not be easy, and sometimes the heart is hardened and deceitful. When things don't work out as they hoped, will they become stranded in the wilderness? Or will each be able to find their way home?

## The Dakota Destruction Series

After a series of coordinated attacks devastate the United States, Katie and Leo sacrifice everything to help their country. But some things aren't as they seem. Is it time to go home and start fresh, or can something good come out of this terrible situation?

## The Lights of the Collapse Series

As martial law descends and society crumbles, families must band together to survive, finding strength in their unity amidst the chaos. But with danger lurking around every corner and the very fabric of reality seeming to unravel, they discover that the greatest threats might be closer than they ever imagined.

## In The October Fall World

In the blink of an eye, an EMP changed everything for Lauren and her family. Now they are in a fight for survival, trying to keep their loved ones alive as society collapses around them. Their once peaceful town of Cody, Wyoming has turned into a powder keg. And with law enforcement a thing of the past, evil lurks around every corner.

## In The As The Light Dies World

Lisa Bentley thought having her daughter attacked and left for dead was the worst thing that could happen. She was wrong. She and her family lived an ideal life operating a bed and breakfast in the perfect Wyoming town. That world came crashing down when her daughter was attacked.

## Nonfiction Books

Millie has penned seven nonfiction, traditional food focused books, sharing how, with a little creativity, anyone can transition to a real foods diet without overwhelming their food budget. Many of her books also include preparedness and food storage tips.

Find these titles at MillieCopper.com

# Join my reader's club!

Receive a complimentary copy of *Wyoming Refuge: A Havoc in Wyoming Prequel*. As part of my reader's club, you'll be the first to know about new releases and specials. I also share info on books I'm reading, preparedness tips, and more. Please sign up on my website:

## MillieCopper.com

# Who's Who

Jake and Mollie Caldwell: A bachelor until age thirty-seven, Jake married Mollie and suddenly became a dad to four girls. A couple of years later they added a son. Malcolm is eleven and is Jake's right-hand man. They've sacrificed for years to build a safe retreat for their children, sons-in-law, grandson, extended family, and close friends. Many times, they thought they were crazy. Now, in a new world full of danger and heartache, they realize their plans weren't enough.

Sarah Garrett: Sarah, Mollie's oldest daughter, married Tate Garrett over five years ago. Sarah discovered she was pregnant early in the havoc. Their son, Tate Keith, was born after Christmas. They recently adopted Marc, Sissy, and Andy after their mom died. Tate's parents, Keith and Lois, and his sister, Karen, were visiting from out of state when the attacks started. Tate and his dad were on a community hunt when they went missing. They haven't been found. Lois passed from natural causes shortly after baby Tate's birth.

Angela and Tim Carpenter: Angela is Mollie's second oldest. She and Tim are parents to Gavin, age three. Tim's dad, Art, reluctantly joined Tim and Angela at the Caldwell homestead. To everyone's surprise, farm life seems to agree with Art.

Calley and Mike Curtis: Calley is Mollie's third born. She married Mike, the boy next door, two years ago. Mike's parents, Roy and Deanne, along with Mike's recently single sister, Sheila Stapleton, escaped Casper for the Caldwell homestead with Calley and Mike. Deanne, along with several others, was murdered during an attempted takeover of Bakerville's legitimate government.

Katie and Leo Burnett: Katie is Mollie's youngest daughter. Before the attacks, she was living away from home while finishing college. After her college town was overrun by people escaping the city, Katie and her then boyfriend Leo Burnett made their way to Bakerville. Leo is a K-State business graduate, construction worker, and Marine. He's now a lieutenant in the Bakerville militia and a member of the elite security team. Katie is part of the medical team.

Alvin and Dodie Caldwell: Jake's parents. They're both in their seventies and fiercely independent. Before the attacks, they lived in nearby Prospect. Prospect has experienced many challenges, including the hospital burning to the ground. Happy to be in Bakerville, Alvin and Dodie now worry about Jake's brother, Robert, and his wife and children living in California. Have they been severely affected by these tragedies?

Doris and Evan Snyder: Neighbors and good friends of the Caldwells. Evan is a retired deputy sheriff, having been part of the county's Specialized Services Division. Evan is a member of the council and leads the elite section of the Bakerville militia referred to as the security team. Always thinking about how to keep Bakerville safe, he was the first to suggest moving to a more defendable location for the winter. Doris is retired from both the Navy and a government job. She always insisted she wasn't a spy or anything. Turns out, that wasn't exactly the truth. Doris's oldest daughter lives in Germany and is assumed safe. Her youngest daughter, recently widowed Lindsey Maverick, lives with the mountain people of Bakerville and is a member of the security team.

Phil and Kelley Hudson: Community members. Mollie considers Kelley one of her closest friends. Phil, retired Coast Guard, is a leader of the community. Kelley is a retired psychiatric nurse practitioner. Her children, Sylvia and Sabrina, arrived in Bakerville with Lindsey Maverick and several others.

Belinda and TJ Bosco: Belinda, a nurse practitioner, is fourth generation Bakerville and related to the founders of the community. TJ is friends with Malcolm. Belinda was recently injured when her mom, Tammy, was killed by mentally ill Lydia. Lydia later took her own life...or did she?

Bill Shane and Aaron and Laurie Ogden: Grandmaster Bill Shane taught martial arts to Jake, Mollie, and Malcolm in nearby Wesley,

Wyoming. Jake invited him to join them at the homestead if the situation deteriorated in Wesley. Bill brought Black Belt and secondary instructor Aaron Ogden as well as Laurie, Aaron's then girlfriend, also a Taekwondo Black Belt, when they escaped Wesley. Along with Evan and Cole Gunderson, Bill is one of the militia leaders.

Ben, Clarice, and Liam Ferguson: Ben, Mollie's former boss, along with his wife, son, and several others, recently arrived from Oregon. Their trip was anything but easy, and all of them are in varying degrees of health. Leanne and her children, who traveled with Ben most of the way, are malnourished and weak. Clarice and Liam, along with Destiny, Leslie, and baby Wyatt, who they met in a small town in Idaho, fared better but still need a time of recovery. Will they be able to return to health before disaster strikes?

June and Sam Mitchellini: After fleeing from their small Wyoming town, they've been hiding out in Bakerville. They and their eight-year-old twins—Abigail and Willie—are now living under assumed names. Chiropractor June is an essential part of the medical team. Before the move to the mountain, retired Navy doctor Sam was shot by an unknown assailant. He succumbed to his injuries several weeks later.

The Cameron and Vasquez Families: Recently escaped from the atrocities being committed in nearby Prospect, the two families and many friends have joined forces with those from Bakerville living on the mountain.

Alina and Victor Quinton: Alina is Sarah's stepmother, having been married to her biological father, Brad. Sarah found out about Brad when he and his family showed up in Bakerville after the havoc began. Brad was part of the insurrectionists who tried to take over the mountain community. He was killed along with most of those attempting the coup d'état.

# Chapter 1

## *Lucy*

"Well, Lucy, I hear everything went just fine."

"Uh, yes." I jump to my feet, immediately regretting my quick reaction. "Yes, sir."

"Please, please. Stay sitting."

I start to nod, then quickly say, "Yes, sir." I've learned he expects formality, even though at times we're way past being formal.

He steps behind me, placing his hands on my shoulders.

I feel myself stiffen.

"Relax. You're much too tense." He kneads my shoulders, then leans close to my ear and whispers, "See? Better already."

I focus on keeping my face calm as I give a slight nod and mutter, "Much better, sir."

He continues kneading for several minutes before saying, "Lieutenant Kruse said she thought this trip may have been too much for you."

"N-no. Not exactly."

"Mm-hmm." His hands move from my shoulders to my biceps. He stops the massaging and gently squeezes my arms. "You performed as expected?"

"I think so, yes."

"Really? Even where the children were concerned?"

I close my eyes and try to block out the screams. I kept expecting one of the children to be Lily, a former student of mine. She lived in Bakerville, and I thought for sure I'd see her there—or see her body. Taking a deep breath, I allow the screaming in my head to be replaced with the boy's face in the second-floor window. He was only eight or nine but was trying to look fierce as he held a toy gun. I pretended I didn't see him, quickly spinning and walking away from the large barn. I couldn't deal with his death on my hands.

1

I take a breath before softly saying, "The children are hard for me. I was a teacher."

"And now you're a soldier. We all must do things we don't like—things we detest, even. But it's the only way. Otherwise, our plans will not be successful and many more will die."

"But couldn't we . . . I was thinking we could bring the children with us. They're still young. We could, um, train them the way we want them to be."

He releases a long breath. "I know you have a good heart—and that's one of the things I like about you, Lucy. But they're tainted. Their parents have already filled their heads with opposition. They had a chance to join us. We went to them in good faith, met with their so-called leader. He laughed in Scott's face, said they were doing fine on their own and they had no interest in sharing their abundance with the good people of Prospect."

"Maybe they could've been convinced?" I ask hesitantly.

He puts pressure on my arms, squeezing them until it hurts. I bite my lip to keep from crying out.

In a rough voice, he says, "You know my mandates. We all work for the good of the county—for the region, even. If they aren't willing to join us, to prove their allegiance, then there's no place for them in Prospector County. They're selfish, thinking only of themselves. How long would people like that be content with what they have? If they're not willing to work with us, eventually they'd be against us. They'd attack us and try to take what we have. You understand this, right?"

"I know this is . . . yes, it's true. I understand."

"Of course you do, Lucy. You're smart and know what's best for our town. No, not just our town. The law-abiding people of our entire county are relying on me to bring us back to a real civilization, where we're not just scraping to survive but where we thrive. Prospect will soon be known as a place of commerce and trade. People will flock to us. If these outliers choose not to be with us, then, frankly, they're against us. When they refuse to contribute for the good of everyone, they're nothing more than traitors—traitors not only to our county but to our country as well."

"But the children!" I cry.

He squeezes my arms until I yelp. "Now, Lucy, you know better than to sass or second guess me. Just because you've been given many

2

special privileges, doesn't mean you can get away with insubordination."

"Y-yes, sir," I whisper.

"I know you have a soft spot for the children. You'll need to sort it out on your own. No more wimping out. You've been put on the acquisition team because you're special to me."

"Yes, sir. Thank you for the privilege."

"Now then, let's put this business behind us and move on to more personal matters."

# Chapter 2

## *Friday, Day 242*

## *Mollie*

I jump at the pounding on the front door.

"What's happening?" my oldest daughter Sarah asks, jerking her head around. Katie rushes to the door, cautiously opening it.

Calley falls in and wraps her in a hug. "It's over! It's over!" Calley says, jumping up and down, dragging Katie with her.

Katie pulls away, looking bewildered.

Still in her snow-laden boots and heavy coat, Calley bounces toward me. "Mom! It's over!"

"What's over?" I ask, smiling at my daughter's excitement.

"We're going to be okay! I heard it on the radio. The president—he's alive and is sending help to people who need it. He's going to have the lights on soon, maybe even before my baby is born. Maybe there will even be a real hospital. For both of us—you can get well!"

"Praise God," Sarah says, grabbing onto her stepmother Alina.

My daughters Angela and Katie are hugging each other, crying.

"Thank you, Jesus," I whisper, pulling Calley into an embrace.

"We will be okay?" Alina asks, her voice questioning yet full of hope.

"We're going to be fine!" Calley answers. "Colonel Shane said to tell everyone. We're going to have a meeting in an hour to talk about it as a group. I'm so glad we no longer have to keep everything we hear on the radio a secret, because this isn't something I'd be able to keep quiet. It's over! It's really over."

Calley grabs on to me again, hugging me just a little too tightly in her excitement.

"You think we'll be able to go home?" Katie asks. "Maybe that's what the meeting is about?"

4

"Maybe," I agree with a nod. "But my guess is we'll stay here until we know it's safe to return home. I can't imagine the announcement about things going back to normal will instantly return people to law-abiding status."

"What you mean by this?" Ukrainian-born Alina asks.

"I mean, we still need to think of our safety. We left Bakerville for a reason, and I'm not sure that reason has changed."

Alina gives a solemn nod. "You think, even with Brad and the others dead, we still have danger." She poses it as a statement, but her eyes hold a question.

Sarah answers in my place, "External threats were our main reason for moving up here. It makes sense we would stay for now."

"Well, if this is so, I should keep with moving my things," Alina says, then turns to me. "Is that good, Mollie? You wish me still to move in with you?"

"Yes, for sure." I reach for her hand.

"Then I go back to packing. We can talk about other bad deeds Brad did another time." She steps toward the coat rack by the door.

"Alina, I'm— " I shake my head. "Thank you for bringing us the things you found. I don't know what it all means, but— "

"It means Brad is what you say he is," she says without turning to look at me. "He is hired killer."

Her frankness is both refreshing and intimidating. While I want to disagree, to say perhaps the evidence she brought means something else, I can't.

"What are you talking about?" Calley asks.

Alina turns to point at the photos and files arranged on the coffee table. "I find things showing Brad hunted down your Dr. Sam. He is the one who shot him."

"Huh?" Calley asks.

"You show her newspaper clippings and things?" Alina asks as she slips on her coat. "I want to get more done before meeting. Thank you again for letting me live in big house with you. It will be good to be part of your family." She gives a rare smile before turning to the door.

As Alina gives a final wave, Angela tells Calley to have a seat so she can look at things. A short time before Calley came busting in with her good news, Alina dropped a bombshell on us. While she was packing things to move out of the tiny house she shared with Brad and

5

their son Victor—Sarah's nine-year-old half-brother—she found some interesting items: newspaper clippings from the school shooting Sam and June Mitchell were involved in.

"Look at this," Angela says. "The people in these articles—he has pictures of them. We think he's the one who killed them. And the sheriff deputy from Groyver, who was killed a few days before the attacks—remember him?"

Calley looks over the newspaper clippings and shrugs. "The deputy was killed in the line of duty, the gym teacher in a car accident, and the school secretary took her own life."

"Well . . . maybe that's the official story. But look—Brad had photographs of all of them, not just newspaper clippings, along with pictures of Sam and June. Who even prints photos? Everything was always digital. Why would he have these?"

Calley's eyes go wide as she shakes her head. "Seems rather . . . unbelievable."

"No kidding," Sarah scoffs. "But it does make sense. He told me he traveled a lot for work. Computers. But he never really struck me as a computer expert. We think he was really a hired killer, and someone sent him to Wyoming to kill those people."

"Why?" Calley asks. "Who would want them dead?"

"Good question. But they were all involved in the school shooting in Groyver. It doesn't make any sense. And— " Sarah stops talking for a minute, seeming to gather her thoughts. "It sounds like a huge conspiracy theory, doesn't it?"

"It sounds like a bunch of bull," Calley says.

"Really?" Angela sneers. "You weren't here when Alina showed us everything. It made sense as she was putting everything out."

"Why else would he have these pictures?" Katie asks.

"Who knows? Brad was a weird dude." Calley meets Sarah's eyes as she says this.

Sarah gives a slight nod and then looks to the ground.

"Besides, what does it matter? Brad's dead. Doctor Sam is dead, and so are the other people in the pictures."

Calley's proclamation puts a bleakness over the room. She's right. Brad is dead, and whatever we think may have happened is nothing more than a theory. And none of it really matters. Those things happened before, when our life was normal.

"I hear what you're saying," Angela says as she gathers up the photos and starts putting them back inside the soft-sided briefcase in which Alina found them. "Besides, the end to all this—the end of the apocalypse—is much more exciting than working on a mystery we'll never be able to solve."

"I thought Brad was here to get help for Victor?" Calley points at Sarah. "Weren't they on their way to Bakerville so you could donate bone marrow or something?"

"Yes," Sarah says. "But they were already here, in eastern Wyoming, when Victor's doctor called and told them the cancer was back and the donation was needed. He'd already contacted Mom by then." She turns to me. "Right?"

"I think so. He'd called me a few times on my work line. The last time I talked to him, I was in Oregon. He said he had business in Wyoming, but according to Alina, they'd been in Wyoming for several weeks before the attacks. I think I talked to him on the day the planes went down, so . . . " I lift my hands. "I don't know."

"So you think," Calley says, "he was in Wyoming working as a hired killer and just thought, 'Hey, I'm in the neighborhood. I'll go talk the daughter I've never met into giving bone marrow to my son.' I don't buy it."

"I would have donated," Sarah bristles. "In a heartbeat."

"That's not what I mean," Calley says softly. "I know you'd help Victor—you'd even donate bone marrow to a stranger if needed. The rest of it . . . that's what doesn't make sense. Why would anyone want to hire someone to kill Sam and the others? What would be the purpose?"

"That's what I've been wondering," Katie says as she again looks at one of the photos, this one of the school's secretary who supposedly committed suicide several days after the shooting at the school.

With a loud sigh, Katie hands the picture to Angela. "Calley's right. We'll probably never know what happened, and there's little reason to speculate. But we should keep these things to give to—well, I don't know who. Maybe the authorities once this is over and our lives return to normal. While we might not be able to solve the mystery of why Brad had these things, someone else may be able to."

"And it doesn't really matter as far as our lives today," Calley says again, driving her point home. "Let's celebrate the president's announcement and not worry about this."

7

The meeting in the dining hall of the ski lodge is just that—a celebration. I'm sad Jake isn't here to join in on the festivities. Jake, along with Evan Snyder and a few others, have gone back to Bakerville proper on a goose hunt. We don't even have a way to contact them with this exciting news. The only ham radio from our community that survived the EMP is on the mountain with us. Our walkie-talkies don't have the range needed to reach from the mountain to the river.

This is their second trip down the mountain to goose hunt. They went a couple of months ago, before Christmas, bringing us home a feast. I suspect, like then, the river people are having their own celebration with our people. Last time they did a culled cow in a pit. Jake talked about the feast for weeks.

Even though I'm missing Jake, I'm swept up in the excitement. With everyone hugging and laughing, it's hard to remember this was a site of murder not long ago. My young children—Malcolm, Tony, and Lily—along with my grandchildren, are all part of the noisy celebration. School was released early today, and the children helped rearrange the furnishings to turn the combination school/dining hall into a meeting room. Although the chairs have been set up to face a pseudo stage, few people are sitting.

"Can you believe it, Mom?" Malcolm asks, with his adopted brother Tony adding, "Isn't it great?"

"I can't believe it. And yes, it most certainly is great," I say.

"Everyone's so happy," my grandson Marc says. "Even happier than they were on Christmas."

"It's better than Christmas," Malcolm answers.

"Will we get gifts?" four-year-old Lily asks.

"It's not Christmas, *Aunt* Lily," Sissy, also four, says. The two girls love the fact they're aunt and niece at the same age. Sissy even gets a bigger kick out of calling Lily *aunt* since she's taller and slightly older. We'll be celebrating her birthday next week, and Lily doesn't turn five until March 31st. I love how they carry on and rib each other over it, though sometimes it does get a little too serious and I have to put a stop to it. They bicker like sisters.

"No gifts today," I say, enveloping her in a hug.

"Too bad Dad's not here," Malcolm says.

As I turn to respond, Phil Hudson calls for the attention of the crowd. "I know we're all pumped about the news," he says in a loud voice. "But let's get settled and we can give the exact details of what's happening, then we'll go back to celebrating."

A cheer goes through the crowd as everyone finds a seat.

After many minutes, Phil says, "Bill, do you want to start?"

Bill Shane, one of the leaders of our security team and militia, steps to the front. "I'll read the actual announcement. It's on a loop and has replayed several times, allowing us to ensure we captured every word."

Bill glances around the room. "My fellow Americans, it is with a full and happy heart I bring you this news. For the last several months, we have been working to restore communication. If you are now hearing my voice, then you can tell we've been successful in our endeavors. While we have been able to communicate with several local groups, this is the first time we've had success using a variety of relays to share the news on an extended scale. You may have heard rumors your government has fallen. These rumors are lies."

"Woo-hoo!" someone yells out, resulting in a spirited round of applause. Then someone starts singing "God Bless America."

Bill smiles and shakes his head, joining in with the song and encouraging us all to get to our feet. As we belt out the words, many voices falter, including mine. I'm completely overcome with emotion.

A rowdier applause happens after the song ends, causing Bill to lift his hands. "Okay, okay. I'm as excited as you are. But let's get through the rest of it."

Phil Hudson lets out a wolf whistle, bringing people to attention.

Bill rubs his ear in jest. "Thanks for that, Phil." He waits several beats as the room quiets, then clears his throat and continues to read. "We're working daily to recover our way of life. In the past few days, under my leadership, we have restored power at my location. This location is our new base of operations after Washington D.C. was destroyed by a nuclear weapon back in June. We will continue working to provide electricity across the United States. The three electromagnetic pulses that took out our power grid— "

"Three?" someone yells out. "There were three EMPs?"

"Seems so," Bill says. "We didn't know until today. There's more chatter on the radio speculating on the fact there was three. We don't know for sure, but the belief is there was one over the middle of the US, one over the eastern states, and another over the west. But we also know parts of the West Coast weren't affected, so . . . " He lifts

9

his hands. "We don't really know much. There's still more from the president. Let me go back to it."

He changes his tone slightly and continues to read the statement. "The three electromagnetic pulses that took out our power grid also affected our neighboring countries to the north and the south. While Canada and Mexico were affected, it was not to the extent of America. They are providing aid as they're able to. We anticipate relief efforts from overseas in the near future. This took some time because of the mass amount of destruction so many of our ports received during the day of the bombs.

"Rest assured, we are doing all we can to reinstate a fully functioning government, and you will soon have your life returned to normal. In the interim, I ask that you remain steadfast. Continue to do what you must to meet your day-to-day needs. We will be providing aid to all areas as soon as humanly possible. The lights will come back on, and these dark days will be but a memory. The United States of America will emerge stronger than before. May God bless you all."

There are several beats of silence as Bill looks around the room, a slight smile covering his face. "That's it. That's all there was."

There's much muttering around the room and many smiles. A small spattering of applause begins again, which soon erupts into whoops and hollers. People are hugging and many are crying. There's also questions as to what will happen in the days to come. While the announcement is wonderful—better than wonderful—the full transcript isn't as encouraging as what Calley shared.

The president did say they're working to restore power, but it sounds rather vague. I glance over at Calley. She's a few chairs down the row from me, sitting next to her husband Mike while holding her nephew Andy on her lap, her small baby bump barely protruding. Her baby will be my second grandchild born since the attacks began. While Sarah and Tate found out they were pregnant in the early days of the havoc, Mike and Calley's child was conceived well into our disaster. There's one other couple in the community also expecting, due the month after Calley.

Our small medical team, now led by nurse practitioners Belinda Bosco and Kelley Hudson, did a wonderful job with the birth of Sarah's baby, Tate. But as Calley said, having the lights back on and a fully functioning hospital before her baby's birth would be a huge relief. And if I can get treated for whatever it is that seems to be plaguing me, that would also be wonderful. The question is, when will this happen?

# Chapter 3

## *Lucy*

"Hey, good looking."

I roll my eyes and keep walking.

"You're looking fine today," Glen says, raising his voice loud enough one of the other snow shovelers snorts out a laugh.

"Dude," he says. "She's out of your league."

"Ha. Lucy Fleming? She's in everyone's league."

I stop and slowly spin to face him head on. "Is that supposed to mean something?" I deliver a pleasant smile.

He opens his mouth slightly, then moves his tongue along his cracked bottom lip. "Mm-hmm, baby. You really are looking fine today."

"This old thing?" I say, motioning to my heavy down jacket and insulated pants as I take a step toward him.

He continues his leer and takes several steps toward me. "That's more like it, *Luuucy.*"

He drags out my name like I'm a redheaded comedian. I sidle a little closer, give him a smile, and grab him by the collar. In a quick and fluid move, I quickly raise my knee into his groin. As he leans into me with an *oomph*, I push him back hard enough he lands solid on his bottom. He crumples to the side, cradling himself as his buddy hoots and laughs.

Gasping for breath, he says, "You— "

"Now, now, Glen. Toad is right. I *am* out of your league. I don't date losers on the *work* crew. Especially not losers I can easily put to the ground."

Turning to Toad, I say, "You might want to get him up and back to work before one of the officers happens by. Wouldn't do for him to be lying on the ground instead of working. And while you're at it, encourage him to take a shower. This town has cleanliness standards,

12

and he's not meeting them. He's as disgusting as those on the hunting crew. Gross."

"C'mon, Lucy," Glen whines. "I thought we were friends."

"Not even. Just because we've lived in the same town forever and happen to cross paths doesn't mean we're friends."

He narrows his eyes at me. "We might have been before you got all hoity-toity."

"Get yourself up," Toad says. "She's right about not wanting an officer to find you on the ground. Remember what happened to Carl?"

Glen makes several guttural noises as Toad turns to me. "You doing okay, Lucy? I heard the raid was— " He shifts his shoulder to one side.

"I suggest you get to shoveling snow and not worry about what happens when our team leaves town," I say in the haughtiest voice I can manage.

He gives me a slight nod before turning back to his work.

Todd Berringer, aka Toad, used to live in the same apartment building as me. I guess he still lives there, but I've moved. All of us who are soldiers on the acquisition team live separately. Even the ones with families moved from their previous homes to the neighborhood designated for us. Not that I hear anyone complaining. It's a gated community known as Creek View Estates and is a collection of the nicest houses in Prospect. I share a three-bedroom home with five other women. It's one of two female-only homes referred to as the women's barracks or dorms.

While families have their own separate dwellings and are often multigenerational, singles are set up in dormitories—two houses for the women, and an entire street of men living four to six to a home. Yeah, the men on the team far outnumber the women. The luxurious clubhouse is our meeting area. We even have a large gym with free weights and nonelectric machines. As part of the infantry, I have some serious perks over people like Toad and Glen.

Anyone not in our makeshift army is doing grunt work: shoveling snow—a never-ending job this winter—cooking, community laundry, and more. Right now, I'm on my way to the laundry to find out why my dorm was shorted three sheets. This is the second time in a row, and I'm not at all happy about needing to make the walk over here. Glen causing me trouble just adds to my irritation.

13

My fists are clenched as I stride purposely away from Glen and Toad. Even though I bested him physically, his implications about the type of woman I've become still stings. Before the attacks, I was a preschool teacher. Well, not an actual teacher with a degree but more of a daycare worker. I was in charge of the three-year-old class at Shining Star School for Tots. I would've loved to be a real teacher, and with rumors of the government possibly giving free college and removing all student loan debt if we could get the right person in office, I'd certainly return to school.

As it was, I was still paying for the one year of out-of-state school. Warm and sunny Florida had sounded like such a good idea. My parents were against it and refused to help me pay. It was easy to get loans, so I didn't need their help anyway. I could've got a loan for the next year, but I spent too much time enjoying college life. I failed more classes than I passed and crawled home with my tail between my legs. My mom was quick to say *I told you so.* My dad was just glad I didn't come home pregnant.

A year or so later, Dad was offered a new job in Arizona. Warm and sunny Arizona sounded as nice as Florida. I was shocked when my parents told me it was time I stood on my own two feet. They planned to get a small place without room for me, saying I was welcome to follow but would need my own apartment.

I moved out of our Prospect home that night, couch surfing for a few weeks until I saved up enough for my own place. They tracked me down to tell me goodbye before they left, which resulted in an intense argument. That was six or seven years ago and the last time I spoke to them. Now, with phones and cars no longer working, I suppose I won't ever talk to them.

As I get near the laundry facility, several sentries run by. I'm off duty today, having just returned yesterday from a raid, but if something is happening, I'll be expected to respond. Out of habit, I touch my hip where my gun sits and then break into a jog.

My fitness level has drastically improved. I used to be pudgy, bordering on more than pudgy. When we received the warning about the missile attack, I'd sought shelter in the basement of City Hall, along with many others from my apartment building and the nearby area. While I was sheltering, my building was looted and all my food taken. Some people had chosen to stay behind, sheltering in our laundry room. When we came out, we found the men had been murdered and

14

the women and children were missing. My fellow soldier and roommate Maddie says she knows where the women were taken.

Maddie says a lot of things—most of it not true. She's the type of person who talks just to hear herself talk. Part of it's probably because she's still young—only nineteen, almost ten years younger than me—and possibly a defense mechanism also, since she's so homely. Being not much to look at, she makes up for it with a slightly outrageous personality. I like her just fine, and she's a good roommate, but sometimes she exhausts me. And other times, after a hard training day or raid, her bubbliness is just what I need.

She might have a point, though. Occasionally, when we go on our acquisition trips, we do take captives. Always women. There was a rumor we'd have a captive on our recent raid, but that didn't happen. I'm not sure if someone made a mistake or what.

"Lucy!" Candace Murphy, the older lady who now works in the laundry, calls as I jog toward her. I've known Mrs. Murphy for years. She was the secretary of the high school and only retired a couple of years ago. She's also the mom of one of my favorite teachers from high school.

"Hey, have you heard what's happening?" I ask in a ragged breath.

"There was another attack—the rebels again."

"Anyone hurt?"

She tilts her head to the side. "Not sure. They hit the sentry post at Taylor's Draw."

We have several sentry stations surrounding Prospect. They have a dual purpose: controlling who enters and preventing townspeople from leaving. Ours is a sealed community. While after proper vetting people are allowed in, there must be a good reason for someone to leave, such as pertaining to their job. Otherwise, if you live in Prospect, you're here for good.

"I better go see if they need me," I say, not relishing the additional half mile to the observation post. "We were shorted in bedding again. I'll need two tops and a bottom."

"Again?" Candace shakes her head. "I don't know how that keeps happening."

"I'll be back for them," I call over my shoulder as I jog away.

When I reach the outpost, I stay on the edge, waiting to see if I'm needed. Susie, one of the girls from my dorm, is part of the response team. I quickly scoot in next to her, where a briefing is already in progress.

"Once again," Lieutenant Knight says, "the cowards have attacked from afar. We found their snipers' nest and some decent tracks. Some of our best trackers have gone after them. You two," he says, motioning to a couple of the men in the group, "will take over watch. The rest of you can haul the dead to the morgue."

I try not to roll my eyes. This isn't the first time I've been tasked with moving a body.

"Who is it?" I whisper to Susie.

"Those two new sentry guys," she says. "No great loss at least."

I give a nod. Not because I agree it's no great loss; both are new to Prospect and I don't even know them, but I nod my understanding of who they are. They're regular sentry people, not on the acquisition team like Susie and me. I used to be a sentry, but that was before Mayor Majors took an interest in me. He put in a good word with General Majors, his son. I still had to test for the team, and, truthfully, I barely made it. And some days, I wish I would've outright failed.

# Chapter 4

## *Saturday, Day 243*

## *Mollie*

The excitement of yesterday's news continues to be the topic of conversation when the kitchen crew arrives for breakfast preparations. Because of my illness—possibly cancer, according to Belinda and Kelley—I'm on restricted work duties. I'm no longer part of the firewood crew, the militia, or anything else requiring physical exertion. *Can't have the Cancer Girl passing out when she's supposed to be chopping wood.* Oh, we don't know for certain it's cancer. There isn't a lot of testing we can do at the end of the world. With our limited medical devices, they base the diagnosis only on my clinical symptoms. And it seems cancer is what everything points to.

Modified duty allows me to be on the kitchen crew, but only at the kitchen in my house—the former lodge of a dude ranch—and doing only prep work I can sit for. For the most part, I'm on the sewing and mending crew. Sarah leads the seamstresses, which consists mainly of the elderly women in our community and one man Sarah refers to as her seamster, who are physically unable to perform any of the other duties. The crew has nine full-time members and another six, including me, considered part-time since we aren't fully housebound and are able to take other work assignments. We each work from our own abodes and have a runner—a teenager in the community—who delivers and picks up the work so Sarah can distribute it.

While Sarah also does the needlework, much of her day is taken up receiving and assigning the work. Sarah and three others are skilled enough to remake garments or, using the limited amount of raw material, construct fully. The rest of us have varying levels of experience with a needle and thread. I usually get the extremely simple things like sewing on buttons or patching. My current project is making mama cloth and family cloth.

With our disposable items either rapidly dwindling or completely gone, alternatives are needed. Even though a small amount were saved to use after childbirths, the bulk of women's personal supplies have been gone for months. Calley is the next person expecting a baby. She'll have the luxury of throw-away items, but then it will all be washable goods. For monthly needs, mama cloth is already the norm. A few women had reusable menstrual cups before the attacks. Many times, Sarah has said she wishes she would've made that change. She'd thought of it, knowing it was an eco-friendly solution, but kept putting it off because of the ewww factor.

There's certainly an ickiness with washable women's hygiene products and cloth toilet paper. Like the women's items, toilet paper is also in short supply. With living so far from a grocery store, most of the homes in Bakerville kept a decent supply of toilet paper, paper towels, napkins, and tissues on hand. Even so, things meant to be thrown away and repurchased can't last forever. The tissues and napkins were the first to be replaced.

Because we were several months into the apocalypse before we moved up the mountain, most families had already switched from paper products to reusable in some way or another. Almost everyone stopped using tissue, choosing to save it for a toilet paper alternative. As a requirement of moving up the mountain, any usable goods became part of the community coffers, causing those stashed items to become public property. As a result, Doris made sure everyone had bandanas or handkerchiefs for blowing their nose.

In addition to the reusable hankies, cloth napkins are now the norm. We were able to scrounge up a decent amount among the empty houses and from residents who moved to the mountain. Lily and Sissy are particularly partial to the hot pink and bright purple napkins. I'm not sure where they came from, but we seem to have a surplus of those particular colors.

I chew on my bottom lip as I remember those first days of living on the mountain. Doris was still in charge of the seamstresses then. Sarah and a few others had helped her with sewing over the summer, but it wasn't the organized team it is now. And Sarah wasn't in any condition to lead anything in our early days of living at the dude ranch.

Her husband Tate, along with his dad Keith, went missing during a fall elk hunt. With both presumed dead, she was in deep mourning. As the fog of grief lifted and her pregnancy advanced, she took over some of Doris's responsibilities with the needleworkers. In January, Sarah gave birth to Tate Keith, named after his father and grandfather. Since his birth and her recovery, she's taken over the entire group. Doris was grateful to give it up, considering how busy she is with the supply house and assorted other duties.

Sally-Anne Hinkle was part of the sewing crew until the attempted coup resulted in her being shot and now fighting for her life. While she did do actual sewing, her artistry was really with her knitting needles. She's made many pairs of wool socks, mittens, and gloves. It's unlikely she'll recover from her injuries, but she's still trying to do her part by teaching others from her bed, in hopes her knowledge will be carried on.

There's already talk of doing the things necessary to shear the few wooly sheep and process the raw product into usable yarn—a lost skill we need to learn. Today was supposed to be a full sewing day, but instead I'm taking a breakfast and lunch shift followed by an afternoon of mending. I was the backup for the kitchen, called into action when one of the other ladies sent word she was ill and wouldn't be in.

Even at this predawn hour, the kitchen is lively with many smiles and teasing. As I sit at the table, peeling the seemingly never-ending pile of sugar beets to be made into porridge, I can't help but participate in the fun. To think this will soon be ending—that we'll be able to flick a switch and have lights again, that we won't have to work from before dawn until after dark and won't have to rely on sugar beets to survive—I can't help but smile.

When the breakfast cooking is done, Sarah and her sister-in-law, Karen, are waiting in the great room with the children to make our way to the ski lodge dining hall to eat.

"Ready to go, Mom?" Sarah asks.

A few months ago, like the rest of the community, we walked the half mile from our place in the dude ranch to the ski lodge. Now we pile in our quad cab diesel. Because of my illness, we've been given extra fuel rations. Though I do still walk on days I feel strong, today the ride is welcome. I suspect it won't be long until I take my meals at the house instead of making the thrice daily trek back and forth.

"Did you check with Dodie and Alvin?"

"They're staying here. Neither has a shift this morning."

My mother and father-in-law, Dodie and Alvin, take most of their meals at home, as do many of the other elderly or infirm. While I don't think of Dodie or Alvin as elderly, based on their activity levels, at seventy-five, they're a bit more cautious about moving about in the snow and ice. Even though we have the truck to use for transport, unless one of them has a shift working in the vicinity of the lodge, they're just as happy to remain warm and cozy while enjoying a little quiet time. Quiet is a rarity in our house of seven adults and eight children—one of them a newborn.

"But we're picking up Doris, right?" Malcolm asks.

"Yep, since Evan's hunting with your dad, she needs a ride." My friend Doris Snyder, whose leg was shattered by a bullet in the early days of the attacks, is unable to put any weight on her leg, making the walk out of the question.

We'll have a snowmobile waiting in the parking lot of the old ski lodge to take us up the steep incline to the dining hall. We're not the only ones who receive this special treatment. That steep hill is difficult for many. This morning, there's also a gentleman with a bad hip—he's able to walk on the mostly flat ground between the dude ranch and the parking lot, but the uphill trek is too hard on him.

After telling my family I'll see them in the lodge, we wait for the snowmobile. The driver's unloading passengers at the ski lodge, so it will be only a few minutes.

Turning to Doris, I ask, "Did you get much sleep last night?"

"You mean because of the excitement?"

"Yeah."

She shrugs. "I just hope we're not setting ourselves up for disappointment."

"What do you mean?"

She shakes her head. "Nothing. I'm sure it'll be fine." Doris pats me on the shoulder. "How's Calley feeling? Is the morning sickness gone?"

"She didn't have much. Just a few days of slight queasiness. With Deanne—well, I'm glad she's doing well."

"And Sheila? Any better?"

"No. Not well at all. You heard she's living at the clinic? She sleeps on a cot set up in the examination area—or she's moved to a new location when they need the space."

"I've heard. It's probably the best way to keep her safe from— "
Doris gives a tilt of her head and purses her lips.

"From herself?" I offer. "Yes, it's basically a suicide watch. I'm glad
Madison and Laurie are part of the medical team. The three of them
became good friends in the early days of the attacks when they were
all struggling with depression."

Since her mom Deanne's murder during the attempted coup, Sheila
has again struggled with her mental health. Last summer was also hard
for Sheila. Adjusting to the new powerless world we found ourselves
in was hard for many, but she really plummeted. When Laurie Ogden
arrived at our homestead on the day of the EMP, along with her now-
husband Aaron and her friend Bill Shane, close friends of ours who
lived in nearby Wesley, she was almost as bad off as Sheila.

Madison came to us in a different way. When I was trying to get
home from Oregon, where I was working when the attacks started, I
happened upon her and her baby daughter at an opportune time.
They, along with Madison's husband, had just been accosted by two
derelicts. Before I completely grasped what was happening, her
husband was shot and killed. With the way Madison was standing, the
bullet passed through her husband and hit her. The murderers, and
me, thought she too was dead. When I heard them say they planned
to kill the baby, I couldn't have that. By the time it was done, they
were dead, Madison was severely injured but alive, and baby Emma
was fine.

The three women, all facing new and difficult circumstances,
formed a bond while living on our homestead. Kelley Hudson, a
retired psychiatric nurse, helped the women come to terms with their
new life. Madison, a veterinarian, and Laurie, a dental student, have
each found real purpose in being a part of the medical team.

While Sheila didn't have the same drive, she had been much better
until the death of her mom. Sheila isn't alone in her struggles. There
are others in the community who've faced difficulties since the attacks.
Kelley's daughter Sylvia has been a huge help to many people, forming
several support groups. Mental health is something we take very
seriously after losing community members to suicide in the early days
of the havoc.

"Has she heard about the radio announcement?" Doris asks as we
watch the snowmobile zip over the bridge. "Maybe that'll help."

"Calley told her. Sheila says she thinks it's a lie, some sort of propaganda to give us hope but will never come true."

"Hmm. An interesting concept," Doris says as the sled comes to a stop.

"Meaning?"

"Mrs. Snyder," Toby James says, offering Doris his hand. "Your chariot has arrived."

"Well, thank you, kind sir," Doris says. Even though each day is the same, with Toby saying the bit about the chariot and Doris always calling him *kind sir*, I can't help but laugh at their antics.

Once we're settled in the trailer, Doris leans in. "I heard one of the kitchen people called in sick today. Seems to be a wave of that happening."

"Is there another virus going around?" I ask, remembering the sickness that fell on our community around Thanksgiving. While it was nothing more than a cold, we took special precautions to cut down on the spread, including having those affected take time off work and eat in their homes.

"I don't think so. I suspect it's more related to the idea of a rescue." She raises her eyebrows at me while I answer with a shrug. "You know, we have rules about everyone pulling their weight. Why bother working if the government is going to swoop in and save us?"

"Oh. I hadn't thought of that. You used to work for the government. Do *you* think they'll swoop in and save us?"

"Ha!" she answers, as we pull to a stop by the ski lodge.

The breakfast is a cheerful affair, with the radio announcement still being the main topic of conversation. As I watch my happy neighbors, I think about Doris's comments. Are we setting ourselves up for disappointment? Could Sheila be right? Is this some sort of lie—propaganda—to give us hope? What would be the purpose? Why would our government tell us help was on the way if there wasn't a plan in place? It's been almost eight months since we've heard anything from those in charge. Why start propaganda now?

"Don't you think so, Mom?" Malcolm asks, jarring me from my thoughts.

"What's that?"

"Tony and I should keep practicing with our compound bows, right? Don't you think, even if we're going to be rescued, it might be a while before the grocery stores are working again?"

"I would think so. We don't know the situation with the meat industry. I can't imagine they'll be able to start sending cattle for processing right away. And even if the lights come back on, we still have the issue of the refineries being destroyed."

"True," Angela says with a bend of her neck. "Gavin, eat your porridge."

"Don't want beet cereal," my three-year-old grandson says with a pout. "Want eggs."

"There aren't eggs today," Angela says patiently, then turns to Malcolm. "Mom's right. I think it'll be a long time before things return to normal. With the refineries being blown up, we won't have the amount of fuel we did before. Even if they're able to process the cattle, how will they get them here? And think about the grocery stores. Many were vandalized. How long will it take to get those operating again? Getting the power back is just one piece of the equation—one I'm certainly looking forward to—but there's still going to be a lot to do."

"How do you think they'll manage it?" Calley asks.

"Manage what?" Sarah asks.

"All of it. I mean, who will do the work? Do you think they have people just standing by waiting to be told they can get the lights back on? Don't you think most people are doing the same things we are? Just trying to survive from day to day? Where will they find the workers?"

I let out a slow breath as Tony says, "I'd help. If they needed people to do the work, I'd do what I could."

"Me too," Malcolm says.

"I know you both would," I say. "And maybe something like that will happen. Maybe the next announcement, or one in the near future, will be a call for people to go and help. But my guess is there will be age requirements. You two won't be old enough yet."

"Do you think— " Tony starts to speak and then bites his lip. "Do you think, if the lights come back, my dad—our real dad—will find his way home?"

"I have no doubt your dad has been working on getting back to you this entire time." I nod.

"That's what dads do," Malcolm says. "But until he gets here, my mom and dad get to be your mom and dad too."

Tony nods as he drops his eyes. Tony and his sister Lily joined our family after their mom, a friend and neighbor, was killed. Their dad was gone for work when the attacks started. He hasn't returned, and with each passing day, the likelihood he'll ever return decreases. Since they had no nearby relatives, we took them in to our family. At first, it was out of a sense of obligation. But now, I can't imagine my life without them.

It's the same with our adopted grandchildren—Sarah's three children, Marc, Sissy, and Andy. Their mom died from, what we thought at the time, a self-inflicted manner. New information leads us to believe she was murdered. Sarah and Tate happily took her children in and loved them as their own.

After breakfast, the children stay at the ski lodge for school. Angela, her husband Tim, and Calley go to their work shifts. Everyone else is on their own duty shifts. I have lunch duty back at the lodge starting at ten, then sewing this afternoon.

"Ready, Mom?" Sarah asks as she gets her baby bundled up. "I want to get the jacket for Cheyre finished today."

"Yep. Let's go."

Though I welcome the ride up, downhill isn't difficult for me as long as we take it slow. With carrying Tate in a sling, Sarah is happy with the leisurely pace.

"You know what I'm most looking forward to?" Sarah asks.

"For today?"

"No, when this is over. No more sugar beets!"

"Amen!" I laugh. "They do get a little old with having them at every single breakfast."

While breakfast is focused on the abundance of sugar beets we harvested in the fall, meat is often the focus of lunch and dinner. We cull livestock—beef, goats, pigs, or sheep—and our hunting teams bring in two elk most weeks. We make the animals stretch by using nose-to-tail cooking methods.

Deanne, who oversaw the kitchen and created the menus before she was murdered, was amazing at coming up with dishes using every single scrap. Some are rather adventurous . . . translation: I hope I never have to eat that stuff again. But for the most part, we eat quite well.

Of course, when feeding a large group, not everyone will be happy with the choices. My daughter Angela considered herself a vegetarian prior to the attacks. She still struggles to eat the meat dishes, but she came to realize food is strictly fuel and the time to be picky has passed. When our world returns to normal, will we go back to our cavalier lifestyles of abundance? Or will we realize how spoiled we were in so many ways?

# Chapter 5

## *Lucy*

"All right, people. Let's get started," Captain Murphy says. "General Majors will be here shortly, and we have a few details to iron out before he presents our next procurement."

As the room settles, he calls on the squad leaders to report their team members' strengths and weaknesses. I hate this part. This is when we're picked apart in front of everyone. I'm squad yellow, which—interestingly enough—consists only of females. *Yeah, there's nothing misogynist about that.*

Janet—or as I'm supposed to call her, *Lieutenant Kruse*—leads our squad. All the squad leaders are lieutenants. And I do make a point of using lieutenant to her face, only occasionally forgetting and reverting to her first name. She's quick to correct me, reminding me no matter what I may think, she is most certainly my superior and any previous relations we had play no part in the current hierarchy. Though it sounds like the Army with our ranks, none of us regular people are given rank.

I'm surprised when Lieutenant Knight brings up haircuts as a problem. It seems a few of the younger men are letting their hair grow longer than it should be and not keeping up with their facial hair. The town has cleanliness standards. I used to find it amusing that Richard Majors passed a mandate on cleanliness, which includes men keeping their hair off their collar and beards kept trimmed. Women can wear their hair any length as long as it looks tidy. And all residents must have a bath at least one time per week, though the word *bath* is rather generous.

Water is hauled or pumped from the creek, resulting in mainly sponge baths. The acquisition team's rules are more stringent: no beards and hair is to be high and tight for the men. Women can have long hair, but it must be kept off our collars. Maddie and I both keep our hair French braided, though I've been really admiring Lorita, one

26

of the others on our team, and her short pixy cut. With perfect high cheekbones and dark eyes, it looks great on her. I lift a hand to smooth the braid of my light brown hair. No way I'd ever be able to carry such a cute cut off. Even though I'm no longer overweight, I still don't have the bone structure Lorita does.

I originally thought the cleanliness standards were stupid. I mean, really, who cares? We're living in unprecedented times; our world has fallen apart. Why should we be worried about haircuts and baths? But as we've traveled to other places that don't care about their hygiene, I've come to appreciate it. Some of the homes we enter are outright rank from the smell of unwashed bodies.

Even with our cleanliness mandate, Prospect does have an unpleasant smell when the wind is just right. In the days after the power went out, the sewer on the east side of town backed up and filled most of the houses with . . . well, nothing good.

When Richard Majors took over, he made it a priority to fix the stench. I don't know the details, but rumor is he used generators and most of the town's limited fuel supply to get the sewer pumps working long enough to remove the worst of the standing sludge.

There's another rumor one of the reasons he killed Mayor Stringer and assumed responsibility of the town was because he couldn't handle the smell. Whatever he did helped, and the stench is better, but it's not completely gone. Unfortunately, where the acquisition team lives is the area affected by the sewer issue. And today is one of the bad wind days. The clubhouse smells awful.

When it's Janet's turn to talk, as expected, she starts with me and only relays my weaknesses. In her gravely smoker's voice, she says, "Once again, Lucy hesitated when it was time to do the job. She finds it . . . distasteful."

"Well, in fairness," Captain Murphy says, "she's not the only one." He searches me out. Meeting my eyes, he gives me a small smile. He was a first-year science teacher my freshman year of high school. That's been many years now, and while he's no longer as youthful as he was then, he still has his boyish good looks that caused most of the freshman girls to have crushes on him. I'm no exception. Even now, with his dark hair greying at the temples and lines at the corners of his eyes, he's terribly attractive. And he's single, having never married.

Though we weren't friends, even after I graduated and moved back from Florida, I'd see him around and he'd always make a point of speaking to me. I was surprised to discover he was part of the plot to overthrow Mayor Stringer and the legitimate Prospect government. He pulled me aside shortly after the coup, telling me if I wanted to do more than just get by, I needed to get with the program and join Richard Majors and his group.

Captain Murphy turns back to Janet and asks, "But did it actually affect her ability to get the job done?"

"She hesitated when pulling the trigger," Janet persists.

"I understand. Did it affect your mission?"

"Not this time," Janet answers sternly, staring at me while she talks. "But it will. If she isn't comfortable with the duties, she ought not be part of the acquisition squad."

I feel the redness of my face, and while I'd like to defend myself, commenting is not allowed. And really, there's not much to defend. She's not wrong. I do hesitate, especially on raids like this one where we sneak into people's homes while they're sleeping and shoot them in their beds. Entire families slaughtered as they sleep. I try and blank my mind, try not to remember the details of what we did. Try not to replay it over and over in my mind—which I've been doing since the raid.

This was the third time I'd been out, but the first time I'd had to be directly in the thick of things. I was put on watch during the previous raids, making sure there were no unexpected people who magically appeared. Thankfully, there never was. But this time, I was part of the attack team. I hated it. And if Janet knew the full truth, that I never directly shot at anyone and only once may have hit someone, she'd really flip her lid.

"Thank you, Lieutenant. Is this a skills issue or a mindset issue?"

"Both. She needs more range time, and she needs to not be such a wuss."

"Make the range time happen then. And get her in to see Doc Bohm."

I inwardly cringe. Doc Bohm isn't a real doctor. He doesn't know medicine at all. I think calling him *Doc* started as a joke. His job is to toughen us up so we're killing machines. I have no idea what he did in his previous life when our world was normal, but he's a scary guy with dead eyes and a monotone voice. He often goes on our raids, too, though he's not assigned to a team. Every time I've had an appointment with him, it's left me feeling almost as dead as he seems.

28

I guess, if I'm to be the killer they want me to be, a part of me must die. Many days I think I'd like to go back to being on sentry duty, not that they'd let me. But now, with the attacks from the rebels, sentries are sitting ducks. And even a peon on the acquisition team gets extra benefits compared to the sentries. Our tier system puts my position near the top—only behind the officers and Mayor Majors. In the case of Mayor Richard Majors, my team is far below. He can get anything he wants.

"Okay, who's next, Lieutenant?"

Janet goes through the other members of our team, giving positive reports for everyone except Maddie, who gets an even more scathing account than I did. Like me, Maddie is an unlikely member of the acquisition team. She was already on the team when I joined, but her skills aren't any more advanced than mine are. I suspect she was allowed on the team in the same way I was, because of who we know and not what we can do. Even though her and I are roommates and friendly, we've never discussed the thing—or rather the person—I suspect we have in common. Richard Majors.

Maddie, too, is ordered more range time and an appointment with Doc Bohm. She's sitting next to me as she listens to Janet degrade her but makes a point of holding her head high and keeping an even look on her face.

As Janet drones on, I think about the last raid. While we did bring home all the livestock—cattle, horses, chickens, and even a few goats—we left some of their fall harvest behind. They had a huge supply of sugar beets they were either using for animal or human food, maybe both, and a good amount of hay and a few other things. We didn't have enough room to bring it all, so we left all the sugar beets and a fair amount of hay. I expected to hear today about a second trip to go and retrieve it; although, maybe they'll send workers for them since it's not something one needs skills for. *Skills!* The acquisition team's main skill is murder. I hate it, but it's a choice I've made. And Janet is right, I do need to be less of a wuss.

When the grilling is finally over, Captain Murphy says, "You all know what you need to work on. We need to start getting ready for the next run. It's— " He looks down at a piece of paper in his hand. "Correction, the next full team run will be within three weeks. Unlike this easy Bakerville acquisition, this will be a multiday event, so make sure your gear is in top shape."

I blink rapidly. Bakerville was not easy. With the fuel shortage, we were forced to walk. Three full days of slogging through the snow each way. We don't have enough snowshoes for everyone, so those of us without follow behind, making sure to stay in the tracks already made. A misstep can result in being buried up to the knee or beyond—postholing—which always results in a hearty laugh among the group.

Believe me, when it happens to you, it isn't at all funny. A moment of inattention, and I found myself in a drift burying my entire leg. Getting out was no picnic either. I thought I could easily pull my leg out, but I managed to fall over and land half on packed snow—thanks to the previous foot traffic over the area—and half on soft snow. When I finally found my footing, my boot was filled and I had snow up under my coat and down my insulated pants.

I'm surprised Janet didn't bring it up. She made sure to berate me at the time, calling me a clumsy ox. That's better than some of the other names she's called me. Not just now, since I joined her squad, but before.

"You okay?" Maddie whispers, leaning in toward me.

I dip my head and give a tight smile.

She responds in kind, then darts her eyes forward as Captain says, "A few of you will be chosen for a special, short run before then. We've found a small enclave holding livestock. The team is being finalized. If you're chosen, you'll be notified tomorrow. This will be a multiteam event led by Major Lassiter."

I stiffen my back at his name; I feel Maddie do the same. He's almost as creepy as Doc Bohm. Looking at him, he's not much. Short and squat with thinning hair, he's an average guy who you'd easily pass over in a crowd. Talking to him, at first, he seems almost normal. But there's something sinister about him, especially the way he acts toward women.

The acquisition team was in its early days when he showed up in town out of the blue. And it was his idea to have a team of women only. He tried to make it sound politically correct by saying we'd function better as a unit if we didn't have to worry about the guys always one-upping us . . . or something like that. I wasn't on the team then, just heard about it through the grapevine. The fact he was given the position of major, only answering to Scott and our mayor, was not lost on me. He must have had some sort of relationship with the father and son from before the attacks and the EMP.

The beginning of Mayor Majors's takeover was hard—full of days where I wasn't sure what I should do, and I'm truly thankful Captain Murphy gave me guidance. I was there the night Mayor Stringer, our properly elected mayor, was killed along with at least a hundred others. I was standing way too close when one of the small bombs detonated. I couldn't scrub enough to get the blood and . . . other stuff off.

Captain Murphy drones on a few more minutes until General Majors arrives. As required, we all stand as he enters the room. It's like he's the president. Same thing happens when Mayor Majors enters a room.

"What's up with his hair?" Maddie whispers.

I stifle a smile. He definitely has a haircut gone wrong. His high and tight is cut to the scalp in a two-inch swath above his right ear. There's even a scab where he was nicked. I knew Scott Majors before he became General Majors by way of his dad taking over our town. He was a couple of years ahead of me in school. I was in the same class as his sister, Shelly. We weren't exactly friends but were friendly—the sister and me, not Scott and me.

Scott was conceited and condescending. He'd go out of his way to bully people. Most likely, if you asked him, he'd say he was a popular jock, which is somewhat true. He certainly seemed to peak in high school. After graduation, he went to the University of Wyoming and was home before the first term ended. There was gossip he was arrested on drug charges or possibly for date rape. I don't know exactly what happened, but he quit school, came home, and then left again. Rumor was he went to serve a jail sentence. It was all surprisingly hush-hush, even without anything in the news. Maybe that's a perk of having a dad who owns and runs a newspaper business.

Afterward, he went from one menial job to another, never holding anything for any length of time. I'd see him working at the mini mart, then washing dishes in a restaurant or something similar. He started several businesses, all of which failed. I think the last was a handyman business, but he got in trouble again when the person he was working for said some of her checks went missing. I guess the EMP was the best thing that could've happened to Scott Majors.

His eyes glance over the audience. He smirks when he sees me. I keep an even look on my face as I meet his glare.

"He sure doesn't like you," Maddie mutters.

I tap my hand on her leg in response. Scott knows about me and his dad. Like his son, Richard Majors finally found his time to shine. While not quite the flunky Scott is, having run a somewhat successful newspaper for years, he has several other failed ventures, many of which he put Scott in charge of. Coincidence?

Richard had political aspirations in the past and even ran to be our legitimate mayor, but he was blown out of the water when Mayor Stringer won by a landslide. He also had a reputation for being handsy. Many of his female employees complained, but to my knowledge, it never went any further than complaints. There was a good story about one of his employees, Milena Maynard, who smacked him and then quit. A few weeks later, she ran into Mrs. Majors in the grocery store, resulting in a full-on fight in the produce section. Prospect could certainly be entertaining at times. Now Richard Majors gets any woman he wants. Not because he is suddenly irresistible, but because we all want to survive.

Scott's speech tells us little. He briefly glosses over the next mission—not the mini mission, but the one for everyone. As usual, he doesn't tell us exactly when the mission will start or where we're going. That's saved until we leave, for fear of the rebels finding out.

I half expect we'll be leaving for a mission and encounter a bomb or whatever they call the things the rebels have been using, some kind of homemade incendiary device that's already killed several from the sentry team when on patrol. They've caused so much trouble, the sentries are now stationary. I asked Maddie how in the world people even know how to make those things. She just shrugged and said, "Some people know things. People make bombs from lots of common items. Didn't you learn that in school?"

I guess I didn't because I wouldn't be able to make an explosive if I wanted to. I did hear there was a construction site that kept dynamite on hand. Janet Kruse said those were what Majors used when he took over the town. Maybe the rebels found their own construction site.

# Chapter 6

## *Saturday, Day 243*

## *Mollie*

Late afternoon, I'm sitting in the great room as Tate sleeps and I work on my sewing. He's in his baby box, a specialty box with a mattress, which works as a portable bassinet, on the floor next to my chair. At about five weeks old, the box is still perfect for him, but Jake has plans for a crib. He hasn't started building it yet but has been working on the drawings and gathering materials. It's to be a surprise, and finding the time to do the work may be a challenge. Sarah put Tate down for his nap before she stepped out to deliver today's sewing jobs. Often, she'll have a runner do the deliveries, but she felt the walk would do her good. Especially with the recent cold snap seeming to have broken.

Today's cooking shifts seemed to really take it out of me, and I'd like nothing more than to stretch out on the couch and nap along with the baby. I wiggle in my seat, trying to get comfortable. My lower back started hurting when doing the lunch preparations, and it doesn't seem to be easing up. I move the small ottoman and try to find a different position.

A loud knock at the door causes me to jump. My sewing, sitting loosely in my lap, indicates I did fall asleep while working on my project. I wipe the back of my hand across my mouth, removing a tell-tale sign of drool. As I stand, the strong knock comes again. Setting my work aside, I give Tate a quick look, the sudden noise causing him to stir. I quickly move to the door.

"Who is it?" I ask as I reach the entry area.

"It's Evan," the voice on the other side of the door responds.

"Evan? What are you doing back already?" I pull the door open. "I thought you guys were going to stay a few days."

33

"Things were . . . we had some surprises," he answers with a concerned look on his face.

"Where's Jake?" Fear spreads through my body.

"He's fine. He's on his way."

"Okay. Good." I motion him to come inside. "He's on his way from the stables?"

"From Bakerville. He's on foot."

"Is he okay? Did he fall off his horse?"

Evan gives me a small smile. "Nah, he did fine on the horse."

I let out a sigh of relief. Jake is not a fan of horses, having always insisted they don't like him. When he and Evan went back to Bakerville to hunt before Christmas, they took a snowmobile under the guise of being able to haul back their load of geese in the trailer. Doris and I knew the truth: neither of our husbands are horsemen.

When they first started talking about this hunt, it was made clear the fuel couldn't be spared again for the sleds and they'd need to have alternate transportation. Both Jake and Evan had a few riding lessons from the Camerons, former hunting outfitters who know their stuff, and somewhat nervously rode off yesterday morning. Jake was given an old gelding named Domino who was said to be the gentlest of all the horses we have on the mountain. Even so, I wouldn't have been surprised to hear Jake had a horse issue.

I wait, expecting Evan to say more. When he doesn't, I prod, "And? Where's Jake?" Even I hear the tension in my voice.

"Don't worry." Evan gives me a small smile. "Jake's fine, and it's good news. Your boss and his family were at your house."

"My boss? Ben Ferguson?"

"Yeah." Evan makes a slight face, encompassing a question and a shrug at the same time.

"What?" I squeal. "Are they okay?"

Tate lets out a cry at my excessive noise.

I motion for Evan to step fully inside as I go to the baby. "Sorry, big guy. Grandma's just happy." I don't even bother wiping away the tears running down my face as I pick him up. "Tell me more," I say to Evan as I sway back and forth. "They're okay?"

"Mostly." He sits on the bench and removes his snow boots.

"And Jake's still with them? At my house?" I'm struggling to understand exactly what is happening.

34

"They're walking back. We didn't have enough horses. Dusty and Dax are going to take one of the wagons and go after them."

"Okay. Good." I let out a sigh. When Dusty, Dax, and the rest of the Camerons fled nearby Prospect, along with friends and families from three neighboring ranches, they brought an old-fashioned chuckwagon and two open wagons plus teams. Those, along with two wagons and teams already in Bakerville, have been a blessing.

The wagons already in our community were rarely used, other than for parades and to take the children from house to house each October for trick or treating. Now we're rapidly thrust back in time to when horses were a necessity and when a wagon or buggy was a mode of daily transportation.

After we moved to the mountain, someone fashioned skis to add to the wagon wheels, turning them into sleighs. They're used daily for wood gathering and other activities that need to haul larger amounts than the snowmobile trailers can. And they don't run on fuel—a huge help.

"When will they be going after them?" I briefly wonder if there's any way I can join the wagon. I'd love to greet my friends sooner rather than later.

"As soon as they get the children situated."

I tilt my head at him. "Children?"

With his snow-clad boots now removed, Evan walks over to the woodstove, warming his hands in front of the heat. "We're keeping this quiet," he says slowly. "We didn't even bring them here, choosing instead to take them to Rudy's place."

"You took *who* to Rudy's place?" Rudy Wallace and his wife were already living on the mountain when our community of Bakerville decided to move up here. Their house is about a quarter mile east of the ski lodge and dude ranch. The Youngs, another couple who also opened their home to our group, live even slightly farther east and are our outermost house. Both outlying homes are housing additional couples—all senior citizens who, by all accounts, are faring well during this time and are working as part of Sarah's sewing crew, with some even on the militia or wood cutting crews.

"They're dead," he says quietly. "The river people are dead."

"The river people are dead?" I repeat, sinking into the sofa. Tate squirms at the sudden lack of motion. As his face wrinkles in preparation of crying, I begin to gently rock side to side. "What happened?"

"It's Prospect. Majors sent his . . . his murderers."

"Everyone?" I ask in a squeak as my eyes sting. There were complete families left behind, banding together to get through the winter.

"We found children—Gabe Griffin's son and daughters plus a little boy and girl who were living in Gabe's shop. Everyone else . . . they were the only survivors."

"Evan, I . . . I don't understand."

He turns from the woodstove to face me, his eyes glistening. In an even voice, he says, "Our friends were murdered. Because of the children and other witnesses, we know it was an attack from Prospect. There's going to be a meeting about it tonight."

Evan saying there will be a meeting tonight reminds me of last night's joyous meeting. This will be nothing of the sort. "What will we do?"

He starts to speak, then shakes his head. "They don't leave us with much of a choice. They'll come for us next."

Evan stays for a cup of tea while he shares what he knows, his news squelching the excitement of my friends' arrival and the radio announcement, the fact this might all be over soon. Doris let him know about what happened during the short time he, Jake, and the others were gone. We briefly discuss what this might mean. Like Doris, he seems less than optimistic about things changing anytime soon.

While devastated over the loss of our Bakerville friends, I have questions about my boss and his family arriving from Oregon. That also includes sadness when Evan tells me Bart, the founder of the business and an energetic seventy-five-year-old, didn't make it. He became ill along the way and passed. Ben, his wife Clarice, and their son Liam, along with an adult female and several children they found along the way, are in varying degrees of health. The worst of the bunch, the other woman and her two children, rode back on the horses. They're also at Rudy's being cared for. Ben and the rest were well enough to begin their journey walking, with Jake as their guide. With the wagon picking them up, they should be here before dinner tomorrow night.

Not even fifteen minutes after Evan leaves, there's another knock at the door.

"Mrs. Caldwell? It's Toby James," he calls out as I make my way to answer.

"Hey, Toby," I say, opening the door. "More sewing?" In addition to often jetting Doris and me up the hill to the ski lodge, he is part of the delivery crew—or as we refer to them, runners—for sewing, food, and whatever else.

"Nope. Mr. Snyder asked me to bring you a note."

"Oh?"

He thrusts it toward me. "I'll be waiting by the bridge to take you up to dinner tonight." He gives a wave and a smile, then turns to leave.

"You were on at breakfast too. Long day for you?"

He spins back in my direction with a shrug. "We had someone call in sick."

"Really?"

"Yeah. Sounds like there's a lot of people sick today." He gives me a shrug and another wave. "See you later."

**The note from Evan simply says: Other than the news of your friends, keep the rest of the discussion under your hat. We're postponing the meeting until everyone arrives.**

I'd barely finished reading when another knock sounds. "Yes?"

"It's me, Mom," Sarah answers. As I open the door, she says, "Sorry it took me so long, that Delores Lancaster was in a mood today." Sarah sits on the bench to remove her boots. "She was going on and on about—oh, I don't even know what. You know how she is. Then Mrs. Gallagher and I got to talking. You know—what's wrong? Are you feeling bad?"

I put on a smile. "Not at all. I'm good."

"You've been crying."

"Yes, we have the most wonderful news. Ben's here. Well, not *here* here, but he was at our house."

"Ben . . . who's Ben? Oh! Your boss?"

"Can you believe it? Evan came back early and told me the news. Jake is walking with Ben and his family, but they're sending the wagon back for them. They'll be here tomorrow night."

"That's amazing, Mom! You must—wow. I can't even believe it. They made it all the way from Oregon? Did they walk?"

"I don't really know. We didn't get into details. All I know is there's a few more people with them. A woman and her children rode up on the horses. Belinda's checking her out. And . . . Bart's dead. He didn't make it."

"Oh, Mom, I'm so sorry." With one boot on and one boot off, she stands and moves quickly, wrapping me in a hug. As Sarah comforts me, my tears return—not only for Bart but for those in Bakerville who were murdered. As requested by Evan, I keep quiet about their deaths.

I'm slightly surprised when nothing's said about the Bakerville proper massacre at dinner. Even though Evan said to keep it quiet, secrets on the mountain are rare. I catch Doris's eye and know she knows. As Evan's wife, it's to be expected. She gives me a nod and lifts her chin slightly before looking away. I swallow the lump forming in my throat.

There's some talk about the hunters returning early, but it's credited to the appearance of my friends—which was not kept secret. My guess is Evan used the news to his advantage, and since they did still bring us a mess of geese, it was glossed over.

I'll admit, there's a few grumbles about how the refugees from Oregon create additional mouths to feed. But overall, the fact they made it here alive gives many people hope. Almost everyone has family and friends in various parts of the country. With our lack of communication, no one knows how their loved ones are doing. For Ben and his family to show up from halfway across the country is a miracle, and we all know it.

And I believe the president's announcement about how this will be ending soon adds to the belief that others may have survived and people will be reunited with their loved ones. Once this is over, a few more mouths won't make a difference. Really, how long will Ben and Clarice even need to be here? Maybe by springtime we'll be telling them goodbye as they make their way back home.

After the meal, Evan pulls me aside. "Thanks for your discretion."

"The wagon got away okay?"

"Yes. Dax and Dusty, along with a new guy, Donnie, were already gone when I got back to the stables."

"Who's Donnie?"

"That's another thing we're being discreet about."

"Okay . . . "

"Things will make more sense tomorrow. I talked with Jude Poppe, and he felt it best we have all the facts first. Because Donnie is one of the witnesses, along with his brother Jerry, he wants to have more details. And he wanted Donnie and Jerry here for questions. He knows them both and feels they'll add value to the discussion."

I shake my head, confused about who these brothers even are. "They'll add value? And you think that's more important than— " I glance around to make sure no one is within earshot. Out of extra caution, I lower my voice to a whisper. "And you think *adding value* is more important than people knowing about their friends' deaths?"

"Does it make a difference? Can they do anything about it tonight they can't do tomorrow night?"

I barely avoid rolling my eyes. "Are they . . . secure?"

"We made sure everyone was inside, if that's what you mean. We'll go back down to Bakerville, maybe move all the bodies to one location and then— " He shrugs. "I'm not sure what we'll do. It's too many graves."

I shake my head as my eyes fill again.

"There's still some supplies the raiders didn't take. We'll either bring those here or hide them. We'll need to come up with a plan. Anyway, I wanted to tell you the ones who arrived today are all going to stay at Rudy's until everyone else returns. We thought it'd be easier this way."

"Easier to keep things quiet?"

"Exactly. We've also started increasing security. I think we're safe for now, but what happened there— " He breaks off and gives an exaggerated shrug.

"Could happen here," I finish for him.

# Chapter 7

## *Sunday, Day 244*

## *Mollie*

The secret was still in place this morning at breakfast, and again at lunch. There were many congratulations directed toward me, which Malcolm gladly answered and told everyone just how excited he was about the new arrivals. Excited is an understatement. He's practically giddy over Liam arriving.

At two years older, Liam is everything Malcolm hopes to be—or at least everything he hoped to be before all of this. I can't tell you how many times in the past I heard about the virtual reality set Liam had and how Malcolm *really* needed one just like it. He also loves Liam's dirt bike, the new laptop he got, and so on and so on. Will any of those things matter now? Will they be able to have a friendship without the hero worship from before?

Tate makes a cooing noise from his blanket on the floor. He's so perfect. Innocent and adorable. There were seventy-eight people living in Bakerville proper when Jake visited before Christmas. They'd lost a few of their elderly in the couple of months since we'd left. Out of those seventy-eight, around two dozen were children, a couple under the age of two. Out of all of them, Evan only brought back five.

I've kept the secret about the massacre from everyone, holding the feelings of loss inside. Once Jake and the others return, we'll mourn together. There have been so many deaths since this all began, plus the thousands upon thousands of people who died in the direct attacks from the planes, bridges, and more. In each address after a new attack, the president assured us they would track down the perpetrators and bring them to justice. Did that happen? Do they even know who's responsible?

40

And what about the nuke producing the EMP or the ones that hit the coastal cities? Was the same group behind those attacks, or was it someone else? How many people died in the bombings? Since the news we receive is so sketchy, we don't even know the exact number of cities bombed; we only have a general idea. And with the high-altitude nuclear detonation resulting in an EMP stretching across the country, the death toll soared as people starved, were murdered, or took their own lives. We've lost so many of our loved ones and community members.

Since we've moved to the mountain, many more people have died. Two teenage girls were targeted by what we believed to be a serial killer. Doctor Sam succumbed to the injuries he received when shot. Several, like Lois, died of natural causes. And then others, like Deanne, were murdered in the attempted takeover.

But to lose so many at one time—good, kind people who were just doing what they thought was best for their family . . . I know Evan's right. I've heard about Richard Majors and the things he did in Prospect, the people he killed so he could take control of the town, plus the people he killed after taking control. The county sheriff was among his victims. And we don't even really know what he's done in the last five months since the Camerons and their friends fled Prospect and we've kept to ourselves.

Remembering the Camerons' arrival reminds me of the two families who arrived with them and stayed in Bakerville proper, living with the river people. I wonder if Pamela Cameron knows? She must since her husband Dusty and son Dax were among the goose hunters who went to Bakerville. Maybe I should go visit her? We can quietly grieve together.

Sarah's in the kitchen working on the sewing team schedule for next week. While we don't really need an actual schedule, since most of us are essentially homebound, I think it makes her feel better to know who's available each day, especially for the few of us who are part timers and also belong to other work crews.

The younger children are playing in the upstairs loft, and Marc, Malcolm, and Tony are with Tim practicing their archery skills. They'll bring back several loads of firewood when they return. The littles are supposed to be drawing or playing with LEGO bricks, but there were plenty of squabbles this afternoon. Both Sarah and I have had to redirect them several times. Their bickering is about to get on my last nerve; I'm about ready to send them all to their bedroom where they can stay until dinner.

"Sarah, I think I'll step out for a bit."

"Are you going to go hang out by the corrals to wait for Jake?"

I give her a smile. "While that does sound tempting, I thought I'd go for a walk. Maybe stop and visit a few friends. You can handle the children okay?"

She shakes her head. "They're something today, aren't they? I think there's some excitement over new people arriving."

"They're something all right," I answer as a squeal pierces the house.

"I'll go check on them, maybe put the younger ones down for a nap. Are you up to walking?" she asks in a motherly voice.

"Feeling good today. Strong," I say with a nod, meaning it. "Plus, I think the walk will help with the kink in my back."

"You said the same about stretching earlier. Did it help?"

"Some." I nod.

"Do you want me to bring the truck and pick you up somewhere?"

"No. No, I'll be fine. Evan thought Jake would be home around sunset, so I'll probably make my way to the corrals to wait for him."

"You're sure?"

"Yes, Mother," I say with a laugh. *Hmm. Maybe she's right.* Honestly, right now, I do feel strong enough to walk home. I haven't had any episodes of lightheadedness or extreme exhaustion in weeks. I'm exercising almost daily with stretches and self-defense, but I'm sure to pace myself so I don't get too winded. The shortness of breath comes on quick, and the feeling of gasping for air is not only uncomfortable but scary. When I'm stretching, it rarely happens. But if I attempt anything resembling cardio, forget it. I'm immediately done.

While I start dressing in my outerwear, Sarah pops upstairs. I listen as she calmly tells Andy, Sissy, and Lily they need to go take a nap. She wisely instructs Lily to go to my room and lie down. If both she and Sissy are sent to the room they share with Sarah and Andy, there will be little sleeping going on, just more playing and arguing.

I'm almost ready to leave when Sarah starts back down the staircase. "Have you thought of where everyone will sleep?"

"For now, we'll use the den and put mattress pads out. I'm not sure what the long-term plan will be. I don't think there are any empty places for them to stay, so we'll most likely move them in with us."

"Things aren't quite the same now, are they? Do you still need to sponsor them?"

I shrug. Our old bylaws required anyone staying in the community in the days after the EMP to be sponsored by an already established family, or they'd go in front of the Bakerville council to plead their case. Following the attempted coup, our bylaws were essentially dissolved, and we're in the process of developing a new form of government. I don't know what will be needed; I guess I should check in with Jude Poppe and see if that's been addressed. I do know, one way or another, Ben and everyone else traveling with him will be staying. I'll make sure of it.

With snowshoes attached to my boots and my body bundled against the cold, I start the half-mile walk to the ski lodge where Pamela Cameron and her husband Dusty live. I didn't even think of asking Evan where the others are. He mentioned Dusty and Dax took the wagon along with the other guy, Donnie. But he didn't say anything about Noah Hammer or Pete Fairbanks, who also left with Jake and Evan for the goose hunt.

Taking the main driveway out of the dude ranch toward the ski lodge is a slight downhill grade. Even though it's an easy walk and I'm taking a leisurely pace, I still feel winded by the time I reach the large parking lot of the former ski lodge. I stop for a few minutes to catch my breath.

Along the creek, the water crew is using a gravity pump to collect the day's allotment of washing and bathing water. Our place, the ski lodge, and three residential homes all have running water of some sort, but the dude ranch cabins, RVs, and camp trailers are all dry. The water crew removes two barrels, three times a day—not an easy task when the creek tends to refreeze between use—taking one barrel to a parking lot at the dude ranch and leaving the other here. Residents fill their containers, giving them water for washing or cleaning up in their homes. Jugs of drinking water are gathered from the ski lodge or our place.

Heath Jefferson sees me and lifts a hand. I raise my chin in response. Heath and I were on a search party together when one of our community members went missing back in November. Sadly, she was

43

dead when we found her. I found him to be odd, but then later discovered he wasn't only odd but had some serious issues. He severely beat his wife, Dot, leaving her for dead before disappearing into the wilderness. Search parties were formed to find him, in hopes of bringing him to justice, to no avail.

Turns out, he'd joined up with Dawson's group that attempted to overthrow our legitimate government. When the coup was stopped, Heath was one of only three agitators left alive. Now he, along with the other two—Shannon and Roscoe—are prisoners. Instead of being locked up, they work on what is essentially a chain gang. Their legs are connected to each other with heavy chains and cable ties during their work hours, and they're kept locked in our makeshift jail when not at work.

We're currently using plastic zip ties—a commodity we still have in abundance, thanks to their usefulness in our rural lives—but our novice blacksmith has plans to make forged shackles. Though he had an interest in blacksmithing prior to our world changing, his skills aren't quite what we need yet. Rumor is he's finally producing a decent horseshoe, but anything beyond that is still out of reach.

Doris has rationed out the zip ties needed for securing the prisoners and given him a May 5th deadline to have actual shackles made. In addition to leg shackles, we need handcuffs. A few of the retired LEOs have their own, but most of us keep the zip ties in our day packs in case we should need to secure someone. Had I realized how useful these plastic fasteners would be, I'd have added even more to our supplies.

I chew my lip, thinking about the stash of them we still have in the garage at home. They weren't on the list of required items to contribute when moving to the mountain. At the time, I'm sure no one realized their value, especially since we never considered we'd have a chain gang.

We were all supposed to get along, living peacefully in our little mountain utopia. That's not what's happened. While there doesn't appear to be any additional threat of insurrection, there's plenty of bickering and arguing. Just like my children picking on each other and carrying on, the adults often act in a similar manner. It's like kindergarten recess some days.

Keeping the three as prisoners was one of our big arguments and was met with much opposition. With the murders from the attempted takeover, many thought it was appropriate to execute them. Heath argued he was never a part of it, all he did was stand guard over Macie Michaelson who was kidnapped by the group to keep her dad Mick in line.

Mick, part of our previous community council, voted in favor of unarming the community. Jon Dawson and his cronies knew, in order to successfully assume control of the community, they'd need the advantage of having us without weapons. I guess he didn't think about how many would ignore the orders and conceal carry against the mandate issued by the council. My lips turn up slightly as I remember how we all went to great lengths to keep our weapons hidden. My son-in-law Mike, who had carried a pocket pistol on his right front side for many years, had it easiest. At least our baggy winter clothes helped with the concealment.

Heath made a good argument, and former attorney Jude Poppe went to his aid. They'll be kept under lock and key until an official county or state government is reestablished. Deputy Clark Thomas, who's in charge of law enforcement on the mountain, added two more deputies to his group so they'd have enough people to monitor the prisoners. Shannon Decker and her brother-in-law Roscoe were also part of Jon Dawson's group, though neither were responsible for any deaths.

Roscoe was still operating on the militia and tasked with keeping our militia and security squad away from the dining hall at the ski lodge where a wedding reception was taking place. The fact Dawson chose to use Harry and Annette English's wedding for the attempted seizure is terrible. Such a joyous day, a day the entire community had been looking forward to, was marred with death. Shannon was complicit in the attempted takeover and, according to Roscoe, was even one of the ringleaders. Thanks to quick action by one of our youth, TJ Bosco, she was unable to perform any murderous acts of her own. As soon as TJ realized we were fighting back, he tackled Shannon, hitting her so hard her head bounced off the floor and knocked her unconscious.

My eyes glance to Shannon. Instead of working, she's staring back at me. She narrows her eyes and makes a rude gesture with her hand. My interaction with her has been minimal. I didn't know her before the attacks changed our lives. I've never even had an actual conversation with her. She shot a few dirty looks in my direction during the time she was campaigning for our disarmament, mainly because my daughter Sarah was very outspoken about keeping our weapons. There were also a few verbal altercations with Shannon and Doris, some of which I witnessed. Her animosity toward me makes little sense. With a shake of my head, I turn my attention to the trail ahead of me.

It's a slight incline to reach the bridge. After crossing, I'll have a steep grade. A year ago, I had zero trouble walking up the hill. Jake, Malcolm, and I would ski here most weekends from December to March. Malcolm was part of a downhill ski club, while Jake and I would alternate between alpine skiing, Nordic skiing, and snowshoeing.

The Nordic and snowshoe trails were well groomed, taking off in various directions from the ski lodge, giving loops or out and backs ranging from 1 to 7K. Some were flat and easy, while others were much more challenging. The resort even had snowshoe and cross-country ski rentals—all of which have come in handy as we've repurposed the ski resort.

Now none of the trails are groomed. While we do use the grooming machine to keep the road between the ski lodge and the dude ranch cleared, plus the dude ranch loops and the main road down to the Young's house at the end. We don't have the fuel to spare for grooming trails. Even without the trails being maintained, they're still used by our sentry team as part of their physical training. And a few community members ski or snowshoe for fun. Although, with as hard as everyone works, off time tends to be spent in front of the fireplace recovering from the physical labor.

I shake my head, thinking about what I used to be able to do compared to what I can do now. Today, just walking up the slope to the ski lodge is too much for me. I take a few steps, very slowly, then stop to breathe. I'm not even halfway when I wonder what in the world I was thinking. My heart is pounding in my chest like I've just sprinted the 7K Nordic trail. Tears are forming in my eyes as I realize I'm woefully out of shape and short of breath. Feeling my head start to spin, I bend my knees and sit in the snow.

"Mollie?"

I jump at the sound of my name. Spinning my head, I give a nod. "Hey, Clark. You scared me."

"Sorry 'bout that. You okay?" Deputy Clark Thomas asks.

"I don't—I'm a little winded. This hill is steeper than I remember."

46

"Yeah, it's a bear somedays. Where you headed?"

"To visit Pamela Cameron. I didn't think about how long it's been since I actually walked up this slope. Last time, well, I guess I was in better condition."

"Why don't I grab the utility sled we have in the office? I'll give you a ride the rest of the way."

I let out a soft laugh. "Maybe just walk with me? That way, if I get lightheaded again, I'll have you to keep me from falling over and cracking my skull open."

"Yep. Happy to help." He gives me a hand to pull me to my feet, then waits a moment to make sure I'm stable. "Ready?"

With a nod, I take a tentative step. I should probably give up this folly and head back down the hill, but being halfway toward the top convinces me to keep going. After only a few steps, I stop to rest.

"Evan said he told you about the situation back home?"

I give a tight nod. "It's terrible."

"Yes, it is. I suppose we were naive to think it couldn't happen, that Majors's people wouldn't come after our community."

"I was surprised when Gabe Griffin and the rest of them still decided to stay after the Camerons told us just how bad things had become. It was one thing when it was just the idea of defending ourselves from a group who just happened upon us. It was completely different when we knew there was a serious threat just thirty miles away."

"True," he says. "But keep in mind, most who stayed were either related or had been friends for years. Many of them had relatives who homesteaded the area."

"Oh, I get wanting to protect your property." I'm starting to breathe hard from the exertion and trying to carry on a conversation.

"Not just that," he says, motioning me to stop. "We, too, lost people we shouldn't have. We were stupid not to realize the threat Dawson and his people posed. We knew from Deputy Fred something was going on, we just didn't put much stock in its validity."

"It still doesn't make sense to me. What did Dawson hope to gain?"

"No telling. People get a taste of power, then they get groupies—like Shannon and her sister—and they like it, they want more. I still feel bad for Dawson's wife and sons. I genuinely believe they had no idea what was happening, but so many people look at them like pariahs now, insisting they were involved. They're essentially outcasts."

47

"Jackson Nicolson's wife too," I say, remembering how Tamra has been treated since her husband was discovered to be responsible for the murders of at least three women—the first when we still lived on the homestead, my adopted grandchildren's mother Lydia, which was staged to look like a suicide. The other two happened after we moved to the mountain. He didn't even bother to disguise those, making it clear it was foul play.

"Yep. And it doesn't help she wasn't a part of the community before the attacks. Rochelle too. Being married to Deputy Fred, and then him escaping after we found what type of person he really was and killing the men taking him to justice."

"I don't notice it as much with Rochelle," I say. "She's got such a pleasantness about her and is always working so hard. I think people respect her. Plus, most people know she was being held against her will and didn't marry Fred by choice but because her and her daughters were his prisoners. And Rochelle goes out of her way to try and include Tamra and her daughters in things. She's definitely a welcoming person."

"Yes, but you heard about them not rooming together, right? Rochelle offered Tamra and her girls to move into their cabin with them so Harry and Annette could have Tamra's studio. Tamra declined."

"I thought the reason behind it was Annette's injuries? With the steps getting into the cabin, they decided it'd be easier for her to have one of the dorms in the ski lodge."

"I think there was more to it. Annette's gunshot wound was a convenient excuse."

I give a shrug, not sure I want to try and decipher the dynamics of people and their personal issues. But I do make a mental note to make a point of talking with Tamra more and including her in things.

*"I'm ready to walk again."* Will we ever reach the top of this blasted hill?

"You've heard she plans to go after her son? PJ Cameron is going to take her as soon as they think spring is on the horizon."

"Rochelle? Her son's summer camp was outside of Billings, right?"

"East of there, yes."

Her son was away at a camp in Montana when the attacks started. Her and her husband, along with their two daughters, were on their way to get him when the EMP hit, stalling their vehicle between Meeteetse and Cody. Determined to find their son, they started on foot, only to be accosted by evil men. Her husband was murdered before their eyes, and Rochelle and her daughters were taken captive. Not long after, Deputy Fred purchased them and brought them to Bakerville. It was several months before we found out she wasn't a willing participant in her marriage to Fred. After the illegal marriage was brought to light, Fred disappeared.

"There was talk, but I didn't know it was decided. I think it's a good idea. I'd want to go after my child if he was missing," I say, before changing the subject. "Do you have plans to increase protection on the mountain?"

"Yeah. Evan and Bill have some good ideas. And Cole, he's definitely knowledgeable."

Like Clark, Evan and Bill are retired law enforcement. Bill was a Prospect County deputy sheriff until he retired a few years ago. Evan is a retired SWAT member of a large metropolitan force on the West Coast, while Clark was a motorcycle cop in Georgia. Cole Gunderson is a Marine. Enlisting straight out of high school and putting in his twenty, he returned to his family home in Bakerville after retirement and started a bail bondsman business. Evan, Bill, and Cole oversee our militia and security team while Clark is in charge of the police force.

After we finally near the hilltop, Clark says, "How about I walk you inside? Pamela and Dusty live on the main floor, right?"

"Right on the backside of the new kitchen. She says it's convenient for her kitchen duty days. Of course, not so convenient on the days she's cooking at my place."

"Yeah. It's a good set up, though. Deanne did a fine job planning and organizing. Pamela and Annette have big shoes to fill."

A pang of grief runs through me at the mention of Deanne, but I shove it aside. "Annette's a natural organizer. She'll do great."

"Need an arm to walk back down the hill?"

I give him an embarrassed smile. "Downhill isn't as big of an issue as uphill is. Thanks for walking with me."

"I'm praying for you, Mollie. Praying you'll make a full recovery."

# Chapter 8

## *Mollie*

After all that, my knock at Pamela's apartment door went unanswered. When the lodge was operating in its original capacity, the main floor had a large open gathering space with tables and a huge fireplace. We've kept the tables to use for our meals, and the fireplace got a woodstove insert, which does a decent job of heating the building. The huge commercial kitchen and large storage space behind it were gutted. We now have a small kitchen used for meal prep, combined with the kitchen at my lodge and an outdoor firepit where most of the meat and flatbread cook. The remaining area became several small dorm-style apartments large enough for a double or queen bed and small closet. The first-floor daylight basement has similar dorms.

When this was a ski lodge, the first floor had ski rentals, a first aid station, ski patrol, and administrative offices. Before we moved up here, Katie assisted Doris with redesigning the building to suit our needs, adding not only the apartments on the first level but also a twenty-four-hour nursery for the younger children in the community. Providing the nursery/daycare space lets the adults work the many needed jobs to keep our society going.

There's even a loft in the building. It used to be my favorite place in the lodge when we'd come up to ski. The windows stretch across the entire space and overlook the slopes. It was fun to have lunch and watch the skiers. The reworked space now houses our men's and women's bunkrooms. With a staircase on either end giving double entry points, a wall was added down the middle, giving separate access to each space.

The main thing this ski lodge was lacking to make it truly livable was full baths. The daylight basement had multi-stall and multi-sink his and her restrooms, and the main level had two family-style half baths, but no showers. Without a decent way to add them and only one small hot water tank surviving the EMP, it didn't make sense to build showers or put in bathtubs. Hot showers are available at the lodge where I live or at ski resort owners Ellen and Zeb's house, which is a short walk from the ski lodge. The bother of a shower is usually skipped, with many people preferring to heat water in the kitchen for a sponge bath in their apartment.

Deciding it smart to visit the women's room before starting my trek back down the hill, I make my way toward the facilities. As I reach for the door to push it open, it widens.

"Oh!" Sabrina Eriksen, my friend Kelley Hudson's daughter, says with a start. "Hey, Mollie."

"Sorry I startled you."

"It's fine. I was just lost in my own world."

"You on nursery duty today?" I ask.

"Not today. I had watch last night and again tonight. I'll be in the nursery tomorrow afternoon."

"You have watch two nights in a row?"

"Yeah. We had someone call in sick, so I volunteered."

"Seems to be going around."

Sabrina gives a shrug. "I'm going back up to my bunk to see if I can get a little more sleep."

"At least this isn't a school day. I don't know how those of you living in the bunkhouse and these apartments sleep when the children are all here."

"It's not easy. Oftentimes, we'll bunk with someone else or sack out on one of the cots at the militia headquarters. I'll see you later." She gives me a wave and a smile before leaving.

After finishing in the restroom, I pass by Pamela's place again, just in case she came in during the last few minutes. Nope.

With a sigh, I stop at the coat rack by the door where I've stowed my winter gear. Clunking around inside with the spikes on the snowshoes would not be okay. Stepping outside, I give an exaggerated shiver. The wind came up and it's considerably colder, almost biting. I slip on the hood of my jacket and button the neck area.

As I clomp back down the hill, I realize Pamela may be at Rudy Wallace's place, helping with the new additions to our community. Had I not had the insane struggle of the incline earlier, I might foolishly decide to walk to Rudy's. No way am I up for that. Thankfully, going down isn't the challenge of earlier. As I cross over the bridge, I decide to visit with Doris at the supply shed. She and her supply team have taken over the garage and a couple of outbuildings at Zeb and Ellen's house to store our necessary supplies. It also acts as a pseudo grocery store, allowing us to get our weekly rations and other necessities. And the driveway reaching the supply shed, though long, is completely flat.

"Hey, how you doin'? Good to see you out and about," Doris calls out from her place behind the counter as I'm leaning against the wall to take off my snowshoes.

"Hi, Mollie," Doris's daughter Lindsey says with a wave.

"Hey, Doris, Lindsey. Is your mom putting you to work today?"

"Nope. Just visiting. She's on her own."

"Not exactly," Doris says. "Shelby and Milena are organizing B shed. Have you seen Shelby's little Hannah lately? She's getting so big."

"She brought her by to visit Sarah and Tate a few days ago. Does Shelby still wear the baby while she's working?"

"Yep. It works well. I think some people stop by just so they can play with the baby—getting their weekly rations is almost an afterthought."

"I need to take off," Lindsey says. "We're having a meeting before dinner. Bye, Mom."

"See you at dinner?"

"Yeah, don't you always?" Lindsey asks, waggling her eyebrows. "You know better than to think I'll skip a meal."

"See you later," I say.

Once we're alone, I ask, "Are you—how are you holding up?"

"Terrible. It's so sad. I can't believe . . . " Doris lets out a long, slow breath. "I hate keeping this a secret."

"Lindsey knows?"

"No. Only the officers and Clark. Evan didn't want to tell Lindsey and have it seem like special treatment."

"I'm ready for Jake to get home."

"And your friends, too, I bet. What a miracle! I'm so sorry for the loss of the father. I know you were close to him."

"Thank you. Yes, he was always good to me, made a point of making me feel like an important part of the team, even though they didn't see me often. The others getting here . . . miracle is certainly the right word."

52

Doris lets me talk about Bart and how much I'll miss him for several minutes before she asks, "How's the new job? Your fingers holding up?"

"Barely! It's hilarious I'm part of the sewing team. You know me . . . I didn't do any kind of crafts or handiwork before."

Doris lets out a small laugh. "I'm glad Sarah's in charge of the sewing. When we worked together over the summer, it was obvious she knew what was needed. And I'm sure she's quite the supervisor, getting you well trained."

"She's doing her best, but I'm a challenge. I've yet to move past the basics, like replacing buttons and patchwork. I can barely even sew a straight hem. Wait until you see the toilet paper squares I made."

"Well, we all have to start somewhere."

"Can I help you with anything?"

"You looking for something to fill your time with until Jake and your friends get here?"

"Exactly."

Doris puts me to work dusting and organizing. After a while, she says, "It's probably getting about time."

"Yep. Thanks for letting me hang out with you."

With a laugh, she says, "Come work here anytime. Once your friends get settled, I'd love to see them again."

"We'll have you over for dinner," I say with a wink. We both know it's a lie since all our meals are community affairs at the ski lodge, but it feels nice to say something seminormal in this abnormal world.

I take my time walking to the small corral, leaning against one of the small tack sheds once I arrive. The wind kicks up as the sun drops, making my layers feel lacking. Cold and wind are common in Wyoming, though this year's snow is something else. Definitely more than I've ever seen in the years we've been coming up here to ski. When Jake and Evan went goose hunting before Christmas, they'd taken the snowmobiles. Jake and I joked he might end up on foot once down at the lower elevations. While each winter we'd see snow in Bakerville, it'd often only last a few days at a time, and only enough for snowmobiles immediately after a good snow.

On that trip, there was more than enough snow for the snowmobile. And there's a considerable amount of snow now. According to Evan, though less snow than what we have on the mountain, it's deeper than any time since he's lived there and is bitingly cold. Just when I think I'll need to return to the lodge for a heavier coat, Art Carpenter, my daughter Angela's father-in-law, comes over.

"Mollie? You're looking chilled," he says as he hands me a wool blanket. "Better pull the gaiter up to your nose. You'll get frostbite."

"You're a mind reader, Art!"

"Not a mind reader. Figured it was time for them to get here and thought I'd help with the horses. Heard your teeth chattering from a quarter mile away, so I went back for the blanket."

"A quarter mile, huh?"

"Must have been," he says with a wink. "I think I hear 'em. Shouldn't be long."

"You hear them? The horses?"

"Yup. Listen."

I close my eyes to focus on my surroundings. One amazing thing about living on a mountain encompassed by snow are the sounds. Everything seems clear and yet far away at the same time. "I still don't hear them."

"You will."

Less than a minute later, the clomp of hooves reaches my ears. About thirty seconds after, as the sun dips behind the mountain, the team comes into view. Jake's sitting up front with Dusty Cameron driving. His son Dax and another man are on horses riding alongside. With my heart pounding, I wave vigorously. Jake shows as much enthusiasm in his return greeting. The five minutes it takes for them to reach the corral stretches on forever.

The wagon has barely stopped when Jake jumps down, wraps me in a hug, and says, "Brought you a gift."

"Hey, Mollie," my former employer Ben says, poking his head above the side of the wagon. He's bundled against the cold with his face covered by a heavy balaclava and a thick hat on his head. Sparse whiskers poke out around the edges of the fabric, and long thin hair hangs almost to his shoulders.

"Hey, Ben." I move toward them as Jake moves to the back of the wagon and lets down the gate. Jake offers his hand to Ben and helps him out. Even with his multiple layers, he's noticeably skinnier than when I last saw him.

Once he's on the ground, he limps toward me, enveloping me in a hug. "You heard about Dad?" he asks in a whisper.

54

"I'm so sorry. So, so sorry," I say through my tears—a combination of grief over the loss of Bart and elation Ben and the others are here.

Ben releases me and says, "Clarice and Liam—they were with him. It was important to him they got to you, where he knew they'd be safe."

"He made me promise," Clarice says, now standing next to Ben. "You look good, Mollie."

I let out a laugh as we give each other a hello hug. Like Ben, she's thin. She's always been lean, but not sickly. Now, as I hug her, I'm certain I can feel her bones. Even in the low light, it's obvious her face is chapped and windblown. Her upper lip's completely raw from the cold combined with a runny nose. Liam, looking much like his mom from the extreme cold, is next—also gaunt and much taller than he was just those few short months ago.

"Hi, Mollie," he says in a deep man's voice. "Malcolm isn't with you?"

"He's at the house. We'll see him soon. Who are your friends?" I ask, smiling at the young girl around Malcolm's age and an older teenage girl holding a baby.

Clarice reaches for the baby. "This is Wyatt." She plants a kiss on his upturned forehead. "And this is Leslie." She motions to the younger girl. "And Destiny. They're—we're family."

"Good to meet you," I say. "And I've heard there's a few others who were traveling with you?"

"Traveling with me," Ben says.

I must give him a dumb look because he continues with, "Clarice and I were separated along the way. She met up with the children. It's a long story."

"How about we get inside where it's warm and then get caught up?" Jake asks.

Getting warm doesn't take too long. Sarah made sure the fire was well stoked, and the lodge is toasty. As Ben removes his facial covering, I get a good look at his sunken cheeks and the scar running from under his left eye to his chin.

My children—minus Katie, who's on duty at the medical clinic—grandchildren, Jake's parents, Karen, Alina, and Victor are all spread out in the great room, excited to greet the new arrivals. The hellos had to be exhausting for the newcomers. Young Wyatt did take particular interest in baby Tate.

55

"Are you his mom?" I ask Destiny.

"His parents were killed," Clarice says.

"Clarice is his mom now," Leslie, the younger girl, says.

I raise my eyebrows at Clarice, who gives a smile and a shrug. "Seems I am. I had no idea you were going to be a grandma!"

"Nor did I," I say. "Sarah found out right before the EMP hit. And Calley is also expecting."

"Leanne and her children?" Ben asks as he looks around.

"I think she's still at Rudy Wallace's house," I say quietly. I have yet to tell any of my family about the others traveling with Ben and Clarice or the children brought back from the massacre in Bakerville proper.

"It's just about time for dinner," Sarah says. "I thought I'd take everyone over in the truck. Your friends might just want to eat here and rest tonight."

"Good idea," Jake says. "Mollie and I will eat here also. Need my help?"

"No," Sarah says with a wave. "We've got it."

Jake nods and turns to Alvin. "Dad, do you and Mom want to eat with us, or will you go to the ski lodge?"

"We'll take our meal in the kitchen and leave you time with your friends," Alvin answers after looking to Dodie for confirmation.

After the family leaves, Jake asks Ben, "Would you all like to shower while we're waiting for the food?"

"You have real showers?" Liam asks.

"We do. And we have four bathrooms, so it should go quickly. Well, five bathrooms, but the fifth is in my mom and dad's room, so . . . " He lifts his hands in a what-can-I-do motion.

"That's fine," Clarice says enthusiastically. "Um . . . where should I put my chickens?"

"Your chickens?" I ask.

Leslie lifts the box she's been carrying, as Jake says, "Clarice found a couple of hens along the way."

"Oh! Should we take them to Art in the livestock shed?"

"They're kind of pets," Jake says. "I thought we could put them in the laundry room tonight and sort out long-term plans tomorrow."

"Put the chickens in the laundry room?" I ask densely. Jake wanting to keep chickens in the house is odd.

"For tonight," he repeats, flaring his eyes slightly.

We sort out who's using which bathroom, and Jake says he'll get the chickens set up while they're showering. I offer to watch the baby while they take their showers.

"Um, he could use a bath too," Clarice says.

"I can give him one in the kitchen sink. Is that okay?"

"Yes, perfect. In fact, let me do it while the others shower, then I'll take my turn."

"Want some help?" I ask.

While the others disperse, Clarice and I take Wyatt into the kitchen. "It might be too chilly in here," I say. "I have a plastic tub we use for laundry. Let's move it in front of the fireplace."

"Good idea," Clarice says with a smile. "Um, Mollie, first . . . " She lets out a sigh. "I just want to . . . I owe you an apology," she says in a rush.

"An apology?"

"For, you know, being how I've always been with you."

I shake my head and shrug my shoulders. "I don't understand."

"I've always found you a little odd."

I let out a hoot of laughter. "Well, you're not wrong."

With her face flushed, she says, "And I've made fun of you for believing in God."

"Oh. I understand you're not . . . don't worry, Clarice. I won't browbeat you into becoming a believer."

"But I am! A believer, that is. When we were on our way here, I realized I need God, I need Jesus, to guide me. I'm a . . . I'm a Christian now. And— "

"Clarice!" I interrupt, wrapping her in a hug that encompasses Wyatt. "I'm so happy for you. And Liam?"

"Liam too. He was first, in fact. Him reading the Bible and talking about God was what got me interested. At first, I hated it. Bart had just died and . . . with the history with my mom and dad . . . "

I give a nod. She'd gone into extensive detail a few years ago about how Christianity was a waste of time. That was right around the time Jake and I had rededicated our lives and our marriage to the Lord. I'd tried to bring up what I thought were valid points, but she had rather venomously shut me down.

"Anyway, I just wanted you to know I'm sorry for the way I've treated you and I'm changing. With God's help, I'm trying to live more like Jesus would want me to. Jake said you have church here?"

57

"We do, twice a day service usually led by David Hammer—you met him at our barbecue when you last visited—or Chaplain Rick if David isn't available."

"Do you think they'll talk to me and Liam? Make sure we did things right?"

"Did things right?"

"To make sure we're really Christians."

"Oh, yes. The Bible tells us we need to believe in our heart and confess with our mouth. You've done the confessing with your mouth, and it sounds like you believe in your heart . . . "

"I do, definitely."

"Okay, then. Welcome to the family, Clarice." I hug her again. "You should still talk with David or Chaplain Rick. They'll be able to give you guidance on how to move forward. They even have baptisms scheduled, but not until the creek unfreezes. And they do in-depth Bible studies. Oh! You should read the Gospel of John."

"John 3:16 is one I know. Bart had me read it to him, and Liam and I have talked about it. We've been sharing a Bible, but Liam usually does the reading. Sometimes we were so exhausted the reading didn't last long, but I did enjoy it."

"We'll find you your own Bible. That way you can study on your own too."

After a couple more minutes of our hugging and chatting, Wyatt begins to fuss. "Let me get the tub and we can get him taken care of." As I step into the laundry room, the two chickens rush toward me. Both hens appear well cared for, though the brown one looks like she's just coming out of her molt. The black one is a smaller hen, probably from last summer's hatch. I manage to get into the room without letting them out, but just barely. They're certainly friendly little things. I take a quick look around the room to see if there's anything I need to move to avoid chicken doo deposits. My eyes land on the metal trash can in the corner. Is the lid askew?

"Watch out little chicken," I say as I move across the room, then push down the lid of our homemade Faraday cage. This cage, along with two others, kept a few of our electronics working when the EMP hit. We left the other two at our homestead, locked in our secret basement safe room, storing an eReader, my laptop, and Jake's tablet along with a few other items. This one holds an older eReader loaded with all sorts of novels and reference materials, an old laptop for

58

playing flash drives or movies, and Malcolm's tablet. We take them out sometimes, but when they're not in use, they're in this special trash can. While it's unlikely we'd have another EMP, we've decided to reduce the risk of losing these resources. Even though the tablet is mainly for reading and games, recently I realized just what a treasure it is.

Malcolm and I were in the great room. I was reading while he was on the tablet. "Mom?" he said. When I looked up, the tablet made a noise.

"What'd you just do?" I asked.

"Took your picture," he said with a shrug.

"You took my picture?" *Of course.* "You can take pictures with the tablet! Malcolm! That's amazing."

"Okay, yeah. I've always been able to."

"I know! I just forgot it did. Will you take a picture of Tate? No, wait. Let's have Sarah dress him up really cute and you can do a photo shoot of him."

"I can . . . sure. But we can't really *do* anything with them. And I only have a small amount of storage on the tablet. I cleared out a bunch of pictures before I took this one."

"Don't clear anymore. We'll go through them and keep the ones we love. I wish I would've remembered this when Katie and Leo got married!"

"Sorry, Mom. I didn't think about it."

That night, we all spent time looking through the photos and wondering why we didn't think of this before. Katie also took the computer out and tested its camera. It works, too, but it's less convenient than the tablet since everything on the computer is done as a selfie. She used a data cable and moved the ones we wanted to keep from the tablet to the computer, and from there she put them on one of our thumb drives. This freed up space on the tablet so it can be used to take more. With the way things are, the pictures are forever stuck in the devices or on flash drives, waiting until a time when digital photography makes a comeback.

"All right, little chickens," I say as I move back to the door. "Stay in here and don't cause any trouble."

By the time Sarah returns with the meals, everyone's washed and in fresh clothes. Jake grabbed some evergreen boughs to make a nest for the chickens. He fretted over them not being able to roost, but

Leslie said they never do; they've been living with them in a box, tents, or the occasional house for months.

We sit around the large dining room table. After Jake blesses the food, there's silence for many minutes as everyone digs in.

"What is this?" Liam asks, a spear of cubed vegetable on his fork.

"Sugar beet," I answer.

He makes a face and then goes back to eating.

"Sugar beet?" Ben asks. "Like for making sugar?"

"Exactly," Jake says. "One of our farmers in Bakerville was part of a cooperative and had some acreage of sugar beets. It's been our mainstay for the winter."

"When will we be assigned to work groups?" Liam asks.

"Not sure. Dusty was going to stop by our medical clinic, see if one of them can come here and check each of you out. They did a house call for your friends and the children yesterday." Jake gives a nod before turning to Ben. "You remember our daughter Katie?"

"The youngest one?"

"Right. She's part of the medical team. And she's not that young anymore. She got married last summer."

"Mollie said she thought Katie had a boyfriend. But marriage . . . so quickly?"

"Well, with the way things are, there's no reason for long engagements and spending months planning fancy weddings," I say. "It was still lovely."

"When's your grandbaby due?"

"Calley's due in June—well, we think June. We thought Sarah would have baby Tate in February, right about now in fact, but he arrived early January, so . . . " I give a shrug. "Who knows?"

"Babies do come when they want," Clarice says. "And I suspect it's much more difficult now without the technology we had before. No ultrasounds."

"Right." I choose not to say the lack of medical equipment weighs heavy on me. "Oh! I bet you all haven't heard the excitement. Jake, did anyone tell you about the radio broadcast?"

"No . . . what broadcast?"

With a wide smile, I say, "It was the president. He said he's sending out help, and they're even getting the power restored."

The room erupts with questions and shouts of excitement. Baby Wyatt jumps and starts to cry. Clarice soothes him, saying, "Mama's just happy. We're all happy."

Listening to her cooing and comforting the baby is amazing. In all the years I've known Clarice, she's never been the warm and fuzzy type. Even when Liam was young, her interactions with him were different than what I'm seeing with Wyatt. There was no doubt she loved Liam, but it was . . . I can't think of a way to describe the difference. Just different. Clarice must feel me looking at her. She lifts her eyes to meet mine. She gives me a broad smile and lifts her shoulders.

"So, things will go back to normal?" Destiny asks, running a hand through her freshly washed hair. Like many of us, she's sporting roots a different color than her ends. Her roots show her natural dark blond color, while the old dye job is a dull faded black. She's a pretty girl and very athletic looking.

"I don't know," I answer honestly. "We haven't heard any additional announcements, though the original one's replayed a few times. There's speculation the rebuilding will start in the cities—the ones not destroyed by the bombs. You know about the bombs? The nukes?"

"We saw one," Liam says quietly. "We think it was Portland."

I let out a sigh. "Yeah, we heard about that one. And Seattle was hit with more than one. Evan's stepdaughter saw two in California. The radio says they hit Sacramento, San Francisco, and several hit LA. On the East Coast, Washington D.C., Baltimore, New York City, several in Florida—pretty much anywhere they could inflict maximum damage. We think there's more, but we don't know for sure."

"Have you heard who did this to us?" Leslie asks.

"Oh, we've heard plenty," Jake says scornfully. "But we don't know what is true. We've had a ham radio set up since we moved up on the mountain. But we don't talk, only listen. And until recently, we were only told what our community council thought we needed to know. Calley's on the radio team, so . . . well, we may have heard a little more than others, but everything is just rumor and hearsay." Jake turns to me. "Did the president give any info on who did it?"

I shake my head. "That wasn't something he mentioned. He did say he has established a new place of government and they're sending a boat to get help from overseas—oh, and parts of Canada and Mexico were also affected by the EMP, but they're helping us as they can. The exact announcement is written down and available to read in the dining hall."

As we're finishing dinner, our family returns. Katie is with them this time, as is Kelley Hudson.

"Your hair looks great," I say after hugging Kelley hello. "Doris's work?"

"Did this myself," she says, proudly running a hand through her closely cropped black hair with streaks of silver shining like tinsel. "I figured, since you cut yours, I'd give it a try myself. I did need to have Phil help me with the neck and around my ears."

"I love it. Maybe I should take mine that short. Then I could go longer between cuts."

"Yours is perfect. You want to introduce me to everyone? I thought Katie and I would do a quick house call." She turns to Ben and Clarice. "Leo went to get the others who were traveling with you. They're anxious to see you."

After introductions, Ben asks, "Are they doing okay? The children have had a hard time."

Kelley nods. "Rest and regular meals will do them good. Should we get started? We'll use the den."

"There's already a fire going in there," Sarah says. "They'll be sleeping in the den, so we wanted to warm it up. Oh, Mom, there's a meeting after breakfast tomorrow. Everyone's asked to attend unless they're on a shift they can't miss."

I give a slight nod as Ben asks, "Will we attend also?"

"Yes," Kelley responds. "We'll be discussing . . . " She pauses a moment while she appears to gather her thoughts before continuing, "Recent events."

Ben and Liam follow Kelley and Katie into the den. After they're finished, Destiny takes her turn. About a minute later, there's a knock on the front door. Leo escorts a worn-looking woman and two scrawny children inside.

The boy gives Ben a smile and says, "Hey, Ben. They have milk here!"

"Hey, Sebastian," Ben answers, wrapping him in a hug. "I had a glass of milk with dinner. Mine was cow milk. Delicious! I hear they have goat milk also."

"They're going to have sheep milk too," Sebastian says. "But Mr. Wallace says they aren't sheep designed for milking, so they don't know how much milk they'll get."

Our dairy animals are a definite plus. Jake and I brought our small Nigerian Dwarf goat herd up, and several are currently in milk while a few others have been bred and will kid within weeks or months. Nigerian Dwarfs cycle monthly, allowing year-round breeding—a definite plus. Another family had three Nubian does, which were bred to our larger buck back in the fall and should be kidding within a week or two. There's also a couple of Jersey cows plus a Brown Swiss.

The amount of milk we get isn't enough to give us an unlimited supply for the community. The children and infirm are given first priority. As Sebastian mentioned, we hope to add sheep milk. We have a new flock of American Blackbelly sheep—what is classed as hair sheep—which will be lambing soon, along with another family's flock of wool-producing sheep. The plan is to train the first-time moms on the milking stand to add to our production. There's also talk of milking some of the beef cattle after they calve. I'm not sure it will be worth the effort, but we've all agreed to give it a try in order to increase the milk supply.

"The doctor said she wants the children on a special diet," the lady says.

"Yeah." Ben nods. "Same with me. Liam, though, he's doing pretty well."

"I'm sure," she scoffs. I raise my eyebrows at the venom in her response. "What about your foot?"

He shrugs. "Job well done. The amount removed was perfect." Ben must feel my eyes on him because he says, "Got a little frostbite and had to have part of my foot removed."

"Oh! Are you—does it hurt much?" I ask.

"Not now, but I've got a limp. Doc Kelley said it will become less pronounced. I've forgotten my manners," he says. "This is Leanne Monroe." He gestures to the lady. "And these are her children, Sadie and Sebastian. We met them in the mountains of Oregon."

"Pleased to meet you," I say while everyone else offers them greetings.

Leanne responds with a stern nod before turning back to Ben. "What will we do now?"

"We'll be able to rest," Clarice says with a smile.

63

Leanne shoots her a dirty look. "I was asking Ben."

"Clarice is right. We'll rest a few days and get our strength back. Then we'll work to become part of the community."

With a roll of her eyes, she says, "Great. We'll be slaves."

I open my mouth to protest when I feel Jake's warm hand on my shoulder.

Ben slowly says, "When we were walking up, Jake told us a little about how things are arranged here. Everyone does work hard, but we'll also have many conveniences. Did you and the children get showers?"

With a softer look and tone, Leanne says, "We did. And . . . I'm sure it'll be fine here. I'm just tired. It's been a long . . . "

"Several months?" Ben offers.

"For sure," Leanne says.

After Kelley's finished with the exams, we visit for only a few minutes before getting the new arrivals settled in the den and great room. My family members not living in the lodge head off to their own homes, and the rest of us make our way to our rooms. Jake and I talk late into the night about the massacre of the river people and the arrival of Ben and everyone else. We both agree there are big changes in Clarice. We also agree Leanne is struggling. We hold hands as we pray for her and thank God for bringing the others here.

# Chapter 9

## *Lucy*

"So, now, Miss Fleming, why are you here?" We're both in straight-backed chairs sitting less than two feet apart, his eyes boring into me.

"By order of Lieutenant Kruse," I say, attempting to keep my voice calm as his dead stare creeps me out. We're in Doc Bohm's office. The woodstove is belching out a tremendous amount of heat, and there's not one but two propane heaters warming the room. At first, I welcomed the warmth. Now I'm uncomfortable. I've removed my heavy coat but really need to take off my insulated pants. I haven't been this warm since summer. Doc Bohm looks plenty comfortable in dress slacks, a long-sleeved button-up shirt, loafers, and even a tie. A tie! Other than Mayor Majors, no one dresses like that now. Even before the lights went out, people in Prospect—in all of Wyoming, actually—rarely wore ties. "She thinks you can help me."

"And what do you think? Do you need help?"

"I—maybe. It would be good for me to be, um, tougher?"

"Good," he says with something resembling a smile, before slapping me hard across the face. My head swings to the side as my eyes fill with tears and I cry out.

"Why are you here?" he demands.

With my hand on my throbbing cheek and my voice high and pitchy, I say, "Janet—Lieutenant Kruse—ordered me to see you."

He smacks me again, this time with a backhand on the opposite cheek, the one not being protected by my hand. I've met with Doc Bohm twice before during my training. While he was creepy, he didn't abuse me.

"Why are you doing this?" I cry.

"Do I have your attention now?" He stares me down with those dead eyes.

I nod dumbly.

He gives me a creepy smile. "Good. Sometimes it takes more than a little tap to get my subject to focus on me."

"Yes, I . . . you had my attention from the beginning. I don't . . . you don't need to— " As his hand twitches, I stop speaking, only giving another nod. My cheeks burn from the abuse and the embarrassment.

"Let's start again. Why are you here?"

I take a breath to steady my voice. "I didn't perform as expected during the raid."

He gives several slow nods. "And why is that?"

I feel the tears welling up again as I quietly say, "It was the children."

"You refused to follow orders for children you don't know?"

"No. Not only children I don't know. I thought one of my former students might be there."

"Go on."

"She was one of my students. Lily Hatch. She lived in Bakerville. Her mom worked at Greater Prospects Marketing Agency . . . um, you probably don't know about that place since you didn't live here when things were normal."

He flares his nose and raises both eyebrows at me.

I hurry on. "Anyway, Olivia started bringing Lily to us when she was only a few months old. I was working the newborn nursery then, and it was—well, I kept getting moved up as she did, so I've known her for a long time. I'm sure you can understand how I wouldn't— " I hear my voice begin to squeak as tears fill my eyes.

I take a deep breath. "Olivia's job changed a few months before the attacks. She started telecommuting and only coming into Prospect for client meetings. She found a neighbor to watch Lily. It was really a better situation for her since she had an older, school-aged son too— better for Lily too." I give him a nod. "Don't you think?"

"I wouldn't know," he says without emotion. "You believe your inability to perform as expected was directly related to a child you used to know?"

"Yes. I didn't want to . . . " I drop my voice to a whisper. "I wouldn't want to be the one. And I didn't want to find her." I start blinking rapidly. "But I don't think she was there. Her dad worked out of town on oil rigs, and sometimes the family would go and stay with him during the summer."

"Or perhaps she is with the other group from Bakerville. The cowards who left their homes and their neighbors behind in an effort to save themselves."

I narrow my eyes and shake my head. "I'm not sure what you mean."

"Really? I was under the impression you had certain . . . shall we say *inside information*?"

"No . . . " I say as my face colors. "I don't have anything like that."

"Mm-hmm."

After many more minutes of talking, verbally abusing me over my failure to perform as expected, Doc Bohm lets out a sigh. "What trauma in your life left you unable to follow orders?"

"Trauma?"

"Yes, there must be some reason you choose to be insubordinate."

Dropping my eyes to my lap, I quietly say, "I just didn't want to kill the children."

My response earns me not one but several slaps—all in a row. When I cry out for him to stop, he pushes me hard, sending my chair flying backwards. The back of my head thumps on the floor as pain rages through my body. I curl into a ball, expecting him to elicit more abuse. After many minutes, when nothing additional happens, I crack an eye open to see him calmly in his chair, examining his fingernails.

"Please pull yourself together and get back into your chair." He's so focused on his hands, he's not even looking at me. How'd he know I was looking at him?

When I put my chair back in place, I make sure to move it farther away, out of his range of being able to smack me.

"All set, Miss Fleming?" he asks, not commenting on the distance between us.

I give a cautious nod. I'm not really *all set*. What I want is to leave this room immediately before he attacks me again. Or . . . I'll be ready. If he comes at me, I'll react. I can't inflict a blow on him. No . . . I can't imagine what they'd do to me if I touch him. I'd probably be shot. But I can protect myself and avoid the worst of it.

"Good, good," he says pleasantly. "Now we're going to work on retraining your brain. There's a reason you don't follow the orders you're given—orders that are for the best of the good people of Prospect. You do know that. The things you must do, what all the soldiers must do, is for the good of all."

67

"Yes," I mutter.

"What was that?"

"I know we're doing what is needed to keep people alive."

"But you seem to have difficulty with this. Why? Why do you want people to die?"

"I don't! I don't want anyone to die. Especially . . . "

"You were going to say children, weren't you?"

I tilt my head to one side. "I want to do the best I can. I know . . . I know what my job is. I can do it."

"Much better, Miss Fleming. Now, I want you to think about the issues you have. What does not performing your duties make you believe about yourself?"

"I don't . . . what is the question?"

He gives me a patient smile. "When you choose to disobey direct orders, does this give you a sense of superiority?"

"No, I just . . . I want to follow orders."

"But you choose not to. We need to get to the source of why you are insubordinate and then reprogram your brain."

I flinch as he pulls out a pen-like item from his shirt pocket.

"Nothing to worry about." He opens his hand to show it to me. "It's a pen light. We'll use this as part of your retraining. I'll turn the red-light feature on. What I want you to do is stare at the light while I move it back and forth. You'll follow the red light with your eyes only—don't move your head—while you think about how you want to follow orders. You did say you wish to follow orders, right, Miss Fleming? You wish to obey your superiors?"

I give a cautious nod.

"Now think about that, think about your desire to no longer be disobedient." He flicks the red light on and moves it back and forth in front of his chest in an arc motion, the red making a small globe against his white shirt. The whole thing seems rather dumb, but I continue to watch the bouncing light as I think about how I'm supposed to obey any commands I'm given by Janet or those above her. After a short while, he turns off the light and says, "What do you notice now?"

"Notice about what?"

"About your disobedience. How does not obeying orders make you feel?"

"I feel . . . bad. I don't mean— "

68

"I want you to think on that. Think about how when you disobey it makes you a bad person. You want to be good, right? You want to be an important member of the acquisition team? An important person in Prospect? You want— " He gives me a lecherous smile. "You want Mayor Majors to be pleased with you?"

"Yes . . . "

"Good. Think on those things as you watch the light." He turns it on again, allowing it to bounce across his chest as I watch it with my eyes.

We continue like this for at least an hour. He bounces the light around, I watch it move, and then he stops and asks me how I feel or what I notice. We talk a minute and then the bouncing light resumes.

Finally, he says, "Let's end there today, Miss Fleming. I think we've made great progress with your issues. How do you feel?"

"Okay. A little tired."

"Very common. I'll write you a note excusing you from training for the rest of the day. I want you to go home and rest. Think about the things we've discussed today. We'll meet again on Friday."

On the walk from Doc Bohm's office to my dorm, I feel calm— almost relieved. The appointment started off a little rough. *Rough!* What an understatement. But then, when he started with the bouncing light, things got better. The questions he brought up and how he helped me with my feelings were good. I can see how, in many ways, my thinking was wrong. By not doing what's expected of me, I'm letting the entire community down. And as Richard mentioned when I met with him after returning from the mission, even the children are poisoned against us. It's up to us, the good people of Prospector County, to do what is needed to usher in our new life. We all want things to be better. To not only survive but to thrive. Richard Majors is the person to lead us to this success.

Back at my house, I shed my parka, insulated pants, and snow boots in the entryway, giving a shiver as I do so. Even though we have a fireplace, it barely keeps the large house above freezing. To keep the fire going while we're training, family members of those on the acquisition team are assigned as fire tenders, going from house to house. There are others who make sure we have enough wood, and also others who do the cooking and even cleaning.

Even though the family members' duties are similar to those in the working class, they're considered part of the acquisition team simply by association. And their help is what allows us to do the things we do and not have to worry about our day-to-day needs.

Although families can live in the Creek View Estates with the same perks as the acquisition team, some still choose not to. Captain Dirk Murphy's mom has her job working the regular laundry and still lives in the home she shared with her husband. He was one of the people who died early in the attacks, when a medicine he needed ran out. Since Captain Murphy's mom doesn't live in here and he's not married, he shares a house with another single officer, Lieutenant Alverez. I'm not sure why they share. As officers, they're allowed their own homes, and it's not even required they live in The Estates.

Janet Kruse, Lieutenant Knight, Major Lassiter, and a couple of others chose homes outside of the gated community. With the deaths of so many early in the attacks, plus people out of town when they happened, there were plenty of lovely homes to choose from. All live in the older part of Prospect near the hotel, close by Mayor Majors so they can do his bidding at a moment's notice. Interestingly, his son Scott lives in The Estates—a less than convenient location should his dad need him immediately.

While I'm glad there's always a warm fire, it's not enough today, and I'm wishing for one of Doc Bohm's heaters. Instead, I grab the quilted jacket I left in the mudroom and slip into lined slippers. Winter clothing is something we have a decent amount of. Just like with the food rations, the acquisition team is given priority on clothing and other goods.

We each have several coats, at least two pair of insulated pants or bib overalls, and multiple pairs of boots. My dormmates and I also have several of the little blanket things with arms, along with sweaters and hoodies. We shed our outdoor clothes and then put on warm indoor items. We're all looking forward to spring.

Taking Doc's advice, I head directly for my bedroom to rest—and warm up under a mound of blankets.

Maddie, already cozy in her bed, turns toward the door when I open it. "Hey. How was the session?"

"It was . . . " I shake my head. "I'm not sure. You had yours this morning before mine, right?"

"Yeah . . . " She lets out a sigh as her voice trails off. "He told me to take the day off. And he hit me."

"Me too," I say with a nod as I slip into my bed. I let out an involuntary shiver as I settle into the cold sheets. "At first, it was bad. I wondered if that was the plan for the entire appointment. But then . . . " I shrug. "It got better."

"Did he do the light thing?"

"Yup. And I think it helped." I glance at the book Maddie is holding open on her bed. "What're you reading?"

"Oh, it's, uh . . . it's a Bible."

My eyebrows shoot up. "Really? Why?"

"I was complaining to someone about running out of reading material. They gave me this."

"You're not supposed to read that."

"It's not forbidden."

"I know, but— " I sit up on my bed. "You remember how Janet made a big deal about the lady and her Bible? What ended up happening to her?"

"That was an accident."

I give her a hard look as I try to remember the lady's name. She was someone trying out for the acquisition team—this was before I joined. According to the Prospect grapevine, Janet found a Bible in her room. Like Maddie said, Bibles aren't strictly forbidden, but Janet took it away from her.

A few days later, there was a training accident. While the team was out on a run, she slipped and fell off the hillside. On the way down, she managed to hit her head on a rock, falling into a coma and never waking up. Rumor was she not only hit her head one time but numerous times.

"Sure it was." I raise my eyebrows. "I'd just hate to see the same *accident* happen to you."

Maddie gives me a hard look before returning to her book. I scrunch back down in my bed, enjoying the warmth of the covers.

After several minutes, Maddie says, "What do you think the bouncing light is about? Is it a form of hypnotizing?"

"Could be. At first, I thought it was weird. But now . . . I think it helped."

"Really? I still think it's weird."

# Chapter 10

## *Sunday, Day 272*

## *Mollie*

"Are you sure this is what you want?" Doris asks, leaning heavily on her crutches.

"We made a commitment," Kimba says. "In the past, that might not have meant much. But now . . . " She shrugs. "Things have changed. Both Rey and I think this is the right thing to do. We want to be people of our word."

Doris gives her a tight smile and a brief nod. "You've changed. You're not the same person I used to know."

"Good thing, huh?" Kimba says with a laugh. "Considering you were ready to shoot me when you saw me last summer."

I look awkwardly at my snowshoes, suddenly feeling I shouldn't be here. Doris and Kimba have had similar conversations in recent weeks as Doris tries to convince her and Rey to stay in Bakerville.

Rochelle is leaving to find her son Christopher. PJ Cameron offered to help. Because of the potential danger of the journey, Rochelle's daughters are staying behind. They've become quite close to Sylvia Eriksen, so she'll be moving into their cabin.

Jennifer Dosen asked if she could join PJ and Rochelle for the first part of the trip, then she and her three sons—twins Atticus and Asher and their younger brother Axel—will continue on to their home outside of Great Falls, Montana. Like Rochelle, she and her family were stranded when the EMP hit. Jennifer's husband was injured and then later died, leaving them stuck in Meeteetse, Wyoming, where they met Sylvia, Sabrina, and the Hoffmanns, who were all making their way to Bakerville.

Kimba and Rey Hoffmann, along with their three children, planned to continue to their friend's house near Bozeman and agreed

72

to travel with the Dosens. They were originally supposed to continue to Montana last summer, but everyone just sort of stayed and rested from the ordeal they'd already been through.

Truthfully, I thought they'd changed their minds. The Hoffmanns and Dosens have been wonderful additions to our community, and I naively believed they felt they'd found a home here. Not that there's really been much rest with as hard as everyone works at their duty stations and on the militia.

"It's not really the same now, though," Doris says. "With the others going, maybe you're not needed."

Kimba gives a slight shake of her head. "Atticus and his brothers are very capable, as is Jennifer. And I'm sure the Dawson boys and their mom will do what's needed. But they don't have the experience Rey and I have."

"It's good Victoria Dawson is going," Doris says. "With what her husband did— "

"She's an outcast," Kimba says. "It's only thanks to Atticus they're going. You know she and Jennifer Dosen were friends before the attack on our community, but with the attack leaving Jennifer's sister dead . . . "

"Right. I know they have issues to work through. But the boys are still friends. It makes sense for the two families to work together as one. But I still question whether you and Rey are needed."

"This goes back to the commitment we made. That hasn't changed, even with the Dawson's being part of the group."

"Mollie?" Doris turns to me. "What do you think?"

Delivering Doris a look for putting me on the spot, I shake my head. What do I think? I think Victoria leaving Bakerville is the best thing for her and her boys. Living in the shadow of what her husband did, and the fact several in the community continually bring it up to them, will never give them the opportunity to forget and move on.

"I'm glad Jennifer and Victoria were able to get past their issues," I say. "And I'm sad that we as a community can't seem to realize Victoria was innocent in her husband's— "

"Murders?" Doris offers.

"Murders," I nod. "No different than Tamra was innocent in Jackson killing Phoebe and Amy."

"And Lydia," Kimba says, nodding vigorously. "He killed her too."

"Yes, it seems he did," I answer. "Jackson killed them, not Tamra. Dawson was the leader of the insurrection, not Victoria. But look how we treat them. We've treated both women so badly they've chosen to leave."

Kimba's eyes travel to Tamra Nicholson. She's helping her oldest daughter put something in the wagon. Even though there was a considerable amount of bickering about the group leaving and being allowed to take provisions with them, an agreement was finally reached. PJ Cameron and his family own two of our open wagons and a chuckwagon, along with double teams for each and several saddle and pack horses, thanks to their previous business as hunting outfitters. They brought these goods with them when they escaped Richard Majors's murderous reign over nearby Prospect last fall. Several in the community believe any private possessions became community property when they joined us. And according to our old bylaws, that is correct. However, those bylaws were voided after Jon Dawson's attempted coup.

While our new rules are still a work in progress, we've moved away from a representative system and now allow every community member of age a voice on matters of importance. Everyone sixteen and older, the age one can be a full militia member, is given a vote. A hearty debate ensued over the wagon and horses leaving. Although PJ and Rochelle intend to return once they find her son, there's no guarantee. We may lose not only people but assets. In the end, about two-thirds voted to let them take the wagon, two horses, and other supplies.

When the group reaches Joliet, Montana, where Tamra's parents live, she and her daughters will stay there. Hopefully, the small town is safe and her parents are fine and able to take them in. I don't believe Tamra has an alternative plan if that's not the case.

Originally, Kimba and Rey planned to break off there and head northwest to the Great Falls area where the Dosens have a small ranch. Rochelle and PJ, along with Robyn Sorensen, one of the widows from the Bakerville proper massacre, would continue toward Billings. Robyn moved to the mountain with us at her husband's insistence while he stayed behind. They lost their only child last summer. She essentially had a breakdown, and he didn't want to risk another without medical staff. Her parents live in a little town east of Billings, near the summer camp Rochelle's son was attending when the attacks happened.

"You're not wrong," Doris says. "I'd leave, too, if I were Victoria or Tamra. I do feel very bad for the children. Even they can't escape some of our people's wrath. I heard you got after Mrs. Lancaster the other day."

I feel the crimson creeping up my neck at the memory. It was the day after the cold snap, and I was irritated anyway when I overheard Delores Lancaster telling the older Dawson boy he was just like his father and should be locked up in our jail along with the others responsible for the coup.

It made me so mad.

I butted right into the conversation and asked Brett if he could find my son-in-law Leo for me. As soon as he stepped away, I gave Delores a piece of my mind. Many pieces.

When I was finished with my rant, she said, "Well, I never," before stomping away.

In too loud of a voice, I called after her, "Well, if someone had told you to keep your mouth shut before now, you might not be the old biddy you are today."

As the people near us turned and stared, I wanted the floor to swallow me up. I was even more embarrassed when the light applause started. Reggie Roberts, who was at a nearby table, said, "'Bout time someone gave that old broad the what for. And you did it without even raising your voice or using profanity. I don't think she even knew you were telling her off until right at the end."

He wasn't exactly right that I didn't raise my voice. I definitely did as she was leaving and wanted to get in one more jab. I felt terrible about it all afternoon. At dinner, I attempted to apologize to Delores, but she just called me several choice names before storming off. Jake reminded me I was sincere in my apology and if she chose not to accept it, that was her choice. She's made a point of avoiding me since then.

The sad thing is, while Brett was completely undeserving of her wrath, I can see how she may have some contempt for Jameson, the younger brother. Even before his dad turned into a murderer, Jameson had begun to show some anger issues. Maybe that's not the right thing to say. It wasn't exactly that he was angry, he just seemed to have an air of entitlement about him. He was argumentative and unwilling to contribute to work groups as he should. After Jon Dawson's death, things became worse. Wearing a permanent scowl, he stomps around ignoring everyone. Kelley Hudson has reached out to him to offer counseling. In response, he went on a verbal tirade. It's really very sad, and I do hope their new life in Montana allows Jameson to work through his anger.

I lift a shoulder at Doris before turning to Kimba. "Knowing how hard it was for Ben and Clarice to get here, I'm glad we were able to work out the travel plans like we did."

"The skis were a good idea," Kimba says. "I'm glad Zeb offered them after the community said no to the snowshoes and the cross-country skis."

"Wouldn't have hurt us any to let you all take snowshoes," Doris says. As hard as some people fought against those leaving to take anything, Doris was a proponent for not sending them off unprepared. "I understand not wanting to give up the horses, but the snowshoes . . . " She shakes her head.

"I don't know," Kimba says. "I think they had a good point about snowshoes breaking. We've had several of those cheaper ones fall apart already, and those are mainly what the Frosts had for rentals. The better snowshoes, like Mollie wears, were owned by individuals. I understand needing to keep what you can. It's not like you can run off to REI and buy more."

"And while the cross-country skis sounded like a good idea," I say, "they would not be great for going uphill. Minor inclines are no big deal, but mountains—*ugh*. The backcountry skis and splitboards are perfect, even if they are older models."

"Not all are old," Kimba says. "The splitboard Atticus is using is from last year, a demo model left by a salesman. All the boards are demos, and most of the skis too. The telemark skis Rey has, though—those are old. He's skied on telemarks before, so it's fine." Kimba lets out a small laugh. "In fact, the last time he telemarked was probably about the same year the setup he has was manufactured. It's like it was meant to be."

As we each laugh at her comment, Doris motions for her to come in for a hug. With her arm around her, Doris says, "You'll always be welcome in my home, whether I'm here or back down in Bakerville. If you don't find what you're looking for out there, come back."

"I know, Doris. And I know you understand we truly believe the right thing to do is take them home. Not just as far as Bozeman, like we originally planned, but the entire way. We'll get them there safely."

"And then what?"

"We'll make the best choice we can. You know we'd like to help with the reconstruction efforts. It seems like something Rey and I could do to give back to our country."

A new radio announcement came out a couple of weeks ago, talking specifically about the rebuilding and how workers will be needed. The restoration has already started in large cities. In our area, the biggest city is Billings, Montana, population just over a hundred thousand before the attacks. We don't believe they're focusing on Billings yet, choosing larger cities not destroyed by the nukes, but perhaps soon.

"Maybe the children should stay?" Doris suggests, her voice tinged with hope.

"And have them miss out on the amazing ski adventure?" Kimba lets out a small laugh. She pats Doris on the arm, knowing she has come to think of Nicole, Nate, and Naomi as grandchildren and loves them like blood. "We've talked about this."

"I just hope—*pray*—you don't get another arctic blast like we had last week."

"Yeah. The cold in January and February was bad. Who would've thought March could be so crazy? This winter feels like it'll never end."

"It does," Doris says. "And we always get snow into May."

"Now seems the smart time to leave before we get another below zero day with crazy wind."

Doris gives a weary nod. "And you'll come back if you can?"

"Lord willing, we'll see you again," Rey says, walking over from the wagon. "It seems we're just about loaded and ready to go. Time to get your skis and skins on."

"I'm glad we practiced with these," Kimba says. "Even though I backcountry skied years ago— " she gives Doris a strange look I can't quite decipher, to which Doris responds with a nod and her own look "—it's been too many years. Nicole and Nate picked it up easily at least."

"And the modified skis Zeb put together for Naomi and the other young kids seem to work well," Rey adds. "I'm glad that guy never

77

throws anything away. Even if some of the bindings and skins are older than dirt, we can make them work."

Part of me is slightly jealous. Backcountry skiing was something Jake and I discussed trying several times. Last winter, we'd even talked about taking a guided snow tour in the Tetons. I wish we would've. While this journey Kimba, Rey, and the others are embarking on won't be all fun and games, getting off the mountain on skis should be a blast. With the skins on the skis, they'll function similar to snowshoes, gripping the snow to make walking—or gliding—easier. Atticus, his brothers, Nicole, and Nate are using splitboards instead of skis—essentially snowboards that break into two pieces for the skinning part and are put together for the snowboarding part.

I look over to the wagon at the gathered group. The day after the meeting and vote, Leanne Monroe—who arrived with Ben and Clarice—announced she and her children would be leaving for Montana. She has an aunt and cousins in Lewistown, Montana, not far from Great Falls where the Dosen and Dawson families are going. Of course, she can only assume they're healthy and willing to take her in.

Doctors Belinda and Kelley, along with Ben and Clarice, tried to convince Leanne to stay. She and the children are still not recovered from their difficult journey to Bakerville. Ben went as far as offering to help them get there when their physical condition improves. Leanne not only refused but became combative, yelling at Ben about how it was his fault she was stranded here with strangers in the first place. As her voice roared through the house, Sarah started to hurry the children upstairs.

When Sarah motioned for Sadie and Sebastian to join them, Leanne turned on her. "Don't you even look at my children!" she screeched. "You and your busy-body family disgust me. This entire place disgusts me. All of you living like you're in some . . . some hippie commune. No. More like some crazy religious sect. You're a bunch of brainwashed lunatics who think some imaginary God is going to swoop in and save you. Or that the president will really come through. *Ha!* What a bunch of hogwash."

My eyes darted to Leanne. I sucked in a huge breath, ready to let her have it. In the month she'd been living here, her snide comments and eye rolls had become progressively more pronounced. The first few days, I figured it was a combination of exhaustion and being amongst strangers. But the nicer we were to her, the worse she'd act.

Before I could say anything, Clarice very calmly said, "You're sure it's what you want?"

"Positive," she said, a little spittle flying from her mouth.

"Okay," Ben said with a sigh. "And you've made the arrangements with PJ and the others?"

"That's right," she said, crossing her arms. "He said they'd be happy to have us."

Adding Leanne, Sadie, and Sebastian to the group resulted in a change of plans. Where the two groups had intended to split at Joliet, they've decided to stick together until reaching Rochelle's son. His camp is north of Billings, off Highway 87—which just happens to be one of the ways to get to Lewistown. The new route will add a couple of days' travel to the original plan of going from Joliet to Great Falls, but Rey and Kimba think being in a larger group and having the wagon for longer makes sense. Especially with the frail condition of the children and Leanne. The Dosens and Dawsons were willing to make the change, agreeing it made sense.

Until today, I didn't realize Donnie McCullough was also going. Donnie and his brother, Jerry, met Leanne at my house when Ben and Clarice were essentially keeping the brothers hostage after the massacre on the river. Once Jake and everyone arrived, their identity and lack of involvement with the gang from Prospect was confirmed.

As I watch my friends and neighbors make their final preparations to leave, I wonder who—if any—I'll see again. Surely, PJ and Rochelle will be able to return. Will their experiences be similar to what Ben found on his trek to Bakerville? He doesn't talk much about the things he saw or did. Clarice said she doesn't really know the details either, but it was bad. She told me how, when they first met Leanne, she was completely different. She was a Christian then and didn't have the bitterness she does now.

"Goodbye, Mrs. Caldwell. I have to go to Montana now," Sebastian says, giving me a small smile.

"Goodbye, Sebastian. I'm praying for you all."

"Did you see my new skis? I have to ride while we have the wagon since I'm still not very strong, but once we leave Mr. PJ, I'll ski and— what's the other thing when we put the special fabric on them?"

"Skin. They call it skinning."

"Right. I'll ski and skin with the big kids. And I'll get to ride with Mr. McCullough sometimes. He's taking his horse and said he'd be happy to have me ride double, but only for short distances. He says I'm getting so big I might tire Gordie out."

"You are getting big. Just in the short time I've known you, you've grown."

He gives a nod, then in a low voice says, "Mom says he's sticking his nose in where it doesn't belong, that he should just stay here."

"Oh?"

"Mm-hmm. Sadie says he has a crush on our mom—that means he likes her. But Mom doesn't like him. She doesn't really like anyone except Mr. Ben. She likes him because he kept us alive. I like other people, though. Mr. McCullough is nice, and so are you. I'm glad you let us stay with you. I really liked living in your den. It was nice to have a fireplace in there so we could keep warm. Do you think, if the lights come back on, maybe you'll come visit us?"

"I, uh . . . I'm not sure, Sebastian. I know I'll be praying for you, your sister, and your mom. And maybe things will someday be the way they used to be and we could see each other again."

"Okay. That'd be good."

"Sebastian," Leanne says in a rough voice. "We're leaving."

I pull him into a quick hug and remind him I'm praying. As he scampers off, I raise my hand to wave at Leanne. She gives me a stern look before turning away. *Okay, then.*

Jake, who was helping load a few things in the wagon, walks over to me as the group says their final goodbyes. He puts an arm around my shoulder. "It's good Donnie is going."

"How'd that come about?"

"Not exactly sure. I overheard his brother telling him it was a dumb idea, but it seems Donnie thinks Leanne might feel all alone. She's not friends with anyone going."

"Sebastian just told me Donnie likes his mom. I guess it should've been obvious, considering he's stopped by the house a few times. I never noticed Leanne reciprocating those feelings, though. Did you?"

"You're asking me?" Jake lets out a low chuckle. "I'm oblivious to those things, remember?"

"True," I say with a smile. "Seems a little strange, though. Donnie's willing to leave his brother and everything to go with a woman who isn't even lukewarm to his affections. And once he gets her there, then what? And he's taking his horse?"

"Someone did mention the horse, but Donnie was quick to point out that whatever happened before, he wasn't a part of and his horse is his property."

I tilt my head. "True."

"And as far as everything else, his brother asked the same things just two minutes ago. Seems they're not in agreement on Donnie leaving, partly because Jerry thinks we'll need him."

"Need him? Oh . . . because of the killers from Prospect?"

"Exactly. They saw the carnage firsthand. And I know Jerry still feels guilty they didn't find the kids hiding out. And he does have a point. We're losing the Hoffmanns and Atticus—three people from our security team. It's a huge blow. Won't be long until we need to send a team back to the valley to start planting the sugar beets. We'll need not only people working the fields but also people standing guard. And we still need to take care of the mountain. We'll be stretched thin. Every person will count."

I let out a sigh. In the past month, our security has been substantially increased. With what the Prospect raiders did to our friends on the river, we need to always be on guard. Jake was part of a team that went back down to Bakerville to retrieve any usable items. There was some discussion of leaving things there to await our return in the spring, but there were concerns about the items disappearing. While they were down there, part of the group worked while the rest stood guard—a process that takes nearly double the manpower. Every person does count.

"Jerry also told Donnie he was being foolish," Jake says. "That he shouldn't be chasing after a woman in this day and age of difficult travel and who knows what. Told him it isn't safe."

I chew on my lip. It isn't safe. Ben and Clarice saw terrible things on their way to Wyoming. Even on my own trip home last summer, I encountered troubles. But considering what happened to our friends on the river, are we any safer here?

# Chapter 11

## *Lucy*

"I'm so tired of being cold," I say as I shiver inside my sleeping bag. "With it being after the middle of March, you'd think it'd finally be warming up." I don't say how weird it is we've had snow on the ground since the middle of November. Maddie and I—all of us, really—have talked about it so many times.

Normally, it will snow and then warm up enough to melt off, then snow again. This year it snows, stays cold, then more snow piles on top. And the incessant wind doesn't help anything. It blows and drifts, so we'll have bare patches in some spots and drifts taller than my height of five-five in others. The wind also makes the already insanely cold temperatures even worse. We've had too many days of bitter cold. Last week, it was so cold we had to delay our raid. Weirdest winter ever.

"Today was bad," Maddie whispers so quietly I can barely hear her. Talking quietly is smart. We're staying in a small tent set up in some kind of an old workout gym. About half the acquisition team is set up here—each in one or two-man tents to help us stay warm in this heatless building. The rest are at a community center down the road. Except the officers, they have better housing somewhere else.

At first, I just let the statement hang there. While she's not wrong— the raid was bad—I know my performance was much better than during the Bakerville raid. And when someone took a shot at me, I did what I had to do and shot back. I wasn't the only one shooting, so I don't know if my bullet was true, but the shots ended as abruptly as they started. That was the closest I'd ever come to being in anything resembling a gun battle. It was unbelievably scary, but I don't think even Janet Kruse could find fault in the way I reacted.

We left Prospect over three weeks ago, with the bulk of us walking to the small town of Wesley where we met up with Club Dauntless— Wesley's version of an acquisition crew. Somehow, they have a mass amount of old work trucks, cars, and passenger trucks still running.

Definitely a perk. We trained with the club for a few days, making sure we all knew the plan for the raid, then the cold hit and all we could do was stay in our tents and shiver. With the building being unheated, it was bad—to the point I wondered if we might freeze to death.

When the weather finally improved, we loaded up in vehicles to travel the final few miles. The group was closer to the town of Pryor, but they'd been causing trouble for Club Dauntless and those in the town of Wesley.

Wesley is mainly comprised of club members and those who have been kept in the town as workers. It seems the outliers have been doing similar things as the rebels hitting Prospect. The club had scouts watching them for weeks, learning their movements and confirming numbers.

They'd planned to take care of the problem on their own but soon discovered the group was considerably larger than originally believed. And based on the guerrilla attacks they'd been doing against the operations in Wesley, they're very well trained. The leader in Wesley, an overly tattooed guy named Meeks with a permanent scowl on his face, sent one of his minions to visit with Richard and Scott Majors, asking for help to eliminate the threat. As such, our original mission was pushed back to allow for this.

Our Yellow Squad is light two people, thanks to a scouting assignment already in progress when we left for Wesley. Thankfully, one of those two is Lieutenant Janet Kruse. We're operating under Captain Murphy for this endeavor. This is much better for me since the assignments he's given me are more sentry-related than anything. There are definite advantages to having a prior friendship with him. Maddie was also on sentry duty, but Lieutenant Knight had her help with cleanup instead. I don't even want to think about the things she saw.

"Did the sessions with Doc Bohm help?" I ask quietly.

Her response is a small sob. I snake my arm out of the sleeping bag and pat her shoulder. She cries for many minutes before saying, "The sessions haven't helped. I know . . . I know what I'm doing is sinful."

"It's not sinful. We're keeping our town alive. Besides, it's our job. We're following orders."

"We shouldn't follow orders that go against God."

"Oh, please," I say, filling my voice with disdain. "We do what we're supposed to do. I don't know much about the Bible, but doesn't it say something about following the law of the land?"

"I'm not sure about that. But I do know the Bible says not to kill people."

"Ha! There's so much violence in the Bible. They're always killing people they don't like. I watched this video about all the genocide in the Bible and how God commanded people to wipe out complete cities because they believed differently. How's it any different than what we're doing? Anyone who spouts stuff about not killing is obviously picking and choosing which parts of the Bible they want to follow."

"You think we're doing the right thing? Killing people and taking their things is something God approves of?"

"How would I know? And why would I care about what God approves of?"

"I'd like to go to heaven, wouldn't you?"

I tilt my head while I consider my response. "There was a time when I may have thought I wanted to go to heaven. But now I think, if there really was a heaven, if there really was a God, He wouldn't have let all these things happen. Even before the attacks, our country, our entire world even, was a mess."

"I didn't think things were too bad," she says.

"Really? You don't think the school shootings and other violence were bad?"

She's quiet for a minute before saying, "So school shootings upset you? But the fact we're expected to kill children is okay?"

I let out a sigh. "The school children were innocent. The ones we're . . . dispatching . . . are tainted. They've been brainwashed by their parents to be against us. We must stop them now, or we'll never gain control of the county and region like Mayor Majors has planned. And without Mayor Majors taking care of things, too many people will die. Innocent people. What's this about, Maddie? Why the sudden interest and concern in the Bible? In God?"

"I wouldn't say it's sudden. I used to go to church with my grandma."

"Is that what this is about? Your grandma dying?"

"No. Although, I'm not going to say I'm over it. It still hurts. Especially thinking she died from something so easily controlled before everything fell apart. And she's not the only one. How many people have died since the attacks from natural causes, suicide, murder, or whatever? Half our town?"

"See? Exactly what I mean. Why'd God allow this to happen? He as good as murdered your grandma."

"She was a Type 2 Diabetic. God didn't give her diabetes."

"Humph."

"Anyway . . ." Her voice drops even lower. "I've been seeing someone."

"And?" I ask, wondering why she's being so secretive about it. I already suspect she's been seeing Mayor Majors. There's no way she got on the acquisition team with her limited skills. The only way she could be here is the same way I'm here, though I haven't heard any rumors about her the way people whisper about me. And we've definitely never discussed it. Cavorting with another woman's husband is not something I'm proud of, and the fact I'm not his only one makes it even weirder.

"And . . . he's a Christian."

"Oh?" I let out a slow breath. That's not good. "So he's the one putting these ideas in your head? Is he . . . he's not on the acquisition team?"

"No."

"Maddie, if it's going to cause a problem for you and with doing your job, you might want to break it off."

"Yeah, maybe. Or . . . maybe I should quit the team?"

"You're not allowed to quit," I hiss.

"Maybe . . . maybe they'd make an exception."

"Ha. You mean like they did for Rob Reynolds?"

"No . . ."

Neither of us says what actually happened to Rob Reynolds. Scott Majors ordered him detained. The next day we all met at the high school where Rob was tied to a post with the brick building behind him. General Majors gave a big speech about how being on the acquisition team was a privilege and considered a lifetime posting unless he released us from our duty. Those unwilling to fulfill their obligation would be swiftly dealt with. When he was finished talking, he shot Rob.

Up until that moment, I had been considering talking with Janet and returning to my position on the sentry team. The rebels hadn't revved up their attacks yet, and it seemed a better fit for me, even if I wouldn't have the privileges and extra rations allowed for the acquisition group. But the main reason I talked Mayor Majors into helping me get on the top tier team was to create a better life for myself in this chaos. Not to end up dead.

"You can't talk about stuff like this," I say in a hoarse whisper. "No one else needs to know about your Bible reading, God nonsense, or thoughts of quitting the team. You need to keep your mouth shut. And I hope you aren't talking to your new *boyfriend* about our team. You know the rules."

"I'm not stupid enough to tell him what we actually do on our expeditions." She leans in even closer. "But don't you think the rest of the town suspects stuff? I mean, you don't think they believe people just *give* us the stuff we bring back, do you?"

"Doesn't matter. We're like . . . like Fight Club. You do not talk about Fight Club, and you don't talk about what happens on the acquisition team."

"I thought we were like Vegas. What happens in Vegas stays in Vegas?"

"Same diff. Either way, you can't be pillow talking with him about what we do."

"We don't . . . " She shakes her head. "Did I mention he's a Christian? We're not like that."

I roll my eyes. "Even so, don't talk to him about our jobs, and don't let anyone else on our team know about your new . . . interests."

"You're right," she says quickly. "I know you're right."

"Is it serious?"

"I think so."

"Do I know him?"

"Probably not. He and his brother were visiting when the attacks started. They were up hiking and didn't even know about anything until they came out weeks later. The lights were already off and their car wouldn't start, so they hiked into Prospect."

"Okay. What's he doing for Prospect now?"

"Just a worker. He doesn't have a permanent assignment, just goes where they tell him."

I roll my eyes again. He's a loser. I would think he'd at least have a permanent assignment or be on the sentry team. He's likely had some disciplinary issues, like Glen, the snow shoveler who's always harassing me, and that's why he's a drifter. And one thing I know about drifters: they aren't worth our time. They're often found dead or mysteriously go missing. Or they're publicly executed as examples of what not to do.

"Be careful, Maddie. You don't want to soil your reputation by hanging out with a drifter."

"He's not one of those . . . those shiftless guys. He just likes to be able to help where needed. He was offered a permanent position working in food distribution, but—oh, what's his name who runs the team? I can't remember it."

"I don't know." Even though I can see his face, his name has never been of any importance to me.

"Anyway. Whatever his name is wanted him to stay on permanently, but . . . uh, *my friend* . . . convinced him not to pursue it. He loves the variety of working in different places."

*Sure, he does.* I'll stick with my original evaluation: loser.

"Just be careful, Maddie. Janet has it in for you—for both of us. You don't need to give her another reason to go after you. And by extension, she'll go after me since we're roomies."

"Don't worry, Lucy. This isn't an issue."

# Chapter 12

## *Wednesday, Day 282*

## *Mollie*

"How's it going?" Doris asks, sliding across the floor on her knee scooter. When her leg was shattered by a bullet over the summer, it was doubtful she'd ever walk again. While she still isn't fully mobile, a combination of her knee scooter, wheelchair, and what we lovingly refer to as her "peg leg" allows her to get around. The peg leg is something like the knee scooter, which allows her to brace her knee on it and not put any weight on the lower leg where the damage was done. It has a rubber stopper on the bottom for indoor use and a crampon that attaches for being outside in the snow. Still, the stability is lacking, so she uses crutches or two canes when on the peg.

"Fine. Just finished organizing this section." After my visit with her on the day Jake returned with Ben and his family, I've taken a shift or two a week in the supply shed. Even though I haven't had any severe issues after climbing the hill up to the ski lodge, I can't risk it by participating in any of the physically demanding work crews. Not only that, but sometimes the exhaustion and shortness of breath will appear without warning. I don't want to be in a situation where I can't easily find a resting spot to recover or where people are relying on me to be at my full capacity. The tiredness I can handle, but feeling like I can't breathe—like an elephant is sitting on my chest—freaks me out.

I'm still off active militia and split my time amongst kitchen, sewing, and supply shifts. Even though I'm not actively taking militia shifts, I'm still doing limited training to keep up my shooting and self-defense skills. Just this morning I trained with Katie on some new moves she's learning in the classes taught by Bill Shane, Aaron Ogden, or her husband Leo.

While the classes are too intense for me, Katie gives me a much less strenuous version. Until recently, Calley would join us for the class, and sometimes Dodie will watch and try a few moves. This morning's lesson was breaker strikes—up close and personal strikes utilizing the elbow to wrist as a weapon. Leo let her borrow a fake knife, a handgun, and an AR rifle they use for training so I could learn how to use the strike to combat against someone trying to take my weapon away. I can see how the breaker strike could do some damage when utilized correctly.

"I hope our Montana-bound people were able to find good shelter for yesterday's snowstorm," Doris says.

"They've been gone, what, ten days? They might've made it to Joliet," I say.

"You think?"

"Maybe. It's about forty-five miles, right? PJ thought they could do six or seven miles a day with the wagon in the snow—if everything went okay."

"*If.* That's a big word sometimes."

"They may have gotten there before the storm hit. Besides, you know as well as I do, a storm here doesn't necessarily mean they got the same weather at the lower elevations—or on the same day."

She lets out a long, noisy breath. "I heard Sheila's doing better."

"Mostly. She doesn't seem to be a danger to herself. But she's becoming a complete recluse. Doesn't want to leave the clinic for anything."

"She's had a rough time for sure."

"Did you hear about Sally-Ann Hinkle?" I ask with a smile.

"You mean about her and Paul Cameron?" Doris says with a laugh. "I heard Pamela walked in on them when they were making out like teenagers."

I laugh. "I'm just glad she's feeling so good. Belinda was sure we were going to lose her, but now— "

"Now she's well enough to play sucky-face!"

"When you're in your seventies, do they still call it that?"

"I don't know but it's funny." Doris hoots again, then says, "I'm happy for them. In this world, they deserve every bit of happiness they can find. We all do."

"Think there will be another wedding?"

"Pamela says there will be. She thinks Paul will wait until PJ and Rochelle return, but Dusty says no way. They'll be married by summer."

"Something to look forward to."

"How are things at home?" Doris asks.

"Good. Much calmer."

"It's amazing Leanne was causing so much turmoil."

"It really is. I guess we knew it was happening, but when you're caught up in it . . . " I lift my hands. "The children were getting almost impossible, especially Lily and Sissy. They're all doing better now, though they do miss Sebastian and Sadie."

"At least you got a new bedroom out of the deal," Doris says with a wink.

"That I did! I have to admit, not taking those stairs multiple times a day is fine by me."

"And your room is adorable. It was smart to take some of the space from the dining room to make a bedroom."

"It really was. Mike and Leo suggesting we build it out of lodge pole pine was brilliant. It's like having a little cabin inside a big house."

"Good use of our available materials too. Do you miss the space in the dining room?"

"Not even. It was useless space. We'd have snacks with the children in there sometimes, and maybe a family meeting once in a while, but we mostly only used the big table. It was still set up for use as a dude ranch dining room with all the extra tables for . . . I don't know, cozy dinners for two?"

Doris lets out a laugh. "A week at a dude ranch would not be my idea of romance, but maybe it is for some."

"Maybe. I do really love the new bedroom."

After Ben and Clarice arrived, I suggested we give them our room and we move into the den. Moving from our upstairs bedroom to the first floor made sense. There were times I could barely make it up the blasted stairs. Belinda was the one who suggested turning part of the dining room into a bedroom. They don't say it, but I know they believe unless I can get proper medical treatment, my days are numbered. Of course, all our days are numbered. God only knows exactly how long I have on this earth.

"And Sarah? Are her and her two youngest happy in the den?"

"Very. It made sense to have Leanne and her children in there—gosh, I can't even imagine if Leanne would've been sleeping in with Karen and Alina. That would've been even more stressful! But at least giving her and the kids their own space meant sometimes we had peace. But now, with them gone, Sarah was more than happy to move her, Tate, and Andy down there."

"Does she love the new crib?"

"So much. You should've seen her face when Jake brought it in. Thanks for finding the mattress for it."

"Well, not a real mattress, but it's enough pieces of foam put together to make something resembling one. The cover was the best find. That ugly old drapery has a new life. Of course, burnt orange and gold is rarely used for crib mattresses."

"Doesn't matter once the sheet is over it. I think Clarice wishes she had something similar for Wyatt."

"Ben and Clarice keep baby Wyatt with them, right? And he's sleeping in the playpen?"

"Yes. And it's fine. He's growing so fast, he'll be ready for a twin-size bed before much longer. You wouldn't even know they aren't his actual parents. They're so good with him. The girls too. They truly are a family. But I know it was hard on Ben when Sadie and Sebastian left. He'd grown to love them while they were traveling together."

"Understandable. Spending time together can make strong bonds."

"For sure. Just like Clarice and her chickens. She still stops by the livestock shed most days to visit them!"

"Rumor is she's not the only one fond of them. I heard Art built them their own house and they don't even live in the chicken coop."

"They follow him around like little dogs! It's crazy."

"That's funny. They sound more like pets than my Danny does—than your dogs too."

"Right. My dogs prefer to spend their days snoozing in their beds. At their age, winter's hard on them."

"I'll agree with that," Doris says, rubbing her leg. "So now that Leanne's gone, are Lily and Sissy better behaved?"

"Much. At first, I was concerned moving Destiny and Leslie into their room was the problem. I'm glad that wasn't it."

"And Liam does fine with the boys?"

"Seems to. I definitely notice a different dynamic between Liam and Malcolm than in the past."

91

"No more hero worship?"

"Very little. Malcolm likes Liam, for sure, and is impressed with how he and Clarice walked all the way here. But it's different now. Nothing I can really put my finger on, but different."

"He's growing up."

"Too fast."

"I'm glad things are calming down," Doris says. "And while I do pray Leanne is doing better, I can't say I was sad to see her go. I just hope she's not driving Kimba and Rey too crazy."

"I can't imagine Kimba would put up with much."

"Truth!" Doris laughs. "Did you hear the firewood crew is scheduled to drop down to only three days a week soon? And it won't be long until we discuss when to move back to the valley for spring planting."

"Mick and Barney said they think we'll be late this year, since spring's taking its time."

"But we can't go too late, or we won't have enough growing season before first frost."

"Barney said his sugar beets need to be planted before the end of April."

"Yeah, but not only do we have the concern of the weather, we also have the threat of the murderers from Prospect."

I give a slow nod. If it's not one thing, it's the other. Moving the full community back to the valley is unlikely to happen until sometime in May, but we need to plan for the planting. There's considerable disagreement over all the proposed plans. Having lost the river people, there's a possibility of losing more if we leave the safety of the mountain. Knowing the danger of going and the risk of not planting in time makes me wonder if there's a right choice. "When are they going down to check out the ground?"

"Evan said probably in the middle of April—earlier if we see signs of warming here."

"I can't imagine Barney is happy. If we don't check the ground before mid-April, how long will it take to get everything organized for planting?" I ask.

"Don't know. If the tractor is running, it'll make things easier. Barney started it up when they were down clearing out the river homes. Good thing the raiders didn't realize we had a running machine. They probably would've taken it."

"Good thing indeed," I say, thinking of the old tractor my son-in-law Tate and friend Aaron Ogden were able to get running last year. It will make turning the ground much easier than doing it manually. Last year, long before the attacks, Barney planted two hundred acres of sugar beets—a small crop by most standards, but more than enough to sustain us over the winter. This year, he plans to plant 125 acres where he had corn planted last year. Between Barney, Mick, and a few other farmers, we'll grow sugar beets, corn, barley, potatoes, pumpkins, pinto beans, and a variety of animal crops, plus we'll have home gardens.

"At least the greenhouses are giving us a head start on some of the plants," I say.

"And hopefully lots to can for next winter." Doris nods. "But I sure don't know what we'll do about flats. There's no way we'll have enough to can the amount of food we need."

"We'll need to dehydrate too."

"Definitely. Sally-Ann says she has a trick for reusing canning flats for water bath only. I don't like it, but . . . "

I make a face. That's a huge canning no-no. Jake and I bought several boxes of reusable canning lids but not nearly enough to meet our needs. I hate the idea of reusing the flats, but it's something we've all known might be needed, so we've tried to be gentle when opening a jar.

"Milena and Shelby should be back from the shed shortly," Doris says. "The additional supplies brought up from Bakerville really made a mess of things."

"Getting it all organized is a big job. And with everyone taking extra militia duty, it seems to make the process go on forever."

"True. There's been plenty of days lately when I'm the only one here. In fact, I can't remember the last time I had three helpers. I've been spending so much time alone, I've taken to talking to myself."

I let out a laugh. "Is that something new? I've been having complete conversations with myself for months."

"Yeah, I guess you're right. It just seems worse lately, especially since Kimba and the children left. I keep thinking I should've tried harder to convince them to stay."

"Maybe. But at the same time, I think her wanting to keep her commitment says a lot about the changes in her. From the little you've

93

spoken about her from when you knew her before, it doesn't sound like she was much for promises."

Doris gives a combination laugh and snort. "No, she definitely wasn't. But like you said, she's changed. I just pray they're having an easy journey."

I spend the remainder of my shift either organizing or helping people who arrive for rations or extra goods. We have a system where, if you need something in addition to the basics, you can take extra work shifts. There's a general list of work exchange, which makes it easy. Although we're given the basics—three meals a day and most of the things each of us needs for daily life—the rations are food or beverage items which are in addition to our regular meals in the dining hall. Those of us with children get snacks to serve at home.

We also get a portion of meat each week to add extra protein to our meals. We've been fortunate our hunting team manages to procure an average of two elk a week. The geese Jake and his group brought back were added to when a second party went down to take care of the river people. It's been a good season for wildlife and is likely the main reason we've done so well.

The supply house has other goods too: things our people salvaged from empty houses. When we moved to the mountain, we had to contribute certain things—high-demand items like batteries, generators and other alternative power sources, popular ammunition, and even some weapons. We could keep any personal goods not on the list of required contribution. Many people now barter those items for goods in the supply house.

"I guess that's it for the day," I say to Doris as my shift ends.

She gives me a nod. "Do you mind checking on Shelby and Milena? They should've been back inside by now. They're shift is over, too, but they always check in before leaving."

"Since Pamela is watching Hannah today, they might be taking advantage of the quiet and putting in extra time."

"That's true! I forgot Shelby didn't have the baby with her. Still, can you ask them to make sure they stop by so we can plan for next time they're on shift?"

I skip the snowshoes for the short walk but still bundle into my multiple winter layers. Although the calendar indicates otherwise, it doesn't feel like spring. I'm with Barney; it better hurry up or we won't get the sugar beets planted in time. The double door on the right is cracked slightly open. Maybe to let in a little extra light so Milena and Shelby can see to work?

"Knock, knock," I say as I approach the shed. When there's no response, I call out to them. "Milena? Shelby?" Still nothing.

Pulling open the door, I'm greeted with a mess. Items aren't only knocked off the shelves but one shelving unit is tipped over and leaning into a second one.

And there's a small puddle of blood on the floor.

# Chapter 13

## *Mollie*

My hand immediately goes to the sidearm on my hip as I move to the edge of the door, putting the thin wall between me and the inside of the building. Entering the building on my own could be foolhardy. I carefully back away, keeping my eyes on the fully open door.

Something's terribly wrong. Since I didn't go inside the shed, I don't know if whoever's responsible is still there. And I don't know the condition of Milena and Shelby. Continuing to move backwards as quickly as I can, I stop only when I bump into the supply house.

Moving around to the door on the back, I yank it open and yell to Doris, "Something happened! I think . . . cover the shed! I'm going for help." Even though my explanation is vague, I have no doubt Doris will do as I've requested without question.

Ellen and Zeb, owners of the ski lodge and the garage and outbuildings we use for supplies, live next door. I hustle there, pounding hard on the door to attract someone's attention.

One of the senior citizens living with Zeb and Ellen answers. "Whatever is the matter, dear?" she asks with a quizzical look on her face.

"Something's happened at one of the supply sheds. Doris needs backup at the main building while I go for help."

She gives me a stern nod. "My husband's home. Be right there."

"Thank you," I say hurriedly as I turn and begin my trek toward the militia headquarters.

While I can't remember the lady's name, both her and her husband are part of the militia, having been approved by Dr. Sam and Kelley Hudson, as required for anyone over the age of seventy. He was one of the Alpha Team sharpshooters on the summer crew, and she was often stationed in one of the guard shacks.

The community of Bakerville consisted of many retired individuals, a surprising number of them being former law enforcement, military, or some sort of government worker. Even with so many people of advanced ages, we have no shortage of people ready and willing to defend their neighbors.

I slow my pace as I cross the slick bridge going over the creek, wishing I would've taken the time to grab my snowshoes. I'm barely a third of the way to the headquarters and already breathing hard. Once I'm off the ice-covered bridge, I speed up, focusing on breathing in and out.

As the parking lot to the ski lodge comes into view, I slow again. Having to stop before I reach my destination won't help anyone. Milena and Shelby could be bleeding to death. I'm kicking myself for not going fully inside to see if they need help.

Moving from the driveway into the parking lot, I see one of our snowmobiles towing a trailer. I start flailing my arms, trying to attract attention. Miraculously, the rider sees me and heads in my direction.

Pulling up next to me, Toby James says, "Mrs. Caldwell? Do you need something?"

Gasping for air, I put my hand on his shoulder to try and steady myself. "Trouble. Militia. Headquarters. Need ride."

"Climb on."

Minutes later, we're zipping over the extra-wide footbridge and up the steep hill to the shed used as militia headquarters. As Toby pulls to a stop, he says, "Wait here. I'll bring whoever is inside out to you."

"Please. Thank you, Toby. I'm— " I finish with a shrug.

He nods as he jumps off the sled and runs inside. Less than a minute later, he is running back outside with Bill Shane on his heels.

"Mollie?" Bill asks.

No longer gasping for breath, I say, "Something's happened at one of the supply sheds. Milena and Shelby were working there. It's a mess. There's blood. I didn't . . . I didn't go in. Doris is covering the shed, and one of the men living at Zeb's place is backing her up."

My abbreviated version of events is enough to get Bill on his radio, calling in his team. He's moving quickly while he talks, then throws a "thanks" over his shoulder as he takes off running toward our police station—a lean-to off the ski lodge where our small police force has their command post.

"Can you take me to the supply house?" I ask Toby.

"You're sure? It might not be safe for you."

"I'm sure."

While we zip down the hill and across the parking lot, he slows the sled considerably as we make our way down the driveway. I realize he's doing it to keep the noise of our approach to a minimum. When we're close to the house, I lean in and ask him to turn the machine off and let me walk the rest of the way.

When I step off, he does too. "I'll walk with you, Mrs. Caldwell."

"Are you armed?" I ask.

"Absolutely."

Together, we slowly make our way past Zeb and Ellen's home. From here, the freestanding garage-turned-supply house is in full view. But from this approach, we can't see the shed Milena and Shelby were working in. The septuagenarian couple, positioned one on either end of the garage, can view the supply shed while using the garage as cover. I don't see Doris, but she may be at the supply house window that faces the direction of the shed.

Toby makes a small noise with his mouth, one of the signals our militia uses as an alert. Both the man and woman turn, with the man motioning us to move toward him.

Once we reach him, he asks, "Where's the calvary?"

"On their way," I say. "Have you seen anything?"

"Nope. Doris is positioned inside. Janey and I have been here since right after you knocked on the door."

"Should we go inside?" Toby asks.

"With Doris?" I ask.

"The shed."

"Best not, son," the man says. "We're smart to wait and let the team do the breach."

It's only a few minutes until a noise like the one Toby made sounds. Evan, Leo, and a few others from the security team are approaching from the driveway.

"What do we know?" Evan asks when he reaches our location.

"Not much," I answer, then tell him what I told Bill. "They could be inside, hurt. I don't know."

"All right. Bill's getting his team around the edge. We'll go in shortly."

Entering the shed happens a few minutes later. My fear of Milena and Shelby lying on the floor bleeding out is unfounded. The shed is empty. Lindsey found evidence of a trail leading away from the shed.

The trail included two separate drag marks. The assumption is Milena and Shelby have been taken—kidnapped.

The security teams immediately follow the trail. The rest of us form search parties in the same manner we used when two of our residents went missing at separate times earlier in the winter. Those two ladies were both found dead. After a freak accident killed Jackson Nicolson, those deaths were attributed to him when his wife was cleaning out his things and found jewelry belonging to the women. Could we have been wrong?

Tamra left our community with the Montana-bound group because of the stigma of her husband being a killer. Was Jackson set up after his death and the killer is still on the loose?

I'm part of the team assigned to search the supply house, various outbuildings, and Ellen and Zeb's house. Once we finish our first look through, we go through each space a second time. At full dark, the search is called to a halt and we make our way to the ski lodge for dinner.

Bill Shane holds a makeshift meeting, updating us on the situation. The security team followed the trail and found many things of interest. The first, about halfway between the supply house and Rudy Wallace's place, well within the boundaries of what we consider our space, was evidence of a camp.

"From what we found, it seems there were six tents set up in a small clearing surrounded by trees," Bill says. "There was no fire ring or any indication they had a fire. These people were being stealthy, making sure they weren't discovered. Their camp was between the ski lodge watchtowers and the eastern tower near the Young's house."

A gasp goes through the room.

"And there's more," Bill says. "They beat in several trails back and forth to our compound. If I had to guess, I'd say they've been spying on us."

The room erupts. Bill lets it go for several moments before saying, "Yep, I know. It freaks me out too. A small contingent of our security team is gearing up right now. They'll track the invaders—the kidnappers—as best they can."

"Why'd they take Milena and Shelby?" someone calls out.

Bill shakes his head. "We have no idea."

"Is anyone else missing?" someone else asks.

"That's a good question, and one we can't answer. Check on your friends and neighbors. If you think someone's missing, report it to me or Clark Thomas immediately. And I probably don't need to tell you this, but we're on high alert. Stay in groups or at least pairs— "

"Milena and Shelby were together. It didn't help them," a voice calls out.

"Stay alert and help keep each other safe."

My eyes search the room, looking for Shelby's family. The Camerons are at their usual dining table. Pamela is holding four-month-old Hannah in her arms. Grant, Shelby's husband, is next to his mom and child. Harry and Annette English and Kirstin Lewis, good friends of the family and the missing women, are sitting with them. All of them are in obvious distress.

As part of the group that arrived from Prospect back in September, Milena often sits with the Camerons. But lately, I've noticed she's been eating with Jerry McCullough. Doris told me a few days ago that, after Donnie left with the Montana-bound people, Milena and Jerry started dating—or whatever the equivalent of dating is during the apocalypse.

I look around the room, trying to find Jerry but not seeing him anywhere. Is Jerry's absence related to Milena's and Shelby's kidnapping? Is he also missing, or could he be involved in their disappearance?

# Chapter 14

## *Lucy*

After staying the night at the gym in Wesley, Meeks had a couple of his old work trucks drive us home. Maddie and I rode in the back of a delivery truck that must have been from the fifties. It was old, and it was a bumpy ride. And cold! We practically froze to death on the drive.

Even so, it was wonderful to be riding instead of walking. What would've taken us three or four days on foot only took us a little over an hour. In the old days, before the attacks, it would've only taken thirty minutes, but out of caution while driving the ancient vehicles, things are much slower. We were fortunate the Wesley guys had been making somewhat regular trips between Prospect and Wesley, so the road wasn't terrible.

Although the drive wasn't bad, there was one time we had to pull over and use shovels to dig out a drift. Our driver told us they usually go back and forth on a four-wheeler with a snowblade attached after a new snow. They follow in a pickup with plenty of guys to dig out the drifts, just as we did today. Sounds like it'd be easier just to stay home, but I guess the connection with Richard Majors and the rest of Prospect is important to them. I don't see Richard having anyone clear the road from our side.

The day after my return, I had an appointment with Doc Bohm. I relished the warmth of his office. He no longer starts the appointments by slapping me around. Now we have a nice conversation before going into the bouncing light therapy. The more time I spend with him, the more I realize I was wrong about him. He's not completely creepy. He's reserved and proactive. He pays attention to what is happening around him, and instead of speaking, he absorbs the events and then does what is necessary.

He wasn't part of my group that went to Wesley. Instead, he stayed in Prospect awaiting the return of the special team Janet is on. Turns

101

out, he could've gone with us. They didn't get back from wherever they went on their scouting mission until two days after we did.

Normally, we'd have a group meeting to discuss the scouting mission. But when I asked Janet about it, she snapped at me and said, "Mind your own business."

Maddie said she heard something awful concerning Major Lassiter. Seems he had a meeting with Mayor Majors that didn't go very well. He huffed out of the building and was having a conniption fit in the middle of the City Hall Park. An older guy, who's part of the work crew shoveling snow in the park, asked him if he was okay. He shot the guy in the forehead.

Knowing about Lassiter's temper tantrum, and his general disdain and poor treatment of women, I was less than excited last night when Janet told me my presence was requested at a special meeting being led by Major Lassiter. She made it clear he invited me. If it were up to her, I wouldn't be a part of it. What exactly *it* is, I have no idea.

Taking a deep breath and a final look in the mirror by the front door, I head out to the dreaded gathering. Normally, our team meetings are in the Creek View Estates clubhouse. This one, however, is at the mayor's old newspaper office, a good fifteen-minute walk. I've allowed myself half an hour to ensure I'm not only on time but early.

I'm about halfway there when I have to stop as one of the snow shovelers pitches a pile directly in front of me. I'd moved off the sidewalk and into the street, when I noticed them ahead of me. He, however, chooses not to pay attention. All I can say is he better be happy I was watching what he was doing. I would've totally lost it if he chucked snow on top of me.

"Hey, Lucy. How you doing?" my former neighbor Toad asks from his scooping spot on the sidewalk.

"I was doing fine," I snap, "until this imbecile decided to start flinging snow around." I point at the tall man with the wild snow shovel.

"Oops. Sorry," the wild snow shoveler says sheepishly.

I put my hands on my hips and give him a full glare. As I begin to verbally assault him, he pulls down the balaclava mask and gives me a brilliant smile. My eyes go wide as I take him in.

He's lovely. His perfectly shaped eyebrows and long lashes frame beautiful hazel eyes. His straight teeth and radiant smile are complemented by his high cheekbones—likely more prominent due to the food rations of the last nine plus months. His body doesn't look overly skinny, but instead lean and well-shaped. He's tall, at least six inches taller than Toad, who's somewhere close to six foot, with wide shoulders that make his waist look tiny. Even his nose is adorable.

I shake my head and straighten my shoulders. "You ought to be more careful."

"You're right. I wasn't paying attention like I should've been. Hey . . . " He pauses and looks over to Toad. "Did he call you Lucy? Are you Lucy Fleming?"

I narrow my eyes at him. "Do I know you?"

"Nope." He flashes his gorgeous smile again. "But we have a friend in common. Maddie Rivers."

"Okay. So?"

"Uh . . . nothing, I guess. Just thought I'd say hello is all."

I wrinkle my nose slightly. Could this be Maddie's boyfriend? I must admit, I'm surprised mousy Maddie could get anyone as good looking as this guy interested in her.

"Fine. Hello. Watch where you're throwing snow next time." I take a few steps closer to him. "And do me a favor, stay away from Maddie. She doesn't need a drifter for a boyfriend. As a member of the acquisition team, she's someone important in this town. I don't care how attractive you are. You need to stay away from her." I spin on my heel, lose my footing on slick snow, and flail my arms out as I try and recover.

He's by my side in a flash, holding me upright. "You'll want to be careful there, Lucy," he says in a husky voice.

I shrug my shoulder to pull away from him, almost losing my balance again in the process. I shoot him a dirty look as I regain my footing and stride away with as much dignity as I can muster. I'm halfway down the block before I take a deep breath and relax my stance. I should've asked his name. I'm sure it's some wonderfully glorious name to go along with his fine physique and gorgeous face. Except some of the most handsome guys have perfectly ordinary names. I let out a sigh. I'll think of him as Ryan. There are some terribly cute Ryan's in the world.

My slight delay with "Ryan" puts me a little later than intended. As I walk toward the former newspaper office Richard used to run, I see Janet stepping in while Major Lassiter holds the door for her. I slow

103

my steps to allow them to fully enter. I'd rather open my own door than have him leering at me during his outdated sexist act. He might think he's being chivalrous; I think it's just another indicator of his chauvinism.

The lobby of the office is dimly lit with a single gas lantern and little natural daylight. A murmur of noise is coming from a room farther back. The high windows of the large room bring in a wash of sunshine. It's also well-lit with several lanterns, both flamed and battery-operated, plus assorted candles. Personally, I think they could forgo the artificial lighting and it'd still be plenty bright.

As I step into the room, I glance around to determine where I should go. Mayor Richard Majors is across the room talking with one of the officers. He's dressed in his usual semiformal outfit of slacks, a button-up shirt, a tie, and a vest, with the chain of his pocket watch hanging loosely. His sparse hair is combed strategically to look like there's more. The way he dresses, I'm convinced he fancies himself as some dapper English gentleman. He sees me and lifts a hand. I give a nod and smile in response. The chairs in the room are set up auditorium style. I move to the last row and take a seat on the end.

After a few minutes, Richard is standing at my side. "Hello, Lucy," he says pleasantly.

"Mayor," I say, getting to my feet.

"I suspect you're surprised to be here."

"Do I have you to thank for the honor?" I ask, wondering if it really is an honor.

"Only partly. Doc Bohm suggested you as an addition to this mission. He seems impressed with the progress you've made during your treatments."

Pride courses through me as I nod. "Thank you. They've been very beneficial."

"Yes." He lightly rests his hand on my shoulder. "I've always known you had a passion for our town. That's why I've paid special attention to you. It's easy to see who can be trusted and given extra responsibilities."

"Thank you, sir." I beam.

His fingers flutter lightly across my shoulder before he takes a step away. But he stops and moves back toward me. "Why don't we meet at the hotel after this is over? We'll privately celebrate your new successes."

"I'd like that, sir." While it's not exactly true that I wish for a private celebration, I do know our hotel rendezvous will involve several luxuries. Almost always included is a bath in the giant tub. When we had running water and electricity, the tub was a jacuzzi-jetted spa. Now one of his lackies heats and hauls water to fill it. Bubble bath formula is added to allow for a luxurious soak.

Richard gives me plenty of alone time while he works at his desk in the other room. He even has several fancy body scrubs, soaps, and shampoos. And lotion for afterwards. Visiting his suite is the only time I ever get any pampering; my normal bathing routine is a washcloth dipped in warm water, quickly applied before I freeze during the process.

After the bath, he'll have food brought up. While the rations my team gets are far superior to the sentries or workers, it pales in comparison to Richard's meals. He not only has a personal chef, but also has people assigned to specialty positions as hunters, gatherers, or gardeners. With a greenhouse at the hotel and another at the nearby Bunn Mansion, which Richard has also procured as his own, he even has fresh greens and tomatoes. As he once said, it's good to be king.

"Give me about an hour after this wraps up," he says with a nod. He talks with several others before making his way to a chair at the front of the room.

Scott Majors makes a show of calling the meeting to order. In addition to Richard and Scott, all the officers and Doc Bohm are in attendance, plus at least two dozen people from the acquisition team. I'm the only regular soldier. The rest are what Maddie and I have jokingly referred to as super soldiers, seemingly more machine than human.

They're the fittest and most ruthless. The only female in the group of super soldiers is Lorita Ceballos. She is, of course, part of Yellow Squad and Janet's favorite. How could she not be? Lorita's completely dynamic in every way. She can run faster, train harder, shoot better—you name it. She's the best of our group and is one of the best people on the entire acquisition team. And she's certainly much more competent than many of the men. Even several of the male super soldiers struggle to keep up with her during drills. It's almost laughable that I'm even here. Whatever Doc Bohm's reasoning is for suggesting me for this mission, I know it's not based on my skills.

"All right, everyone," Scott says. "I suppose you all know why you're here."

Doc Bohm loudly clears his throat, then Richard says, "Remember, son, we have a new addition to the group."

Scott's eyes find me in the room. The look he gives me raises the hair on the back of my neck, as every head in the room turns in my direction. I clench my fists and keep my eyes forward, trying to remain calm. I catch a glimpse of Lorita as she lifts her head slightly in my direction, sending me what may be a smile—or maybe a smirk.

"Oh, yes, the illustrious Miss Fleming. I forgot you were added at Doc Bohm's request. It seems he thinks you may have some contribution to make."

Janet lets out a snort of laughter. My cheeks burn from being singled out.

"General Majors, if I may?" Doc Bohm says.

"By all means." Scott flutters his hands.

Doc Bohm stands and turns to face the gathered crowd. His dead eyes bore into Janet as he says, "Miss Fleming may have a different skillset than others in the room." He pauses a moment. I expect another snort of divisiveness from Janet, but she surprises me by keeping quiet. "In the time I've gotten to know her, I've seen a dedication to our town—to our cause—unmatched by anyone else I've met with. She is a true patriot, and we're lucky to have her on this mission."

I feel my back lengthen as I lift my head a little higher. I struggle to keep a smile from my face as the compliment washes over me.

"Well, then," Scott says as Doc Bohm returns to his seat. "I guess we should be grateful for Miss Fleming's willingness to join our mission."

Without Doc staring her down, Janet once again feels free to have a laugh at my expense.

Even though I expect the meeting to include some discussion on what the mission might be, it's all rather vague. We'll be training as a unit for a week, then we'll be driven to a drop-off location and hike in the rest of the way. Where we're going is a mystery to me, but the others seem to know. Instead of a raid for supplies, we're performing guerrilla warfare, much like the rebels are using on us, to instill fear and take out key players.

I assume we're hitting Cody, a town south of us. This must be where they went to do their reconnaissance during the last few weeks and why they couldn't join us on the raid with Club Dauntless. I must admit, Cody seems a rather bold move. I know Richard's goal is to rule over not only Prospector County but also Park County—where Cody is located—Big Horn County to the southeast, and then Hot Springs County to the south. His desire to be not only mayor of Prospect but de facto king of the entire region, maybe even the whole state someday, isn't a secret.

After the meeting ends, I stay seated for several minutes and wait for the small crowd to clear out. Janet walks by, making eye contact while shaking her head and sneering. She stops and walks back to me. "You may have crazy Doc Bohm fooled, but you don't have me fooled. I know how you got on the team—I suppose it's the same way the Doc recommended you for this special group. There's a name for women like you."

I watch as she walks away. Arguing will do no good. And she's not wrong about how I was originally allowed to test for the acquisition team. But Doc Bohm—no. Not happening.

I walk around the park surrounding the old City Hall. Richard uses the hotel for his mayoral duties, preferring the opulence of the historic building as opposed to the starkness of City Hall. Besides, the building only had central heat, which doesn't work with the power grid destroyed. And it was determined putting in woodstoves didn't make sense. So the building stands empty now. Last summer, it functioned as one of the daycare centers and housed a few other offices of those in charge of the working crews. They've been moved to easy-to-heat houses. Thinking of the work crews reminds me of Maddie's snow-shoveling boyfriend. He is gorgeous—too bad he isn't a more suitable catch.

When my hour wait is almost up, I head in the direction of the hotel. In the early days of the attacks, the hotel was used to house people who had no place else to go: visitors to the town, people who were staying at the hospital when it caught fire, and residents of the apartment complex next to the hospital, which was also damaged during the fire. In August or September, I can't remember which, Richard decided to clear it out so he could use it as his headquarters and home. The large fireplace in the lobby and fireplaces in many of the higher-end rooms helps keep the building warm. The kitchen has been reworked to be usable in our electricity-free world.

I let myself in the main door. Standing by the fireplace, elegantly dressed in skinny jeans tucked into her knee-high boots with a fluffy sweater and puffy vest, is Mrs. Majors. She turns and gives me a fake smile. "Hello, Lucy, dear."

"Um, hello, ma'am," I say quietly. She knows about Richard and me. Before the world fell apart, she seemed to care about the other women he had or wanted to have. Everyone in Prospect knows about the fight she had in the SuperMart with Milena Maynard, one of the former newspaper employees. There were also rumors of her driving women out of town, paying them off to stay away from her husband. Now I guess she's decided that if Richard is king, she's the queen and is willing to accept me as—what? A concubine? Is that what kings have?

"Did you have an appointment with Richard?"

"I—yes."

She narrows her eyes and lets out a slow breath. "I suspect he won't be keeping your appointment. But please go on up. I'm sure Bernard has more information than I do about such things."

"Yes, ma'am," I say as I move toward the staircase.

At the top of the third floor, Bernard is sitting in his usual spot. He's a combination butler and personal guard for when Richard is at the hotel. While the rooms on the second floor are used for various meetings and official business, the third floor is for *unofficial* business. These are the more extravagant rooms and suites—perfect for private entertaining. The fourth floor of the hotel is Richard and Mrs. Majors's private residence. The hotel was built in the early days of Prospect and is where Emerson Bunn, the first mayor of Prospect, lived after the death of his first wife. The original lavishness was thanks to him, but there have been many other updates over the years.

Bernard sees me and raises a hand. "He asked me to reschedule your meeting," he says.

I give a nod. "Did he give a time, or will he send for me?"

"He'll send for you."

"Thank you, Bernard."

# Chapter 15

## *Friday, Day 288*

## *Mollie*

After a careful census of the community, only Shelby and Milena were missing. The local search went on for days, with a small contingent from the security team doing a far-off search. Leo was part of that group, only returning this afternoon.

A meeting has been called for before dinner. As we wait for it to begin, the talk around the room is focused on what we might learn. Because we expect details inappropriate for the children, the downstairs nursery is full, with even the older children going there. Only the babies are in the dining hall. Sarah's holding Tate; Hannah, Shelby's baby, is being held by her grandma. As I look around the room, besides for the babies, it's militia-aged teens and adults only.

Evan, who led the search team Leo was on, calls for our attention. The chatter immediately ceases.

"I know there are rumors going around about what we found and what we didn't find. Let me start by saying, as I'm sure you've heard, we weren't able to bring Milena and Shelby home."

Evan pauses and looks around the room. Several people nod their understanding. We all know, if they had been brought home, we'd have heard about it and this would be a celebration as opposed to an informational meeting.

"We also found no indication they're no longer alive," Evan continues. "We believe they were taken against their will but aren't seriously harmed."

"You mean you didn't find their bodies," Jerry McCullough says loudly. "You don't know whether or not they've been harmed. You just didn't find them dead."

Evan nods several times. "Correct."

109

"Who took them? Where are they?" asks Janey, the woman who backed up Doris with her husband on the day the women went missing.

Evan takes his time as he looks around the room. Just when I think he's not going to respond, he says, "We believe it was a group from Prospect."

There's a huge eruption of noise as he delivers this news. I can't say I'm surprised. Jake and I have spent many hours talking about who could've been watching us. Prospect people are the most likely candidates. How they got inside our defenses, bypassing our easternmost guard station, is concerning.

In the days since the kidnapping and the discovery of the camp, we've added additional roving sentries and two hastily built twig shacks, which are now being used as observation posts. What was an easy guard schedule before, has been ramped up. With the increase in guards, I'm even back in rotation, being placed in one of the close guard towers. Since a portion of the security team has been out searching, we've been stretched thin this last week. I don't imagine it's going to improve anytime soon.

"Okay, folks," Evan says after several minutes. "Let's get it together so we can finish."

"After you let so many people leave for Montana, your security team doesn't have the strength it once did," one of the men in the audience calls out. "How do you think we can protect ourselves?"

He's not wrong. Losing Kimba and Rey was a huge blow to our security.

"We're working on training more people, and Bill set up a new watch schedule and rotations. We'll continue with those and see what else we can improve. We can only assume, if they were watching us once, they'll return and do it again."

"What about Shelby and Milena?" someone asks.

"We don't know where they are," Evan says bluntly. "We followed as best we could, but we lost the trail once we reached the heavily traveled areas."

"Let's go to Prospect and get them," Paul Cameron, Shelby's grandpa by marriage, says.

"That's a plan we're discussing," Evan replies. "The problem, Paul, is we're severely outmanned. And we don't know where they are. We

110

assume they're in Prospect, but we have no idea of their exact location."

"They probably took them to the place Deputy Fred bought Rochelle and her girls from," another man says.

"Possibly," Evan says. "We believe the place is somewhere around Prospect, but we don't know where. Folks, I hate to say this, but it'd be like looking for a needle in a haystack. We just don't know where to start."

"So that's it then?" Jerry says venomously. "You're just giving up on them?"

"No. That's not it," Evan says forcefully. "We're going to look at this strategically and figure something out."

"Why were they watching us?" Sarah asks.

"Good question. It could've been strictly for the kidnapping. Many of you have heard Milena used to work for Richard Majors at the newspaper. Apparently, there was some bad blood between them after she quit. And we know she was among the people Majors planned to publicly execute before she and a few others managed to escape. It's possible her kidnapping was out of revenge."

"Majors does hold grudges," someone says loudly.

"Right." Evan nods. "And if that's the case, Shelby was probably in the wrong place at the wrong time, which is why she was taken too. Or perhaps, it was a scouting crew to determine our weaknesses— which we know they easily discovered. Milena may have been an afterthought, someone snatched her knowing she could be of value if brought back to Richard Majors. We simply don't know."

"Could have value?" Jerry asks. "He tried to hang her. Me too. We were to be publicly executed. Don't you think, if he is behind this, that's his plan now?"

Evan shakes his head. "I don't know, Jerry. We're going to do what we can. You know two people from our team stayed back. They're keeping eyes on Prospect. Tomorrow, we're sending two more to relieve them. We'll keep that up, rotating people back and forth so we can monitor what's happening in the town."

"And you think that's enough?" Jerry sputters.

"It's all we can do for now."

The meeting lasts almost half an hour longer with no new details given, simply rehashing what we know and don't know. What we don't know far outweighs what we do know. Finally, Evan calls an end to the conversation, and the room is transformed into our dining area while the children are brought up. With the children now in the room, the conversation over dinner is much more guarded but still mainly focused on the same subjects: the missing women, the fact we were being watched, and how both could happen again.

Back at our home, our children have been put to bed. Yesterday, we celebrated Lily turning five. We tried to make the party as wonderful as possible for her, and she seemed to love it. We were able to get a cake mix from the supply house. Katie put aside a piece in hopes Leo would return in the next few days to enjoy it. As he eats his treat, the rest of us who aren't on duty have peppermint tea as we sit by the fire in the great room.

Sarah is rocking Tate when she says, "Belinda cleared me to go on militia duty."

I close my eyes. While I know my children need to be a part of the security of our community, I still don't like it. Sarah has been excused from our fighting force since her pregnancy started to show. Before that, she had only minimal training. Angela, Katie, and Calley all served on militia teams over the summer. Now, at six and a half months pregnant, Calley is part of the radio crew, listening for transmissions on the ham and helping coordinate any needed militia efforts via the handheld radios. Katie, while officially a militia member, is part of the medical team, which keeps her somewhat out of battle. Angela is on the regular militia and trained to be in the thick of it.

Tony and Malcolm will become a part of the junior militia when they turn fourteen, taking jobs as runners or helpers until they're sixteen. Of course, our prayer is things will be closer to normal well before then and we won't have a need for the militia like we do now.

"Well, I suppose it can't be helped," Alvin says with a slight quiver in his voice. "What will you do with the baby?"

"If Mom or someone else can't keep him, he'll go to the nursery. I start training tomorrow."

"I have range time in the morning, then supply from ten to four," I say, shifting in my chair to relieve the ache in my back and hips. I've started seeing Doctor June for minor adjustments and massages. As both a chiropractor and a massage therapist, she has a variety of treatment ideas to help with the aches I can't seem to get rid of.

Belinda and Kelley have increased the amount of turmeric, ginger, and garlic I'm taking, plus added a tincture of willow bark, which is

112

essentially aspirin. Kelley's alternative medical knowledge, a hobby of hers before the havoc of our world, has given us many alternatives for over-the-counter and prescription meds. Even though Kelley does have wildcrafting knowledge, the willow bark she uses in the tinctures is from white willow bark she ordered from an online source before our world fell apart.

There was a concern about the alcohol needed for making tinctures being in short supply. But Gabe Griffin's hidden moonshine still, not found by the raiders that killed him and the rest of the Bakerville river people, helps with solving that need. We're exceedingly grateful his son Chandler knew where the still and many other useful things were hidden.

Now we just need more willow bark. While willow trees do grow in Wyoming, none are the preferred species for making aspirin tincture. We'll use what's available but expect it to have less medicinal qualities than the white willow native to Europe and western Asia do. As soon as the trees begin to bud, the harvest will start. The bark will be dried for use in either a tincture or tea. Teas require more product over time, but Kelley thinks maybe they'll work well with these varieties of willow.

"Dodie and I are both off shift tomorrow," Alvin says, looking to his wife, who gives a nod. "I'll need to take a turn on the shooting range, though I think it's a little ridiculous we go to the range so much but aren't actually shooting."

"We're conserving ammo, Dad, and developing muscle memory and practicing maneuvers," Jake says.

"Psh. I know all that. Just seems we spend a little too much time there for the little shooting we can do. Anyway, Sarah, Dodie and I could keep the little squirt for you."

"Thanks, Grandpa Alvin," Sarah says with a small smile. "It's hard for me to think about being away from him for any length of time. I've had it pretty good with the sewing. I'll still be managing that team. The training and militia shifts will be in addition to those duties."

Alvin lets out a loud sigh. "We had it easy for several months. Too easy maybe. We've become complacent, allowing them to sneak up on us, watch us going about our business, and then taking two of our own. I sure as shootin' hope Bill and Evan have a plan, because I'm not okay with leaving those girls out there to those . . . those monsters."

"Amen to that, Dad," Jake says. "Amen."

# Chapter 16

## *Lucy*

I've been training with the super soldiers for three days. Even though Janet was at the meeting, she's apparently not part of the team going. Major Lassiter and Lieutenant Knight are the only officers involved in the training and planning. It doesn't take a genius to quickly realize I'm way out of my league. Surprisingly, the team is incredibly considerate. Lorita Ceballos even offered to work with me outside of the group on things I'm struggling with. Hand-to-hand combat is my biggest weakness, so we start there.

"You are too timid," she says in her mildly accented voice. She's originally from somewhere in South America but has lived in the US since she was a child. Like most of the super soldiers, she served in the military at some point. She's probably a few years older than I am, but she looks younger. "You wait for the attack and then you do too little to defend."

I give a nod of understanding.

"Unless there's a reason for being stealthy, you should use your voice. This time, when you respond, I want you to make noise. Scare me into submission."

She comes at me with a quick kick. When I put my arm down to block it, she quickly follows with a vertical punch. I'm too slow to move or block the punch, and it lands on my shoulder. I lift my elbow in response as she shouts, "Make noise!"

I make a quiet sound, not even close to resembling any real threat.

Lorita lets out a whoop and does some kind of spinning back kick thing, which lands not very gently on my hip.

I cry out in pain and bend over.

"Keep going!" she orders. We spar for several more minutes before she finally calls a halt to it. "You need to work on your speed. You think too much about what you should do instead of just doing. Show me your roundhouse."

I step into fighting position and give a halfhearted kick.

She shakes her head. "You broadcast your intentions as you move in slow motion. You do want to lift your kicking leg first, but then, as you swivel on the ball of your stable foot and open your hips, it should all be fluid. Your kicking leg should fully extend and barrel through using all your power—don't stop midway. And your foot . . . which part of your foot should make contact with your target?"

"The top," I say quietly.

"Yes. Even though it's not easy in these shoes, you still must practice. And remember, if you're using the top, you make your foot strong like a knife. You can connect the ball of your foot, but it's more awkward, even in shoes."

"More awkward than I already am?" I ask.

"Not much," she says with a smile. "Let's do it again."

We practice the roundhouse with my right leg, kicking until the top of my foot stings.

"Just imagine if we were barefoot," Lorita says. "Now your left."

When we're done with roundhouse kicks, she switches to side-kicks and then to punches. After a while, she asks, "Do you know how to roll?"

"Somewhat, from the time Lieutenant Alvarez showed us."

"But you haven't practiced?"

I shake my head.

"Okay. Watch. I keep both my hands near my head when I roll. I want to protect my head. See? I tuck my chin and look at my belt. I want to become a . . . a tire. Something round and rollie."

"Like a donut?"

"Sure. Donut is fine. Hands up. Tuck your head. Exhale and become a donut. Make the roll fast and get back on your feet."

"Easy for you to say," I mutter. Rolling across the ground is a painful experience.

Finally, Lorita says, "Good enough for today. You are much better but need to keep practicing. You can do these at home on your own. Practice without shoes and with shoes. With boots too. Kicks and punches don't have to be pretty, but they need to have power behind them. If you're in a fight for your life, pretty won't matter. Tomorrow, we'll meet again. We'll work with the knives."

I close my eyes and nod. The knives are awful. In group training, we often practice against each other with fake knives. Today, we had to use a real one on a dummy bag made just for this purpose. We're supposed to learn how to sneak up behind someone and slit their throat without any sound.

"Will you be going back to the dorms now?" Lorita asks.

"I, uh . . . no. I have an appointment in town." I pull the watch out of my pocket. Another advantage of being on the acquisition team: we have personal time pieces. The rest of the town relies on bells sounding on the hour. We can't hear them from our housing complex, and instead of having an additional bellringer set up nearby, they've outfitted us with watches or something similar. Mine is only a windup watch face. The band was broken and useless, so I removed it to create something like a pocket watch.

Lorita gives me a wave and walks toward our housing complex—the opposite direction I'm going. Richard sent a note earlier today requesting I join him for dinner at 6:30. I round a corner and smack right into a body, losing my footing and thrashing about. Strong arms grab me, keeping me upright. "You okay?"

"I–I'm fine," I say, shaking my shoulders to remove the hands.

"Oh, hey," Maddie's boyfriend, "Ryan," says. "Fancy bumping into you again." He gives me a small smile, not the brilliant one that shows his teeth. "Where you headed?"

"Really? You plow into me and think you can ask where I'm going? Just because you're dating Maddie doesn't mean we're friends."

"I'm not . . . let's start again." He gently touches my arm and tries to guide me back around the corner of the building.

I allow him a few steps before I say, "Let go of me."

"Sure. I just wanted to, uh, talk a bit." Again, he reaches for me.

I slough him off and start walking.

"Lucy," he says loudly. "I'd really like to know you better."

I stop walking and turn around. "That sounds like a come on. What would Maddie think?"

"Maddie would be happy. She's suggested several times a double date might be fun." I raise my eyebrows at him as he rushes on with, "She and my brother Chance. You and me. I'm Chase, by the way."

"Maddie is dating your brother?" I ask.

"Yes, right. If you'd like, we could go to the cantina on Vining. We could get a cup of tea."

I watch his perfect face. I'll admit, I'd like to get to know him better. He's more than pleasant to look at and seems nice enough, even if he is a clumsy oaf, but . . .

"Sorry. I have an appointment. And—Chase was it?"

He gives me a nod.

"Being seen with you isn't in my best interest. Maddie might be okay dating beneath her class, but I'm not."

I turn quickly and start toward the hotel. I can feel my cheeks are hot and flushed. I hated the words I just said, the snotty way I delivered it. But it's true. There's no way for me to survive in Prospect by chasing after some cute guy. Chase . . . that really is a perfect name for him. *Stop it, Lucy. Do what you must do.*

I nod to myself. I'm going to survive this. I'm going to make sure I not only survive but flourish. The things I've already done would be for naught if I let a pretty face sway me. Maddie can do what she wants. She may have got where she is the same way I did, via Richard's attentions, but if she thinks she can keep her privileges by sharing her affections—affections Richard is clear belong only to him—she's mistaken. While Richard can have numerous relationships in his position, he has zero desire for those of us chosen by him to see anyone else.

I check my watch. I still have twenty minutes before my appointment. I walk the long way around City Hall, taking one of the sidewalks through the park. Every time I walk through here, I think back to summer, shortly after Captain Murphy convinced me to join Richard and his quest. I was walking home one night, right before curfew, when I noticed one of my friends quickly walking down the sidewalk—well, not really a friend but someone who'd been nice to me when we were sheltering in the basement during the missile attack. By her side was a little boy who lived in my apartment complex. Not her little boy, Annette was single with no children, but he was practically running to keep up with their fast pace. I watched as she disappeared around the edge of the building.

For whatever reason, I decided to step behind a tree and waited to see if she returned. Why did she have the boy? He was young, around two or three, and always with his mom and baby brother. The three of them lived in my building and also sheltered with us in the basement. I hadn't talked with the mom much before then, but we'd been friendly since. I'd seen Annette earlier in the evening at the community meeting—or rather the community execution. At least that's what it was supposed to be. I glance at the gallows still in place after being constructed during the summer. The first time they were to be used was the night when the former Sheriff Jason Spieth and several others were to be publicly executed.

But things hadn't gone as planned. Right after Richard declared them all guilty, Milena Maynard started singing. Other prisoners joined in, and even many people in the crowd.

It all went crazy from there. There was shooting and screaming. I threw myself on the ground, waiting for it to end. Afterward, I found Captain Murphy—who at the time I still called Mr. Murphy or, when he insisted, Dirk. He quietly told me they'd shot two in the uprising, but the rest had escaped. Richard had an idea where they'd gone, and teams were being formed to go after them. He said since I was new to the team and hadn't trained with anyone, I should go home. I was terribly restless, so I went for a walk before curfew.

Seeing Annette caused a delay, and I was at risk of being late for curfew. Just as I stepped out from the treed area, I saw another person walking on the path. This time it was Kirstin, the boy's mom, carrying her baby close to her chest. She was looking around furtively and seemed very nervous.

On a whim, I started moving quickly to catch up with her. I was a few feet away when I called out. She answered and we chatted a few minutes. With her demeanor, I knew she was up to something. I also knew she was friends with escaped convict Milena Maynard. Annette, who I'd seen only minutes earlier with Kirstin's son, was also friends with Milena. At that moment, I realized I might be able to help myself.

After we said our goodbyes, I found a new place to hide in the shadows, where I could watch Kirstin. I moved with her as she made her way to the basement entrance of City Hall. After she disappeared from view, I weighed my options. There was no reason for her to be going there, especially when we only had fifteen minutes or so until curfew. I could've walked away, left Kirstin and Annette to do whatever it was they were doing, but . . . I didn't.

I went looking for Dirk Murphy. He'd been staying on this side of town with a friend in one of the neighborhoods near City Hall, but I didn't know the exact location. I did know Richard Majors was operating out of his former newspaper office. I wasted no time getting to the office. Dirk wasn't there, but Richard was. And so was Janet Kruse.

When I went inside the door, both heads turned toward me. "What are *you* doing here?" Janet asked.

"I, uh . . . I think . . . I'm looking for Dirk Murphy."

"Of course you are," Janet said. "He told me he convinced you to join our endeavor—like you really have a choice in the matter."

Janet was a friend of my mom's. Even though she's around a decade younger than my mom, they'd known each other for ages. My mom even used to babysit her when she was a child. When I had the falling out with my parents, Janet went out of her way to search me out and make my life miserable. Even after my parents moved away, she'd been unnecessarily cruel when she'd seen me in the grocery store, on the street, or wherever.

"Why are you looking for Captain Murphy?" Richard asked. Unlike Janet's voice, which was dripping with hate, he was kind—almost fatherly sounding.

"I think . . . I saw something, and I think it may be related to the missing prisoners. At least one of them. Milena Maynard. I saw a couple of her friends sneaking around."

He quickly jumped to his feet. "Tell me more."

After I quickly told him what I knew, he placed a hand on my shoulder. Looking deep in my eyes, he said, "I won't forget this. We need more people like you as we strive to create our new country."

He turned and ordered Janet to follow him. Even though my information didn't result in finding the prisoners, Richard didn't forget my help. Two days later, he sent Bernard to find me, and that was how our rendezvous started.

A few weeks later, Sheriff Spieth was killed while perpetrating an assault on the town, killing several of our people. As far as I know, Milena and the rest of the prisoners were never found. And I haven't seen Annette, Kirstin, or her children again. Another couple from my building also disappeared around the same time.

I've wondered if they might be part of the rebels who started causing trouble then. There was a rumor early last fall that the instigators were eliminated. Our people had attacked a group of ranches west of Prospect. We lost a lot of people after an ambush and several explosions. But we were told the ranches had been wiped out. Dirk shared with me in confidence the announced story wasn't exactly true. While the homes were destroyed, he believed the bulk of the people fled unharmed. His belief was confirmed when he identified several people killed in our Bakerville raid as having lived at one of the ranches.

I glance again at the gallows. Though they weren't used to hang Milena Maynard, Sheriff Spieth, and the others, they've been used many times since. Public executions are quite popular. I let out a sigh as I start walking toward the hotel.

I round a corner, admiring the beautiful building, when I'm suddenly thrown back. A loud percussion causes my ears to ring. I scramble to my knees as I look back toward the hotel. The lovely façade is now a gaping hole with smoke and fire billowing out. I'm again thrown backwards as everything goes dark.

# Chapter 17

## *Lucy*

Someone's shaking my shoulder. I open my eyes to see his lips moving, but there's no sound. I shake my head, causing a wave of pain through my body.

"Are you hurt?" he seems to mouth.

"I don't know," I answer.

He straightens and lifts a hand, calling someone toward us. Within a few minutes, I'm on a slab of wood and being carried to the infirmary. One of the town medics looks me over. After several minutes, she taps me on the arm, so I look at her.

"Can you hear?" she mouths—this time there's a slight rumble to her words. She says something else I don't catch.

"What?" I ask.

She puts her hand to her lips. "You don't need to shout." I still don't really hear the words, just read her lips and hear a rumble of noise.

"Oh, I didn't realize I was," I say in what I believe is a whisper.

She gives me a smile and nods. "The explosion may have damaged your hearing." At least that's what I interpret when reading her lips.

"For how long?" I ask.

She shrugs. "You seem fine otherwise. Probably sore."

"I am sore," I answer. "Can I have something for the pounding in my head?"

"Sorry," she says, shaking her head.

"I'm on the acquisition team."

"Oh, I didn't realize. Yes, of course."

She returns several minutes later with two white tablets and a burnt orange one. She helps me sit up, offering me water while I take the meds. Making sure I'm watching her, she says, "We've sent for someone. They'll take you home and someone will check on you tomorrow. You'll be more comfortable in your own bed."

Thirty minutes later, I'm being helped into my house. One of the sentry guys transported me and several others to our homes via an old, rusted sedan. My hearing has started to return, allowing me to pick up snippets of the conversation. Several people are dead from the explosion. Among the dead are believed to be Mrs. Majors and Richard's bodyguard, Bernard. Richard was injured but is expected to be fine in a few days. It's not lost on me how close to death I came.

Inside the house, Maddie lifts her eyes from where she's reading by the fireplace. She jumps to her feet. "Oh no! Lucy, are you okay?"

Like I'm in a tunnel, I hear the sentry say, "She was injured in the explosion." He hands me off to Maddie before taking his leave.

"I'll help you to our room," she says, tears streaming down her face.

"I'm okay—just sore and can't hear right."

Maddie not only helps me to my room but into pajamas and then tucks me into my bed. "Do you want a cup of tea?" she asks.

When I agree tea sounds good, she disappears for many minutes. While she's gone, I cry. Bernard was always nice to me. Even Mrs. Majors, who knew what I was to her husband, treated me kindly. I'm pretty sure one of the other names of the dead mentioned was the lady from the kitchen who brought meals up to the suite when I was with Richard. She was also nice. At least Richard is alive. Was he in the suite waiting for me when the explosion happened?

It had to be the rebels. There's no way, without electricity and other amenities, it could've been accidental . . . at least I can't figure a way it could've been. My ears feel like they need to pop. I move my jaw several times, trying to help the process.

When Maddie returns, she has the mug of tea in one hand and a wedge pillow in the other. "I thought this might help make you more comfortable," she says.

After getting me settled with the pillow and tea, during which time I manage to pop one ear, relieving not only the pressure but also helping with my hearing, she sits cross legged on her bed. "Why were you there?"

I give her a long look before asking, "Could you hear the explosion all the way out here?"

"Yes, at least that's what Mae and Susie said. They heard it. They headed to City Hall Park to hear the gossip firsthand, I guess. I was at the cantina when it happened. We heard it there."

"The one on Vining? Were you with Chance?"

She visibly pales before letting out a long breath. "How do you know his name?"

"I met his brother. He asked me to go to the cantina for a cup of tea."

"Oh."

We sit in silence for several minutes before she says, "I guess I do know why you were there. He sent for you, right?"

I meet her eyes before giving a single nod.

She returns my nod. "Rumor is he's fine, but his wife was killed."

"That's what I heard too," I say quietly. "Even though she *knew*, she was still nice to me."

"Yeah. To me too. Do you think . . . will things change for us? For women like us?"

"You mean with his wife dead?"

"Yes. Will he still call for us? Oh! Bernard, he's dead too. I liked him."

"Me too, he even walked me home when it was past curfew."

While I sip my tea, Maddie examines her fingernails. After many minutes, she says, "I don't want to see him anymore. It's not . . . it's not right."

"You think you can break up with him?"

"Probably not." She sighs. "Too bad the blast— " She stops speaking abruptly, then meets my eyes.

"Then Scott would be in charge," I say quietly. "And I know for a fact he hates me. He probably hates you too. You think that would be better?"

"No," she whispers. "I suspect . . . he'd probably take us to the gallows."

"It must have been the rebels, right?"

Maddie answers in a shrug.

"Maybe they'll be able to catch them this time and put a stop to the attacks."

She gives a small nod and then pulls a book out from underneath her pillow. I notice what it is right away. "Maddie," I hiss. "You really should get rid of that thing."

"If they outlaw them, I will. But until then, I'm going to keep reading it and keep going to church with Chance. You should come too. I think you'd see— "

"Not interested," I say quickly.

"Chase goes."

"And?"

"And . . . I think you guys would make a nice couple."

"You're kidding. Have we not just been discussing the fact I'm—we're both—mistresses? Is your boyfriend okay with that?"

"Well, no . . . "

"I wouldn't imagine. Especially if he's a churchgoer. Isn't that a big sin?" She tilts her head to the side in something like a nod. "I can guarantee I wouldn't want a boyfriend okay with . . . with sharing me." I'm surprised at how my voice has raised in volume, even with my wonky hearing, I can tell I'm practically yelling.

Maddie puts a hand to her lips and makes a shushing noise. "You want the others to hear us?"

I roll my eyes. She's right. Mae and Susie could return anytime. And our other two dormmates, Althea and Char—I don't even know where they are. I didn't ask Maddie. They might even be in their room right now.

In a quiet voice, I say, "I just think it's weird your boyfriend's okay with it."

"He's not. But what choice do I have? You know as well as I do, until Richard breaks it off, I'm stuck. And Chance and I, we don't . . . we're waiting."

"Well, that's good at least," I scoff.

She looks down at her Bible. After several moments, without looking up, she says, "I know I'm a sinner. And I want to ask God to forgive my sins, to ask Jesus to be a part of my life. Did you know there are prostitutes and adulteresses in the Bible?"

"No . . . I don't read the Bible."

"It's true. It's full of people who do questionable things. Their sins were forgiven. Mine can be too."

"Well, there you go then," I say with considerable snark.

"Yeah. But I can't, not until Richard lets me go. I can't just ask Jesus into my life and keep sinning."

"Why not?"

"Because . . . because Jesus says to turn away from our sin. And I want to turn away from it. I'm just . . . I'm scared." Maddie begins to cry.

I snuggle down in my covers and stare at the ceiling, listening to her sob.

125

After a while, she says, "At first, Chance didn't understand. He thought I didn't want to give up the privileges we have. He didn't know how I got these privileges. It was a huge thing when I finally told him—when I explained it's not about the stuff, it's about thinking Richard will likely kill me if I try to break it off. He was pretty upset. We even stopped seeing each other for several days. Maybe . . . probably not seeing him would be for the best."

"Undoubtedly," I agree. "If Richard finds out, the end result is likely the same."

"Yeah."

"And he'll probably kill Chance too."

"You don't think he would, do you? Not really."

"Seriously?" I let out a harsh laugh. "In a heartbeat. You and me? We're property. And Richard likes his property. You need to grow up and grow up fast."

I attempt to flip myself over, but the pain in my body squelches my quick movements, resulting in a slow, agonizing turn. I can't believe Maddie can be so naive. Does she not understand Richard owns us?

# Chapter 18

## Sunday, Day 299

## Mollie

"This was a good idea," Angela says as she watches her three-year-old Gavin rolling down a hillside with Sarah's same aged son Andy. The children, along with Art, brought sleds and are having a great time.

"It was," I agree, as I lift my face to the warm sun. "Even though we're only a mile from the lodges, it feels like a whole different world."

"The ride getting here was a little rough," Doris says, rubbing her back in mock agony. "Especially zipping down the hill. Man, that was steep! I thought Mike was going to topple us right over."

I let out a laugh. Getting down into this basin was heart-pounding. Like Doris, I thought Mike took it a little fast. Doris, Calley, and I were driven via the snowmobile and trailer. Calley and I both insisted we could snowshoe like the others, but since Doris was riding, we gave in and joined her. Even though the last bit was harrowing, I'm glad I did. While the walk here was mostly downhill, the walk home won't be. And going uphill continues to be a challenge for me.

Last week, after our Easter service and lunch, Doris suggested we have a picnic this week to celebrate spring. Spring! Though the thermometer is slowly creeping upwards, we still have many feet of snow on the ground. "We've all been working so hard and under too much stress," she said. "When David was preaching today, he said we need to remember to enjoy the life we have. It may not be the circumstances we want, but Jesus' death on the cross gives us hope. That's what I want to do—enjoy life. So, let's have a picnic next week."

I nodded my agreement, and she took over from there, making sure we had everything in place. While our food will be our normal rations

127

of precooked elk roast warmed near the fire and corn and barley flatbread, eating it outside makes it seem almost exciting. And it's a beautiful spring day, with temps somewhere in the high thirties or forties. We're hopeful the spring melt is finally beginning.

We're on the east side of the dude ranch at an old cabin in a small valley surrounded by hills. The cabin and outbuildings were used as a hideout for Jon Dawson's band of mutineers. They'd stolen many supplies out from under us and had the sheds filled with goods, even taking a few of our chickens and rabbits. One of Mick Michaelson's children was kidnapped and held here to ensure Mick, part of our community council, voted the way Dawson wanted. Now, with their murderous mutiny squelched, the buildings have all been emptied and our supplies returned. The wide-open meadowlike space makes a wonderful spot to have a bonfire and gathering.

A gentle slope to the west, with a clear path where the trees have been carved out, is being used as the sledding hill. We could do all these things back at the ski lodge. There's even a magic carpet powered by solar to give sledders a ride up the hill. They make a point of firing it up every Sunday, so I'm sure they're having a blast right now, just like we are. But being away with just family and close friends is a special treat. We invited Ben's family to join us, but they decided to skip it this time. Alvin and Dodie also chose not to come, citing they'd prefer to stay at home and enjoy the quiet.

"I'm surprised so many of us have time off to get together," Angela says. "Tim and I have barely seen each other these last couple of weeks."

"I know what you mean," Doris says. "Evan and Lindsey are always on duty, training, or conditioning. I can't believe they're both here today."

"Yeah, but they look like they're ready to go if needed," Angela says. "Leo too."

All three are in their full tactical gear, including weaponry. One of the rules for being on the security team is being ready to roll at a moment's notice. My sons-in-law Mike and Tim are also dressed for duty since both have a guard shift later today and they didn't want to be rushed to leave so they could get ready.

"Lindsey's going to Prospect tomorrow?" I ask.

"Yeah," Doris says, her word coming out as a sigh. "She and Carol Mathers are taking their turn watching Prospect."

"They're cold camping?" Angela asks.

"Right. No fires or hot food."

"So what do they eat? Just the militia rations?"

Militia rations are what we've taken to calling the snacks militia members are given to carry in their packs, things like jerky, pemmican, hardtack biscuits, and sugar beet crackers. Those are nobody's favorite. We shred the sugar beets, use the smallest amount of flour and water possible to get them to hold together, cook them like pancakes, and then set them on a hot rock by the fire pit so they can continue to dry out until they're hard crackers. It's much-needed calories, but *blech*.

Also not on the top of anyone's list: pucks of rendered fat. The fat is either tallow from an elk or culled goat or cow, or lard from one of the pigs. At over a hundred calories per tablespoon, the fat can provide some much-needed energy on a long shift.

In the fall, when we had more milk, we made yogurt and dehydrated it into curds for a snack. Those were a tasty treat. When the cow calves in the next few weeks, we'll do those again. Dehydrated bone broth was also part of the rations until the weather made dehydrating outside nearly impossible. If we're smart, we'll stockpile the bouillon like cubes over the summer so we have them for next winter. Same with the yogurt treats.

"They take those, yes. But we also have the small stash of MREs we put aside for things like this. Plus we can send them with already cooked and frozen meat they can thaw with their body heat."

"Sounds terrific," Angela says making a face.

"Did I hear you're taking militia shifts too?" Katie asks Doris.

"How you going to do that?" Calley asks, motioning to Doris's leg propped on a log acting as a footstool. Doris brought her peg with the crampon attached and crutches; all are leaning against the cabin since she's not walking around. Instead, her husband lifted her from the trailer and carried her to her chair, making sure she was comfortable.

"I'm doing what your mom does, getting a snowmobile ride to one of the easy-to-reach lookouts. I'll act as a sharpshooter."

"At least you don't have to go to the new guard shack up on the hill," Angela says, gesturing to the makeshift structure visible from our picnic area. "Getting up *that* hillside is a challenge, and the new one on the southside isn't much better."

"Isn't that why they extended the shifts to twelve hours?" Calley asks. "So people don't have to go up and down so often?"

"One reason," Doris says. "The longer shifts also help with our limited numbers and the extra duties. More people on roving patrol and two extra lookouts—with two guards each—is stretching us thin." She lifts her hands in a *what else can we do* motion.

"I guess it's all hands on deck," Sarah says as she cuddles Tate. "And I agree with Angela, it's nice so many of us were free at the same time."

"It's also nice that firewood gathering is now only two times per week," Calley says. "Though, I thought I might see Mike a little more often. But less firewood shifts mean more militia shifts."

As Calley and the others continue to discuss duty shifts, I look around our group. While the children are enjoying the sledding slope, the adults are relaxing near the fire. My girls, Doris, and me are sitting in camp chairs we brought along. Evan, Jake, my sons-in-law, and Lindsey are standing by the fire, laughing and having a great time. Even some of our extended family members have joined us.

Getting Art Carpenter here wasn't easy. He'd much prefer the company of the goats and chickens in the livestock shed than us humans. But our shared grandson Gavin convinced him sledding could be fun. He's the only adult on the sledding hill but seems to be enjoying it. Mike's dad Roy and sister Sheila are even here enjoying the bonfire. Sheila joining us is a surprise. While she's doing much better, she has become such a recluse she rarely leaves the medical clinic where she now lives.

Somehow, Kelley Hudson convinced her she'd have fun, and she walked over with the group. Kelley, Phil, Sabrina, Sylvia, and Rochelle's daughters—currently under Sylvia's care—should be here anytime. Phil and Sabrina were both on a shift this morning, so they're running a little late.

I visited with Sheila a few days ago and was completely surprised by her progress. She excitedly told me about a new treatment she's been doing with Kelley: EMDR, which stands for Eye Movement . . . and something I can't remember for the DR part. She said it's known to help with traumatic memories.

Then she got really quiet as she said, "Kelley told me I'm doing great and I should be able to move home soon. I think she's right. I feel better. I'm so surprised she's able to treat me like this—no need for drugs or anything. She just has me watch a light and it helps to reprogram my brain. I can't believe it's actually working. Kelley—

she's great." Sheila's had a terrible time since Deanne's death, and Kelley has become a lifeline of sorts. To hear she's feeling ready to move out of the clinic and back to her cabin is great.

I watch as Sheila, standing next to Lindsey, glances to the top of the hill and the path down to our picnic spot. My guess is she's watching for Kelley. Her dad taps her on the shoulder to get her attention, causing her to jump. She gives him a broad smile, then gets a look of surprise as she grabs at her thigh, collapsing to the ground. The percussion of a large caliber round shatters the festivities.

"Get down!" Doris yells as she dives to the ground. A series of additional shots echo through the snowy meadow. All of us in the chairs are suddenly on the ground, scrambling to crawl toward the protection of the cabin.

I grab Calley's arm, pulling her behind me. As I move, I'm yelling at the top of my lungs, "Malcolm! Tony! Get down—all of you! Get to cover!"

A blur of a body runs by me, zigzagging as they go, in the direction of our children. "Get down, Mollie!" Jake yells over his shoulder.

I scream out as I watch him fall when another shot sounds off. He grabs at his right arm and stumbles to his feet, heading again in the direction of the children.

"Stay behind the porch!" I shriek at Calley. "I'm going after the children."

I'm several yards behind Jake, following his wavy tracks and blood trail. Almost as quickly as it started, the shooting stops. The laughter of the children on the sledding hill and the adults around the bonfire is replaced with cries of fear and pain. Gasping for breath, I scurry to Jake's side as he grabs for Andy with his uninjured arm. Andy's screaming while sitting next to a scrub brush at the bottom of the hill. Jake pulls him behind a larger tree and motions me to join them.

"Where is everyone?" I cry out, looking for my children and grandchildren.

"Here, Momma!" Lily says somewhere up the mountain.

From the other side of the sledding slope, Art says, "I have Gavin and Sissy. Malcolm? Tony?"

"We're here," both boys say in unison as they come down the hill, staying in the trees about ten feet above Jake and me. "We were trying to get to Andy."

"Marc!" I yell, my voice in a near panic. "Marc? Marc!"

"Grandmo!" Marc calls out, popping his head out from behind a tree at the very top of the hill. "I'm here. Is Andy okay?"

"Stay where you are." Jake says. "He's fine. Just scared."

I watch as Jake seems to sway slightly. Moving quickly toward him, I grab Andy and say, "Sit down." Turning back toward our group. "Katie! We need a medic! Katie!"

Searching her out, I find her behind the cabin, already working on someone. She lifts a hand in acknowledgment before returning to her task. It's Sheila on the ground, and she's not moving.

Angela and Calley are at the edge of the porch. Calley has her sidearm aimed toward the guard shack where the shooting originated. Angela has a rifle. I'm not sure where she got it from, but since her husband Tim was carrying one earlier, it might be his. She's looking toward me. I respond with a lift of my hand. She nods and turns her head to also look at the guard tower. I don't see Sarah with baby Tate or anyone else from our group.

"Do you have a bandage in your pocket?" I ask Jake, kicking myself for taking off my daypack and propping it next to the cabin along with all the snowshoes and Doris's peg leg. *Why didn't I grab it?* "Where's your emergency pack?"

"Just a bandana," Jake answers. He's pale, and sweat is beading up on the swath of his forehead, peeking out from under his stocking cap. He fishes the fabric out of his pocket. "My backpack is leaning against the cabin."

"It's a handkerchief, barely big enough for anything," I say. "Did you blow your nose with it?"

"No, it's clean."

With a nod, I form it into a triangle to make the fabric stretch as much as possible before tying it around his arm.

"Is Dad hurt?" Malcolm asks. "Dad, are you hurt?"

"I'm okay, Buddy." Jake meets my eyes and gives a solid nod before saying, "I don't think it's too bad."

"We need to get you to Katie and Leo."

"Not yet. Let's make sure this is over." Jake raises his voice. "Kids, stay where you are. We'll wait until Evan gives us the all clear."

Quietly, I say, "Sheila was hit."

"Yeah. I don't think she was the only one."

"Do you have a crinkle blanket in your pocket?" I ask.

132

"Yeah, inside pocket—oh, hey, I bet there's one of those homemade bandage strips in there too." Jake gives a visible shiver. "Sorry, Mollie. I'm— " He moves the hand on his good arm to his forehead and gives a slight shake of his head.

"Lean against the tree," I say. "Malcolm, can you grab Andy? Take him up there with you."

"Can I go after Lily?" Tony asks. "I won't go out in the open."

"Yes, get her and bring her to where you and Malcolm are now."

"I'm okay," Jake says again. "It's okay."

I unzip his jacket. "Which pocket?"

He reaches in and fiddles for a minute before taking his hand back and patting his chest. "Here. I . . . maybe you can get it out."

I retrieve the strip of cloth, folded neatly and placed in a zipper bag, along with a silver emergency blanket. I place the blanket over him and then take the bandage and put it over the already soaked-through handkerchief.

A few minutes later, I'm getting concerned. We've yet to be given the go-ahead to move, I haven't seen Sarah, and Jake's new bandage is already starting to show blood. Under the blanket, he's shaking.

I unzip my jacket and start to remove it when he says, "You need it."

"I'm not shot," I say. I take a deep breath and feel the crushing on my chest. *Not now!* I revert from trying to breathe deeply to just trying to breathe. The imaginary elephant on my chest moves off slightly. I give Jake a tight smile.

"Just for a few minutes," he says as I slip the coat over his shoulders. His lips are blueish, and his eyes are dilated.

"Grandmo!" Marc calls from his spot on the top of the hill. "Someone's moving through the trees."

"Art?"

"Not me," Art yells back.

"It's me—It's Kelley Hudson. Marc, it's Kelley. Mollie, where are you?"

"It is Mrs. Hudson! I can see her," Marc says.

"Kelley! We're at the bottom of the hill, opposite Marc. Jake's been shot—others too."

"I'll be right there. I'll bring Marc down with me."

It's many minutes before the rustling of the brush indicates Kelley is almost to us.

"Hi, Marc," Lily's young voice says when she sees him. "Mrs. Hudson, my dad's been shot. You need to help him."

"I'm going to do that," Kelley says. "Are you okay?"

"I scratched my face, but it's not bleeding now."

"I'll clean it for you after I take care of your dad, okay?"

"Jake?" Kelly says as she slides down next to us.

"I'm okay," he says. "The children? They okay?"

"I brought Marc with me. He's not hurt at all. Lily has a scratch, but the others look okay. I didn't go to Art but heard him over there. Does he have Gavin and Sissy?"

"He does," I say. "I don't think they're hurt. He would've said something."

"Caught one in the arm," Jake says. "It's not bad, though. You might go see if anyone else is hurt first. There was a lot of shooting and— "

"I'll take a look at you first," Kelley says while she opens her pack.

"Where's Phil?" I ask. "And the girls?"

"Sylvia took Kerryanne and Cheyre back to the house. Phil and Sabrina went to the militia headquarters. No doubt they'll be sending out a team. We were just at the crest of the hill when the shooting started. We could see them right next to the new guard shack."

"Not our people?" I ask, appalled it could be.

"Doubtful," she says. "Our guess is they took out our guards. There were other shots in the distance. Could you hear them?"

"What?"

"Phil thinks it was a coordinated attack."

"You've got to go back, Kelley," Jake says as she takes out a second cloth bandage from her bag. "They'll need you."

"You need me. I saw you go down on your way to get your kids, Jake. I'll take care of you and then see if anyone else here is in need, then I'll go back. Belinda, Laurie, Madison, and Doctor June can handle it until then."

I close my eyes. Katie is the other member of the medical team. And Sheila, while not officially a member, has been doing some training, but both are here. Sheila herself is being tended to by Katie. I look over to where they are, still against the cabin, hidden from view of the guard shack where the shooting originated. Roy is now there with Sheila. He's holding baby Tate. Sarah is at the far side of the cabin, pistol at the ready. Angela and Calley are still in their positions by the porch. Still no Doris or anyone else.

Kelley fiddles with Jake's arm for several minutes before asking, "Too tight?"

"It's fine," Jake says through gritted teeth.

"Sure it is," Kelley answers. "All I've done is add another bandage to what you already had in place. That'll keep the bleeding down until we can give you proper care back at the clinic. I don't want you walking that far, so— "

"We have a snowmobile," I say, pointing toward it.

"Don't know if we can use it," Jake says. "Pretty sure it was hit."

"Really?" I say as my heart sinks. Losing the snowmobile will make things more difficult for us, especially as far as getting our injured home.

"We're clear!" Mike calls out as he comes around the side of the cabin. Calley jumps up and runs to him, almost bowling him over as she launches herself into his arms. Angela sits the rifle on the porch and then turns and runs toward us, no doubt after her son. Sarah holsters her weapon, says something to Roy, then is also running toward us.

"Dad?" Tony says. "Can I help you?"

"Good idea," Kelley says. "Malcolm, you help your dad too. Keep him steady as we make our way to the others."

"My legs work fine," Jake says as he stands. He's shaky and needs to use the tree for support.

"See?" Kelley says.

"Put your coat back on, Mollie," he says, handing it to me while he gives Kelley a nod. "It's too small to do me any good while I'm moving anyway."

Art's making his way down the hillside, carrying Gavin and leading Sissy by the hand.

"Mom?" Angela hollers. "You okay?"

"Jake's hit," I say, while Jake simultaneously says, "We're fine."

"You got this?" Kelley asks. "You can get Jake and the children to the cabin?"

"Go," I say.

Kelley practically sprints in her snowshoes, following the packed trails toward the cabin. As we get ourselves together to follow, I watch as she first runs to Sheila. She spends only a few moments there before

135

patting Roy on the shoulder and darting around the end of the cabin. The brief interaction tells me little of Sheila's condition.

Angela reaches Art as he and the children make it to the bottom of the hill. Sarah's still several yards away when Andy sees her and goes running to his mom. Sissy and Marc also quickly make their way to Sarah.

"You were all so brave," Sarah tells her children. "I'm so sorry I couldn't get to you."

"Grandpa got shot," Sissy says, tears choking her voice.

Sarah's eyes meet mine.

I give a slight nod. "He'll be okay."

"I'll be okay," Jake adds through chattering teeth.

As we slowly make our way back to the group, a sense of foreboding comes over me. We've been attacked. Not just here but at other locations on the mountain. How bad will this be?

# Chapter 19

## *Mollie*

My question of how bad this will be is partially answered as soon as we reach the cabin. "Mom?" Katie says. "Have Jake sit next to the wall. Put something under him. Everyone should stay on this side of the cabin, just in case. Kelley went to check on Doris. Then we need to get Jake and Sheila out of here."

"How is she?" I ask, as Calley puts her daypack on the ground and then motions for Jake to sit on it. He's shivering again. I put the blanket back over him and tell the younger children to sit close to him and help warm him up.

"Drink this," Calley says, thrusting a water bottle at him.

"Can I sit on your lap, Grandpa?" Andy asks.

I start to say no, but Jake says, "Sure you can. Just watch my arm, okay?"

"'Kay," Andy says as he climbs on Jake.

"Sheila needs fluids. I don't have an IV kit with me," Katie says. "At least we got the bleeding stopped quickly, so . . . " She gives a shrug.

"We're the same blood type," Roy says. "Kelley's going to do a field transfusion if we can't get back shortly."

"Ugh, Dad," Sheila says in a quiet voice. "I already have enough of your crazy blood in me."

Roy smiles at her attempt of humor. "A little more won't hurt."

"I could give you mine," Mike says.

"No thanks. I'll stick with Dad's. Besides, you're not a donor for me."

"You're no fun," Mike says.

I'm surprised to hear Sheila so calm and joking. After the way she's been the last several months—since the attacks started, really—I would've expected her to be hysterical. Once Jake is situated, I move to Angela. She's hugging Gavin close to her while Art stands nearby.

"Tim?" I ask quietly.

"They went after the shooters. He's with Evan and Leo."

"He left you his rifle?"

"No, it's not Tim's. They left Mike here to help us."

I turn to Mike and ask, "How'd you know we were clear?"

"Leo left me his radio." Mike taps his pocket. "Evan called when they got to the lookout. And we're not the only ones who were attacked."

"How bad is it?" Jake asks.

"Um . . ." Mike says. "I don't know exactly. I'm only catching bits and pieces on the radio. The reception down here isn't great with the line-of-sight thing. I do know our snowmobile is toast, so getting you two out of here . . ." He lifts his arms in a shrug motion. "Evan asked for them to send help. And— " Mike tilts his head. "Mollie, you should maybe go see if Doris needs you. She's by the smaller shed."

"Needs me? Was she hit?" I ask, starting to move.

"Not her. Lindsey."

My mouth forms an *O* as I look at Mike's face. The slight shake of his head speaks volumes.

I swallow hard. "I'll be right back."

At the shed, Doris is holding Lindsey's body as she rocks back and forth. Kelley is sitting next to them, her hand on Doris's shoulder. When Kelley sees me, she motions me to them.

"Doris," Kelley says, using what I think of as her shrink voice; it's calm and welcoming. "Mollie's here. I'm going to have her stay with you."

As Kelley stands, she wipes at her eyes and gives me a shake of her head. "I'm going to get Sheila and Jake ready to leave. Hopefully, someone will be here soon."

I give a nod before sinking down next to Doris.

She's pushing Lindsey's hair out of her vacant eyes. "She didn't even get a chance to fight back," Doris says between her tears. "Evan went after them. He'll find them and make them pay for taking our girl."

I sit with Doris as she cries, my tears joining hers.

It's many minutes before Mike comes over and says, "Uh, I thought you should know they're on their way. They're sending a machine for Jake and Sheila. They'll bring horses, too, so we can take— " He lets out a sigh. "We can take Lindsey back."

"Thank you, Mike," I say. "I'll come over as soon as I hear the snowmobile."

"At least she gets to be with Logan," Doris says. "A part of her died the day he did. She's tried to get past it, but you never really do. You know that and I know that—we both lost our first husbands."

"Yes," I say quietly. Doris's husband, father to Lindsey and Doris's older daughter Jessica, was killed in an auto accident when her girls were very young. My first husband, Jamie, died of a heart attack. Even though we both knew loss, we also found love again. Perhaps Lindsey would've someday too.

This new world we live in is plagued with death. We've lost so many since the attacks started. I remember when Jake and I were in heavy prepper mode. We studied all kinds of charts and theories about the suspected death tolls related to various end-of-the-world disasters. We tried to look at it without emotion to better make ourselves ready for whatever may happen. We failed.

The snowmobile to take Jake and Sheila arrives quicker than I expect. The trailer we rode down on is attached to the new ride. It was hit also but has only a single-entry hole in the wooden side. The slug mushroomed and buried itself in the opposite side. Sheila is positioned in the trailer with Katie riding next to her. Jake sits behind the driver. Roy left on foot while Sheila was being loaded so he can be there as needed for giving blood. Kelley went with him.

"Mom," Sarah says as the sled pulls away, "they'll either send the machine back for you or you can ride one of the horses. I guess the rest of us should start heading back." Everyone already has their snowshoes on and daypacks gathered.

"Calley will wait for a ride," Mike says quickly. "I'll stay with her until she can go back. With Mollie and Doris too."

"Thanks, Mike," I say.

"The bonfire has mostly burned down, but I want to finish putting it out before we go," he says.

About half an hour later, two riders are making their way down the trail, each ponying a horse behind them. They take the downhill trail slowly, finally reaching the meadow.

Grant Cameron slides off his horse. "We heard about Lindsey. Mom sent a shroud. We'll wrap her first. Where— "

139

"Behind the shed," I say. I'd been sitting with Doris until Mike notified us of the riders. She told me to go ahead, saying she wanted a few more minutes with Lindsey in private.

"Doris?" I call, raising my voice.

"I'm ready," she replies weakly.

Grant gives a nod. With his wife missing for almost a month, he too is no stranger to heartache. The other rider, his younger brother Bryce, helps prepare Lindsey. Even though Doris was an absolute wreck before the riders arrived, she manages to pull herself together and help wrap Lindsey. Once the cloth is in place, they wrap twine around it to hold everything tight. A low whimper escapes from Doris as the last knot is tied. Mike helps them get her in position before helping Doris stand and hobble to her horse.

By the time we're ready to go, the sun is low on the horizon. Calley rides behind Bryce while Doris rides behind Grant. Lindsey is on one of the ponied horses, and I'm on the other. Mike walks back to us, telling Calley he'll meet her at the lodge where I live. We take the necessities back with us, deciding the chairs, snow sleds, and other extra items we brought for our day of fun can stay behind. There're three pairs of snowshoes still propped against the cabin—the ones Evan, Leo, and Tim were wearing.

Although Doris is obviously devastated over the loss of her daughter, she holds her head high on the ride back to the dude ranch. When we reach the lodge, Sarah comes running out.

"Any news on Jake?" she asks.

"He's not here? I thought he'd be here since we're used for overflow when the medical clinic is too full."

Sarah shakes her head as Bryce says, "There weren't many injuries, ma'am. The, uh . . . the shooters were precise."

"What do you mean?" I ask.

"Our three watchtowers on the east side were all overrun," Grant says slowly. "The one near where you were, the new shack to the south, and the lean-to shack near the farthest house in our compound. All six guards were killed."

Doris and I both gasp at the news.

"And, like in your case, the infiltrators became snipers. As far as I know, only Ms. Stapleton—Sheila—and Jake survived their wounds."

"How many?" Doris asks quietly.

"Three at the Young house— "

"The Young house!" Sarah cries. "Why would they be targeted? They're some of our most elderly."

I shake my head. "Which three?"

"Mrs. Young and also the gentleman who uses a wheelchair and his wife."

Sarah begins to cry as I give a nod. I know who he means. The gentleman had been on our militia last summer, more of a figurehead than anything. He had made a point of saying for us to set him up where he could shoot and he'd help defend his neighbors. Last summer, he was mostly using a walker. He went downhill over the winter and worked on Sarah's sewing team.

"Who else?" Doris asks.

Bryce lets out a slow breath. "They shot at the sledders."

"What?" I cry.

"Three dead. Toby James and Chaplain Rick, plus one of the children—Willie, Angelo Master's grandson."

"Not one of the children," Doris says quietly. "And Toby? He's such a sweet young man."

I shake my head as my tears again flow freely. Angelo lost his daughter Tricia during the attempted takeover. He'd been caring for her children since then. Toby James, who's often my snowmobile chauffeur, has become a friend, always polite and an asset to our community. And Chaplain Rick is a cornerstone of our group. Today's losses are huge.

"How?" Doris asks. "How'd they get close enough?"

"That's just it," Grant says. "They were shooting from the new shack we built to the south."

"What?" I ask again, shaking my head. "The new lookout is over a half mile away."

"A trained sniper," Doris answers. "Do you know where Evan is?"

"No, sorry," Bryce says. "We didn't see him. After securing the area, we were told to come after you." He lowers his voice to almost a whisper; I strain to hear him but can barely make him out. "Will you want to take Lindsey's remains to your cabin?"

"Yes," Doris says quietly.

"I'm going with Doris," I say to Sarah. "Then I'll go see Jake. Are the children okay?"

"Shaken up but physically fine."

"Okay," I say as Bryce holds Calley's arm so she can slide off the horse.

Once she's on the ground, she says, "As soon as Mike gets back, I'll send him to the clinic to see if you need anything. He'll want to check on Sheila anyway."

I respond with a nod. Calley and Sarah remain on the porch as we ride away.

"Tell Jake we're praying," Sarah calls out.

When we stop at Doris and Evan's studio cabin, they help her off and inside first. I follow them, sitting next to Doris on the couch while the men move Lindsey in. I'm anxious to go to the clinic and check on Jake but want to make sure Doris doesn't need anything first. When they enter with Lindsey, Danny, their black lab, lets out a low moan.

"I know, boy," Doris says. "You're going to miss her, aren't you?" She rubs his ears as he lays his head in her lap.

As they gently place Lindsey on the bed, I ask Doris, "Can I help you?"

"No . . . Bryce said he'd send his mom over to help me get Lindsey ready."

"She should be here shortly," Bryce says. "We'll leave you be for now, okay?"

Doris nods. Both men mutter their condolences again before stepping out.

"I was hoping—will it be okay if we bury her at your place next to Logan? I mean, when we go back down in the spring?" Doris asks softly.

"Absolutely."

"Thank you." She nods as her eyes fill again. "Go. Go be with Jake. Please give him my best."

"I can stay until Pamela arrives."

"No. I need to be alone. Can you move my wheelchair over so I can get in it?"

After helping Doris from the couch to her chair, I tell her again to let me know if she needs anything.

I'm almost to the door when she says, "I think our shooters weren't as well trained."

"What do you mean?" I ask, turning back toward her.

"They took out the guards at each lookout—oh! We didn't even ask the names of the guards killed."

"No. I wanted to, but after hearing about Toby and Tricia's boy— " I shake my head. "I just needed to wait a bit."

"Understood. Anyway, they took out our guards, then each sniper team took out three people. We know the ones shooting at us fired more than three shots since they made sure to hit the snowmobile too, but they only shot three people. I suspect we'll hear there was other equipment shot up as well."

"Three people? What is the significance?"

"I don't know. But why only three is my question. Were they limiting their shots?"

"There were a lot more than three shots where we were," I say.

"And at our location," Doris says, then visibly swallows, "Lindsey was, thankfully, the only fatality. That's why I say our shooters weren't as well trained."

It's a short walk from Doris and Evan's cabin to the clinic. When I step inside, Bill Shane and two others from the militia are in the reception area.

"Mollie, Jake's in the hospital room," Bill says. "Sheila's in surgery."

"How are they?" I ask, moving toward the closed door of Jake's room.

"Katie came out a few minutes ago, checking to see if you'd arrived. She said Jake's asking for you."

I give a nod. "I just left Doris at her cabin. Is Evan back? She needs him."

"They went after the shooters—the ones that hit your group."

"Leo and Tim are still with him?" I ask, concerned for my two sons-in-law.

"On last contact, yes. The radios don't work well at that distance."

"And the other shooters? Did anyone go after them?"

"Tried. But by the time we got to the guard shacks, they were gone, and they cleared their tracks so they couldn't be followed."

"They covered their tracks? In the snow?"

With his lips pulled tight, he gives a nod. "Sort of. The ones who killed Mrs. Young and the couple at her house used the ridgeline. We had a small group tracking them, but the snow gets thin from the way the wind blows and then turns into hardpacked bare ground and rocks. They're still out looking."

"Doris said she thought there were two snipers in each group. Is that true?"

"They were in groups of three. Two shooters and a spotter, we think."

"How'd the southside shooters escape?"

"They were brilliant," Bill says, slight awe in his voice. "I never would've thought of this, but they set off a small avalanche behind them."

"An avalanche? Why?" I ask, remembering how an accidental avalanche killed one of our community members a few months ago.

"To cover their tracks. That and slow us down. Our people were already a good ways behind them because of the distance to the lookout. They planned this well."

"Okay . . . maybe the attacks on the other two lookouts were planned, but how'd they know where we'd be? How'd they know we'd go to the old cabin?"

"I doubt they did. They must have just taken advantage of the situation."

"You're sure?" I drop my voice to a whisper. "Are you sure there isn't someone inside our community feeding information to them?"

Bill pats my shoulder. "Go see Jake. I'll want to get a statement from you later."

"You're not sure. We just lost over a dozen people, including a little boy, and it could be another inside job?" I hear my voice starting to squeak with a combination of anger and fear.

In his calm cop voice, Bill says, "Right now, I'm not sure of much. Except for your husband is asking for you."

I shake my head and walk a couple of steps. I stop and turn back to Bill. "Why are you here?"

"Because, like I said, I'm not sure of much. Seemed it might be smart to spend some time here considering only two people survived their wounds."

"Do you think they're still in danger?"

"Doubtful. But . . . " He shrugs.

"Doris said she thinks our snipers weren't as well trained as the others."

"Makes sense. Maybe they were watching us and saw your group leave. They put together another hit squad—those not as skilled as the

144

others. After you visit with Jake, we'll talk. Maybe you saw something helpful."

I shake my head. "I didn't. I was watching Sheila when she was shot, but I didn't see the shooters." With that, I continue the short trip into Jake's room. I crack the door slightly and ask, "Can I come in?"

"Come in, Mom," Katie says. She's standing next to the bed where a pale Jake is propped on several pillows.

"Hey," he says. "How's Doris?"

I shake my head. "About how you'd expect. She's a wreck but is trying not to be."

"Yeah. Did you talk to Bill?"

"A little. You?"

"He asked me what I saw, but I didn't see anything. He asked Katie the same thing."

"I wasn't looking at the guard shack," Katie says. "We were just talking— "

"I know. How's the wound?"

Katie gives a slight shrug. "They're working on Sheila first. Jake's stable."

"How's Sheila doing?"

"I don't know. Roy's in there so they can give her blood. I expected them to be finished with him before now. I have a cot set up over there for him to rest. Let me grab you a chair."

Once I'm sitting, I realize how exhausted I am. It's a good hour before the door to the surgery room opens.

# Chapter 20

## *Mollie*

June Mitchellini escorts Roy out, supporting him as he moves carefully. Katie runs over to offer an arm.

"I'm okay," Roy says. "Just a little woozy."

"Sheila?" Jake asks.

"Holding her own," June replies.

"She lost a lot of blood," Roy adds.

"Katie did great getting the bleeding stopped in the field," June says quickly as she helps Roy sit on the cot. "She's getting intravenous fluids now in addition to the transfusion."

Both of them purchased reusable IV fluid bags a few years earlier when hospitals across the country had a shortage due to a hurricane interrupting the manufacturing of them, making them realize reusable bags were a good idea.

Kelley, a longtime prepper, purchased hers after reading an article about the shortages. Belinda, who didn't consider herself a prepper, already had filled bags as part of the supplies she kept on hand as one of the few medical people in our rural community. Living so far from a hospital and without local ambulance service, she's had to administer emergency care many times over the years. She added the empty bags after realizing the supply chain could so easily be interrupted. I have no idea how many people have had her homemade IV solution since the havoc began. I know my own daughter's life was saved thanks to their foresight.

"Will it be enough?" Roy asks as he moves to a reclining position.

"Keep praying and stay positive," June answers. "You heard Belinda."

"Yeah. It's just . . . it's a lot with losing Deanne such a short time ago, and now my little girl's hurt."

June and Katie help Roy lower to the bed.

Once he's down, he asks, "Where's Mike?"

"He should be here anytime," I say, surprised we haven't seen him yet.

Roy gives a nod. "I'm going to take a short nap. Wake me if anything happens with Sheila or when Mike gets here."

June fiddles with a few things on a shelf before walking toward the door to the reception area. She motions for Katie to follow her. Jake and I share a look and a shrug. We sit quietly, me still holding on to his hand while tears stream down my face. The deaths are heartbreaking.

At some point, I realize I've fallen asleep when a noise causes me to jump. As I look around the room, I'm surprised to see Mike sitting next to his dad's cot. Katie is on the other side of Jake in a chair. The door from the surgery room opens, and Belinda exits the room behind Madison.

"Okay, Roy. Mike," Belinda says, removing her fabric surgical mask. "Sheila's doing fine. Blood loss is still a concern, but not as much as it was. The bullet was embedded. I'm fairly confident we got it all and . . . well, after an open wound, our biggest worry is always infection."

"You have antibiotics for her, right?" Roy asks, moving to a sitting position.

"Not a lot. Mollie's friends brought fish antibiotics with them. We're using those."

Even though Belinda isn't talking to me, I give a nod. Clarice had a container of single-dose powdered erythromycin used for fish tanks. She and Liam found them at a house they were staying in when Bart was injured. They tried them for a few days, but when it didn't make a difference and he kept getting worse, Bart insisted he stop taking them so they'd have them if needed.

They didn't need them, but now we do. Those, along with other medicines and a small amount of food and supplies they found in their salvaging along the way, are now added to the community coffers. One of the biggest surprises they had with them was coffee. Two containers had yet to even be opened. We're saving those for something special. I'm not sure what that might be, but something.

"And you think they'll work?" Roy asks. "Fish antibiotics?"

"We'll know more in a few days, but I'm cautiously optimistic. And as a precaution, we'll keep her in the surgery room for now. At least one of us will stay with her. Kelley and Laurie are with her now.

Once we have Jake taken care of, we'll clean this room before moving her to the more comfortable bed. We'll treat this as an ICU with visitors limited." She turns and looks in our direction. "So, Jake, let us wash up and we'll get you sorted out. Katie, you'll take the lead on this."

Katie jumps to her feet. "I'll scrub in the reception area bathroom."

With a nod, Belinda motions to Madison and they move into the small bathroom off the hospital room. Although this cabin—like all the cabins—is without running water, they've set up water coolers in each of the two bathrooms of this former vacation duplex. The insulated coolers keep the water warm for washing up. The woodstove in the other section of the duplex has large pots on it with more water heating. After a few minutes, the three return and begin their examination of Jake.

"Belinda, does Laurie know about Toby?" I ask as she puts on exam gloves.

"She does," Belinda answers with a frown. Laurie knew Toby when they both lived in Wesley. He was severely injured and taken to Prospect early in the attacks. He was there when the hospital caught fire. Laurie assumed he'd died in the fire. She was surprised when he showed up last fall with the others from Prospect. "She and I went there as soon as we could after the shooting. There wasn't anything we could do for Toby, Chaplain Rick, or Willie. Same with the people at the Young's house."

Belinda gives a nod as Katie indicates she's ready to examine Jake. "Okay," Belinda says. "Tell me what you see."

As Katie begins her report, I can't help but smile at my now grown-up little girl professionally detailing her clinical observations. Before the attacks, Katie was an art major. At then boyfriend Leo's urging, she took first aid courses as part of their personal preparedness efforts. Early in the attacks, due to his EMT training, he was added to the medical team. He suggested Katie also join, but she originally declined. She finally gave in when she realized there was a need and she has an aptitude for medicine.

When she was shot last summer and fighting for her own life, she got an up close and personal view of the dedication of our doctors. After her recovery and marriage to Leo, she began her training again. Now, it's completely clear Katie is doing what she was meant to do. While she's an amazing artist, she certainly has a knack for medicine.

Once Katie is finished, Belinda says, "Good. And what do you think we should do?"

"Clean the wound. There doesn't appear to be an obvious break in the humerus, but there may have been a nick. And even though there's an exit wound showing the bullet passed through, we don't know if fragments may have been left behind."

"And if there were fragments left behind?"

"We run the risk of infection. But like Sheila, the more we mess with the wound the higher the risk of infection."

After discussing their options for a few more minutes, Belinda says, "So, Jake, we'd better take a look. The problem, as you've heard, is infection. Not only that, but we also have a space shortage with Sheila in the operating room. What I think we'll do is scrub down the reception area and examination space and then move you in there for the procedure. Then, once we get you put back together, we'll send you home. Mollie, you'll need to get your bedroom ready for him. Because of the type of wound, and the fact we won't have to do as much digging around as we did with Sheila, I'm comfortable with him healing there. Just give the room a good cleaning and put fresh sheets on, like if you were having company. And let's have you sleep on the couch or a cot for the first couple of days as an added precaution."

"What?" Jake asks. "Are you afraid my wife will give me cooties?"

I squeeze his hand and say, "All right, no cooties for Jake." As I start to stand, the room begins to sway. Madison, who's closest to me, is immediately by my side and gently guiding me back to the chair.

"Put your head between your knees," she says, moving me into position.

"I'm okay," I mutter, as things continue to spin. I squeeze my eyes shut tightly to try and get my bearings. *Not now.* As the room rotates, the voices become far away. I can hear Jake saying my name and Katie telling him to stay in his bed. The fogginess seems to go on forever before I'm finally able to raise my head without feeling like I'm going to keel over.

"Sorry," I say once I'm no longer in danger of landing on the ground. "Sometimes . . . " I give a slight shrug.

"You're okay?" Jake asks.

I attempt a smile. It's weak, just like I feel. "I'm okay." Madison is still at my side. Belinda's at the foot of Jake's bed, giving me the hairy eyeball. "I'm okay," I say again, directing it toward her.

"Really? Doesn't seem like it."

"Lots of emotions today," I answer. "It all just . . . I don't know."

"Madison, walk her home. Put her on the couch and get whoever is at her house to set up the bedroom for Jake. I'll examine her when we bring Jake home."

"I'm right here. You don't need to talk to Madison as if I'm elsewhere."

Belinda raises both eyebrows at me. "Fine then, *Mollie*. Let Madison escort you home, and I'll be there shortly."

I give Jake a kiss goodbye and tell him I'll see him soon. Madison walks next to me but doesn't try to hold me up or do anything weird. As quickly as the wooziness started, it's gone. While I feel completely exhausted, and the ache in my back is terrible, I don't feel like I'm in any danger of passing out.

As soon as I walk into my house, everyone wants to know how Jake is. I let them all know he'll be fine and home soon. Then I hug each of the young children, starting with Lily, who's thrown herself at my legs.

"And Sheila?" Calley asks. "Are Mike and Roy still with her?"

"Roy gave her blood," Madison answers. "He's resting, and Mike is there. Sheila did well in surgery. Before Jake comes here, can you give his room a good cleaning and disinfecting plus fresh sheets?"

"Yes, sure," Angela says, giving me a questioning look.

I answer with a slight shrug and an eye roll, while Madison says, "Your mom had another event, and Belinda wants her resting until she can be checked out."

Of course, everyone starts fawning over me, especially Malcolm and Tony, who both help me to the couch. Malcolm offers to get me a glass of water.

"You'd rather have tea, right, Mom?" Tony asks.

"I'm okay for now," I say, while Madison says, "She needs a big glass of water, then she can have a cup of tea. There's a good chance she's dehydrated."

Once Madison makes sure I plan to stay put on the couch and let the others wait on me and get things ready for Jake, she returns to the clinic.

"Tim and Leo aren't back yet?" I ask.

Angela shakes her head. "I'm pretty worried."

I give a slight nod. It's been hours since the massacre.

150

"Anything more about the others?" Sarah asks.

"Nothing more than what we already knew."

Marc gives me a sad nod. "My mom told me about Willie. He was my friend."

As I sit on the couch with my feet up on the coffee table, Angela and Sarah, along with help from the younger children, get the bedroom ready for Jake while Malcolm and Tony wait on me. Marc sits with me and talks about Willie and how much he'll miss him.

It's about twenty minutes later when there's a knock at the door and a voice calls out, "It's Leo and Tim. We're back."

Malcolm runs to let them in. Stepping inside, they both look like they've been through the wringer. Their clothes are dirty, and Tim has twigs in his hair and is holding his right arm across his chest.

"Are Angela and Gavin here?" Tim asks.

"Tim?" Angela says, stepping out of the dining room. "You're back!" She runs over and hugs him. I watch as he winces in her embrace. "What's wrong?"

"I'm okay. I slipped and hurt my arm. I wanted to tell you I'm back. I'm on my way to the clinic to have it checked out."

"Is Katie at the clinic?" Leo asks.

"She is," I say. "What happened? Did you find them?"

"We found them," Leo says with a nod.

I wait a couple of beats for him to say more, but when he doesn't, I prompt, "And?"

"Not good, Mom," Tim says. "They . . . we . . . " He shakes his head.

Leo claps Tim on the shoulder, which results in a grimace. "Sorry. I'm going to walk Tim to the clinic. I'm sure his wrist is broken. I did what I could in the field, but Belinda needs to take care of it properly."

"And Evan? Did he come back with you?"

"He did. He went home to check on Doris."

"Do you know about Lindsey and the others?" Angela asks.

"They were assassins," Tim says in a harsh voice. "Is Sheila okay? I saw her go down."

"She's been operated on and was fine when I left the clinic," I say. "Jake should be okay too."

"Jake?" Tim and Leo respond simultaneously.

"He was shot," Angela says. "You didn't know?"

"No, sorry." Leo shakes his head. "Sorry, Mollie. We should've checked to make sure no one else was hit before we took off."

"Was anyone else hit?" Tim asks.

"Not from our group," Angela says.

Leo gives a grim nod. "We got a little on the radio."

"My friend Willie was killed," Marc says.

"I'm sorry about that," Leo answers, walking over so he's standing close to Marc. "I'm sorry you lost your friend. If you feel sad, I'll be around to talk, okay?"

Marc leans his head against my arm. "Too many people have died since we lost the electricity."

# Chapter 21

## *Lucy*

The day after the explosion, a time of mourning was declared. Eight people, including Mrs. Majors and Bernard, were killed immediately. Three more died within hours. Of those killed, one was a sentry and the rest were workers assigned to the hotel.

Two days after the deaths, a special memorial service was held at City Hall Park, right next to the gallows. Although I was still sore, I was well enough to attend.

My hearing had returned to normal, and the headache was well-controlled with mild pain relievers. I'm very thankful to be part of the acquisition team. The medical team has taken great care of me, making sure I have pain relievers and even special healing foods. There were several workers injured, and I know they received extremely limited treatment, only enough to stabilize them and send them home to recover.

The service was nice. People, even workers, were able to talk about their lost loved ones. I was surprised to see time devoted to those in our lowest class. It was almost like before—before the attacks, the EMP, and Richard taking over the town by force and changing everything, including how we look at each other. Although many workers have died in the months since Richard became mayor, we've never done anything to commemorate them. Even when sentries were murdered by the rebels, there were no public funerals.

Out of fear of another attack, extra security measures were put in place before the service. Not only was the area thoroughly checked for explosives, but there were also sentries and acquisition team members on hand and ready if needed. A new podium was added, which had a small piece of plexiglass at the top. Maddie said she even heard sandbags were put inside the lectern. While the sandbags would probably do the job of stopping a bullet, would the plexiglass?

Scott seemed completely distraught over the death of his mom, but Richard was without emotion. Scott gave a true eulogy, talking about his wonderful memories of his mom. Richard, with his arm in a sling but otherwise looking perfectly healthy, delivered more of a war cry. While I expected him to blame the rebels for this, just like the shootings of the sentries and other attacks, he surprised me by saying it was another community responsible.

He blamed Bakerville—the same town we raided several months back, killing everyone in sight. Doc Bohm said only part of the town was there and the rest was hiding out. It does make sense, considering we killed around seventy people and there were close to four hundred living there prior to the attacks. At the time, I assumed they'd had a large die off like Prospect did.

Richard ranted for almost half an hour, promising to find the murderers from Bakerville and bring them to justice. Understandable, but it's odd. As I listened to his accusations, I found myself wondering how people from Bakerville managed to sneak into town and plant the bomb. Are our sentries not doing their job? People coming in and out of town is a big deal. Although Richard had plenty to say about the killers and the revenge he has planned, he gave no tribute to his wife. He shared no memories, no personal tidbits, and didn't even acknowledge the length of time they'd been married.

The special team I was supposed to be on left as scheduled. Even though my injuries were mild, it was decided I'd be more of a hindrance than an asset—not that I truly think anyone considered me an asset when I was well. Lorita stopped by after one of the medics told me I wasn't going. She was exceedingly kind and assured me she'd be happy to continue working with me on improving my skills when she returns.

"Why?" I asked.

"Because the better trained you are, the better for all of us."

"Do you work with anyone else?"

She shrugged. "If they need it or one of the officers asks me."

"So someone asked you to work with me?"

"No . . . not exactly. Have you heard about that Meeks guy from Wesley wanting us to go on a mission with him?"

"Are they having trouble again?"

"Meeks said someone from around Billings reached out to him, said there's some kind of warlord or something up there. He thinks we should all team up—his town and our town—to eliminate the warlord."

"Why?"

"Because Meeks wants to be a warlord!" she said with a laugh. "He doesn't want competition."

I smiled but didn't think it was as funny as she did. We're fortunate we have Richard looking out for us. I waited, expecting her to say more.

Instead, she asked, "Did you ever imagine this would be our life?"

"Well, no. Who would think we'd be attacked like we were? I mean, really?"

"For me, the attacks are no surprise. Coming from Columbia, I understand how bad things can be. I was young when we escaped, but my mom and dad told me much about what it was like. And then we watched as Venezuela fell. It was . . . concerning. I'm glad my parents died before they could see their beloved America turn into . . . whatever we are now. And I'm glad they don't know the things I'm doing in this new world."

"What do you mean?" I asked.

She stared at the floor and said, "I'm sure they'd be embarrassed how I willingly have gone along with the things we've done."

"I doubt it. They'd probably be happy you're a strong leader for us and you don't have to scramble the way the workers do."

"Do you think your parents would be happy?"

"I have no doubt," I said with a scoff. "My mom was good friends with Janet—Lieutenant Kruse. No, let me rephrase that. I'd probably continually hear what a disappointment I am since that's what Janet thinks. So I guess my parents would only be happy about the benefits of what I could give them as part of the acquisition team. And I suppose, if they were here, I'd have a house instead of living in the dorms. I guess that'd be a benefit."

"Do you not like living here? I'm sure you could move to my dorm if you think it's a better fit."

"Oh no, this is fine. Although, Maddie has been— " I slammed my mouth shut.

"Yeah. I know. She's a sweet girl, but it's going to get her in trouble. Having a boyfriend, especially one who isn't a good fit for our lifestyle, is risky."

"You know about him?"

"I don't *know* anything, but I hear talk."

"I've tried to tell her."

She gave a nod and said, "The best thing we can do, considering we've already made our choices, is to keep our heads down and not draw attention. We need to obey the rules and do what is needed."

"You don't keep your head down. You're amazing."

"Well . . . thank you. But that's not what I mean. I do what's necessary. I won't shirk my duties and make others have to do something I should be doing. If I don't— " She took a deep breath. "If I don't do the hard things, as distasteful as they are, others like you or Maddie will need to do them. And I know how difficult this is for you."

"I do my job," I replied crossly.

"I'm not saying you don't. You're a part of our team, and you do well at obeying orders. That's not what I'm saying. I'm able to compartmentalize things better. I despise the things we do, and I know I'll eventually pay for these choices. But for today, I can keep my wits about me as I follow orders. I'm not going to worry about tomorrow when our rightful government is reestablished. I know— " She shook her head. "I'm not sure you, Maddie, and a few of the others can keep your minds right. Of course, your appointments with Doc Bohm have made a difference. I can see a new toughness about you that wasn't there before."

"Thank you?"

She gave me a small smile and a nod. "Anyway, I hope you're feeling better, and I'll be happy to work with you again after the team gets back. How much longer are you excused from training?"

"Someone from the medical team will be by the day after tomorrow to see if I'm ready to be released. They've hinted I'll be on modified duty for a week or two, but I don't really know what that will entail."

"Keep practicing the things we've worked on."

Lorita and the special team have been gone a few days. The same medic stopped by a couple of days ago and released me to modified training, saying he'll see me again in two weeks to check how I'm healing. Janet has been less than understanding about my limitations and refuses to let me train with them since I'm not able to do everything. Instead, I'm on my own. I don't really mind. I'm pacing myself while I get my body back in shape. I'm also able to spend extra time at the range when the rest of them are off doing other things, and I spend time working on the punches and kicks Lorita taught me. Some movements still hurt, so I try not to overdo it.

I have an appointment with Doc Bohm tomorrow. He searched me out yesterday, saying he thought it'd be a good idea for us to do a check in, make sure I'm mentally doing okay after the explosion. I almost laugh when I think about how he used to creep me out. He genuinely seems to be a caring man. And I'm sure those times he got physical with me was for my own good, a way to get me focused on what was important.

With it being the middle of April, maybe the weather will start warming up. It's still cold enough I have to wear multiple layers and insulated pants when out and about. And there's still drifted snow combined with bare ground. I'm beginning to think it's never going to melt. Maybe there's something to the rumors floating around all winter about the nuclear attacks changing our weather. I don't know. I'm just ready for the snow, wind, and cold to end.

Back at my house, all my dormmates, except Maddie, are in the living room. After saying my hellos, I head to the bedroom. Maddie's sitting on the bed staring at the wall, not even acknowledging me when I walk into the room.

"Almost time for our dinner to arrive," I say, digging in my closet for my comfy clothes.

"I told him no."

"Told who no?"

"He sent for me. I . . . I refused."

I quickly turn to look at her. "Are you nuts? What do you think he'll do? Just— "

"I don't care. I've decided, and I'm sticking with it. It's time I was known by my fruit, not my sinful behavior."

"What's that? Christian mumbo jumbo?"

"I guess you would call it *mumbo jumbo*. But I mean it. I'm going to change. This time I didn't come right out and say I won't ever see him again—even though I won't. I just had the messenger wait and I wrote on the note this week was bad for me."

With my hands on my hips, I shake my head. "So you're just going to put him off? What happens when he sends for you next week?"

"I'll have the flu?"

"Good luck. If your plan is simply to put him off for a few weeks, maybe it'll work, but I can't imagine it will be sustainable."

"I think he might lose interest in me. Did you hear he moved into the Bunn Mansion? Or . . . maybe you've already visited?"

"No. I haven't heard." I give her a pointed look before adding, "Or visited."

"Chance's brother helped salvage usable things from the hotel. He thinks Richard is going to make some big changes. He even has a woman living there."

"Really? Chase said that?"

"Well, he didn't actually see the woman, but one of the other guys did and told him about her."

"So it's a rumor?"

Maddie responds with a slight lift of one shoulder.

"Thought so. I'm pretty sure it's nothing I need to hear then. About Richard, I sure hope you know what you're doing."

# Chapter 22

## *Monday, Day 300*

## *Mollie*

As Leo suspected, Tim's wrist is broken. Without the ability to do x-rays, Belinda could only assume it was a clean break. With Madison's help, she was able to reset and splint it. Not only is his arm in a sling, but it's also taped to his body to limit his movements. In a few days, he'll likely be put in a proper cast.

Belinda, Kelley, us, and one other family had a small amount of casting supplies stocked up before our world fell apart. A few years ago, I was focusing on our medicine cabinet supplies and was surprised to discover just how easy it was to get just about anything over the internet, including casting supplies. I ordered a short arm fiberglass cast kit in black, along with a black long leg cast. When Doris was shot in the leg, breaking both bones in the lower part, I thought Belinda and Doctor Sam would cast her, but they chose to use an air cast so it could be removed to check the wound from the gunshot.

When I was buying casting supplies, I was sure one of each would be enough. Now, I'd go back and buy a dozen of both kinds, along with several other things. It was so easy then to think Jake and I were just being ridiculous. Sometimes it seemed stocking up on food, gear, and goods was little more than an exercise in futility—even a waste of money. Really, when would I ever need a cast kit? Well, at the end of the world, that's when.

And with no substantial updates from the president, even though there was a new vague announcement with no new information, I can only assume the end of the world is still here. The deaths of our friends certainly confirm my feelings.

The memorial service for our dead is planned for late afternoon before our evening meal. I haven't seen Doris since I left her yesterday but did hear from Leo, who spoke with Evan, who said she's doing as well as can be expected. Although Leo and Tim were slightly cryptic yesterday after they returned, they have now been given permission to share their experience. We're having a family meeting now, followed by a community-wide discussion after lunch. New plans are being made and will be shared then.

With Leo on a break and the younger children in school, those in our family unit not on duty are gathering in our dining room. There was talk of cancelling school today because of the death of Willie and the others, but it was decided keeping them on a normal schedule and able to grieve as a group might be best.

I was part of the group in favor of cancelling. Truthfully, I don't want my children and grandchildren to leave the house! I'm not the only one who feels this way. Out of caution, the children are being driven to school using an old diesel car and one of the trucks as school busses. Then the snowmobile and trailer zooms them across the bridge to the lodge. Zeb Frost says, if we get a little more snow melt, we'll be able to take four-wheel drives across the bridge and up the steep hill. They normally do that in the spring and summer to ferry supplies back and forth during zipline season, their summer business at the ski lodge during normal times.

This morning, Cole Gunderson assured worried parents they are acting to prevent a similar attack and these measures are only temporary until more precautions are put into place.

Jake's propped up on pillows in our bedroom with the door open. He argued that he's well enough to join us at the table, but I put the kibosh on that. He's been grumbling at me ever since.

"I'm still replaying yesterday over and over in my head," Tim says. "This was really the first time I'd been— " He shakes his head. "I'd never done anything like that before. I wasn't even up close and personal, but it was still— " He lifts his hands in a surrender motion.

With a nod, his dad Art says, "You'll work through it."

"Tim told me a little about it," Angela says. "But since we're here . . . "

"I'd rather Leo give the details," Tim says. "I'll add things when it seems appropriate."

"I caught a glint of something, movement or . . . I don't know," Leo says. "The sun wasn't in the right spot to be reflecting off the scopes, but in my mind that's what I think I saw. It happened right in

160

the instant before the shooting started. Lindsey was talking and then she was down. I heard Sheila scream at the same time. Tim and I both dove behind the bonfire—not a great place to take cover, but it's what we had. I pulled Lindsey with us, but she was already gone."

I squeeze my eyes tight as I remember looking at Lindsey as Doris held her. She'd been shot center mass, likely piercing her heart.

"There was a pause in the shooting, and Evan started barking orders," Tim says. "A couple more shots flew off, but as soon as it was over, we went after them."

"My nose was a little out of joint when he demanded I stay and help the rest of you secure the area and tend to our wounded," Mike adds. "At the time, I didn't realize Lindsey was dead or Jake had been shot. I only knew about Sheila. I guess Evan thought I might be upset about her getting shot, which is why I wasn't allowed to go along. My dad and I took Sheila around the backside of the building, and Katie went right to work."

"Sheila's doing better this morning, right?" Sarah asks.

"I stopped by on my way to breakfast," Mike says. "She had a good night and was talking this morning. Dad's still with her. Belinda asked me to just stick my head in and talk from the door—because of germs and all. I'll go see her again before I head out this afternoon for my wood cutting duty."

Mike glances around the room before continuing, "After getting Sheila out of the line of fire, Dad and I went back to Lindsey. Doris was already there, having crawled from her camp chair to her daughter's side. That's when we saw she was dead. We helped move Doris to the shed first. She didn't have her peg leg, so she wasn't mobile. Then we took Lindsey over. We still didn't know Jake was injured. Calley yelled she and Angela had the southside of the cabin covered— "

"Tim told me to grab Lindsey's rifle," Angela says. "I knew then she wasn't okay."

There's several beats of silence before Mike says, "So I went to the northside to watch for any additional threats, telling my dad to go be with Sheila. I watched as Evan scurried up the hill, with Leo and Tim hot on his heels."

"Man! I had no idea Evan could move like that," Tim says. "Even the deep snowy spots barely slowed him down. He'd posthole and almost like magic pull himself out. It was impressive."

"He's an animal," Leo agrees with a nod. "And he was running on pure anger and adrenaline. You saw what he looked like after we were finished?"

"Yeah, true. He was pretty wiped out. Of course, so were we. I still am," Tim says, rubbing his arm through the sling.

"When did you break your arm?" Destiny asks.

"Not long after we reached the top. Even though Evan had little trouble with the incline and the snow, I was really wishing for the snowshoes we had. Going up was hard, but going down was worse."

"That's for sure," Leo says. "When we reached the tower, we slowed down and checked it out."

"I guess it shouldn't have been a surprise to find our people dead," Tim says. "But it was still hard. The killers were gone, but with the snow, they left us an easy trail. We took off after them. I hadn't gone ten feet when I lost my footing and tripped over a fallen tree. It's like the snag just reached out and grabbed me. I knew right away my arm was bad, but what could I do?" He gives a shrug as he looks around the table.

There're many mumbles of "nothing you could do" or "you did what you had to do."

Angela gives Tim an adoring look before saying, "He's tough." She then narrows her eyes and adds, "But not always smart."

"That's probably true," Tim says, putting his good hand on her arm. "And I'm certainly glad we've been training to shoot with both hands. I was able to slide my paddle holster to my left and reposition my rifle so it was slinged on my left shoulder. It was awkward, but I was still functional."

As we discuss yesterday's event, in which thirteen people from our community were murdered, it strikes me how odd our conversation is. We're all heartbroken, that much is true, but we're also detached. We understand this world we live in is full of danger. Talking about it, processing it all in a seminormal conversation, feels wrong.

We should be hysterical, wailing over what has gone on. If this would've happened before the attacks, if thirteen people from our small community lost their lives in such a violent way, we'd be in extreme disbelief. But now, as much as I hate it, I can believe it. Like Marc said last night, too many people have died since we lost the electricity. Have we become immune to it?

162

"I didn't even realize Tim was hurt," Leo says. "Other than a slight gasp when he fell, he didn't say anything. He was back on his feet almost instantly. It was then Evan motioned us to stop. He could see the shooters making their way down the hill. They were moving, but not nearly as fast as they should've been. My guess is they didn't expect us to follow—at least not immediately."

"Probably thought you'd be confused about what was going on," Clarice says. "And with the children there and in danger, they might have thought you'd stay to protect the kids and not follow at all."

"Maybe," Leo says with a nod.

"But they've been watching us, right?" Sarah asks. "They knew about our training, so why would they even think we wouldn't fight back?"

"They should've realized we would," Leo says. "But the fact they didn't was definitely in our favor. Evan spotted them. And, well, that was their downfall."

I chew on my lip as I think about his statement. Evan is a retired sniper for a metropolitan sheriff department. He's exceedingly well trained and precise. While the weapon he was carrying wasn't his favorite sniper rifle with an amazing scope, it was still more than adequate with him at the trigger.

"Evan used one of those awful snags as a rest," Tim says. "Three shots—*bang, bang, bang*—and all three were down. I'd never seen anything like it. Even on the range, he's never been quite so quick. And accurate. Wow."

"Well . . . " Leo says slowly. "The way he tells it, he could've done better. One of them did manage to get to his gun and take a wild shot."

"So Evan shot again," Tim says. "That ended that. When we got close enough, we could see he was still alive. Evan had shot the gun out of his hand, taking a few fingers with it. One guy was dead and the other was bleeding out. Leo started first aid on the one with the missing fingers." Tim's suddenly pale. He takes a deep breath and then raises his chin in Leo's direction, indicating he should take over.

"The fingers were the least of his worries. The first shot was fatal, just not immediately. It was . . . it wasn't good. When I motioned to Evan there wasn't anything I could do, he squatted down next to the guy. He was younger than us, around Katie's age. Evan asked him what his name was, but the guy was still playing it tough and answered rather bluntly."

"I'll say," Tim says. "I learned a few new phrases in his tirade, ones we didn't even use in the oil field."

"That's when Evan told him he was going to die and there wasn't anything we could do about it. I thought Evan would ask who they were. Even though we suspect they were from Prospect, it would've been smart to get confirmation—interrogate him a bit and get us some info." Leo looks around the room, nodding, which results in most of us nodding back. "And his group had just killed Lindsey, so you'd think he would've said something about that, right? Instead, he said, 'In these few minutes you have left, it's time to get right with the Lord. Do you know who Jesus is?'"

I feel my eyes filling with tears as the corner of my mouth lifts slightly. I've known Evan for years. Before the last few months, I would've never thought of him as an evangelist.

"That resulted in even more interesting words out of the guy," Tim says. "Evan waited until he was done with his string of profanities before saying, 'I'd be happy to introduce you to Him—all you have to do is ask.' After a little sputtering, the guy got really quiet. Then he said his name was Bowe."

"Yeah," Leo said. "He took a deep breath and started coughing. Then he asked how we caught up to them so quickly. Evan said we just did. Then Bowe started telling us all kinds of stuff. How they were sent here to watch us, but then their major decided to turn it into a mission and cause some bloodshed."

"Yep," Tim says. "It wasn't even his first time here. He was part of the group who kidnapped Milena on Richard Majors's orders. Seems he knew enough about Milena and the others who escaped Prospect last fall to know she was in Bakerville. They were supposed to bring her back on the raid of the river people, but when she wasn't there, they had to rethink things. Shelby was taken only because she was in the wrong place at the wrong time."

"Do you know where they are?" I ask. "And what about Milena? Is she okay?"

"To his knowledge, both are fine," Leo says. "Milena is being kept by Majors, and Shelby is in what he called the bordello. Evan urged him along with several leading questions about where the bordello is. From the description, we're pretty sure it's the same place Rochelle and her girls were kept. It's not only for, uh, onsite entertainment but people make trades for the women and take them with them. It's disgusting, to say the least."

"How'd they know about us living up here?" Sarah asks.

"Sounds like they were watching the river people off and on for months before the slaughter," Leo says. "Bowe didn't know much, but he said they knew for a fact part of us were living up here."

"And just like with the river people," Tim jumps in, "they'd been watching us for several days before taking Milena and Shelby. They wanted to learn our habits. Same thing this time. He said they'd been in camp a week, finding different locations to watch and plan. We never had any idea. Originally, they were just supposed to watch and gather intel. Shooting at us was spontaneous. Yesterday, they decided to take out the eastern and southern watch towers. But when they saw our group leave, they shook things up, sending the trio to take care of us since it was a good opportunity, especially since we had children." Tim's voice chokes on the final words. He swallows, then shakes his head.

Leo takes over. "That was their plan. Not just to kill our guards but to take out soft targets. He used that phrase, *soft targets*. Said they knew it'd cause fear. We didn't know at the time about Willie being killed, but when he said it, we were worried other children in the community might have also been— " Leo sucks in a breath. "And we left in such a hurry, we didn't know if our own children were safe."

My hands go to my mouth. I hoped Willie's death might have been an accident, bad aim. But to know they were purposely targeting our children . . . with the Sunday sledding, we easily could've lost many more. It could've been a complete massacre.

"I was kicking myself," Tim says. "My heart was in my stomach. I was so worried about Gavin. I knew Angela was okay—she yelled at me to go and told me she'd take care of our son. But she couldn't know he was okay. I'd seen Jake and Mom as they started running toward the sledding hill, but I didn't stick around to make sure everything was okay."

"Gavin was fine, Tim," Angela says. "You can't beat yourself up over something that didn't happen."

He scrunches up his face before nodding. "Hearing him say they were targeting our children was almost too much for me. I completely lost it. I barely remember it happening, but the next thing I knew, Leo

165

was holding me back. I'm not proud of it, especially since Bowe was already dying, but I would've killed him with my bare hands if Leo hadn't stopped me."

"That's when I realized Tim was injured, the way his wrist just sort of flopped when he let out a roar and launched himself toward Bowe."

"Leo took me to the ground, and once he had me settled, he fixed me up."

"Did he tell you anything else about Milena or Shelby?" I ask.

"No, Evan tried to get more details, but we don't think Bowe really knew. He didn't seem to know where the bordello is or who's there."

"So we don't even really know if Shelby is still there?" I ask, dread filling me to my core.

# Chapter 23

## *Mollie*

"We don't know," Leo says. "Whether Shelby is still there or has been sold to someone as a— " He clears his throat. "That was the topic of conversation this morning, plus what was discovered yesterday, which was a whole lot of nothing. Other than Bowe and the two with him, the rest made a clean getaway. We do know from Bowe their orders were to hightail it to a meeting spot and then they'd go back to Prospect. Evan gave Bill Shane the information last night, and he took a group out at first light, but we suspect they're long gone."

"But now we know where our people are. Let's go after them," Mike says. "Did he give you the location of the place he thinks Shelby is? Or where they're keeping Milena?"

"He doesn't know where the bordello is," Leo says, "And it isn't where Milena is now. Seems there was an explosion at the hotel Majors was staying— "

"What hotel?" Jake calls from the bedroom, while everyone else shakes their heads and gives other expressions of disbelief.

"Prospect Hotel," Tim says. "They're having trouble with rebels, and they blew the place up. Mrs. Majors and several others were killed. Milena was staying there. She's fine. Bowe was one of the ones who helped dig her and Richard Majors out of the rubble. He was in her room when the bomb went off."

Paul Cameron told us there was a group of rebels, besides his own, operating to bring down Richard Majors, but he had no details. They'd decided the safest thing for their family and the other families living in his area was to leave, join forces with others, and then go after Majors and his henchmen. When they arrived in Bakerville, we were in the process of moving up the mountain. All plans of retribution were put on hold for the winter, but the murderers from Prospect have changed that.

"They evacuated both of them to the newspaper building Majors owns," Leo says. "A medic was treating them. That's the last Bowe saw of Milena. Their guerrilla team left a few days after the explosion. Seems their team is smaller than it was supposed to be too. One of the team members was injured, and a few of their officers stayed behind. He didn't know why."

"Officers?" I ask. "They went with a military system too?"

"Guess so. It's an easy way to recognize the leaders."

"Anything else you should tell us?" Alina asks. "I must prepare to do kitchen work."

"Yeah," Angela agrees. "We'd better wrap this up. The lunch crew will arrive shortly."

"Probably nothing that won't be covered at the meeting," Leo says.

"Do you expect Bill and his team to be back by then?" Sarah asks.

"Doubtful. There's, uh . . . this will be announced at lunch, but they'll go on from the rendezvous spot Bowe told us about toward Prospect. We're going to rework the observation post overlooking Prospect.

"But two did leave today?" I ask.

"Bobbi Newton volunteered to go with Carol. They'll keep watch for now while we form our new plans."

"And Bowe?" Clarice asks. "Did he accept Jesus?"

Leo and Tim both shake their heads. "Evan asked him again when it was evident his time was ending," Tim says. "He let out a big sigh and said it wouldn't make sense for him to go begging for forgiveness now, not after the way he'd lived and especially not after the things he's done since he became part of Majors's acquisition team—that's what he called their group, *acquisition team*. But anyway, he died right after."

Clarice gives a nod. "The Lord doesn't want anyone to perish but wants everyone to come to repentance. That's from a verse Chaplain Rick was talking about the other day at Bible study. I can't remember where to find it, though. Does anyone know?"

I shake my head, feeling like I should know, but I can't remember.

"The Lord is not slow in keeping His promise, as some understand slowness. Instead He is patient with you, not wanting anyone to perish, but everyone to come to repentance," Jake says in a powerful voice. "Second Peter 3:9."

I smile at my Bible-spouting husband. Before, when our lives were terribly busy, he'd often talk about wanting to learn verses but never took the time. This winter, living on the mountain has given him not only time but a desire to learn more about our Lord through His Word. He'll have verses written all over the place and carry them around with him when on guard duty or doing other jobs. This wasn't one I knew he was working on, having not seen it on any of his paper scraps.

"That's it," Clarice says. "Chaplain Rick said the first part is important because it's God's mercy that delays His judgment. He's waiting to allow people the opportunity to repent. At least Evan was there and gave Bowe the opportunity. I'm not sure I'd be so— " Clarice scrunches up her face as she shrugs her shoulder.

I nod my agreement. I'm not sure I would've offered him salvation either.

"I'm really going to miss Chaplain Rick," Sarah says with a sigh. "He had such a wonderful way about him. And Toby James too. He was always so kind and such a help to everyone."

"We haven't talked much about the sentries they murdered," Angela says. "Gina was in the watchtower by us. She was only accepted to the militia after Shelby and Milena were kidnapped. You all knew her? She was one of the women rescued by Lindsey and Logan on their way to Bakerville."

"That's why Bobbi went out with Carol," Leo says. "Bobbi and Gina were together when Lindsey found them. She felt she'd be honoring both Gina and Lindsey by taking watch."

"Gina had a hard time," Sarah says. "Lots of terrible things happened to her before Lindsey found her—rescued her. Annie Bond was also killed. Her husband was massacred along with the other river people, having sent Annie and their three children up here while he stayed behind. Three more orphans."

"Who cares for the children now?" Alina asks with a frown.

"I don't know. She didn't have any family."

"They were in the nursery when she was murdered," Leo says. "I don't think any other arrangements have been made yet. We're running out of potential parents."

I give a nod as I think about how Pamela and Dusty took in the five children brought home from Bakerville. They're around the same age as Jake and me—too old for young children. But Pamela grew terribly attached in those first days she was helping care for them. After relocating the couple to Tamra Nicolson's now empty studio cabin, their small dorm apartment in the ski lodge had a minor remodel, connecting the two apartments. The second apartment was divided into two small rooms, with a set of three-high bunk beds in one room for the girls and a regular set of bunks in the other room for the boys. Dusty and his sons custom made both sets of bunks, and they're quite the works of art. Little things like that have helped the children feel special and know they're loved.

Where will Annie's children go? With so many in our community being retirement age, it's hard to find adoptive parents. And the ones who aren't older are often single or widowed. When Sarah took in Marc, Sissy, and Andy, her husband was still alive and she was pregnant with their baby. Now she, too, is widowed with four youngsters. It's really not uncommon. And if my fears are correct, we can expect many more losses as we defend ourselves against those from Prospect who wish to harm us.

"I'm sure we'll hear more soon," I say. "Like Alina and Angela said, we'd better wrap it up for the kitchen crew. And Belinda should be here shortly to examine Jake."

"And you too," he says.

"Yeah." I sigh. "Me too."

As everyone begins to break up, there's a knock at the door. "Not a moment too soon for adjournment," Mike says. "I'll go answer it."

Several kitchen crew people solemnly enter, their usual laughter and ribbing absent on this sad day. One asks how Jake and Sheila are doing. Another points at Tim's arm, asking what happened.

Tim simply says, "I slipped," and gives a small shrug. The rest of the story will come out at lunch.

As they move into the kitchen to begin their duties, another knock sounds. This time it's Belinda. "You're looking a little better today," she says when she sees me.

"That's good," I answer, not realizing I didn't look okay yesterday.

"I'll check Jake over first and then it'll be your turn."

"Can't wait."

After she gets her boots and coat off, I join her in the bedroom where Jake's still propped on his pillows. The first thing he says is, "I know you didn't want Mollie sleeping in here because of my stupid arm, but I don't think she should be on the couch. It isn't comfortable for her."

"It's fine," I say, though he's right—it isn't comfortable. Of course, with the way my back and hips have been hurting, the bed isn't great either. June worked on me yesterday morning before we went on our picnic, and I'll see her again tomorrow for a massage. Maybe she can alleviate the intense ache that seems to have been exacerbated by the night on the couch.

"We'll discuss that after the examinations," Belinda says.

After washing her hands and gloving up, she checks out Jake's arm, unwrapping the bandages put in place yesterday, cleaning it, and looking it over. A few minutes later, she declares him healing much better than she'd hoped.

After Belinda rewraps his wound, she turns to me. "Now we'll see what's up with you, Mollie. Why don't you have someone bring one of those cots in here."

"She can use the other side of the bed," Jake offers.

"I want to be able to get to both sides of her."

A large storage closet between the two main floor bathrooms holds several camping cots, along with various other medical items. The lodge was setup to be used as a backup medical clinic in case of overflow. Up until now, it's only been needed during Dawson's assault.

"Okay, let me grab one," I say.

"That's not something you should be doing," Belinda says.

I give her a look.

With her own look, she says, "Bending over and picking things up can lead to you falling over and passing out."

"They're propped against the wall," I say, the exasperation evident in my voice. "I'm pretty sure a slight bend isn't going to make all the blood rush to my head."

Belinda sighs and shakes her head. "I'll help you."

After getting the cot set up in the room, she asks me to undress to my underwear and put on my robe, then excuses herself to go wash again.

With a wry smile, Jake says, "I guess she told you."

"Ha! Sometimes there's a thing or two I'd like to tell her."

171

"Like what? She does have a point. Passing out could result in you hurting yourself. You might need stitches or even get concussed. Then where would you be?"

"Reclining in the bed next to you?" I tie my robe and then plant a kiss on his lips.

"I wouldn't complain. And I'm serious about you sleeping in here. You'd sleep better than on the couch, and I'd sleep better with you next to me. Last night was weird. With no one yanking the blankets off me, I kept waking up too hot."

"I'm not the one who yanks blankets," I say, putting my hands on my hips. Since our honeymoon, he's accused me of stealing the covers.

"Really?"

I give him a pointed look and then crack a smile. "I can't help it if I get cold."

"See? That's my point. Besides, when I need a drink of water in the middle of the night, I can wake you up to get it for me."

"I left a glass by your bed last night."

"Yeah, but I had to contort my body to reach it. My right arm is closest to the nightstand, so I have to reach over with my left—the uninjured one."

"Oh? I'm sorry, I didn't even think it might— "

"I'm just harassing you, Mollie. It was fine. But I really do want you to stay in here tonight."

"We'll talk about that in a bit," Belinda says, entering the room. "Socks off, Mollie. I want to see your feet."

Unlike with Jake, Belinda is bare handed for my exam. Disposable gloves, like everything else, are in limited supply and used only when necessary. The examination starts with her looking at my toes and then my fingers. She has me sit on the edge of the regular bed as she checks my jaw, where a few months ago I had small bilateral tumors, which have since subsided. Then she examines my throat, arms, and shins.

"Okay, untie your robe so I can check your back." She pokes at my lower back in a few spots, eliciting a jump from me when she reaches a tender area. "Still hurting, huh? Do the massages help?"

"Some." I shrug. "The shortness of breath is better. I'm not winded nearly as easily as I was a few months ago."

"Mm-hmm. That's good. Maybe the warmer weather is making it easier to breathe. You're still doing the deep breathing exercises?"

"I am, along with the regular walking. Slight inclines aren't terrible. I made it up the hill to the ski lodge a couple of days ago."

"How many times did you have to stop?"

Choosing to ignore the question, since the answer is *a lot*, I say, "And I can do more of the martial arts moves before having to stop. Katie and I have been working on— "

"I'm pleased to hear that," she interrupts. "But I'm still concerned about the dizziness and, well, everything else."

After a few more minutes of checking my back, she has me turn to lie on my back on the cot, where she pokes and prods my stomach. Unlike the lumps along my jawline, the masses found in my abdomen have yet to subside. She takes her time checking the known spots and then other areas. Finally, she helps me sit up and tells me I can get dressed. She's going to go wash up and then will be back so we can discuss.

Once I'm dressed, Jake pats my side of the bed. I crawl up and sit next to him. When Belinda comes in, she pulls a straight-backed chair we have in the room to the foot of the bed where we can both see her easily.

"As I've already said, I'm very happy with how Jake is healing. The wound looks good. It's healing to the point I'd expect in the time since yesterday, and there's no indication of infection or issues."

"Excellent," Jake says. "Mollie will be sleeping in here tonight."

"Sure. That's fine." Belinda takes a very loud, long breath and lets it out slowly and just as loudly. "It's not as good for you, Mollie."

I blink a few times as the tears threaten. "I know," I say in a wobbly voice.

I feel Jake's hand reach for mine. We've talked about this—about how I'm getting worse instead of better.

"After your appointment with June yesterday morning, she brought her concerns to me. She felt a lump on your lower back and another on your hipbone. I feel both too. You also have a new lump under your left armpit and one behind your ear."

"The stomach lumps?" Jake asks.

"A little more pronounced," she answers with a nod. "And you're losing more weight. I'll have you get on the scales, but I can tell just by looking at you."

"So I guess there's no doubt then?"

"I don't think there is."

# Chapter 24

## *Lucy*

"What do you think this is about?" Maddie asks, leaning too close to me.

"We'll find out soon enough," I answer, shifting in my seat to put distance between us. With her decision to put an end to seeing Richard Majors, I don't want to appear too friendly with her. Especially if Richard should happen to be at this meeting. She might be ready to reform and let her fruit be known—or whatever weird phrase she used—but I know what's best for me. And keeping all the benefits I have now is it.

"Chance said the super soldiers returned in the middle of the night."

"How does he know? And when did you even see him?"

Maddie lifts her shoulder and scrunches up her face. "Saw him before breakfast. He hears things."

"Don't you think we'd know if they were back? We live in the same community—and do you see any of them here? We were *all* called to meet at the clubhouse. Don't you think they'd be here too?"

"He said they were taken to the newspaper office for debriefing. Maybe they'll show up soon?"

I lean close to her. "I think there's something not right about your secret boyfriend knowing things like this. And it's definitely not right you snuck out to see him this morning. I thought you'd gone for a walk."

"I don't think our team's movements are as classified as you think. You should spend a little time in the cantina. The acquisition team and especially the super soldiers are huge topics of conversation."

I tightly grab her leg as I glance around. "You want to have it all end right now?" I hiss. "If Janet finds out you've been seeing him and going to the cantina, she'll not only kick you out but—Richard or no Richard—she'll make you pay."

"You're hurting me," she mutters. "Besides, I'm done. I meant it when I told you."

Shaking my head, I release my grip and lean away. I give her a hard look and then cross my arms. She leans toward me again but stops when the side door to the clubhouse opens. She flares her eyes at me before turning straight in her chair.

General Scott Majors strides in with Major Lassiter hot on his heels. There's a gap and then Captain Murphy, Janet, and the rest of the lieutenants enter. When the door closes, I realize I'm disappointed Richard wasn't part of the group. I also realize Maddie's boyfriend must be correct. The super soldiers, which were being led by Major Lassiter and Lieutenant Knight, must be back. Scott walks to the podium while Major Lassiter plops himself in a chair at the front. Instead of looking at the gathered crowd, he stares right through us, his face contorted in anger.

"Uh-oh," Maddie mumbles.

Scott waits a few moments for the officers to take their chairs before beginning his address. "All right, people. Let's get started." He pauses a couple of beats to make sure all eyes are on him. "The team who went out to surveil the group we heard rumors about—the ones causing trouble in the area, a group from Bakerville who've been hiding in the mountains—met some difficulties. This group has been stealing from travelers and people who refused to join their group . . . or perhaps *cult* is a better word.

"We started hearing complaints about them last summer. Our February excursion was supposed to take care of the problem, but it seems the worst of the bunch moved to the mountains and have been hiding out. We know they're hoarding goods and supplies. Things our town desperately needs. Until they planted the bomb that killed my mom, we had plans to wait until the weather cleared before making first contact, encouraging them to stop their heathen ways. To turn over a new leaf and join us, instead of being a threat to the peace-loving people of Prospector County, the ones you've sworn to protect.

"But after the attack on us, we had to reevaluate our plans. Major Lassiter led a scout party to determine their numbers and assets. He was still under orders to bring a peaceful resolution if at all possible. We don't believe the entire enclave is corrupt. Many people there are nothing more than slaves. Our plan was to watch and observe, and if the major was presented with an opportunity to make contact, he'd take it."

Scott's sad eyes wander the room, making eye contact with as many as possible. When he reaches me, he blinks but doesn't give me his usual smirk.

"This cult," Scott says slowly, "they discovered our team—our team who was only sent to gather information and find a peaceful resolution. But instead of even being willing to talk like men, they attacked." Several gasps go through the room.

"Ha," Maddie mumbles.

"Without any provocation, our soldiers were fired upon, leaving three dead and the rest barely escaping with their lives."

This time, my gasp is included among the group. While we've lost a few people on the acquisition team since I joined, none have been during a scouting mission. We're so much better than most of the derelicts we've encountered, it defies belief any of our own could've been killed.

"Who?" several people call out.

I hold my breath, fearing Lorita might be one of the dead.

"Jeremy Lambert, Cory Banner, and Bowe Nelson," Major Lassiter says from his chair. "There would've been more of us dead had we not been quick on our feet." Lassiter stands. "I know these people. General Majors's characterization is accurate. They're more like a cult than anything. Except not the peaceful hippie dippie cult you may have seen on some TV show. These people are murderers. Not only murderers but kidnappers. They stole my wife and children from me."

Another gasp passes through the group. Movement near Major Lassiter catches my attention. Lieutenant Janet Kruse puts her hand to her face. At first, I think she's covering her mouth in shock, but from the look of her eyes, I quickly decide she's covering a smile.

"That's right. And I'm not the only one," Lassiter says as he walks toward the podium. He puts a hand on Scott Majors's shoulder, who gives him a nod as he steps away. "They've kidnapped children, keeping them as their slaves," Lassiter says. "In fact, other than a few of their higher echelon, most of the poor people are slaves or have been brainwashed into believing the things they're spewing— brainwashed into believing we're the enemy. Part of our mission was to devise a way to rescue them, to bring them into the safety of Prospect."

"Can you believe him?" Maddie whispers.

I tap her leg to silence her.

"This was supposed to be a special mission," Lassiter says. "We rescued two of the hostages when we were there on the first scouting operation."

A slight spattering of applause starts, which is quickly encouraged by Scott and the officers. Except Captain Murphy. He suddenly looks tremendously uncomfortable. He catches me watching him, raising his eyebrows at me before he joins in the applause.

"We saved two," Lassiter says. "Two women who were in very unfortunate circumstances. The things they told us . . . " He shakes his head. "It's even worse than we imagined. Now those women have a chance at a better life, a life here in Prospect surrounded by comforts instead of being treated as property. But there are still more for us to rescue, including my wife and children, who were taken from me in a violent manner. This will be a special mission. Not only will you, our well-trained soldiers, be involved, but we'll be enlisting members of the sentry and even workforce."

I feel my eyes go wide.

"This cult is evil. Their leaders are without mercy. All the good we've done up to now, they're trying to undo. We've done what is necessary to protect those who are too young, too old, or too infirm. All has been in preparation for this, for this mission of ridding Prospector County of a community laced in wickedness."

Lassiter returns to his seat as Scott steps back to the podium. "What Major Lassiter says is true. We'll begin choosing additional members for the team beginning tomorrow. While these people will be hand-picked to serve on this mission, most will return to their current positions after we eliminate this evil cult."

He looks back at Lassiter, who gives a nod of agreement. "There may be a few people who prove themselves worthy of promotion to join your ranks on a permanent basis. And because of other circumstances that have recently become evident, there will be some rearrangements of the teams. We'll start with those details tonight. Then, tomorrow, the recruiting of the new members will happen. They will, as always, be moved to this community for their training time. We know having all of you immersed and living together is the best way to nurture teamwork. Our officers already have some ideas of who will be joining you, but if there's someone who would be a good fit, please speak to your supervisor. Any questions?"

Susie, one of my dormmates, raises her hand. When Majors calls on her, she asks, "Will there be a funeral?"

"We'll have a memorial after our evening meal tonight," he says. "Major Lassiter was unable to recover the bodies since they were in a life-or-death situation. Cory Banner was a family man. His wife and young son have suffered a great loss. As always, we'll be there for them. They're family, and as such, they'll be allowed to stay in their current home for a month while they grieve. We'll then make sure they're set up in new, suitable housing, and Mrs. Banner will be given a new work assignment. We take care of our own. Any other questions?"

As we're released to go, Captain Murphy motions me toward him. Before I can move in his direction, Scott Majors is standing in front of me.

"Miss Fleming. Miss Rivers."

"Uh, hello, sir," Maddie says as she takes a step away.

"I wish to speak with you," he says. "With both of you. Please stay behind. I'll be with you as soon as the room clears."

"I have training," Maddie blurts. She crooks her thumb in my direction and says, "She's on light duty, but I'll be expected to arrive with the rest of my squad."

"You've been cleared from training." He turns on his heel and strides to the front of the room.

With wide eyes, Maddie asks, "What's happening? Are they kicking us off the team?"

Being booted from the team is what I think too. Janet's had it out for me, for both of us, forever. But with seeing Doc Bohm and my getting a placement on the team with Lorita, I thought I might be moving up and she'd leave me alone. With the mission going to pieces, maybe she can get her way and kick me off. But kicking us off can't be good. Will they reassign us or . . .

Shaking my head, I say, "We'll find out."

From across the room, Captain Dirk Murphy signals me again.

As I take a step toward him, Maddie grabs my arm. "Where're you going?"

I shake her loose. "Don't worry about it."

When Murphy sees me walking toward him, he makes a *follow me* motion and then turns in the direction of the clubhouse's small kitchen.

Inside the room, I lean against the counter while he positions himself so we can talk in low voices and he can see out the open door. "General Majors is reassigning me," I say.

"I've heard. Did he tell you about it?"

"Will they execute us?"

"No. It's not that. He didn't give you any details?"

I let out a slow breath. "Not yet. He asked me and Maddie to stick around until everyone leaves. No one gets demoted. How . . . why us?"

"Look, Lucy." He scrubs his hands to his face. "You listened to me months ago, when I told you to get behind our new government, right?"

"Yes, of course. You were right. It's been the best thing for me."

"You trust me?"

"What's this about?"

"Soon enough, more things will make sense. And you'll need . . . things will make sense. When it's time, you'll know more. I just need to know you trust me to always do right by you. You're going to be okay. You need to go. They're all clearing out now." He motions to the almost empty room. "What Scott tells you, it's a good thing. Look at it that way, okay?"

"I just want to survive. That's all I've ever wanted. To live through this . . . this disaster and then build a life."

He reaches for my hand. "There's surviving and there's living. And if we're going to live, then maybe we need to think about helping others live too."

"Isn't that what we're doing? The work we do is helping our entire town. They depend on us."

"Is it? Go on. He'll be looking for you soon."

I give him a final look. I want to be angry with him—angry he's questioning what we're doing and angry because he isn't just telling me what's happening.

"Go," he says, making a shooing motion.

In the main room, Maddie's sitting, chewing on her thumbnail. I slide into the seat next to her.

She leans over and asks, "Is this it for us?"

I open my mouth to answer when Scott bellows from across the room, "Fleming, Rivers. Front and center." He motions to a separate space of the clubhouse.

"Here we go," Maddie whispers, an obvious tremor to her voice.

"We'll be okay," I answer with more conviction than I feel.

"I pray you're right."

Captain Murphy, Major Lassiter, and all the lieutenants except Alvarez are gathered on sofas and easy chairs in front of the now useless giant television perched above a fireplace.

This clubhouse must have been a great perk when the power was still on. I can imagine having a birthday party here, with the huge open space, the cozy sitting area, and a separate large room with a pool table, ping pong table, and even a foosball table. Outside, there's a Wyoming rarity: an inground pool. There're also three hot tubs. Of course, like the TV, they're now useless. Most of the water in the pool and hot tubs was scooped out before winter. What was left turned green with algae and froze solid. Now, with the weather warming, it's a disgusting slush.

"Have a seat," Majors says, motioning to three meeting chairs pulled into the space. They're set slightly separate from the comfy furniture, making it apparent we're different—outcasts. "Where's Alvarez?" Majors asks, looking around. "He should've been back by now."

"Should be," Janet agrees. "Would you like me to go after him?"

"Go."

With more flourish than warranted, Janet stomps to the door. As she reaches for the push bar, it opens. "About time. We're waiting."

"Sorry," Lieutenant Alverez answers, not sounding at all like he means it. Reluctantly following him is an older teenager from the community. Alverez takes his time removing his coat and hanging it on the rack, motioning for the girl to do the same.

She gives a slight shake of her head and wraps her arms around her body. I can't remember her name, but I know she's the sister of one of the men on the acquisition team, a recruit who joined us a couple of weeks ago after he was promoted from sentry along with three or four others. She and her parents live with her brother in one of the family units.

"Miss Perez, thank you for joining us," Scott says. "Please have a seat." While staring at the floor, she gives a partial nod and shuffles to the chair next to me.

"Can we get on with it?" Lassiter asks.

Scott pierces him with a hard stare before turning toward the three of us outcasts. With a smarmy smile, he says, "You may be wondering why we're here."

Maddie nods vigorously while the Perez girl seems to shrink within herself, her long black hair covering her face. I hold my head high and give him an even look.

"It seems the mayor is a special friend of each of you."

Maddie and me, okay. We're both adults. But this girl, she can't be more than sixteen. And she's scrawny and awkward. Her face is cute enough, but she's so shy I don't think I've ever seen her make eye contact with anyone.

"And as special friends, he wanted to give you each the first opportunity to be part of a new— " he purses his lips and looks to the sky "—venture. The mayor's starting a new team, I guess you'd say. This team is, as of yet, without an official name. But for clarity's sake, we'll refer to it as the hospitality team."

Janet lets out an ugly laugh. "Hospitality. That's rich." The rest of the officers, minus Captain Murphy, join in on her teasing and laughter. Scott even allows himself a broad smile.

Tears sting my eyes as I realize they're laughing at me, at each of us outcasts. A whimper escapes the girl, but Maddie seems to sit up straighter and jut out her chin in a challenge. Even though I can feel my eyes are wet and my cheeks are red, I choose to imitate Maddie.

"Okay, okay," Scott says, waving his hands. "We shouldn't laugh at their expense."

"Why not?" Janet asks. "We all know exactly how Fleming and Rivers got on my team. It certainly wasn't because of any soldiering skills. Even Bobby Perez didn't make it by his own abilities, but rather what his little sister Alyssa could offer your dad. Moving those two— " she uses two of her fingers to point at Maddie and me, reminding me of a striking snake "—off my team and out of my life will be doing me a huge favor. I'm definitely getting the best end of this deal."

"Enough, Janet," Dirk Murphy says.

"I don't think it is." Janet spins her head toward him. "You have no idea what it's like to have these two incompetent fools— "

"It is enough," Scott interrupts. "Now, ladies, this new team includes lodging. You'll be moving from the houses in this complex to the mayor's new house on the creek. You'll have tonight and tomorrow morning to get your things together. Workers will arrive at 3:00 to take your belongings. Right now, you'll each go straight from here to the mayor's home to begin the transition to your new team. Captain Murphy, please escort them."

# Chapter 25

## *Lucy*

"Wait," Maddie says. "I'm not interested in going to a new team."

I turn my head quickly and motion for her to be quiet.

"Humph," Janet says. "The choice isn't up to you."

"Lieutenant Kruse is right," Lassiter says. "We go where we're assigned."

"In addition, this new team will be much more suited to your specific skills," Scott says. "And the luxuries you have now will be increased."

"My specific skills?" Maddie asks.

I roll my eyes at her and again urge her to shut it.

"Do we really need to spell it out for you?" Janet asks.

"Am I . . . are we to be some sort of . . . "

"Seriously?" Alyssa Perez says, whipping her head toward Maddie. "Are you that dense?"

"Enough," Scott says. "Dirk, please see them to where they need to go. And gather Fleming's and Rivers's personal weapons. They won't need those in their new position."

Janet snorts out another laugh.

Alyssa Perez may have slinked into the room, but she walks out like a warrior. I hustle to my feet, attempting to imitate her determined walk. As an afterthought, I turn and motion to Maddie. She gives a shake of her head as she stands. I yank her by the arm and hustle after the Perez girl, grabbing our coats from the rack as we pass by.

Outside, Alyssa is leaning against a portico column, casual and carefree. Lifting her chin in acknowledgment, she asks, "Did you two know about each other before today?"

"We did," I answer as I slide into my coat. Even though it's nearing the end of April, there are still patches of snow on the ground, and it's too cold to be without a jacket for long.

"But you didn't know about me?" she asks, looking at both of us.

183

I shake my head.

"Figures. How about the one living in the hotel with him?"

"I'm not naive," I say. "Neither of us thought we were the only ones. We just didn't know who else."

"Seriously? Don't you get out of this walled community and hear people talk?"

"I go to the cantina," Maddie says, puffing out her chest.

"The Christian place? Why would you go there?"

"Ready, ladies?" Captain Murphy asks as he walks out the door.

"Will this . . . we'll be okay?" I ask him, my eyes searching his face.

He gives me a tight smile. "You'll be okay. Today is an introduction."

"An introduction?" Alyssa asks. "You do know we *know* Mayor Majors, right?"

"Shall we?" he asks as he steps away.

Dirk sets a brisk pace, leaving Alyssa gasping for air before we're halfway there.

"You're going to have to slow down," I say. "She's not conditioned like we are."

"Are you . . . calling me . . . out of . . . shape?" she asks.

"Sorry, Alyssa," Captain Murphy says as he noticeably slows.

After we've walked at the reduced pace, I ask the question I've had since Alyssa sat next to me. "How old are you?"

"Old enough."

"She graduated last May, before the attacks," Dirk says. "She was one of my students and on her way to UM."

"University of Montana in Missoula?" Maddie asks. "I would've loved to have gone there."

"Yeah," Alyssa says. "I would've too. But nope. The universe had other plans, and I'm stuck in Prospect. It was a dump before the attacks. It's worse now." After half a block of silence, Alyssa asks, "Are we going to the Bunn Mansion? I heard the mayor's living there now."

"You'll be living there too."

A thrill of excitement runs through me. The Bunn Mansion is a historic landmark. The home was built in the early days of Prospect becoming a town by our original mayor, Emerson Bunn. Bunn's first wife, born in London, was behind the design, making it a replica of a London estate. It seems, though a close likeness to the original, she was known to have said it was not quite as gawdy and more to her liking. The biggest difference: the original home was made of brick and this one of wood harvested in the nearby forest and locally milled. The two lived there together only a short time until she died during childbirth along with the baby. Mr. Bunn then moved to the top floor of his nearby hotel but kept a full staff on hand so the house was always perfect should he choose to move back.

When he married his second wife, she and the children lived in the mansion, but he still lived in the hotel, choosing to only visit. The general belief about Mayor Emerson Bunn is he was a bit eccentric. The house now belongs to the town of Prospect. Up until the time of the attacks and our world changing, it was a museum with guided tours. I've been on the tours many times as a schoolgirl and when friends or family would visit from out of town.

It's really no surprise Richard Majors would move in there after the explosion at the hotel. He'd talked about it often and mentioned how perfect it'd be for his needs, especially since so much of the original, old-fashioned things were still in place. There're even oil lamps attached to the walls, an old wood cookstove in the kitchen, small woodstoves in each of the bedrooms, and several other conveniences of the 1800s. When Mayor Stringer was still in charge, before Richard killed him, he had several displaced families living there. Richard cleared them out right quick after taking over and even had a team of workers in to scour the home from top to bottom.

When we're less than a block away, Murphy says, "Look. I think it's important for each of you to remember you've done the things needed so you can best get by. This is no different. Do what you must and keep your heads down. Maddie, Lucy, this will be better for you— less dangerous, especially with the new mission coming up. You'll be able to stay here and stay safe. Alyssa, you'll have improvements too. I know you're often in the team kitchen now, so no more of that."

"Whatever," Alyssa says. "I've already made it clear I'll do what I must to make things easier for not only me but for my family. But, really, Mr. Murphy—excuse me, *Captain Murphy*. Don't you feel a little like a pimp walking us here?"

He stops abruptly and causes Maddie, who was following too close, to bump into him. He doesn't turn to look at Alyssa, or any of us, but his shoulders drop as he says, "More than a little. Just remember what I've said. Keep your heads down. Things aren't always what they seem."

At the front door of the house, Murphy uses the big brass lion's head knocker to announce us. Feeling nervous, I run a hand through my hair. I haven't seen Richard since before the explosion killed his wife. Well, I've seen him, but not up close and personal—only at the memorial when he was angry and filled with hate. Expecting Richard, I'm surprised when the person opening the door is Candace Murphy.

"Hello," she says pleasantly while delivering a nice smile.

"Mrs. Murphy," each of us women say with varying degrees of surprise in our voices.

"Hey, Mom," Captain Murphy says. "Are you ready for us?"

"Yes, your timing is perfect. Please, come in." The hardwood floors of the sumptuous foyer gleam with the look of fresh wax.

"Why are you here?" I ask.

"Lucy, it's lovely to see you. Maddie, Alyssa, you two also. I'm essentially your den mother."

"Den mother?" I repeat.

"Is that like a madam?" Alyssa asks.

"Alyssa," Captain Murphy warns.

With her smile unwavering, Candace Murphy says, "I look forward to you meeting the others."

"So there's more than just the three of us?" I ask.

"Duh," Alyssa says. "I've tried to tell you that."

"Please remove your boots and let me take your jackets. Then I'll show you your rooms and we'll have a discussion as to what your new position entails."

In stocking feet and without our outdoor clothing, we follow her to the amazing parlor off the entryway, still decorated and furnished in the period pieces from when the massive home was a museum.

"You'll each have your own room," Mrs. Murphy says. "As you know, if you've taken the tour, all the family and guest rooms are on the second floor. The family rooms were in the west wing, and the guest rooms the east. You'll each have a room in the east wing. Mayor Majors is in the west wing. There's maids' quarters off the kitchen and more staff rooms on the third floor, though we don't have many of those occupied."

"Do you live here?" Maddie asks.

"Yes, I'm also in the east wing."

"Who else?" I ask.

"You'll meet them soon. Let me show you to your rooms. Dirk, will you be leaving now?"

"Yes, as long as you don't need me for anything else."

"I think we're fine, dear. You've been invited to the welcoming party?"

A look passes between mother and son, one I can't quite decipher but seems to speak volumes. "I've been invited but will need to send my regrets," Dirk responds with a nod. "I'll be back tomorrow to help move their things."

"Goodbye, Captain," Maddie says.

"You're no longer under my command. There's no need to refer to me by rank."

"You want us to go back to calling you Mr. Murphy?" Alyssa asks with a smirk.

"If you wish. Or Dirk will be fine, considering I'm no longer your teacher—or anyone's."

At the top of the massive staircase is a huge sitting area with oversized windows, allowing panoramic views. We turn to the right, toward the east wing. "Please use the main staircase and not the smaller set for the domestics. Mayor Majors wants to make sure each of you feel like you're part of the family and not hired help."

"Humph," Alyssa snorts.

"This is my room," Mrs. Murphy says, pointing to the first room on the right. "The room across from me is occupied by a lovely young lady you'll meet shortly. Lucy, you're in the second room on the left." A smile tugs at my lips. The rooms on the left all have beautiful views of the creek, the back garden, and Prospector Peak, where the rooms on the right overlook the front of the house and the mountains in the distance. "Maddie, you're in the room next to Lucy, and Alyssa will have the last room on the creek side. Go ahead and check your rooms."

"Where's the staircase for the hired help?" Alyssa asks, looking around.

"There's a door between your room and Maddie's. Please take only ten minutes to look over your room, then meet me at the second-floor sitting area." Mrs. Murphy stops at the door of the room next to hers, knocking softly. "Shelby? May I come in?"

I stand at my bedroom door a minute while I listen for a response.

"Shelby? It's Mrs. Murphy, I'm coming in."

I step into my room, trying to think of who Shelby is. It's not a common name, and the only Shelby I can think of is a girl a few years younger than me who lived with her husband in my apartment building. My eyes go wide. She and her husband disappeared last summer, the same night my other neighbor Kirstin and her friend Annette left. The two women I'd seen acting suspicious in City Hall Park. The same day Milena Maynard and several others, including Sheriff Spieth, escaped custody. When I took the information to Richard Majors, that was the start of our relationship. Could this be the same Shelby?

Setting my memories aside, I take a look around the room. During the time this was set up as a museum, the tours only allowed minimal access. You could step into the room, but other than a small alcove area, the rest was sealed off with plexiglass, allowing us to see in but not touch, in order to preserve the period furniture. Now, with the barrier down and the antique furniture still in place, I walk from piece to piece, touching the wood and caressing the upholstery. I tentatively sit on the bed. I'm surprised when the mattress, which I expect to be either hard as a rock or too soft, is a perfect contemporary one. The room's huge—much larger than the room Maddie and I shared in the women's dorm—bigger than any bedroom I've ever had.

The closet's a problem. There isn't one. Instead, there's a large freestanding armoire. Next to the armoire is an old-fashioned dressing screen and then a door. I slowly open it to find a compact and tidy bathroom with a clawfoot tub, pedestal sink, and toilet. I didn't see this room on the tour but did see a similar-looking bathroom shared by the two rooms at the end of the hall, one of which Alyssa was assigned. I knock on a second door in the bathroom. "Maddie?"

Seconds later, the door opens. "It's pretty strange thinking about living in this house," she says. "I used to wonder what it'd be like."

"Yeah, I guess we'll find out."

She shakes her head. "Nothing has changed for me. I'm not— " Her head sways rapidly from side to side. "It's not happening."

I put my finger to my lips and motion her to step into the bathroom. In a whisper, I say, "Living at Creek View Estates, you might have put Richard off for another week. But now, there's no choice. Whatever this new team is, you are on it."

"*Whatever* this team is? Really, Lucy? The *hospitality* team?"

"You heard Captain Murphy. We just need to keep our heads down. And with Mrs. Murphy here, she'll help us."

"Mrs. Murphy acting as a madam is seriously wrong. I read a book my grandma had by a Christian writer. She inherited a place like this—like it sounds Mayor Majors is turning this into—and the women there . . . they . . . *you know*. They called them doves. Soiled doves. I'm not going to do it. I've turned my life around— "

"I've heard all this before. You went into great detail about how you're going to live like Christ. What I don't think you realize is you won't be allowed to live. He'll take you out and shoot you."

"Then that's what happens." She retreats into her room, saying over her shoulder, "Our ten minutes are probably up."

# Chapter 26

## *Lucy*

Mrs. Murphy is waiting for me at the end of the hallway. "Perfect, I was just going to see if you were ready. Alyssa and Maddie are already in the sitting room. Come, let's meet the others."

Maddie gives me a smile and raises her eyebrows. I choose to ignore whatever signal she may be trying to deliver. Sitting next to Alyssa on a small old-fashioned love seat is another girl around the same age as her. Where Alyssa's hair is dark, this girl's is very blond, to the point of being white, which fits perfectly with her light blue eyes and very delicate, almost elf-like features. Like Alyssa, she's cute but tiny and almost frail looking. Mrs. Murphy introduces her as Star.

On an identical love seat is Shelby Cameron, formerly of my apartment building. As I look at her, I realize she was pregnant the last time I saw her. She'd been a big girl before she became pregnant. And even when food rationing started, she was still good sized. Not now. Now she's way too thin for her large frame. Her cheeks are sunken and sallow, and her hair is in desperate need of a wash and comb. She looks terrible. She stares straight ahead, not even acknowledging mine or anyone else's presence. Sitting next to her is the infamous Milena Maynard—former employee of Richard's, then condemned prisoner who escaped the gallows.

Milena looks considerably better than Shelby—at least she isn't a total mess. Her red hair is smooth and pulled into a single braid. Her pale skin and freckles look healthy enough. She's holding Shelby's hand and appears to be ignoring everyone else, off in her own little world. As I stare at the two of them, I wonder, are they drugged?

"Why don't you take this chair, Lucy?" Mrs. Murphy says, directing me to an uncomfortable looking seat next to Maddie. She introduces each person, saying where their room is. Milena is the *lovely young lady* Mrs. Murphy referred to occupying the room next to mine. "Okay, ladies," she says. "This is us for now. Mayor Majors will be adding one additional person in the next few days."

"Who?" Alyssa asks.

"I'm not sure. That information has yet to be shared with me. I only recently learned about the three of you. Milena moved in first, then I arrived two days ago. Shelby and Star arrived just this morning. This has all happened rather quickly."

"How'd you get the job of pimp?" Alyssa asks.

With a serene smile, Mrs. Murphy says, "I'd prefer we go back to den mother. Dirk is responsible for my being here. I'm sure you're aware—you, Maddie, and Lucy anyway—my son's rank and position would allow me to live in the gated community. I chose to live on my own and run the eastside laundry service. Unfortunately, my age is catching up with me, and the work was becoming exceedingly difficult. When Scott Majors told Dirk about this new endeavor, he was able to make arrangements for me to be here."

"Why would you want to do something like this?" Maddie asks, a tinge of disgust in her voice.

"They planned on having someone in this position. Dirk thought I may be able to make things a little easier for you—for the women."

"Why us?" Alyssa asks. "From the sounds of things, the way Lieutenant Kruse referred to the new *team* being created— " she makes sure to use air quotes around team "—we're going to be entertaining more than just Mayor Majors, right? But those two," she says, pointing to me and Maddie, "and me, we already have a *thing* with the mayor. Now he wants to share us? That's gross."

"Humph," Milena Maynard snorts.

Mrs. Murphy taps at her chin a few times, before she says, "I believe he thinks he's doing you a favor. The three of you are special to him. When he heard about the possible dangers the acquisition team may encounter on the upcoming mission, he thought this would be a safe place for Lucy and Maddie."

"And me?" Alyssa asks. "I'm not on the team. Will he make sure my brother's safe?"

"I can't answer that. I do think he believes moving you here will be better for you, give you a few additional luxuries. He does have some rather grandiose plans for the future."

"So we're going to be high-class prostitutes?" Star asks from her spot next to Alyssa.

Mrs. Murphy smiles at her.

"Even her?" Star asks, pointing to Shelby. "She's nuts. She was with me in the bordello." She turns to Alyssa. "You may have had a *thing* with the mayor, but believe me, whatever you did was a thousand times better than living in the bordello. I'll take this big fancy house and the thought of an easier life any day."

My stomach turns sour at the thought of where she used to live and what she used to do. I thought the bordello was just a rumor. I'd even made fun of Maddie when she'd told me about how women, and sometimes their children, were kidnapped and taken to the house between Prospect and Wesley. She'd even speculated several times where the bordello might be located.

"Shelby just needs a few days and some nutritious meals," Mrs. Murphy says. "Milena's going to help me with her."

"The druggie?" Star laughs. "She's so strung out she won't even be able to help herself."

As I wonder where she's even getting drugs in the end of the world, Milena lifts her head slightly. "I didn't do this on my own," she says quietly.

"Okay, so . . . " Mrs. Murphy says. "Lucy, Maddie, and Alyssa will be moving in tomorrow."

"Why not today?" Alyssa asks. "I'm ready today."

"Tomorrow is the planned move. There's still a few changes we wish to make."

"Like maybe getting some more comfortable furniture in the bedrooms?" Star asks. "Those chairs are even worse than the ones in this room."

"Perhaps," Mrs. Murphy says. "Go home now and get your personal items packed. While you can certainly bring your clothing, much will be provided for you."

"Are we going to walk around in negligees or something?" Alyssa asks.

"No, dear. You'll walk around properly clothed. It's much too cold to wear too little. And that isn't the . . . *impression* Mayor Majors is looking for."

"Who will we be entertaining?" I ask.

"That's a good question. I don't know if there will be many guests, at least in the beginning. Likely, you'll be here for your convenience and for Mayor Majors."

"Wait." Alyssa lifts her hand in a stop motion. "Will there be others, or is this more of a harem?"

"At this point, I'm not entirely sure. But he believes there will soon be travelers and trade starting up. I think he envisions a spot more for dignitaries than— "

"The kind of people who show up at the bordello?" Star asks.

"Maybe I'm missing something," I say. "But there's already a *place* for . . . " I lift my hands, encouraging someone else to finish my sentence.

"I already told you," Star says. "We're going to be the high-class hookers. Most women at the bordello are in about the same condition as her." She points to Shelby. "Though I did hear she was somewhat normal when they brought her there. I guess most of them were."

"How long have you been there?" I ask Star.

She shakes her head. "A couple of weeks."

"How'd you get there?" Maddie asks.

"Okay, ladies," Mrs. Murphy says. "You'll have plenty of time to get to know each other better. Tomorrow night, we'll have a celebratory dinner."

"You can't be serious?" I scoff. "You want us to celebrate our new . . . *status?*"

"Lucy, you've always been smart about things. Please try and look at this as an opportunity and an advantage. Things aren't always as they seem."

I blink rapidly. *Things aren't always as they seem.* Dirk said that too. I respond with a nod. At least I won't get shot at and I won't have to put up with Janet Kruse each day.

"Hello, ladies," Richard Majors says, entering from the west wing. "I'm so glad to see you. Lucy, are you recovered from your injuries?"

"Yes, sir," I say, standing as he reaches for my hands. He's no longer wearing the sling, and he squeezes both of my hands with just a slight amount of pressure. "You look well. Your arm is better?"

"Fine, fine. I was concerned when I heard you were injured. The medical staff took good care of you?"

"Very good, sir."

"Excellent." He leans in to kiss me on the cheek before releasing me. "And Maddie," he says as he goes to her. I watch her stiffen before she allows him to take her hands in the same manner and pull her to her feet. "It's been a while since I've seen you. You have a lovely rosy glow."

"I've been getting some of our spring sun," she answers.

"I'm sure. Do you like your room?"

"It's very nice. I'd seen it before on the tour."

"Yes, I'm sure you have. I suspect you never imagined you'd be living here, though."

She shakes her head as he leans in to kiss her, causing him to miss her cheek and catch her ear. He ignores the mistake and moves on to Alyssa.

"And you, my dear." He offers her his hand to help her stand. "How's your brother liking his new position?"

"It's fine," she says quietly, once again the milquetoast version of herself. Weird how she goes from strong to frail in an instant.

"Only fine? Is he not pleased with the accommodations and other perks?"

"I'm sure he is. I thought you meant the job itself."

"Oh? And it's only fine?"

"No, I'm sure he likes it. Thank you for helping him get on the acquisition team. My parents also very much like the new house and their new duties."

"Of course they do. You've all met Star, Milena, and Shelby? Perhaps you knew Milena and Shelby from when they used to live in Prospect. I don't know if you heard, but they were both kidnapped by a terrible cult living in the mountains. We were so very fortunate to be able to bring them back to the safety of Prospect. They've both had a rough go of things, so they'll need your patience, all of our patience, while they recover."

"Where'd the cult come from?" Maddie asks.

"Excuse me, dear?" Richard asks.

"Where'd the cult come from? Did it start after the attacks, or was it already in place before?"

"Well . . . both. We knew there was a fringe element living in the county, some people with some very outlandish ideas. We just didn't realize how extreme they were, and we let them become too powerful after the EMP. When I was working so hard to save all of you, I should've paid better attention to what was happening in our backyard. Major Lassiter warned me and wanted me to step in last fall, but we had so many other pressing things. It was only after we were able to rescue Milena and Shelby that I realized just how bad it was. And then, when they attacked us, killing my lovely wife in the process . . . " He shakes his head. "I'm sure you heard at the briefing this morning we'll be bringing them to justice. Saving more poor women and children will be our goal."

"Where's her baby?" I ask, pointing to Shelby.

"Her baby?" he asks with a tilt of his head.

"We used to live in the same building. She was pregnant last I saw her."

"Oh . . . sad story there. Part of the reason she's so . . . disheveled. As soon as her baby was born, they took it from her. Didn't even let her see it once."

My eyes go wide. "And her husband?"

"Dead. They killed him long ago. They kept her prisoner until the baby was born, barely giving her enough food to survive, then once it was out, they put her on their work crew. It's a miracle we found her when we did."

"How do you know this?" Maddie asks. "Did she tell you?"

"In one of her more lucid moments, she told Major Lassiter, and he told me. It's really a very sad story."

I give him a small smile. While I may believe there's a cult operating in the mountains, it seems strange they'd take Shelby from that bad situation just to put her in an equally bad one. From the little Star has said about the brothel, it's not a place anyone should be. Why take her there?

"Lucy, Maddie, Alyssa, I'll let you get back and start your packing. Did Mrs. Murphy tell you we'll be having a special dinner tomorrow night? We're going to celebrate our new household—our new family. That's what we'll be. One big family." He delivers each of us his most winning smile before turning back toward the west wing. As he walks away, he begins to whistle. It takes me a few notes to place the tune: *I'm a Yankee Doodle Dandy.*

"Please, ladies," Mrs. Murphy says. "Will you let yourselves out? I'm going to help Shelby and Milena back to their rooms. Star, please go to your room."

Once again dressed for the cold day, the three of us begin the walk back to the community.

"Milena Maynard," Maddie says, shaking her head. "I thought Mayor Majors hated her. She was one of the people he condemned to death last summer, remember?"

"I guess things change," I say.

"No doubt, but why make her one of his— " She tilts her head and widens her eyes. "And why go on and on about how they were able to save her? That doesn't seem at all suspicious to you?"

"Richard has a good heart," I say. Both Maddie and Alyssa make a snorting noise. "He does. He probably realized he was wrong to . . . to want to . . . anyway, when he heard how bad it had been for her and Shelby, he wanted to do something to make their lives better."

"He was going to hang her last summer," Maddie says, speaking slowly like I'm a two-year-old to whom she's trying to make a point.

"A change of heart," I insist.

"Believe what you want," Maddie says.

After we walk a block or so, Alyssa says, "There's worse places to live, though it really freaks me out Mrs. Murphy is there."

"Did you know her?" I ask.

"From my freshman year. She retired after that. I guess it makes sense, though. I never would've thought Mr. Murphy would be a killer either. People sure can hide their true selves."

"He's not a killer," I say.

"Really? He's a Captain in your so-called army—your acquisition team. Everyone knows what you all do to get the stuff you bring back. How many people have *you* killed? How many children?"

"No children," I say quietly.

"Yeah, really? How many people?"

"We're usually on watch," Maddie says. "And Captain Murphy is on watch too. We're not—we're different than some of the others on the team. Besides, your brother is on the team now. Are you going to harass him about doing his job?"

"Nope. And I guess it doesn't matter. Whatever your job used to be, you've got a new one now. Yee-haw." She picks up her pace, leaving us behind.

"I'm not sure I like her," Maddie says after Alyssa is well ahead of us.

"Never mind about her. You need to get your head screwed on straight. Forget your boyfriend and your new God."

"Not happening. I can't do what Richard wants. I won't. I'm going to figure out how to get out of this."

# Chapter 27

## *Saturday, Day 305*

## *Mollie*

In the predawn, I feel Jake's arm wrap around me. "Be careful," I whisper. "You're still injured."

He snuggles close to me, burying his face into my neck. "They're wrong."

Several times a day since Belinda told me she believes me to be terminal, he's said the same thing. Every day, I give the same answer. I move my hand to cover his forearm. "I don't think so."

He pulls me closer, wincing slightly as the motion affects his gunshot wound. "I don't want you to be part of the attack."

"We've talked about this. It makes sense for me to go."

"It makes sense for you to stay here," he says with more force than the quiet of the morning requires.

I run my hand up his arm. "You're still recovering from a gunshot wound, and you're going."

"What if you have an episode? What if . . . what if it prevents you from getting to safety? You'll be a sitting duck."

I slowly flip over so I can look at him. "You know what is happening to me. You know I'm— " He starts to offer a retort, but I cut him off, whispering, "No, Jake. We don't want to say it, we don't want to call it cancer, but that's what it is. You see me changing. I'm still losing weight, the masses are growing, the pain is increasing. There's no getting around it. It's in my bones now. Belinda told us what I can expect—more pain and the possibility of easy breaks. And even if the lights came back on tomorrow, it's unlikely they could do anything for me. Once it's spread to the bones— "

"Don't, Mollie," he says in a ragged voice. "Don't tell me I have to go on without you."

"But you do. We have three young children counting on you to keep things going after I'm gone."

He puts his hand on my face. "How? My heart feels like it's being ripped out of my chest just thinking about— " He makes a gulping noise as he breaks down.

We hold each other; he doesn't even try to control his tears while I fight to keep mine at bay. I don't want to die. I want to stay with my husband—my love—and my children and grandchildren.

A few years ago, Jake and I had troubles in our marriage. Such bad troubles we came close to separating. The road back to each other was difficult. When the attacks happened, we were better than we'd been but still had challenges. After the lights went out, things changed for us. As we learned to trust completely in God, we started growing closer than ever before.

Even now, with what I believe will happen—I'll waste away little by little until God ushers me to His home—I have faith Jake and the rest of my family will be all right. Even so, I hate the idea of them watching me die bit by bit, watching helplessly as I writhe in agony. I'm truly frightened by the pain I'll experience and the scars it may leave on my family.

When his breathing returns to normal, I ask, "Do you want to pray?"

"I don't know what else to do, other than pray and bawl like a baby. It seems that's how each of my days are spent."

I give him a squeeze. "Well, today will be slightly different," I say in as cheerful of a voice as I can manage. "You get to go back on sentry duty, even if it is modified."

"I'm not complaining about work. Something else to occupy my mind will be good. It wasn't easy yesterday with you being at the supply house. I like having you around me as much as possible."

I let out a breath. "Yesterday was crazy busy."

After Lindsey and the others were killed, Doris took several days off, keeping the supply house closed. I've been a backup for the kitchen crew but haven't been needed, so I'm either spending time on the range or sewing. Where previously I was mending or making more products for our daily needs, now I'm sewing ghillie suits.

Yesterday, everyone refilled the personal items they may need. In just a couple of days, we'll begin our assault on Prospect, and backpacks needed to be restocked. After our hectic day was completed, Doris broke down. Through her tears, she asked how she could do this day in and day out. How can she help people with their needs, while keeping a smile on her face, when her daughter is dead?

"All I want is revenge," she said through gritted teeth. "I want to go after the rest of the murderers and make them pay. I want to watch Richard Majors squirm the seconds before he knows he's a dead man."

I swallowed hard while thinking of a response. I have no doubt, if Doris's leg weren't still injured, she'd be leading the charge to bring the Prospect butchers to justice. And she's not the only one. Mrs. Young's husband has also spoken a lot about revenge. As a not very spry seventy-seven, he's a member of the militia but, like me, only in stationary positions. And he won't be going to Prospect.

Me, though, I'll be one of the overwatches, essentially a sniper, just like those who killed our friends. Since last summer, when I was a designated sharpshooter, I've focused on long shots and maintaining the control needed for those shots to be successful. Now I'm training to take extra-long shots. My trusty .308, which I used as my hunting rifle before our world fell apart and then in my militia post as a sharpshooter—similar to my new overwatch position but shooting at closer distances—has been passed on to Angela, my spotter. I'm now using a specially developed rifle for long shots made by a company out of Cody, marketed as being proven for accuracy up to a thousand yards.

Paul Cameron and his sons brought four of these specialty rifles, which they owned in their outfitter business, when they moved to our community. There were a couple of long-range rifles in Bakerville, including one owned by Gabe Griffin, who was killed along with the rest of the people still living on the river. Gabe, too, was a hunting outfitter and guide, though his business was much smaller than the Camerons'. The rifle was one of the things Chandler, Gabe's son, was able to direct Jake and the others to find. Gabe and Dina Griffin were smart to cache things so the Prospect raiders didn't find them.

While I don't relish the idea of being a sniper and what it means— I've taken human life before, and it's not easy—I'm glad to be included in the plans. Not in the same way as Doris, not for revenge. But because I know, if we don't stop Majors and his gang, they will come after us again. When that happens, my children and grandchildren will again be in danger.

"What do you think about the information Bill brought back?" Jake asks, rousing me from my thoughts.

"Not sure what to think. Other than there's a whole lot more of them than there are of us."

"Yeah, that's why— "

"Don't, Jake. I'm going. Especially considering our children will be a part of this attack. I'm not going to stay home while they're in danger."

"I don't like them going. We should've at least talked Sarah and Angela out of it. Katie won't be on the front line, and with Calley being pregnant— "

"Yes, I'm glad she isn't even being offered a spot on the militia. Angela will be with me, so she'll be out of the immediate danger."

"I know you think that, Mollie, but Evan said snipers are often targeted. That's why you only take a few shots and then move."

"You'll be with Evan, Jake. If I'm in danger, you'll be too."

"I know. Me acting as his spotter is the same as Angela acting as yours. There's still danger. But Sarah, she shouldn't be going at all. She was given the choice of staying here."

I close my eyes. After Annie Bond's death during the sniper attack left three more orphans, Sarah, and others like her—or those who have a spouse going to attack Prospect—were given a pass from the invasion. We have too many orphans and not enough able-bodied caregivers now. Annie's three children have found a home with Mick Michaelson and his wife, adding to their five biological children.

Sarah talked about it with all of us, adamantly stating how she didn't want to shirk the duty she felt was hers, both in caring for her children and in helping to defend them. In the end, after confirming one of her sisters would care for her children should she not return, she chose to go. Sarah's stepmom, Alina, who's also exempt from going, decided to stay. Her son Victor has fought cancer for half his young life. While it's believed he's currently in remission, Alina doesn't want to risk him getting sick again and someone else needing to be his caregiver.

I let out a long breath. "I don't want her to go either—I don't want Angela, Katie, Mike, Leo, or any of our family there, including you. But Sarah's choice is hers to make."

"I guess, but I don't like it. And, like you, I'd prefer none of them went—especially you."

"But we have to. We can't just sit back and wait for them to pick us off. We must eliminate the threat Richard Majors and his henchmen pose."

"We could wait, keep watch like we're doing and wait it out. The president's latest announcement gave more information."

"Did it?" I ask. "It still sounded to me like a whole lot of nothing."

"I think he's in Texas."

"The president? Why?"

"Don't know for sure, but his voice almost sounded to have a southernness to it this last time. Sounded a bit like David Hammer and his family. Maybe he's picking up a regional accent."

"Oh, okay," I say with a laugh. "I didn't notice. And I don't really think he gave us enough information to believe the government is going to swoop in and take care of Prospect for us."

Jake lets out a long sigh. "I hope the part of the team Bill left behind are able to gather more information and can ensure no additional guerrilla teams are sent in our direction. Going on the offensive is the only way. I just don't like it being necessary. And if I'm being honest, I hate I'm relegated to spotter while our daughter will be a full-on soldier. That doesn't seem right."

"Is your dad still going?"

"He's passed all the tests to be able to go. Mom's not happy about him going either, but she understands he feels the need to do so."

At seventy-six, Alvin's one of the oldest to be going, as a hiker as opposed to joining later and riding in via snowmobile or horse and buggy. While I know he has the stamina for the walk, he's developed a bit of a totter over the winter. He, along with several of the other seniors who wanted to be part of the hiking group, had to pass an agility test, showing they could remain upright on the snowshoes in a variety of conditions.

With warmer temps, the snow is melting in heavily traveled areas around the dude ranch and ski lodge. We expect less snow in the valley where Prospect is located, but the snowshoes will be helpful with getting our team off the mountain and through the untouched snow. When the snowshoes are no longer needed, the team will leave them and then retrieve them later.

"He's not the only one. I'm amazed at how so many in the community are willing to do this, especially the seniors."

"I'm pretty sure some of them are going just so they don't have to move into the ski lodge."

I let out a small laugh. "That may be true, especially in your dad's case. I know your mom is less than happy about having to leave our place and move up there."

"It's smart, though, to move everyone into the lodge and have the home guard, ensuring their safety."

"Whose idea was it to call them *the home guard*?" I ask.

"Not sure. But it makes sense and says exactly what they'll be doing—keeping our children and others safe."

"Aaron Ogden didn't seem happy about being put in charge of the guard."

"No, he wasn't happy. Especially since his wife is going to Prospect on the medical team. He'll do it, of course, but it's not what he wants. And Tim's broken arm puts him at a disadvantage. We needed someone not injured in charge."

"Will Aaron and the others be able to keep everyone safe while we're gone?"

Jake gives a small shrug. "We'll have the team of watchers to make sure no one leaves Prospect to attack us. The biggest concern is an unknown entity. You've heard what Roberts keeps saying. He thinks the whole thing is foolish."

"Reggie Roberts never likes any plan," I say, thinking of the crusty Vietnam veteran.

"We'd better get going," Jake says, reaching for my hand. "Let's pray."

Jake's voice takes on an almost dreamy quality as he asks—no, *begs*—our Heavenly Father to bless our endeavors and keep our family and community safe. My eyes well up again when he says, "And please, Lord, touch Mollie with a miracle. Take her pain away and give her peace. Let us grow old and grey together." He squeezes my hand, indicating it's my turn to speak.

I clear my throat before saying, "Lord, I know Your Word tells us there is a time for war and a time for peace. If there's any way for this to be a time of peace, please, Lord, make it so. If war is what must come, please place Your powerful shield around us, safeguarding us who advance on Prospect only to protect the lives of the innocent. Lives like Willie, Annie, Toby, Lindsey, and all those living on the river. We didn't— " I suck in a breath as tears threaten to overwhelm me. "We didn't ask for this. We wanted nothing from Prospect or Richard Majors. We were living in peace and . . . " I let out a slow breath as I realize my prayer is turning into a rant. "Please, God, we need You."

Jake and I echo our amens. For many minutes we lie in bed, staring at the ceiling through the dark.

Jake finally says, "Maybe the team will bring back good news and we won't have to do this."

"That's my prayer," I say needlessly.

"You still planning on waiting to tell the family until afterwards?"

"I think it's best. I don't want them thinking about their poor, sick, dying mom when they need to be focused on what they're doing."

"And you don't think they already know?"

I turn my head to meet his gaze. "We haven't hidden my illness. So, of course, they know. And Calley has said many times that she's sure we'll have a hospital before her baby arrives and we can even have side-by-side beds while I get well. She's joking, but not really. I just don't think telling them I'm terminal is necessary. Not right now. And I certainly don't want the younger kids to know. Until the only thing I can do is lie in bed, they don't need to know. And even then, I want to wait. I just— " I let out a sigh. "I don't want to ruin the little bit of childhood they get in this world."

# Chapter 28

## *Mollie*

"Did you say something?" I call out after hearing what sounds like muttering. When Doris doesn't respond, I return to the dusting.

This morning's rush was almost as crazy as yesterday's, with people lined up at the door right after breakfast. Today, there was plenty of grumbling directed toward Doris regarding the new housing arrangements. She took it in stride. Although, when the last person cleared out about an hour later, she did say, "I sure get tired of everything being my fault."

Now Doris is working on organizing the open shelving under the customer counter and the employee-only storage section behind the countertop, while I take care of the layer of dust coating the surfaces. During the heavy days of winter, with several feet of snow on the ground, the dust was less. These last few days, spring has slowly made an appearance. While it's still cold at night, it warms up during the day, and we haven't had fresh snow since before the sniper murders.

The daytime snow melt is ushering us into the next season. Some people call it spring; we call it mud. There are many places where the wind came in and swept the snow away. And now, as the piles and drifts melt, the runoff is streaming toward any low spot, many of which were showing dirt. There's one such spot on the long driveway to the supply house, resulting in a good-sized mud puddle. When I attempted to walk around the puddle, I ended up in the soft dirt, which was also plenty muddy. I can only imagine how the ground will be by the time I walk home. It must be in the midforties today. There may be more mud than snow.

This time of year, it wouldn't be unusual to have a heavy snowfall, so who knows what we'll encounter in the time between now and when we make our attack. Thinking about the raid on Prospect hurts my heart. The dangers our family and friends face are almost overwhelming.

A muffled *oomph* followed by a thump breaks me out of my thoughts.

I open my mouth to call out to Doris and ask if everything's okay. The hairs standing on the back of my neck prompt me to stay quiet. Removing my pistol from the holster at my waist, I quietly stand. Making sure I have my balance, I creep to the end of the shelving. A loud crash is followed by a shout. I pull my sidearm to the ready position while keeping my finger indexed. My pulse is pounding in my ears, and my vision's beginning to narrow. I focus on staying alert, then slide up against the shelf with my back to it to ensure no one is sneaking up behind me.

I'm less than a foot from the end of the aisle when a body jumps out, grabbing my gun and pushing it to the side. Without even thinking, I tighten my arm to turn my forearm and elbow into a weapon. Using the breaker strike Katie taught me, I jab my elbow into my attacker's cheekbone. As brown hair flies, my eyes widen as I recognize her. She lets out a scream. I lift my right leg and deliver a forward push kick, throwing her against the shelf behind her and knocking several things to the ground. With distance between us, I regain my balance, now in shooter's position.

"Shannon?" a man's voice calls out as she regains her footing.

"Don't do it," I hiss.

Shannon Decker sneers at me. There's a loud crash across the room, followed by a gunshot and then a man letting out a scream like a little girl. Shannon's eyes narrow as she lets out a guttural roar. I squeeze the trigger of my .40 caliber Springfield Armory twice in quick succession, slamming her into the shelving—this time knocking the entire unit over. As she lies there on top of the mess of shelf and goods, gasping for breath, she says, "Pretty tough . . . aren't you? You didn't . . . even     wait . . . until     I     pulled . . . my     weapon. You . . . executed . . . me."

"Mollie?" Doris calls out. "You okay?"

"Shannon's down."

"Secure her and then come help me with Roscoe. He's down, too, but I'm hurt and can't . . . I need your help."

I feel myself pale. Doris is down? *Shot?* After the shooting at our picnic, I've made a habit of keeping my everyday carry on me. The crossover bag is balanced on my left hip and contains a couple of zip ties, in addition to homemade battle dressings and a few other first aid items and essentials.

I watch for a few more seconds to confirm there's no need to secure Shannon. Both shots were fatal—delivered center mass. She takes a rattled breath, then stops.

With my gun still trained on her, I pick up the pistol lying on the floor next to her. I never even saw her holding it, but she must've been. I tuck the 9mm semi-auto into my own holster.

With my sidearm by my thigh, I quickly move toward the counter area. As I step near it, I say, "I'm stepping behind the counter."

"You're clear," Doris responds.

She's sitting on the ground, leaning against the open shelving of the sturdy counter. Roscoe is on the floor several feet away. A quick look over Doris doesn't result in any obvious serious injuries. Roscoe's curled in a ball, his eyes tightly closed, his body heaving as he gasps for breath, and his hands pressed against his stomach. There's a spreading puddle of blood underneath him.

"Does he have any weapons?" I ask.

"My main pistol and one on his hip," Doris answers. "I shot him with the stash gun from under the counter."

"After she hit me with a pipe," he says through clenched teeth, opening one eye. "I think my leg's broken."

"That makes two of us," Doris says, her own teeth clenched.

"Roscoe, slide the gun away," I order.

"I dropped it when she hit me."

I quickly glance around, spying the weapon against a wall well out of his reach. "The one in the holster."

He slowly moves his hand from his wound to his hip. "Don't shoot me again, okay? I'm going to take it out and toss it away."

"Best be smart about it," Doris says slowly. "We're both trained on you."

Without ceremony, he removes the gun and puts it on the floor before sliding it in my direction. I pick it up and put it on the shelf behind me, setting the 9mm I retrieved from Shannon next to it.

"Were you hit?" I ask Doris, as I take a couple of quick steps toward the gun laying against the wall.

"Not shot."

"Where's the radio?" I ask as I hand Doris her weapon. She gives me a nod.

After the day I had to run for help when Milena and Shelby were kidnapped, we once again have a radio while on duty. Doris used to have a full-time radio, but with battery shortages, she gave it up when someone declared it a luxury. The kidnapping proved otherwise.

"Not sure. Shannon took it when they got the drop on me—that's when they took my gun too."

"Let me tie him up," I say.

"He's bleeding pretty good," Doris says. "I'll keep him covered. See if you can find the radio and get the medics here, then you can start patching him up."

It takes me a couple of minutes to find the radio. I had to move Shannon's body to locate it on the back of her belt. Her dead eyes stare at me accusingly as I replay how she thought I didn't fight fair, how I should've given her a chance to draw on me. Shaking my head, I make the call for help, giving as many details as I can, as quickly as I can, then go back to Doris and Roscoe.

Pulling a couple of bandages from my bag, I move over next to him. "Move your hands, Roscoe."

"Too late, I think," he says quietly. "Too much blood."

Looking at the massive puddle surrounding him, I have to agree. "Move your hands," I say again, lifting one out of the way as I press a heavy cloth square into place. "Press here while I put the battle bandage in place." It takes a minute or so to get it in position and ready for tightening. "All right, move your hands." He's shaking as he pulls his hands away.

"How'd you get free?" Doris asks. I glance up at her when she points to Roscoe. "Roscoe, how did you and Shannon escape?"

He mumbles something, then lets out a cry when I pull the battle bandage tight.

"Okay?" I ask.

"Hurts," he mumbles.

"Yeah," I answer. "Let's try and get you warmed up." I quickly go to the bedding section of the supply house, bringing back two blankets. I cover Roscoe with one and then turn to Doris. "Did you break your bad leg again?"

"Seems I might have," she answers. She's also shaking and pale with a small cut above her eyebrow and a second at the top of her cheek, the backup gun lying next to her. "Roscoe, how'd you get free?" she asks again.

He doesn't answer as I cover her with the second blanket. "Any blood?" I ask. "From your leg, is it bleeding?"

"Why are you here?" Doris asks Roscoe.

"Needed supplies. Then we planned to disappear."

"Doris. Is your leg bleeding?"

Before she can answer, the front door opens and a voice calls out, "Are you clear?"

"We're clear!" I yell back. "Mollie Caldwell and Doris Snyder behind the counter. Two attackers down and disarmed." Within seconds, we're surrounded by security team members as they come in not only the front door but also the back door in our storage area.

"Mollie, are you injured?" Leo asks.

"Not me. Roscoe and Doris. Shannon Decker—she's dead."

Leo's team does a full sweep of the room, then they begin treating Roscoe and Doris. After a quick triage, it's determined the bandage I put on Roscoe is the best we can do for him here. Leo doesn't say it, but the slight shake of his head speaks volumes about Roscoe's chances. Leo checks Doris's leg, agreeing it's likely rebroken. As they start making plans to transport them to the clinic, Doris asks, "How'd they escape?"

I slide down the wall I've been leaning against to sit on the floor.

"We're still working that out," one of the team members says. "Can I get you a chair, Mollie?"

I wave him off. "I'm fine."

Leo shoots me a look.

"I am. Really. Where's Heath? We didn't—he isn't in here."

"Not sure," Leo answers.

Katie and Madison show up a few minutes later, carrying a skinny wooden door we use as a stretcher. Roscoe will ride in the trailer of the snowmobile, which I heard pull up outside right before Katie came in, and Doris will be carried on the stretcher. With her broken leg, it's likely the more comfortable option.

"Mom?" Katie asks, raising her eyebrows. "You're okay?"

"I'm not injured."

"Okay. Let's use the stretcher to get Roscoe to the trailer and then bring it back for Doris," she says.

Madison helps load Roscoe as Katie looks over Doris. When I called for help, I told them about Roscoe being shot and Doris's leg likely reinjured, so Katie brought an inflatable leg cast with her—the same air splint Doris wore for weeks last summer during the early stages of her healing.

"Oh, great," Doris mutters. "My old nemesis. I hate that itchy thing, Katie."

"Best thing we can do for today, especially until we get you to Belinda."

"Leo, will you make sure your team locks up when they leave?" Doris asks. "We'll worry about cleaning up later."

"No problem, ma'am," Leo answers. "Mollie, are you going to the clinic?"

"She is," Katie answers for me. "Even though she says she's fine, she's going to be examined."

# Chapter 29

## *Mollie*

The security team, along with Katie and Madison, scramble to get Roscoe ready, leaving only a few minutes after the stretcher arrives. It's about half an hour later before Doris is being carried to the medical clinic and I'm riding behind one of our teens on a snowmobile. It never fails; each time I climb on one of the machines, I remember Toby James and his cheerfulness. Losing him has left a void in our community.

We'll be taking all but one of the snowmobiles with us when we attack Prospect. This boy, one of our runners, is joining us on the expedition, delivering us to the overwatch staging area. Then he'll take the snowmobile to where a watch crew will be camped. Liam, him, two other teens, and David Hammer will be at the watch spot. David will act as overwatch, staying behind to slow down any attack from Prospect, while the teens notify our home guard. Even though the watch team will be out of harm's way, they aren't completely safe and have all had training in gun handling and safety. Liam was already an experienced marksman, thanks to his dad Ben's love of hunting.

Ben and Destiny are part of the regular militia and will be on the front line. Clarice is staying behind, not only for Wyatt but because Kelley and Belinda won't medically clear her. While she's considerably better from her winter trip, they're concerned her rapid weight loss combined with years of being underweight has taken a toll on her heart. Even though she's not going to be part of the mission, she's still getting basic militia and guard training as part of the home guard.

Could Reggie Roberts be right? Could this futile effort not only get everyone going to Prospect killed but also those staying behind? We're all well aware, with the bulk of us gone, we're leaving our community vulnerable. While it's unlikely we'd see an attack from Prospect, mainly because we're watching them and don't think a large group can sneak up on us, we suspect there are others around who may wish us harm—wish anyone harm.

One reason we're planning our attack sooner rather than later is the weather. Our hope is, during this season between winter and summer, not as many people will be looking to invade, choosing to wait until better conditions. Of course, that didn't work out for our friends on the river. Prospect attacked them in the dead of winter.

The snowmobile ride allows me to reach the clinic well before Doris. As I climb off the sled and thank my driver, the front door of the clinic opens and Belinda steps out onto the porch.

"It'd be nice if you'd try and stay out of trouble," Belinda says.

"Yep, I agree. How's Roscoe?"

She shakes her head. "He passed before they got him here."

I give a nod. "Doris will be here shortly. Katie told me Jake was here. Is he inside?"

"He arrived when the first snowmobile bringing Roscoe did. He said to tell you he's helping at the murder scene."

"The murder scene?" I ask slowly. "Where I killed Shannon? He wasn't there when I left."

"The prisoners were on firewood duty. As soon as you called in about the attack, Evan sent Leo and his squad to take care of the supply house while he went to the woods. Laurie went with them, but right after Roscoe arrived—when Jake was here—Evan called on the radio for Kelley to come, and I sent Madison too. Jake went with them."

"Why?"

"Security. Him and two other militia members. Pete Fairbanks took them with the wagon and team. We're going to need your house."

"My house? Why'd you call it the murder scene?"

"Shannon and Roscoe killed their guards. They were working with the firewood crew when they escaped. From the sounds of it, there are also several injured crew members. Pete will bring them back in the wagon. We'll need your house for overflow."

"Who?" I ask quickly. Mike is on firewood duty this morning.

Belinda shakes her head. "I don't have any names."

I close my eyes and look down at my toes, blinking rapidly. "Where's Heath?" I ask.

"That's what the security is for. Heath isn't at the murder scene or the supply house. I'm not sure if anyone knows where he is at the moment."

"I'm here," a voice says, stepping around the corner of the clinic.

Lifting my shirt with my left hand, my right is simultaneously moving toward my gun.

"Whoa, whoa," Heath says, holding his hands up.

I don't stop my motion and quickly have my weapon trained on him.

"I'm not armed. I wasn't part of that. It's all Roscoe and Shannon. See? They hit me!" He points to his head and the blood dried on his collar.

"Cover him, Mollie," Belinda says. "I'm calling for help." She removes the walkie-talkie from her waistband.

"Put both hands on top of your head and sit on the ground," I command.

Heath gives a nod and complies, plopping himself directly in a mud puddle. "I promise I didn't have anything to do with it. They knocked me out. When I came to, Hendricks and Murdoch were dead— they're our guards today. Others were hurt and, well, maybe dead too."

"Did you try and help them?" I ask.

Shamefaced, he gives a slight shake of his head. "I thought I'd try and escape." He frowns. "But I didn't want to leave and never see Dot again."

I narrow my eyes at him. Dot is his wife. He beat her and left her for dead a few months ago. As far as I know, she's had nothing to do with him during his incarceration. "Are you armed?"

"I have a rifle," he says. "I left it around the building, propped against the wall. There's a small gun in my pocket. I took it off one of the woodcutting crew." A look passes over his face as his mouth makes an O. "It was, uh . . . "

"Mike?" I ask in a whisper.

"I think he's okay, just knocked out, like me. I didn't even know he had it, but with the way he fell, it was hanging out."

With my heart pounding, I snap, "But you didn't bother to find out or to help him, did you? You didn't check anyone to see if you could help them. But here you are, showing up at the clinic, for what? Treatment?"

He wisely clamps his mouth shut and looks at his knees.

"You okay, Mollie?" Belinda asks, stepping off the porch.

"No. No, I'm definitely not." She gives me a look before I add, "He left my son-in-law for dead."

Belinda binds Heath's hands behind him, then gets him to his feet and removes the gun from his pocket. She gives me a small nod as she hands it to me. "We'll wait until someone shows up before taking him in for treatment," she says.

The words are barely out of her mouth when we see Katie and the crew carrying Doris move up the road. Right behind them are Leo and several others running toward us.

"And here they are," Belinda says.

"There's the wagon," I say, pointing toward the corrals where the team has just come into view. Evan's riding next to Pete.

"It's about to get busy," Belinda says. "Can you make sure your house is set up? I'll cover dufus here."

"Will you send someone to tell me about Mike?" I ask as I holster my weapon and step away.

"I will. Are you well enough to do this, Mollie?" she asks.

Without turning, I lift a hand in response.

At the house, Sarah and Karen help me move the furniture in the great room against the walls and set up cots. Okay, I only sort of help as they do most of the work. Even though I feel fine and am not having the severe shortness of breath or anything, my body is reacting to the stress from the day and threatening to crash. The brief fight with Shannon and then shooting her pumped my adrenaline too high. I close my eyes as I replay it.

"Mom?" Sarah asks.

"Yeah?"

"I said, why don't you sit on the couch. Tate's starting to wake up. You can hold him."

"It's going to get crazy here in a minute," I say.

"Sit there until it does," she answers. Within a minute, Tate is in my arms as I rest on the couch. As I prop my right elbow up on the arm of the couch, there's a slight pain on the boney spot right below my elbow. I flash back to the brief altercation with Shannon when I used my elbow as a weapon against her face. No wonder I'm tender. A minute later, there's a bang at the door and the wounded start arriving.

Mike is with the first group. He's walking and has a bandage on his head.

At his side, Katie says, "He'll be fine. We're keeping him for observation." She leads him to one of the cots.

As the busyness of the room increases, I move with Tate into the former den—now his, Sarah's, and Andy's bedroom. Early on in the attacks, Doctor Sam asked me to be a part of the medical team. I declined but do help as needed, and like everyone on the militia, I have basic battle training. Today, though, the best place for me is out of the action and holding my grandson. We're both asleep on the small loveseat when I hear my name being called.

"Mm-hmm?" I ask, dragging myself out of the fog of sleep.

"You doing okay?" Kelley asks.

"I'm fine," I say, straightening up. Still asleep but not happy about being disturbed, Tate makes a face and then stretches. "How bad is it?"

"Three dead in addition to Roscoe and Shannon, their guards and one of the firewood crew."

"How'd it happen?"

"We're piecing it together. Seems Mike and Kevin Breene were working closest to the prisoners while the other four were farther away. Mike says one of the guards, Scott Murdoch, had to use the bathroom, so he stepped off behind the trees. Roscoe started a fight with Heath. When Larry Hendricks stepped in to break it up, Shannon got the drop on him. She'd managed to get herself disconnected from the chain. She used it as a garrote. After that, things went bad quick and Roscoe hit Mike in the head with a log.

"Kevin Breene was the crew member killed. Shannon used Larry's gun on him, then shot Murdoch when he came rushing over to see what happened. When the other four from the firewood crew came running, they were all shot too." I let out a gasp as Kelley nods. "Thankfully, they had bad aim. Only one of the gunshot wounds is serious. Well, let me rephrase that. If we were in a normal hospital situation, we'd consider one serious. Here— " She lifts her hands.

"Yeah," I say. "They're all serious."

"Your friend Aaron Ogden is one of the injured."

"Aaron? How bad?" Aaron and his wife Laurie lived with us on the homestead. Back when things were normal, Aaron was one of my martial arts teachers.

"The shot barely grazed his bicep, but it caused him to fall. He broke his leg."

"Bad?"

"Bad enough. Right below the knee. Belinda and Madison are still working on him. They're in surgery trying to set it."

"Is Laurie holding up okay?" I ask, wondering about his wife.

"She's great, staying focused right now. I'll keep an eye on her. Now, I'm under orders to make sure you're okay. Any injuries?"

"My elbow's tender. Otherwise, I'm fine. A little tired." I shrug. "But I'll tell you, it's a good thing Shannon went down so easy. There's no way I could've come out ahead in any kind of a prolonged fight. She taunted me. Said I was shooting her in cold blood without giving her a chance to defend herself."

"She didn't give you a choice, Mollie. You know that, right? When she and Roscoe chose to go to the supply house instead of just taking off, they had to know what could happen."

She looks at my elbow, which is already sporting a silver-dollar-sized bruise where it connected with Shannon's face.

Tate, now wide awake, announces his need for his mom. There's a rap at the door and Sarah pokes her head in. "Should I take him out?"

"C'mon in. I think your mom's fine," Kelley says, then turns to me. "If you start having any trouble, let us know."

"And?" I ask.

She lifts a shoulder. "And we'll see what we can do."

216

# Chapter 30

## *Lucy*

"Lucy Fleming?"

I spin at the sound of my name. It's that Chase guy, without his heavy jacket, wearing only a slightly too tight long-sleeved T-shirt—which looks like it was made to fit his sculpted torso. In my opinion, it's still too cold to be without a coat. I straighten my back and put my hands on my hips. He might be cute, but unlike Maddie, I know better than to go slumming behind Richard's back. Besides, with my planned move into the Bunn Mansion today, a boyfriend is certainly not in my future.

"You know my name," I snap.

He lifts his hands in mock surrender. "Wasn't me."

"It was me," the man standing next to him says. I was so caught up in looking at Chase in his tight shirt, I didn't even notice the completely disheveled guy. Is this his brother?

"And you are?" I take a good look at him. He not only seems unkept but looks completely distraught. Even though we have certain cleanliness standards in the town, many of the workers let their hair and beards go longer than allowed until they're reprimanded to clean up, but not usually to this point of filth. But his sadness is what gets me. It's exaggerated almost to hopeless. What's the Christmas show where the guy is going to jump off the bridge? He reminds me of him. A man teetering on the edge. Even so, there's something familiar about him.

"You don't recognize me?" he asks in complete monotone. "I guess that makes sense. I've lost some weight."

Chase lets out a snort. "We've all lost weight."

"Yeah," the guy agrees with a nod. "I'm Jason Hatch. You used to watch my daughter Lily. My wife is Olivia—do you remember?"

My eyes go wide. It *is* him under the beard and long hair. And as he said, he has lost weight—lots of weight. "What are you doing here?" I hiss, looking around to see who might notice me talking to him. "You shouldn't be here."

He lifts his hands and shakes his head. "Why not?"

I turn to Chase. "Are you just going to let him walk around talking to anyone he wants? Do you know what they'll do to him?"

In a low voice, Chase says, "No, I don't know what they'll do. What are you freaking out about?"

Of course Chase doesn't know. Unless Maddie lied to me and she does tell Chance about the things we do when we go on our raids, how we never leave witnesses to what we've done, he wouldn't know. Not for sure. There's talk, there's always talk, but never proof. But doesn't he remember Richard at the memorial service saying they thought it was the community of Bakerville who planted the bomb in the hotel and killed his wife? "He's from Bakerville," I say between gritted teeth. "They're our enemy."

Jason pulls his head back and widens his eyes. "What are you talking about? Bakerville is wiped out. The houses are empty, and the buildings are burned to the ground. My house is gone. Did— " He steps into my space, putting his face next to mine. "What happened to my family?"

"I didn't think— " Chase says quietly. "She's right. If they know where you're from, even though you haven't been there, it won't be good for you."

"I don't care," Jason says. "I just want to find my family. I thought they might've moved into Prospect."

I take a step back with my left foot and lift my hands slightly into ready position. My heart is pounding. "I haven't seen them. I don't know where they are. I was hoping maybe they might be with you. You know, how they'd go along with you sometimes?"

"They were planning to come with me on my July hitch," he says. "They were home. I talked to Olivia the morning the phones stopped working. Told her I was trying to find a way back—the supervisors of our crew took our company trucks the night before. Each left without even telling any of us. I guess they thought getting back to their own families was more important than helping us get home too." The bitterness in his voice causes me to cringe.

"I don't know where Olivia and Lily are—or your son." I shake my head and give a shrug. "I'm sorry I can't help you."

"But you know what happened to the rest of them?" Chase asks, giving me a look I can't quite interpret.

Keeping my eyes on Jason and my face neutral, I say, "You need to leave, Jason. I heard a rumor some of the people in Bakerville moved somewhere. They're hiding out for the winter up in the mountains. I'm not exactly sure where, but . . . " I give a shrug.

"Do you have an idea where they moved to?" Jason asks. "Up in the mountains—oh . . . " He gives a nod. "That'd make sense, but it's kind of tight for all of them."

"What are you two talking about?" Chase asks, looking at each of us in turn.

"There's a ski resort at the end of the road operating on a forest lease," Jason says. "There's a few other houses up there, too, including an old hotel or something. But it hasn't been operational for years. They could be there."

I give a slight nod. "It'd make sense. I don't know if that's where they are, and I've also heard they've got some whackados leading the place. They're doing some weird stuff."

"Whackados? Who?"

"I don't know. But people are calling it a cult. It might not even be actual Bakerville people in charge anymore. Maybe someone came in and took over?"

"Like here?" Chase asks.

I give a shrug. "I don't know much. Nothing really."

"I'd be surprised," Jason says. "Someone taking over Bakerville? Unlikely. It's a unique place. Lots of retired military and law enforcement. And it's clannish. There are the original people who've lived there for generations and the newcomers. Newcomers, according to the originals, are anyone who hasn't lived there at least thirty years. Combined with the servicepeople—no . . . I don't buy someone came in and took over."

"But you don't know," I say.

"I'm going to find out. If there's a chance my family is there, I'll find them."

"How?" Chase asks.

"What do you mean?"

"How will you approach them?"

With a smirk, Jason says, "Walk right in like I own the place."

"Great," I say, thinking that sounds like a good way to get himself shot. "Go find your family. But while you're here, don't tell people where you're from. And definitely don't tell anyone you know me. Got it?"

He gives me a nod. I look from him to Chase before turning to leave, being careful of a puddle of melted snow. After a couple of steps, I stop and walk back to them. "How did you get inside town, anyway? Didn't the sentries try and stop you?"

Jason sheepishly says, "Snuck in last night. I've had some experience sneaking around. When you travel through what I have, you learn to be a ghost. I'll leave the same way I arrived."

"It's only late morning. You need to find a place to go and stay out of sight until then. You shouldn't be on the street. And you— " I point to Chase. "Shouldn't you be working?"

He gives me a smile and a wink, both melting my insides, before he says, "Day off. We get those once a week."

"Well, so . . . fine."

"My offer for a cup of tea still stands."

"No, thank you." I spin and leave, managing to stumble over my feet in the process and plopping right in the water with my left foot. I let out a low growl and mutter several choice words.

"You okay?" Chase asks.

"Of course! No thanks to you." I keep walking without looking back, my cheeks hot and my foot wet.

As I go, I hear Jason say, "Man, she sure doesn't like you."

"Yeah, I guess not," Chase answers.

I can't help but throw him a dirty look over my shoulder, which results in a chuckle from both of them.

"See?" Chase says.

I quickly turn, hiding my smile.

I should've returned home to change out of my wet boot, but I decided to continue with my intended mission. With my packing finished, I'm doing a favor for the rest of the dorm. After several weeks of no issues, we were shorted on bedding again. I'm beginning to think it's someone messing with us.

With Candace Murphy no longer at the laundry, I deal with a rather unpleasant lady with a hawk nose. She's someone I've seen around the last few months, but I don't know her or even recognize her as being from Prospect before the attacks. She launches into a big tirade on how her people would not make a mistake and it must be something we've done. I wonder if I'll have to go find missing sheets once I move into Richard's place.

Back at my dorm, it's terribly quiet. Everyone but Maddie and I has regular training and group lunch at the clubhouse. When they returned from training yesterday and our evening meals were delivered, things were tense. Where there's usually lots of laughter and talking after training day, last night there were stink eyes sent toward Maddie and me.

Finally, Susie said, "You two have been sleeping with Richard Majors, and that's how you got on our team?"

While I looked at my plate, Maddie calmly said, "Yes."

"I guess it makes sense," Mae said. "Neither of you were really acquisition team material. Wish I would've thought about sleeping my way to the top, maybe I'd be an officer."

I swallowed hard to keep from crying. She wasn't wrong, but it sounded terrible the way she put it. The others had their own comments to add, some even more terrible and blunt than Mae's. I finally got up and left the table.

My mission today to fix the sheet issue was in hopes of making amends for the deception to my teammates. They're right, I never should've been on this team. Even so, they're all dedicated and kind and, up until last night, each have done what they could to help both Maddie and me. I write a quick note and put it on the pile of sheets. Maddie and I will be gone before they return from training.

In our room, Maddie is sitting on her bed. When I close the door, she motions me over.

"What?" I ask, not moving.

She flips her hands again. With a sigh I move to my bed, sitting on the edge so I'm facing her. She shakes her head and then scurries by my side, sitting way too close.

"Give me some space, Maddie," I say with a huff.

"I'm leaving," she says in a quiet voice.

"Meaning?"

"Chance and I are going with Chase and Jason—the one you saw today."

"How do you know about that?"

"Duh. I popped over to the cantina to see Chance when you went to check on the laundry. Chase showed up right after you saw them, and he talked. Both agree they're going with the guy to find his family. I think the cult sounds phony, and they need to know what Scott Majors and Lassiter are planning." She gives a shrug. "It's smart to go, don't you think?"

"To give them a warning they're going to be attacked? It's only smart if you want our friends to be killed. Is that what you want?"

"It's smart because it can give them a chance to run."

"Oh . . . where would they run? It's not like there's really anyplace they could hide."

"I was thinking about that. Jason told Chance he thinks—you also think—they're probably at the little ski lodge."

"It makes sense. It's not far from Bakerville, and Scott said they've been hiding in the mountains."

"Yeah. I think so too. I skied there on a class trip a few years ago. I even went ziplining there the summer before the attacks. What a rush! You ever go?"

"No. Never skied either, but I've driven up there before just to look around."

"It'd be a good place to hide, but I don't know about living in the lodge."

"Think about the ski lift towers," I say. "They could get in one of those and see for a long distance. It'd be good for keeping watch. And if they saw Lassiter and his team coming before, they'd need good locations for watching."

"Do you believe that? That they were attacked without provocation?"

In a whisper, I say, "Lassiter is a strange one. And I definitely don't believe his wife and children were kidnapped. She probably realized he was a creepy loser and left him."

Maddie nods. "I thought you might want to come with us."

"What? No!" I screech.

"You want to stay here and become a . . . you know."

"You're crazy. Absolutely certifiable. Why would you think I'd consider leaving here?"

"Because all of this is wrong."

"We're trying to survive. How is that wrong?"

"Do you really not see it?"

"Oh, I see plenty. I see Jason Hatch, who used to be robust and slightly overweight, is nothing but skin and bones and looks—and probably smells—like he hasn't bathed in months. Do you see Prospect people looking that bad? Our cleanliness standards keep people looking decent at least."

"Most of the workers are skinny."

"Not like Jason. If we get a good wind, he'll blow right back to South Dakota or wherever it was he was working when the attacks started."

"North Dakota. Chase said he walked from North Dakota."

"Not the point. We have it good here. We have it good because of Richard Majors. Do you think Mayor Stringer would've done nearly as well? You heard about the plans they found. He was willing to sacrifice part of the town, especially the elderly."

"We've still lost the elderly," she says quietly. "My grandma died because her medicine ran out. How many senior citizens do you see in town?"

"Most of them stay inside because of the weather."

"Do they? What about the secret burial crew?"

"Secret? No, just the regular. People do die—and as always, I'm sorry about your grandma."

"There's a secret burial crew too. I heard about it at the cantina. These aren't the people who die of natural causes. They're euthanized. And not just the elderly. Those who have injuries. The paralyzed lady—I can't think of her name, but she was hurt when she fell down the stairs a few years ago. She died."

"And?"

"And she didn't die of natural causes. They killed her. They're killing anyone with anything wrong. Even Down syndrome."

"No, they didn't! Richard wouldn't do that."

"He did—or he ordered someone to. I'm sure of it. We had two people with Down syndrome in Prospect, right?"

"I don't know."

"Sure you do. Remember the lady who worked at the hardware store? Everyone loved her. And there was the teenager. Remember him? They've both disappeared—even their families are gone."

"Maybe they left, snuck out and went someplace else."

"All of them?"

"Rumors," I say, shooing her away like she's a fly. "The cantina is nothing but a rumor mill. And you shouldn't believe everything you hear. You're too gullible."

"No, I'm not. It's really happening. They're starting to do it to the people with autism too. Several have already vanished. Chance and his brother care for an autistic girl. They're worried for her."

I shake my head. "You're a conspiracy theorist."

"You wait. If you won't leave with me tonight, then you'll find out soon enough. How long do you think they can keep it a secret?"

"Keep what a secret?"

"The deaths! Seriously, Lucy. They're killing people and hauling them off at night to bury them."

"No one is even getting buried right now. With the frozen ground, it's all on hold until everything thaws out."

She stops for a minute as she absorbs what I've said. "Well, maybe you're right. But there is a group taking the people who are killed somewhere. Besides, do we even really know when someone dies? It's not like there's an announcement, other than with the explosion. How many have died this winter?"

"No idea. All I know is it's not me. And not you—yet. But if you leave . . . " I shrug.

"Come with us," she pleads. "You're not like some of them."

Could it be possible? Could we leave here and find someplace to hide out, to survive until this is all over? I shake my head. When will it be over? We've heard nothing about FEMA or anyone else coming to save us.

Richard is the only one. He stepped up and made a difference. Yes, we've had deaths, but most of us are strong and healthy. And Captain Murphy, I owe him too. He's the one who told me to join Mayor Majors. "We're set to move into the Bunn Mansion. The Bunn Mansion! Did you ever think you could live somewhere so luxurious?" I ask. "We'll be living comfortably in the middle of the apocalypse."

"I'm not doing it. I've told you. I've changed. Christ has changed me."

"Well, He hasn't changed me."

"Have you asked Him to?"

"That's not something for me. You can be a Christian if you want, but I prefer to get by on my own merit."

"Like how you got on the acquisition team?"

"You got on it the same way!"

"I'm aware, Lucy. I know exactly who I used to be. But now I'm different, and I have Jesus to thank. You could too. All you have to do is ask Him to forgive you and choose to follow Him."

I drop my head and let out a sigh. "I can't go. I won't say anything about you leaving, and if they ask, I'll play dumb. How are you planning to get out? We're supposed to move in just a few hours."

"I don't know." The way she says it makes me think she does.

I slip my arm around her shoulder. "You've been a great roomie."

# Chapter 31

## *Lucy*

Dirk Murphy arrives a few minutes before 3:00, driving a rickety old pickup, the kind that was probably just as ugly when it was new as it is today—at least sixty years later. "Ready to go?" he asks.

"Ready."

"The moving men were at the gate when I drove up. They should be along shortly."

"You probably didn't need to bring a truck," I say. "It's not like Maddie and I have much stuff."

"Probably true. And I doubt Alyssa has much either, but I do have a stop to make along the way to gather a few other items. There are the men now." He points toward a throng of five at the end of the block.

I recognize all of them as part of the working crew, including my former neighbor Toad and Maddie's boyfriend's brother Chase. I bite the inside of my cheek to keep the smile trying to make itself known at bay.

"Maddie ready?" Dirk asks.

I lift a shoulder. "Seems to be. She's in the backyard."

"It's a good day to get some sun. Maybe this hold winter has on us will finally let go."

"We'll see more snow," I say knowingly.

"No doubt. But at least it won't stick around forever. I was beginning to wonder. I can't remember ever having a winter like this one. Blizzards, sure. And snow on the ground for weeks—a month or two even. But this year it started snowing in, what, September? And we've had snow on the ground since then."

"I guess it's from the nukes."

"Yeah, must be. I wonder if it'll be like this next year too, and if we'll have a shorter summer than we should. It'll make it hard for growing the gardens and crops."

226

"We put in a nice garden at my apartment building last year—part of Mayor Stringer's Victory Garden plans." I wrinkle my forehead at the memory of the garden. Shelby Cameron, the girl who's part of our new hospitality team, was the main person who tended our garden. With her ready smile, she was always a pleasure to work with. Now she's an absolute wreck. What could've happened to her? Was her child really stolen from her? If so, it could explain her condition.

"Well, here they are," Dirk says when the men are within speaking distance. "We'll get you loaded."

I grab Maddie from the backyard while the men begin moving our things to the truck. While that's happening, Dirk tells us they'll get Alyssa's things and then it will be about an hour before the truck is at the Bunn Mansion. He tells us both we should keep our daypacks with us and walk over, meeting him when he arrives with the truck and our goods.

After Dirk drives the loaded truck away, the men fall in on foot behind him. Chase makes a point of turning around and giving me a wave and a wink—which I smartly ignore.

Maddie hoists her pack on her back and says, "I'll see you at the mansion."

"Where are you going? I figured we'd walk together. Maybe get Alyssa too."

"To see if I can find Chance. I'll meet you there."

I give her a long look. This is it. She's using this time to break out. I shake my head. "I hope you know what you're doing."

"I'll see you at the mansion. We're having a celebratory dinner tonight, right?"

As she practically trots off toward the entry gate, I grab my pack and head in the direction of Alyssa's house. She's not the most pleasant person, but maybe if I get past her rough edges, we'll . . . what? Be BFFs? Not likely. I do have to wonder about Richard Majors and his preferences. As I think of the six of us sitting with Mrs. Murphy yesterday, we're all very different.

Milena Maynard is a natural beauty, but she's really the only one of us. Not only is her face nearly perfect with a cute little button nose, but she's always been trim and athletic looking with an easy style about her. Alyssa and Star are each attractive but not in the same way as Milena. Their good looks are mostly youth related. And both are too skinny. Maddie is thin, too, but looks healthier—maybe it's because we get better food as part of the acquisition team.

Before Alyssa's brother moved to the team a few weeks ago, she wouldn't have been eating as well as she is now. While Maddie may look healthy, she's terribly plain, from her dishwater hair, uninteresting face, everything. There's nothing remarkable about her. Sure, she's pleasant and fun to be around . . . most of the time. But she's not attractive.

Neither is Shelby, not really. When things were normal, she was rather over the top. She wore a full face of makeup and outlandish clothing, which was way too form-fitting for her oversized body. She even wore ridiculous high heels—not at all normal for Prospect. She was already too tall, and with the heels, she towered over everyone, especially her short and scrawny husband. She was almost like a cartoon character with the way she dressed and even with some of her mannerisms. And like me, she was overweight, even heavier than I was. We're such a motley crew. Why would Richard choose women so different to be part of his . . . whatever it is he's putting together? It makes little sense.

When I reach the block where the newest families live, I take a quick look for the truck Dirk's driving, finding it parked in front of a light beige house with brown shutters. Its two-story design is like the house I live in . . . or I should say *lived* in, but its entry is more dramatic, and it has a huge three-car garage. Not that a garage is of much importance these days.

Dirk is on the lawn talking with Alyssa and an older man and woman. The woman is one I recognize from the kitchen, and the man is one of the do-it-all guys. I've seen him delivering wood or meals and shoveling snow. When Alyssa sees me, she leans into the group and says something before walking toward me.

"What are you doing here?" she asks.

"Do you want to walk with me to the mansion?"

She wrinkles her nose. "My parents want to walk me over. They're hoping to get inside and— " She gives a shrug. "You know, check the place out."

"Are they okay with you moving there?"

"What do you think?"

I shake my head. "It was a dumb question. Sorry."

"It's not like they have a choice in the matter."

"I would think they'd be happy you're going to be so well cared for."

"Yeah, well . . . I'll be walking over with them."

"Will they be allowed inside?"

She narrows her eyes. "Mr. Murphy said he'll see what he can do, but I know my dad, and he's not going to take no for an answer."

I lift a shoulder. "You did just say they don't have a choice about you moving over there. What makes you think— "

"Stop. Okay?" She turns and storms back toward her parents.

**Jeez. Testy much?**

Movement at the porch catches my eye as Chase walks out carrying a box. With his hands full, he lifts his chin in my direction. I shake my head and turn to go.

To give Dirk the time he requested, I take a circuitous route, choosing to walk along the creek instead of through town. There's a paved path starting from Creek View Estates and ending right before the old part of town. As I walk, I try not to think about anything, to just enjoy the moment, deeply inhaling the fresh smells.

Part of me feels I should be upset about this new team I'm being placed on. But I'm not. Like Richard said, it's safe. And I won't have to kill anyone. I've done my best to avoid actually pulling the trigger, but I haven't got out of it completely. I don't know if my aim was ever true enough for me to be the actual cause of someone's death, but I've tried. I've done what Doc Bohm and Richard both say is my duty as a soldier.

What if Maddie's right? What if the best thing to do is to escape Prospect and start a new life? She seems to think she can. Her God and her boyfriend are seemingly both okay with the things she's done. I think back to what she said about the soiled doves. It's not what I want. Neither was raiding people's homes, killing them, and stealing their property.

I could've done something different maybe—maybe left months ago when things started going bad. But Shelby left. She and her husband left, and look at her now. She's right back here and is now a complete basket case. No. I've made my choices. And really, how bad can it be?

When I reach the mansion, the pickup is out front. A quick glance in the bed shows it's already been emptied. Either I took longer than

I thought or Dirk was quicker than he said he'd be. As Dirk did yesterday, I use the heavy lion's head knocker to rap on the door.

After Mrs. Murphy invites me in, she suggests I may want a bath and then a nap before dinner.

"Do you have running water?"

"No, dear. But we have helpers who will bring water up for you. We've been preparing for your arrival, and it should only be a minute before it's brought up."

"Should I wait until Alyssa and Maddie arrive?"

"Alyssa is already here, and I'm sure Maddie will be along shortly. There's no need to wait."

"Oh . . . are her parents here? Alyssa's?"

"Alyssa rode over with Dirk. Her parents will visit another time. Go head up to your room. Please remove your shoes and carry them with you. There's already shoes in your room that are acceptable for wearing inside to help preserve the lovely floors."

My room is warm and cozy, thanks to a fire burning gently in the woodstove. The bath and nap are both wonderful. I'm still groggy when there's a knock on my door. One of the ladies who brought up the water sticks her head in and says dinner will be in an hour.

"Thank you, Donna," I say. Donna used to work at the SuperMart as a cashier. We weren't friends, but I'd try and choose her line when I'd shop. She was always friendly and efficient. She was exactly the same today, greeting me with a smile and quickly bringing up enough water for a decent bath, with help from an assistant. Unlike the huge, jetted tub at the hotel, this is a deep clawfoot tub. It's a little on the short side but still wonderful.

"Mrs. Murphy says you should dress smart casual."

"Smart casual," I repeat with a nod. When I arrived in my room earlier, I was surprised to find not only the clothing I'd packed, but also several things already in the closet, including a couple of cocktail dresses, a long formal dress, and several other pieces from blue jeans and sweaters to office attire. There are so many wonderful clothing choices, I wonder why I even packed the things from my old house. Those are all heavy-duty work clothes designed for training, hiking, and raiding. Not the kind of clothing one would wear in the Bunn Mansion. I certainly didn't pack anything I'd consider smart casual. Smart casual was my official dress code at the preschool. It meant I usually wore well-fitting jeans or trousers with a button shirt or sweater.

"She suggested the makeup on the vanity might be to your liking too."

"What's that mean?"

She tilts her shoulder. "I guess she wants you to put makeup on?"

I let out a laugh. "Who does that these days?"

She lifts her hands in a question and gently closes the door.

All the makeup is new. There's also perfume, lotion, and several different hair ties and clips. There's even a beaded headband thing I'm sure Maddie would love. I wonder where she is. Will she stay wherever Chance lives until they figure out a way to sneak out? Jason Hatch didn't seem too concerned about sneaking out, and he did get in easy enough, but it sounds terribly risky.

I choose my outfit first: skinny jeans in an impossibly small size I would've only dreamed of fitting in a year ago, a silky sleeveless top in white, and a long black velvet jacket. The jacket is amazing, shorter in front and longer in back, with a chiffon ruffle along the hem. I add a pair of chunky fashion boots from the closet and a long necklace, leaving my freshly washed hair loose and flowing. I strike a pose in the large mirror. Letting out a giggle, I decide I don't look too bad.

"I wonder what Chase would think?" I say aloud. The mirror reflects an immediate frown. What do I care? Besides, it's not Chase who's letting me live here. It's Richard Majors. I straighten my shoulders and head for the door, extinguishing the battery-operated lantern—one of the items I brought from my old house—on the vanity before I go.

The hallway is lit up and lovely, with flaming wall sconces lighting my way, the gentle fire combining with the glass covering it to make beautiful patterns as it bounces off the wallpaper. Although homes of this caliber may have been built with electricity in the year the Bunn Mansion was constructed, electrical lines had yet to be put in this far west. Electricity was added at some point and used during the tours, but the oil lamps and sconces were put in as part of a restoration to return to the original authenticity and preserve the history. Plus, it makes sense. If you're going to get people to spend money on a tour, it should be legit and how it used to be.

I'm steps from the bottom of the staircase when I stop and listen. Maddie's laugh is filling the parlor room off the entry. A pang of sadness overcomes me. Something must have gone wrong and she wasn't able to find a way out. But . . . she's laughing. Why would she be laughing? I paste a smile on my own face and smoothly stride in the direction of the festivities.

Like the hallway, the parlor is beautifully lit with wall sconces and oil lamps in various places. Maddie is talking with Star; both seem excited about something. Milena and a now very put together looking Shelby are sitting on one of the uncomfortable loveseats. Shelby visually looks much improved, with her hair now combed and piled stylishly on top of her head, plus a small amount of makeup that really brings out her cheekbones, but she's still staring off into space and holding onto Milena. Likewise, Milena has a vacant look about her as her free hand fiddles with a piece of loose yarn hanging off her sweater.

Alyssa is standing by the fireplace next to another woman a few years older than her who's wearing a red slinky dress, knee-high black boots, and a short leather jacket. She must be the final addition to Richard's new *endeavor* Mrs. Murphy mentioned. I wonder how she feels about being here. From the look on her face, my guess is she's happy.

"There you are, Lucy," Mrs. Murphy says, offering me her hands in greeting.

"I didn't realize I was late."

"You aren't. Everyone else was early. I guess the idea of a party brought out their excitement."

"Indeed."

"Mayor Majors will be around shortly. In the meantime, we'll have appetizers and cocktails in here before we move to the dining room."

"Cocktails?"

"We have a small number of spirits reserved for occasions like this."

"Oh, of course." While I know about the stockpile of alcohol, I also know there's a town-wide ban on the consumption of it—one of Richard's rules. It didn't turn out well for the few who've ignored the ban.

"Now, now. Don't worry about the mandate on alcohol," Mrs. Murphy says with a smile. "The mayor has a clause allowing it under very specific circumstances."

"It's good to be king," I mutter.

Mrs. Murphy gives me a tight smile before turning away.

# Chapter 32

## *Lucy*

Four members of the staff, dressed in black dresses or suits, walk around with trays of food and drinks. I wonder how many people Richard has brought in to act as help at the mansion. The cocktail turns out to be some sort of red wine and bourbon drink. I can't say I'm a fan; neither wine nor bourbon has ever been my thing. The appetizers, though, they're to die for. I quickly eat way more than I should and wonder if I'll even be able to have dinner.

From Mrs. Murphy's conversation with Dirk yesterday, I thought others would be joining us, but it's only us ladies and Mrs. Murphy. Alyssa, Star, and Red Dress, who introduces herself as Rebecca, are onto their second drinks when Richard arrives. Just like yesterday, he walks around and greets each of us.

"It seems you all are getting along famously," he says, a broad smile covering his face. "I'm so pleased. I want us all to be like one big family. Mrs. Murphy? How close are we to dinner?"

"About fifteen minutes, sir."

"Excellent. Excellent. Have the ladies seen the entire house?"

"No, sir. Only the east wing of the second floor and the parlor. I know you wanted to take them on the tour of the rest."

"Yes, thank you. Let's do that now. We'll, of course, avoid the kitchen where they're working and also the main floor servants' quarters."

The condescending way he says *servants* grates at me. Those spaces are on the first floor of the west wing, which I know from the historical tours. The main-floor east wing has many public and private rooms, including a library, three offices, a less formal parlor, a sunroom, and two half baths. Richard seems to marvel in describing each room in detail. So much so, we're well beyond the fifteen minutes allotted before dinner. He finally walks us to the palatial dining room where the much too large table is beautifully set.

233

"You'll each find a spot with your name on it," Richard says, seeming to enjoy playing the host. As we move to our seats, he asks, "And where is Miss Maddie?" I look around the room, not noticing she didn't walk into the dining room with us. "Mrs. Murphy, please send one of the servants to locate her. She must have become turned around in her beautiful new home."

"Right away, sir," Mrs. Murphy says, giving a look and raised chin to a man dressed in a smart-looking black suit standing near the kitchen door. He responds with a small dip of his head before disappearing into the kitchen.

"Let's take our seats while we wait," Richard says.

Like a mother and father, he's at one end of the table with Mrs. Murphy at the other. I'm on one side with Milena and Shelby. Alyssa, Star, and Rebecca are on the opposite side. Maddie's empty chair is next to Rebecca. After many minutes of small talk, in which Richard constantly checks his pocket watch, the suited man—who I've decided must be the butler, though he was never introduced—returns through the same door he exited.

When Mrs. Murphy sees him, she says, "Excuse me a moment."

"No need," Richard says, directing his gaze to the butler. "Where's the girl?"

"We were unable to locate her," the butler responds.

"Keep looking," Richard booms. "We'll begin our meal and she can join us when you find her."

"Uh, yes, sir. It's just—I don't believe she's in the house."

"Of course she's in the house! The daft thing just got herself turned around. Assign some of the servants not needed for dinner to find her. Then you will promptly return to begin the service."

I feel a smile threatening. She was smart to wait until after dark to make her escape. Hopefully, she has a good plan to get out of Prospect without being discovered by the guards. Jason seemed confident, but one person sneaking in is different than four people sneaking out.

As the dinner service begins, Richard becomes increasingly agitated when they fail to return with Maddie in tow. Missus Murphy, on the other hand, is the epitome of congeniality and influences the conversation in a positive direction.

Although Milena and Shelby fail to participate and seem to eat by remote control, the other three seem to enjoy themselves. I doubt any have ever had such a lavish dinner. I know I haven't.

234

The butler takes great pride in announcing each dish with a flourish as the staff scurries around—from the first course of mild yet flavorful soup, to a salad with lettuce and thinly sliced tomato, thanks to several greenhouses Richard commandeered for personal use, to a pasta made from butternut squash and slathered in browned butter.

"And now for the entrée," the butler says. "Smoked cheddar stuffed chicken with a green apple slaw."

"Yes, yes," Richard says impatiently.

"Will there be much more food?" Rebecca asks with wide eyes. Even though none of the portions have been large, it's been too long since any of us have eaten this much.

"Just the main course and then dessert," Mrs. Murphy says with a nod.

"I thought the entrée was the main course," Rebecca mutters.

"It's important for you to learn these things," Richard says. "There will be times when we entertain, and you'll need to at least pretend to be sophisticated. Tonight is a trial run to see how each of you behaves. Mrs. Murphy is keeping a keen eye on you, so she'll know where improvements are needed. So far, I'd say you have your work cut out for you, Candace."

Mrs. Murphy tilts her head in his direction.

Feeling terribly self-conscious, I gently dab at my lips with my napkin. While I know the basics of table manners, growing up, my family ate in front of the television with our plates propped on our laps. I've eaten in plenty of restaurants but never anything on a grand scale. And certainly never any more courses than a salad, main dish, and dessert.

The main dish following the chicken entrée is pork tenderloins with a cream sauce and gratin of root vegetables. By this point, I'm so full I can't even really savor the flavors. And Richard's demeanor has degraded drastically with each refill of his wine glass, making it exceedingly uncomfortable. Even Mrs. Murphy struggles to keep a lighthearted conversation going.

After dessert, a very dense pumpkin cake and actual coffee in tiny cups, Richard instructs the butler to send someone to Scott Majors's home and bring him to the mansion immediately. Scott, unlike Janet, Lassiter, and a few other officers who live near the mansion, lives in the Creek View Estates. He has the most lavish house in the development all to himself. Mostly to himself. It's no secret he *entertains* on a regular basis.

"I'd planned on all of us retiring to the den after the meal," Richard says once the butler leaves. "However, with the seeming disappearance of Miss Rivers, I'll excuse you to your rooms. Please be prepared to have your rooms searched within the hour." He stands and stomps out of the room.

"Please go ahead, ladies," Mrs. Murphy says. "We'll get past tonight and have more time tomorrow to get to know each other. I know creating a family is very important to Mayor Majors."

"Yeah?" Alyssa asks with a smirk. "I guess one of our *family* has run away."

"Can you blame her?" Milena asks quietly.

"Let's save our assumptions for another time," Mrs. Murphy says as she slides her chair away from the table.

My room is cozy warm with someone having stoked the fire while I was at dinner—possibly Donna, since she wasn't part of the meal serving. I change into yoga pants and a sweatshirt, then check the small bookcase in the room for something to read. I've barely settled into an easy chair and ottoman, which were added after I viewed the room yesterday, probably thanks to Star's suggestion, when there's a knock at the door.

"Come in," I call out proudly, like the lady of a fine manor.

"Miss Fleming," Doc Bohm says as he enters my room.

I immediately sit up straight, pulling my feet from the ottoman. "Oh, uh, hello. I didn't realize— "

"Of course you didn't. The mayor and the general have enlisted my assistance in locating your former roommate. I'm to look around your room and then ask you where she might be. My guess is we can skip the looking around. I'm sure she's left the premises. And I'm confident you know where she went."

As his eyes bore into me, I swallow the lump forming in my throat. Anyone but Doc Bohm and I'd be able to fake it, to lie and say I don't know anything. But with him, he has the ability to see right through me, to look deep inside me and know exactly what I'm thinking.

Maddie disappeared while we were on the tour. Richard took his time sending for help, letting us go through our entire extended dinner. Surely, by now, she's made her way out of town. And if they're still looking for her, she wasn't caught by one of the sentries. I clear my throat. "I think she may have gone to visit a friend."

"Chance Morgan?" Doc Bohm gives me a sly smile. "The mayor is aware of her *friendship* with the drifter."

"She probably just wanted to tell him goodbye, since we're . . . " I shrug.

"Yes, perhaps. I do believe the general has sent someone to his quarters to see if she's with him. But I suspect we won't be successful in locating them there."

I straighten my shoulders and meet his gaze. "She went to Meeteetse," I say in a rush. "She has a friend living there and thought it'd be a way to . . . to start over."

"Meeteetse?" he asks, raising his eyebrows.

"It's a little town south of Cody."

"I'm aware of its location. Why would she choose to go there?"

"She thinks it's out of Richard's—I mean, Mayor Majors's reach with it being in Park County instead of Prospector County." I nod vigorously.

"I see. And why didn't you go with her?"

"Why would I?" I ask, crinkling my forehead. "I don't—she's different. Over the last few months, she's found God or something. She thinks this . . . uh . . . she thinks this is sinful."

"And you don't?"

I give him a hard look. "I think I had the best meal of my life tonight. And by living in this house, no one is going to shoot at me, and I don't need to shoot at anyone either."

With a broad smile, he says, "That's one of the things I respect about you, Miss Fleming. You're practical. Unfortunately, Miss Rivers has her head in the clouds more than she should. I cautioned Mayor Majors about this." He lifts his hands. "But his decision is his to make. Is there anything else you wish to share with me?"

"Such as?"

"Perhaps the name of her friend in Meeteetse?"

I shake my head. "She didn't say."

"Of course not. Good evening, Miss Fleming."

"Doc Bohm," I say with a nod. As soon as he closes the door, I collapse into my chair. Saying she went to Meeteetse was an impulse. I think he may have even believed me. Leaning my head back against the chair, I think of Maddie and hope she's well away from Prospect.

237

If she's not, and they catch her, it won't go good for her. Especially considering Richard knows about her boyfriend. I just hope it's quick and she doesn't suffer. After several minutes, I try to return to my book. When my mind starts to wander, I decide moving to the bed is a good idea.

After changing into proper pajamas, thick flannel pink ones left in the dresser for me, I prop up the pillows for a comfortable reading position. My hand hits something hard under one of the pillows. Lifting the pillow off it, I find a Bible. *Maddie.* That girl just doesn't know when to quit. I pull it from the bed and plop it on the nightstand. As I return to my reading, my eyes keep drifting to the Bible. Maybe she left me a note in it?

Picking it up, I fluff it so any paper will fall out. When nothing does, I set the Bible on my lap. It's probably better she didn't leave me a note. If she had, I'd need to read it and then burn it in the woodstove. I thump the top of the Bible. It's a nice one, I guess, with a brown leather cover and a series of small cuts labeling the different sections. I put my finger into one of the grooves, opening to John. *The Word Became Flesh.*

Sure it did.

I shake my head but continue reading. "In the beginning was the Word, and the Word was with God and the Word was God. He was with God in the beginning." Even though I have no idea what *the Word* is, I keep reading about how through Him all things were made and how in Him was life and light.

Then I read about a man named John and then Jesus and how He was baptized by John. John called Jesus the Lamb of God. I've heard it before, among churchy people. The Lamb of God saves. Maybe Maddie even said it once when going on about how Jesus changed her life.

As I read, I decide I kind of like Jesus. He turns water into wine and even throws a bit of a fit in the temple, tossing over the tables. As I keep reading, I find a quote I've heard before about how God loved the world so much, He gave His only son so people could live forever. Blah, blah, blah. I almost quit reading there, but my attention is captured by the next section, which starts talking about light again.

"Light has come into the world, but men loved darkness instead of light because their deeds were evil. Everyone who does evil hates the light, and will not come into the light for fear that his deeds will be exposed. But whoever lives by the truth comes into the light, so that it may be seen plainly that what he has done has been done through God."

I can see how darkness and evil go hand in hand. When we attack an enclave, we do it while it's still dark, counting on the darkness to hide us. Before, I thought it made sense from a tactical standpoint, but I can also see how it could be truthful from an evil standpoint. But what we're doing, it's not evil. We're just doing our best to care for our town. Our scout teams always go and make contact in advance; they encourage the group or community to willingly join us.

## Do they?

I snap my head around. Letting out a small laugh, as I realize I'm hearing things. Closing the Bible, I reach to set it on the side table. No. That's not a good place for it. What would Mrs. Murphy or Donna think if they saw it in my room? Best to toss it in the fire and forget about it. As I start to move from my bed, I decide to tuck it under the mattress instead. I'm warm and don't want to get out from under the covers.

After it's in place and I settle back in, I think about the whisper I heard in my head. *Do they?*

Yes, of course they do. Scott always tells us about how they contacted a group and were turned away. The groups always think they can get by on their own. They don't seem to realize, if they were to join us, they'd be much better off. And alive.

Richard's rules are clear. They're either with us or against us, and he doesn't take any chances. If they're against us, they could attack. We only attack first to save the lives of our people. Richard always says that if we can save even one life, it's well worth it. Surely, he's right.

# Chapter 33

*Mollie*

Tomorrow, the militia involved in the offensive attack on Prospect will leave the mountain. I look across the table at Sarah. She's holding Tate while talking softly to Andy. She's nervous about going but still insists it's the right thing. The plan is to have our troops arrive at different times and in different locations. With people like the Camerons, who know the area extremely well, we're hopeful we can find well-hidden spots to cold camp until it's time to begin the assault.

Mike, Roy, Katie, Leo, and Art are also all leaving tomorrow. Mike's injury last week almost prevented him from going, but we're so short on people, Belinda reluctantly cleared him. Other than a minor headache, he's recovering well from being knocked in the head. Alvin, who was originally accepted on the assault team and part of the hiking group, is now on the home guard. With Aaron breaking his leg, his mobility issues make overseeing the guard next to impossible.

Alvin's now co-leader. It's odd to me they'd pick Alvin for the job, but Evan's reasoning made sense. Alvin's an experienced hunter and stays calm under pressure. Aaron will still be able to do a good amount of the coordinating, but he needs someone able-bodied, and Alvin fits the bill.

As has become the norm, we're staying behind after lunch to discuss the operation. We learned our lesson after the first meeting, which started before lunch ended and the children were still with us. We now wait until everyone's finished and the children are moved to the nursery. Things can get a little heated, and the discussions tend to be brutally blunt, especially from some of our elders who have gone to war before. And as Reggie Roberts has said many times, we should make no mistake—this is war.

"All right, let's get to it," Evan says, standing by his table. "Doris, do you have the new lodging assignments?"

"Such as they are," she answers from her wheelchair, her rebroken leg propped up. "Everyone who's leaving tomorrow and lives in this building must have their personal items stowed before you go. Your neighbors will be sleeping in your bed and pawing through your drawers."

The way she opens her eyes wide and gives a wacky expression results in a few complimentary laughs. Though, with the seriousness of recent events and what's about to happen, no one really feels like laughing. The tension surrounds us. The killings by the Prospect teams, then by Shannon and Roscoe, combined with our need to go on the offensive, has everyone on edge.

The supply house was cleaned and then closed. It's being used to store gear for the militia members who live in the ski lodge while they're gone. With everyone moving into this one building, we need all the space we can get. Since only a small portion of our residents live in the ski lodge, with most living in cabins, their own recreational vehicles, or one of the houses, we'll be tight on space. Beginning tomorrow, we'll move in additional beds after the foot soldiers head out, using part of the dining room as a giant dorm.

"And remember," Doris says, "home guard should expect to hot rack. The bunk beds on the second floor and in two of the dorm apartments are being rearranged for your use. When you're off duty, just find a bed to sleep in. We'll try to keep the children in their own spaces so they have the familiarity."

To help with the familiarity, the nursery is remaining unchanged. Someone originally suggested that'd be the best place to put the new beds, and it certainly would be, compared to right out in the open. But we still need a place to care for the children, now more than ever since so many of the parents will be gone.

"Anything else, Doris?" Evan asks.

"Other than the obvious—keep praying—we're set for tomorrow."

Evan gives a nod. "Okay, for the home guard, I know some of you are less than happy about staying behind." He looks directly at Tim and then glances to Alvin.

From his own wheelchair, with a splint cast from his ankle to his hip, Aaron raises a hand. When Evan acknowledges him, he says, "I think we're in good shape. Alvin and I have a first draft of the schedule. We're ready to have the home guard as sentries starting tomorrow."

Tim opens his mouth to say something but seems to think better of it as he gives a shake of his head. Alvin chooses to speak his mind. "While I did think you were just putting me out to pasture," he says with a hard look. "I can see the necessity of staying here. But I think you're off base. We've got eyes on those butchers from Prospect. With our team watching, it's not likely they'd sneak up on us."

"If they leave as a large group," Evan says evenly. "It's unlikely they'd get past our team. However, if they were to go out in smaller guerrilla units of one or two— " He lifts his hands. "The Prospect henchmen are not our only concern. You're all well aware we moved up here because it's more defensible than Bakerville, which was too spread out. When we first started the plans for the move, it was because of attacks from small groups of raiders. We didn't even know about the threat from Prospect until Paul Cameron and his party came riding into Bakerville."

"I know all that," Alvin says. "I'm old but not senile. I'm just saying, it seems to me the more of us you have with you, the better our odds of ending Richard Majors's murderous reign once and for all."

There's a general mutter through the room, mainly from the ones who've been ordered to stay behind. There was some disagreement early on when Clark Thomas and his deputies started training with the militia. The general consensus was they should be the ones staying behind and overseeing the home guard. After much back and forth, it was finally agreed that having them as part of the attack team made sense. Well, maybe not agreed but it was accepted. While the home guard group isn't large, it's vocal.

Like Alvin, most of them are older but still capable. All of them started intensive training after Lindsey and the others were murdered, in anticipation of being part of the assault. And other than a few, they made the cut to go to Prospect, having to be medically cleared, performing basic self-defense moves, and passing an agility test. Everyone going to Prospect or on the home guard was tested on the range, not only dry firing but also using our precious ammo.

The home guard isn't only the aged. Tim with his broken wrist wasn't cleared, and neither was Grant Cameron—husband of kidnapped Shelby. In his case, there was concern he wouldn't be able

242

to stick with the mission and would instead go in search of Shelby and possibly not be able to contain himself properly. Begrudgingly, he admitted to this and now seems to accept the need to defend the people at the lodge, including his young daughter.

Plus, everyone over the age of fourteen staying behind has been given a refresher course on weapons training and basic self-defense. Even the less mobile in wheelchairs or using walkers, canes, or other aids will be expected to fight as needed. Our young sons have also been practicing their archery and self-defense as backups. Just like they did what they needed to do with their pocketknives when Dawson's goons attacked, they'll do what is necessary. And I hate it. I hate my children can't just be children.

"You're right about how we need the numbers," Evan says. "And I'll admit, taking more of you would probably be smart. But I can't in good conscience leave us vulnerable. And not just vulnerable for the time of the attack on Prospect. Most of us in the room have never gone into a real battle before. Cole Gunderson and a handful of others have seen warfare. Reggie Roberts, Walt Pritchard, Dick Johnston—they've been in the thick of it before. And they'll tell you, not everyone comes home. We will lose people in this attack. There will be bloodshed. There will be deaths. You, Aaron, Tim, Grant, Noah Hammer, and the others who have been chosen to stay and defend our people will be needed in the future."

"You're going in as attackers," Walt Pritchard says from his chair, his walker sitting next to him. "That gives you an extreme disadvantage. No one should be under the impression this will be a cakewalk."

"True," Evan agrees. "We've all talked about how we'd be in a better position to let them come to us. But we don't have the luxury."

"It's a fool's errand," someone calls out. "You're going to get everyone killed."

"Reggie, I know how you feel about this," Evan says. Reggie Roberts has been vocal from the beginning about the plans to go after Majors. As a veteran who made the Army a career, he's seen the worst of the worst. Even though he's against the assault, he's still part of the group leaving tomorrow. He says he feels it's his duty, even though he's confident all of us will be wiped out.

"Just so we're clear," Reggie says. "And once we're dead, your little home guard isn't going to be enough."

"That's why we have the watchers," Cole Gunderson says. "If things go bad for us and Richard Majors sends his troops after the families, the watchers will see them coming and everyone will bug out."

"Psh," Reggie says. "You're under the mistaken idea he won't pursue them. People like Majors don't quit. You ought to know that, Gunderson."

"I do know. Which is why I completely support us going after him and ending this for good. Otherwise, we live in fear, waiting for him to come after us, the way it's been since the shooting. How much longer can we keep it up?"

"Fair enough," Reggie says as he lifts his hands in a surrender motion. "Not like you're going to listen to me anyway. If we were smart, we'd hightail it out of here—move the whole community as far from here as possible."

"And you think that will guarantee safety?" Clarice asks, a slight quiver to her voice. "I've seen what's out there. Cooke City, Montana—which as the crow flies isn't far from here, right? You heard about the condition of their town?"

I close my eyes. I've tried not to think about the people I met in Cooke City last summer when I was trying to make my way home. I was accidentally injured, and they cared for me. Clarice, Liam, and the girls went through there. The town was gone; all the buildings were burned to the ground, and they saw several bodies. I can only assume those helpful to me, whom I considered friends, are now dead.

"If it's not this Richard Majors character," Clarice says in a stronger voice. "It will be someone else. There's no place to hide."

"Clarice is right," Evan says. "Right now, we need to stand firm and deal with Majors. If we're not victorious, the watchers will know and hightail it back here to take people to safety. It's the best we can— " His voice cuts off as the radios he and Cole are wearing sound. Evan motions to Cole, who gives a nod and starts walking toward the door, while Evan turns his radio down.

Because of the arrangement of the tables, Cole's weaving around one when the voice on the other end plainly says, "We've got visitors."

Someone at a nearby table cries out, "We're under attack!"

Evan shakes his head. "That's not what they said. Cole, just take it in here. Everyone, pipe down so he can hear."

Cole raises the radio to his mouth and asks for a repeat.

"This is Andrew Hammer. I'm in the south tower with a relay from the east. They tried to call you directly, but— "

"Go ahead, south tower," Cole says.

"They have five people approaching—three males and two females—on the main road less than a mile from the Young's house. East tower is requesting a greeting party."

# Chapter 34

## *Mollie*

As the room explodes with voices yelling and crying out that we're under attack, Evan calls for quiet. He takes his own radio off his belt and responds the greeting party is on its way. To those of us in the dining room, he yells, "Listen up. Foot soldier team Alpha, you're with Major Gunderson." He turns to Cole. "Set them up as back up."

"Yes, sir," Cole says, then he calls out, "Militia room, now." The militia headquarters is near the ski lodge and houses backup weapons for this purpose—when they're needed and people may not have a rifle on them. In the dude ranch area, we have an armory set up for the same purpose. While almost everyone has a sidearm on their hip, not everyone on the militia carries a rifle around. A group of around twenty, including Mike and his dad Roy, are immediately on their feet and moving to the coat rack.

"Security team, you're with me," Evan says, his voice elevated above the people moving around. Unlike the regular militia, the security team is always ready to go, wearing their full gear and outfitted with complete weaponry. They'll grab their jackets on the way out, but other than that, they're ready. "Alvin. Aaron. Your home guard is on. You'll have the rest of the foot soldiers to use also." Evan starts to turn but pauses and says, "Overwatch and spotters, to the militia room."

I suck in a breath and meet Angela's eyes as Jake, sitting next to me, squeezes my shoulder. We quickly move to grab our coats and get to the militia room, where the specialty long-range weapons are stored. The .308 Angela uses is in our lodge since it's my personal rifle, as is the 7 Mag Ultra Jake uses.

"I don't even have my binoculars," Angela says as we go out the door.

Evan is right behind us and says, "There's extras in the militia room. Get a rifle too. Jake, get a 5.56 and catch up to me. You'll be with my team." At the militia room, Evan has a brief conversation with Cole and is again on the move.

Jake's grabbing an AR when Cole Gunderson says, "Jake, we need your truck. Where are the keys?"

"On the dashboard," Jake says as he hurries to catch up with Evan. He takes a few steps, turns, and mouths, "I love you," before spinning on the ball of his foot and hustling off.

Angela is also given an AR to use. "Overwatch and spotters, along with you five," Major Gunderson says, motioning to a group of his foot soldiers, "take Caldwell's truck and hightail it into position. I want two snipers on either side of the road, high and hidden. Dusty and Pete, you're taking the north side at the knoll where we saw those wolves a few months ago. You know where I mean?"

When both say they do, Cole says, "Space out with your spotters and put these three between you." He motions to three of his foot soldiers who were singled out earlier. "Dax, you're across the road on the high spot between the two houses. You'll have these two with you." He motions to the remaining foot soldiers. "Mollie Caldwell, park your truck in the wide spot between the two houses and set up there."

I narrow my eyes at him, thinking the road is a terrible place for me and Angela to be because it's out in the open. He quickly says, "Use the terrain to your advantage. Keep the truck on the downhill side so it's not visible. If you go up slightly, you'll have a clean view down the road."

I nod as I think about the area. There's an incline there with a ditch off to the side to keep us hidden.

One of the other foot soldiers says, "Maybe we shouldn't have cleared the road so far and people wouldn't be walking up it." Since we moved up here, the snow grooming machine has kept the main road cleared to the Young's house so we can easily get them back and forth for group events at the lodge and so they can get their food.

As we've started planning for our insurrection into Prospect, the machine has cleared the road many miles down to make our approach on Prospect easier. They stopped clearing when the snow melt was enough so our few running vehicles won't have any trouble. While we've had some decent melt of the winter snow, the lower elevations are melting much faster.

"The rest of you," Cole says, choosing to ignore the man, "we're double timing. Let's move."

As we get to our truck, Angela announces she'll drive. The rest of us pile in the cab and bed. Everyone else can easily reach their stations from where Cole wants us to park. Angela starts off faster than she should and fishtails out of the parking lot.

"Slow and easy," I say. "Let's put it in four-wheel drive."

Angela gives a nod, lets off the throttle, and engages the four-high. The road between our lodge and the dining hall is so well traveled we rarely need to gear down, except after a fresh heavy snow, but with Angela's adrenalin pumping and having to drive on the main road, extra traction makes sense. Minutes later, she stops the truck where Cole ordered, turning it slightly so the nose is facing the shallow ditch. She has the truck at the beginning of the pull out where it'll be hidden from those approaching.

As everyone bails out, Dusty Cameron says, "Don't get itchy fingers. Remember, we always watch for the signal."

"Got it," I say, wishing we'd been given radios. Evan has trained us on hand signals, but the radios are what we've been using while getting ready for the Prospect incursion. I don't worry about getting *itchy fingers*, as Dusty said. One thing I've practiced over and over is to keep my finger away from the trigger until go time.

"And remember," Pete says, "Know your backup locations. Mollie, your best option is going to the other side of the road."

"Yep," Angela says. "I noticed a good setup there when we were driving up. Then slightly up the hill from there for spot three."

"Should work," Dusty says. "Let's move, folks."

"Grab the small shovel," I say to Angela. She gives a nod. We walk hunched over to the top of the hill. Once we're there, we scoot down in the ditch.

"You want me to dig out a spot? Or we could scoot up the hill a little." She points to the right of the ditch. "There's a boulder."

"The boulder isn't big enough for both of us. Think you can see from the ditch while I use the boulder as a rest?"

Angela nods and then points. "Across the road is a fallen tree. For our secondary position, we move back down the hill and then hustle across the road? Use the ditch to get to the tree?"

"Yep. As good a plan as any. See a third spot for us?"

She glances up the hillside. "Just like we thought. Halfway up the hillside right before the road crests. Can you make it?"

I look at the hill. *Can I?* I give a slight nod. "And then we bug out. Get back to the truck and retreat to the high spot by the edge of the corral. That's where we make our stand."

"I hope it doesn't come to that," Angela says. "Can you crawl into position? I'm ready."

I stay low and crawl up the hill on my stomach, then turn until I'm at the boulder. Angela crawls into the ditch, moving until she can see but is still hidden. We're lined up next to each other, though I'm on a higher grade.

In a low voice, she says, "They're still a good distance, but it looks like everyone's waving a white flag."

I let out a breath I didn't realize I was holding. I move so I can see. "Let's hope they mean it." Just in case they don't, I get into a comfortable position. The rock isn't ideal, making it more of a rest than allowing me to lie prone, my most stable position.

As they continue to walk slowly yet purposely up the center of the road, slight movement in the trees on the north side catch my eye. "There's the team," Angela says in a low voice.

Within seconds, Evan calls out, "That's far enough." The five people in the middle of the road stop. Each of them wave their flags of surrender and make sure their other hands are visible. "State your business," Evan demands.

The five are still far enough away. I can't hear the answer, but it's one of the men who responds.

"Say again?" Evan says. After listening for a few seconds, he asks, "Tell me your wife's name."

"What's going on?" Angela asks.

"I'm not sure, but I think it's someone looking for their wife."

"Who could it be? None of the women living here are without their husbands—well, who don't know where they are. Except— Mom! Do you think? Could it be Tate?" She quickly moves the binoculars back up to her eyes.

My heart skips several beats as I look through my scope. Tate— could it be him? I look for the man whose lips are moving, trying to determine if it's Tate. A quick glance over the other two men and I quickly confirm neither is Tate's dad, Keith, who was with him when they went missing. And I don't know the two women at all. I look again at the man talking. He's got a full beard and seems skinny. He's shorter than the other two men but is considerably taller than both women.

"It's not Tate," Angela says sadly.

"No . . . it's not," I agree. "But he does seem familiar—just the one guy. The other two, they must be brothers with as much alike as they look."

"Twins even," Angela says. "The woman and the girl, though, they don't seem related."

"Girl?" I ask, looking again at the women. She's right. One is late teens or early twenties and the other is younger, midteens maybe.

"Throw the flag on the ground," Evan says. "Then you step forward. Keep your hands visible and remove your jacket."

After the man talking does as asked, Evan directs each of the other men, then the woman and the girl, to follow suit. When he's satisfied, they're spread out on the road away from their jackets with several feet between each of them. Seconds later, his team appears out of the woods and is on them. The young girl screams loud enough it's almost piercing, even at this distance. She tries to run—which results in the other four yelling what I assume is to "calm down" or "hold still." She's grabbed and, like the others, taken to the ground, not in a violent manner but assertively.

"I guess that's it?" Angela asks.

"Might be. We'll wait until we're told to stand down."

"I hope that's soon. I'm not wearing enough clothes today to be crouching in this ditch."

As a shiver runs through my body, I nod my agreement. It was almost springlike this morning, but now the wind is picking up. It's not uncommon to have snow well into the middle, even the end of May. Since I've lived in Wyoming, I only remember one Mother's Day without snow. Right now, even though I'm wearing my winter jacket with a sweatshirt underneath, I'm without insulated pants or gloves. At least I have a neck gaiter and stocking cap on. Angela isn't even wearing a heavy coat. She's only in a hooded sweater with a turtleneck underneath.

We watch as Evan, Jake, and several members of the security team start marching the prisoners up the road. Once they're within a hundred yards of us, Evan searches me out and motions me to stand down. I tell Angela we're moving, then slide out of my spot. The ache in my back is so bad I can barely stand upright.

"You okay?" Angela asks.

"Yeah, I'll be fine." She gives me a piercing look, which I return with a tight smile. "Really. It's just from being in the same position too long." I give a vigorous nod. "And the cold. The cold makes it worse."

Standing on the side of the road, we wait for Evan and his crew to reach us. Up close, the youngest girl looks even younger, maybe only twelve, and she also looks terrified. The woman and one of the tall men seem to be speaking to her. I focus on the oldest man. He's the same height as Jake's six feet. The two men with him—definitely related but not identical—are much taller, over six-five. The man's probably in his forties, with his hair and beard both overgrown and unkept.

The tall men, while also bearded, lack the scruffiness. Their hair is tidy with nothing sticking out from under their stocking caps, and their beards are even trimmed and neat. They have the look of city folk who dress up as lumberjacks, where the other guy looks like an actual lumberjack. He looks like our men look. Up close, his skinniness is even more pronounced, much skinnier than the other four, resembling Ben and his group when they arrived malnourished.

He gives me a slight smile. When the smile spreads to his blue eyes, tears sting my own as I recognize him. I quickly look to Jake, my face a question: *am I seeing who I think I'm seeing?*

Jake lifts his shoulders slightly, then gives a tilt of his head followed by a very weak nod. He thinks so too. It's our former neighbor Jason Hatch—husband to Olivia, who was killed by Dan Morse in the early days of the havoc, and father to Tony and Lily, our informally adopted children.

I start to walk toward them when one of the security team says in a rough voice, "Keep your distance."

"Hey," Jake admonishes him.

I shoot the security guy a look, then turn to Evan. "It's Jason Hatch."

Jason's smile grows wide as he says, "That's what I've been telling him."

"Yeah," Evan says. "He's told us. I didn't know him but in passing. Jake thought so, but said you'd know for sure since you knew him better. And with the *situation* . . . " He lifts his hands.

I turn to Jason. "It's a miracle you're here."

"I told Olivia I'd be here soon," he says with a nod. "Just didn't expect it to take me the better part of a year." He turns to Evan. "Let's get on with whatever you need to do to vet me. I'd like to see my family."

I chew on the inside of my upper lip as I try and keep my face straight. I must have failed because one of the other men quietly asks, "What's wrong?"

# Chapter 35

## *Mollie*

"Load them into the back of the pickup truck," Evan says. "Leo, Harv, Watson, you're with me as guards. The rest of you are on foot. We'll take them to Clark's accommodations until we can sort this out." Clark Thomas's accommodations is our jail. I start to protest—at least about Jason—when Evan raises his hand. He lifts his radio, and says, "Gunderson, report."

Within a few seconds, Cole Gunderson responds, "Nothing happening."

"Copy that. East tower, report."

"All clear."

Evan then asks the south and north towers for their reports. Because of our location and the way the radios work, the east tower does a relay to and from the south before we find out they're also clear. Evan tells Cole to keep his team in the field until he's had a chance to talk with the newcomers. That's what he calls them, newcomers, instead of prisoners. He sends word via a relay back to the home guard, letting them know they're returning.

"Did you want Angela and me to stay here?" I ask Evan as they begin to load into the truck.

"Not necessary. I think you and Jake might as well join us as we have our chat. You probably knew him better than most."

I raise my eyebrows. I knew Jason in passing only. He and Olivia had moved to Bakerville a few years ago from the West Coast. They rented a small house over the hill from me. While I'd talked to them when we'd seen them at community events—and our sons would play together—I didn't really *know* them. In fact, other than the people they rented from, who were away on vacation when the attacks started, they weren't close with anyone in the community. Like many of us, they were busy.

Jason worked in the oil fields and was gone for weeks at a time. Olivia worked in Prospect until a few months prior when she switched to telecommuting. And believe me, telecommuting isn't a great way to get to know your neighbors. Besides, what does it matter how well we knew him? I have no doubt he is who he says he is, and his children will be able to confirm the fact instantly.

Jake touches my arm and says, "Hop in, Mollie. We'll let Evan figure this out."

Once we're inside the truck, with the security team and prisoners in the back and Jake driving, from the back seat, Angela asks, "Is it really Tony and Lily's dad?"

"Absolutely," I answer. "And I don't know why we aren't taking him straight to his children."

"Evan thinks it's suspicious he's showing up now," Jake answers.

"Why would it be?" Angela asks.

"It isn't," I scoff. "You know how hard travel can be. If he were on foot—which from his frame, I'd say he was—then it'd take a while."

"How'd he find us?" Jake asks. "It's not like we left a note in his house saying we were moving up to the ski lodge."

"Their house burned down," Angela says.

"I know," Jake says. "I'm just saying it seems a little suspicious. And we don't know who the others are. Jason introduced them. The girls are from Prospect, but none of us knew them. The men were vacationing in the area when the attacks happened. There are questions we need answered, especially considering what Prospect has done to us and what we plan to do to them."

"I agree," I say. "But that *is* Jason Hatch. And his children—*our children*—need to see their father."

"I guess . . . " Angela starts. "I guess they'll— "

"Yes," I say quickly. "I guess they will. And I'm so glad Tony and Lily will have their dad back. But I'd be lying if I didn't admit to feeling like I'm losing something."

"They'll always be our children, Mollie," Jake says. "Whether they're with us or their dad, we'll still love them the same."

I stare out the window as tears fall down my face. The dichotomy of emotions almost overwhelms me. I'm praising God for Jason's return, while feeling like I'm losing a piece of my heart. My hand goes to my mouth as I realize this is the answer to one of my prayers—my concern Jake will be overwhelmed taking care of three young children when I'm gone. I knew God would make a way, but I figured it'd be with the rest of our extended family pitching in as everyone does now.

"Thank you, Jesus," I whisper quietly.

As we get to the parking lot, Jake cranks down the window of our old ranch truck, asking Evan, "You want me to drive across the bridge and try and make it up the hill? Or you want to walk them?"

"I'm not feeling that adventurous today. Let's just walk."

Jake turns to me. "Should I get the snowmobile to zip you up?"

"I'm going up to find Tim and Gavin," Angela says as she opens her door.

I get out of the truck as Evan and his team unload Jason and the others. "I can walk," I say to Jake. "I'm still feeling fine."

"You sure?"

"Yeah. I walked up before lunch, remember?"

"A lot has happened since lunch."

"No kidding," I mutter.

Once we're across the bridge, I take a deep breath. It smells like spring. The ice melting off the creek and some of the deciduous trees growing along the water are beginning to bud. I want to cherish this day, the memory of the children of my heart's father returning from the dead. I only need to stop and catch my breath twice before we make it to the top of the hill and the jail. Jake opens the door for me, and we step inside the sparsely lit room, giving our eyes a minute to adjust. While waiting, I remove my hat and neck gaiter. The room is plenty warm, thanks to the roaring fire in the woodstove.

At the back of the building are two makeshift cells—the same ones we used to house Shannon, Roscoe, and Heath in the months since the insurrection. Now only Heath remains. Currently, he's in his cell while the other five are in the second. After we finish with Prospect, we need to determine what to do with Heath for the long term. Mike supports Heath's statement that he wasn't involved in the escape. He seemed completely surprised when Shannon and Roscoe began their attack. But his attempted escape, beating his wife, and involvement in Dawson's uprising can't be ignored.

"Hey, Mollie. Jake."

"Hi, Clark," I say as Jake and Deputy Clark shake hands. It's always funny to me how often men who see each other on a regular basis still shake when greeting. Clark's that way, though, always respectful and seems pleased to see his friends.

In a quiet voice, Clark says, "I know Evan was waiting for you and Kelley Hudson to arrive before talking to Jason. It's definitely him."

"We know," Jake says with a smile.

I give a nod as tears again fill my eyes. "Where's Kelley?" I ask.

"Not sure. We sent for her. You've done right by his children, and I know you've loved them as your own."

"So he doesn't know about Olivia yet?"

"Not yet. Thought it'd be best with— "

"Mollie? Jake? C'mon over here," Evan says. Only Leo and Harv from the security team remain with Evan.

Clark walks with us to the lockup. As we near the area, Jason says, "Mollie, could you go get my wife so we can clear this up?"

"Step to the door, Jason," Evan says. "The rest of you, go against the far wall."

The cells, added in the early days of our move to the mountain, are reminiscent of an actual jail but modified to use what we had available. The building was already in place, built as a large lean-to type of structure against the ski lodge and used for storage.

The back of the building butts up against the ski lodge but was reinforced with six-inch logs to prevent any prisoners from busting through, same with the already existing sidewalls. The front walls of the cells were added out of poured concrete to four feet, then rebar to the roof so there's at least a partial view of the occupants. Then, on each cell is a steel door salvaged from buildings in Bakerville. It must be secure, or Shannon and Roscoe would've busted out when locked up instead of on work duty.

"Yes, sir," one of the tall men answers.

After Jason is quickly taken out of the cell, Heath, who's watching with rapt interest, says, "Hey. I know you. Your wife was that tiny little blond girl, right?"

"That's enough, Heath," Clark orders.

"Why do you have him locked up?" Jason asks, jutting a finger in Heath's direction.

"We can discuss that later," Evan says.

Jason blinks a few times and then looks at Heath. "You're Dot's husband, right? Tell them you know me."

"Your identity is no longer in question," Clark says, while Evan says, "Step over here, Jason."

"Wait a minute," Jason says, a look taking over his face. He turns back to Heath. "What do you mean *was*?"

"Over here, Jason." Evan motions to the table and a chair he has pulled out.

Jason spins toward Evan. "He said my wife *was* that tiny blond girl. Is my wife—where's Olivia? I want you to bring her to me right now."

"Have a seat," Evan says, pulling out a chair. He's using his cop voice, a tone that leaves no doubt he's in charge.

"She's dead, isn't she?" Jason asks as he sits limply in the chair. "My children?"

"I'm sorry, Jason," Evan says. "Olivia—we lost her last summer."

Jason raises his hands to his face and scrubs at his eyes.

"Your children, though, they're fine. They've been living with Mollie and Jake."

"Thank you," Jason says, his voice quiet and haggard. He lifts his face so he can first meet Jake's gaze and then my own. "What happened— " His voice cracks. In a near whisper he asks, "Olivia?"

"There's time for that later," Evan says, then turns to Jake and me. "Have a seat?" he asks, motioning to the other two chairs surrounding the round table. Jake pulls out my chair before taking his own.

"I think I knew about her. About Olivia," Jason says. "I had a feeling." He lets out a long, slow breath. "Did she suffer?"

"We don't think she did," Clark answers—not the answer I would've given, considering she was kidnapped prior to being murdered, but it's the right answer to give her grieving husband.

Jason nods and again puts his hands to his face.

Once we're seated, Evan says, "We'll answer all your questions, and as soon as we know you're not here to mean us any harm, we'll let you see them."

He drops his hands and looks at Evan with narrowed eyes. "Mean you harm? I came home for my family. I found my house burned down and Bakerville deserted. I've been looking for them. I just want my family. I'm not here to *harm* anyone."

"And your friends?" Clark asks.

"They're from Prospect."

"Prospect!" I cry out.

"Mollie," Evan says in a warning voice.

I shut my mouth with a nod. We're watching Prospect, and yet here they are.

"Do you know what Prospect's like?" Jason asks. "It's a rathole. Worse than a rathole. They're euthanizing people, killing the elderly and the disabled. They had to get Joely out. She's on the spectrum. It was only a matter of time."

"Which one is Joely?" I ask, which earns me a look of reprimand from Evan. I lift a shoulder in apology.

"That's Joely," Jason says, pointing to the girl. Unlike the other three who are standing at the front where the half wall is filled in with rebar, she's sitting on one of the cots. I can only see her head, but she seems to be fascinated with something on the ground. "She's only thirteen. Her parents were killed months ago. The brothers—Chance and Chase—they've been looking out for her. And now with Maddie . . . she knows things. She'll tell you."

I look to the cage where the woman is nodding vigorously. "I will. I was— " She takes in a breath and looks to one of the brothers.

He gives her a nod.

She turns back to us. "I was on the acquisition team."

Evan's face goes hard as he spins toward her. With a voice like ice, he asks, "You were on the team that attacked us?"

"No," she says, shaking her head vigorously. "I wasn't on the mission. But I know about it. We had a meeting, and Major Lassiter told us. Uh, his version of events, anyway."

"Major Lassiter?" Clark says slowly. "Fred Lassiter?"

I feel myself pale. Fred Lassiter. Former jailer for Prospector County Sheriff Department who advanced to Deputy of Bakerville early in the attacks. Deputy Fred was our law enforcement until we discovered he was a criminal himself, having purchased a wife and children. We only discovered his horrific deeds when Cheyre, the youngest girl, escaped. After Fred was captured, a group was transporting him to Prospect for justice when he killed his guards and disappeared. Many believed Deputy Fred had fled the area, but now . . .

"I think Fred is his name," she says in a hesitant voice. "We don't call him by his first name. He, uh . . . he wouldn't like that."

Evan and Clark share a look before Evan asks, "What else can you tell us?"

"There's a resistance."

"We've heard about it. One of the murderers sent here said there was a bomb detonated in Prospect Hotel, killing Majors's wife."

"Ha," one of the brothers scoffs. "That wasn't the resistance. Majors planted the bomb himself."

"What?" I exclaim. "Why would he do that?"

"To blame the resistance and get rid of his wife. He has a— " He pauses and looks to Maddie.

"He has a group of women," Maddie says. "Being one of his group gives extra privileges. But I think his wife was probably preventing his full plans."

"And now, he's moved a few women into the Bunn Mansion. That's where he's living now after the explosion at the hotel."

"A few?" Evan asks. "We heard about one."

"Right," the man says. "She was kidnapped from here?"

Evan tilts his head. "You tell me."

The other brother nods and takes over. "We heard a rumor she was kidnapped, but we don't know where from. Majors knew her before and ordered her found. Then, a few days ago, Maddie was told she and another lady used to live here."

"What about the other one?"

"She'd been living at the bordello, but after the explosion, Majors claimed her too," Maddie says. "I've seen them. Talked to both. They're . . . alive, living at the Bunn Mansion."

I feel myself smile. We were worried Shelby might have been sold and taken elsewhere, resulting in us never finding her. If this is true, if Milena and Shelby are both living with Richard Majors, we can get them back. There was already a plan in place to retrieve Milena based on the information acquired from the attacker Bowe gave before he died. The position I've been given for my overwatch job is part of the rescue mission.

"Both Milena and Shelby used to live in Prospect before the attacks. I didn't know them then, but one of my friends did," Maddie says. "My friend lives in the mansion too. There're three others—or there was. I don't know the number now. And lots of staff. Most of them are nice people just trying to get by."

"The staff or the other women?" Evan asks.

Maddie chews on her thumbnail for a moment. "Both, I guess. You need to understand, the women . . . they just . . . " She lets out a sigh.

"There's no choice, really. If Richard takes an interest in you, it's not like you can say no."

"I'm sure they understand," Chance says, narrowing his eyes at Evan. "Right?"

Evan lifts a hand. "I'm not here to judge. Just gathering the information we need."

"You're going after them, aren't you?" Maddie asks with a look of determination. "If you do it right, you could end this once and for all. There's only a few who are extremists. If you— " She takes a breath, then gives a nod. "If you kill them, you can take the town back."

"And if you connect with the resistance, they'll help," the brother standing next to her says as he reaches for her hand. "They've been picking people off one or two at a time. The ones who they know were faithful to Majors and his son."

"Why not just kill Majors?" I ask, cringing as I hear how heartless I sound.

"They'd like to," he says.

"Are you part of the resistance?" Clark asks.

The brothers look at each other before the one holding Maddie's hand says, "Jason doesn't have the full picture of why we're here."

# Chapter 36

## *Mollie*

"What do you mean I don't have the full picture?" Jason asks, spinning in his chair to look at the man in the cell. "Chance, explain."

With a nod, the man says, "Yeah, it's time for that. Chase and I were visiting when the attacks started." A look passes between the brothers.

The second brother, Chase, jumps in. "For several days, we had no idea there was anything going on. We'd spent some time in Yellowstone and then moved into the national forest, camping and climbing. We were in the backcountry for almost two weeks. We didn't even know there was a problem until we got back to our car and it wouldn't start."

"You were in the backcountry for two weeks?" I ask, raising my eyebrows. "You were able to take that much food in with you?"

"We were using our SUV as a basecamp," Chance says. "We went back once to reload on food. We didn't see anyone, and everything was fine with our car. We even started it up to make sure the battery was good."

"Plus, we stretched our food with fish," Chase adds. "There's several creeks and small lakes up there. Our plan was to stay another week or two, but when we went back to resupply, the car wouldn't start."

"Didn't you have phones with you?" I ask. "Didn't they stop working?"

Both shrug. "Yeah," Chance says. "But we thought the batteries just went dead. It was weird it happened at the same time, but at the time . . . " He lifts his hands. "Even when the car didn't start, we thought it was a battery issue. We were parked up a forest service road, so we walked down to the main road, thinking we'd stop someone to give us a jump. After three hours without any traffic, we started to think something might be up. We went back to the car and camped

261

overnight, then started walking into Prospect the next day. That's when we discovered all we missed."

"Did you hear how things were before Richard took over?" Maddie asks. It doesn't escape my notice she refers to him by his first name instead of Mayor Majors, Mr. Majors, or even Richard Majors. The look shared by Evan and Clark suggests they caught it too.

"We were good," she continues. "Mayor Stringer had plans and was making them happen. Then everything changed. Now there's a few people completely loyal—not as many as there were before, but still some. If you were to combine forces with the resistance and take out most of the acquisition team, plus the few remaining on sentry and Scott Majors, the workers would join the revolt. Most of them anyway."

"And I suppose you have an idea of how we can connect with the rebels?" Evan asks, giving the brothers a hard look.

"That's why we're here," Chase says.

"Wait," Jason says. "You're part of the rebellion? I thought—you said the three of you were tired of living under Majors's rule and we had to get Joely out of there."

"That's true," Chase says. "With the genocide, she'll be targeted. When we found out where the rest of the Bakerville people had moved and knew you were part of them, well, it seemed we might have an in—a way to make contact and, uh, recruit help. Especially considering half of your town was slaughtered by Majors's thugs."

Maddie hangs her head on his final words.

"They'll be coming here next," Maddie says. "The plans are already in the works. There was a meeting before I left. The scouts returned home, and we heard about how you attacked them."

"We didn't attack them!" I blurt.

"Figured," she says with a nod. "But that's the official story. They were surveillance only and you caught them and attacked. Did you kill three of our people?"

"Why would they say we attacked?" Jake asks.

"Because it fits their narrative. Oh, and you're a crazy cult who holds people as hostages and slaves."

I let out a laugh, while Jake says, "Really?"

Evan and Clark just shake their heads.

"They're mounting a full attack. They'll send the entire acquisition team, and they've even recruited others to bolster their numbers."

"And you were the ones who killed our friends? The people from Bakerville still living on the river?" Jake asks.

She meets his eyes. "The acquisition team is tasked with procuring the things the town of Prospect needs to survive."

"So that's a yes?" Jake asks with a quiver in his voice. "You're one of the murderers?"

She gives a slow nod. "I was on the team, stationed as a guard. My job was to shoot anyone who tried to run away. There wasn't anyone in Bakerville who was able to run. While I'm responsible for their murders, I didn't pull the trigger. I'm, uh . . . now I'm . . . my life has changed recently, and I'm trying to make amends for the awful things I've done."

"You're part of the rebellion too?" Clark asks. "If you're on the— what do you call it? Acquisition team? It seems to me staying in Prospect would've been smart. You'd have an inside man."

"We still do," Chase says. "Maddie is with us because she and Chance are a couple. With her *position* in Prospect, they can't be together. And she was recently moved from the acquisition team to a new posting. Her place in the rebellion is more by relationship than anything. She didn't even know we were part of it until we were on the way here."

"I had no idea," Maddie says, shaking her head. "I wasn't—I was kind of mad Chance told me."

"Chance didn't tell me," Jason says. "Sure would've been nice to know."

"Sorry," Chase says. "We do have someone on the inside, part of the acquisition team."

"You're sure?" Evan asks. "You're sure he's loyal to you and not just using you to squash the rebellion?"

"Positive. And who said it's a he?"

As our group stares at the people in the cell, Heath pipes in with, "Sounds like you'd better team up so you can end this once and for all."

"That's why we're here," Chase says.

"What's in this for you?" I ask.

"Pardon?"

"You were vacationing when everything happened. Why didn't you just keep on hiking and head for home?"

"We planned on it. But when we arrived in Prospect, they were doing good things and we thought we could help. Joely's parents let us stay with them. Besides, we didn't figure we'd have enough time to make it home before winter, and we didn't want to risk it."

"Where's home?" Clark asks.

"Upstate New York. When Joely's parents were killed in the takeover, we knew we couldn't leave her. And at the time, we had no idea how bad things could get. Had we known, we would've taken her and left, even without someplace to spend the winter."

"When did you join the resistance?" I ask.

"It wasn't long after Majors took over. Then, there were only a handful of us."

"And now?"

"I'm not exactly sure. Over a hundred but probably less than two hundred. We have groups that operate independent of each other. It's a safety measure, so in case someone is caught everyone isn't exposed."

"And one of your people is on the acquisition team?"

"There may be more than one. I only know what I know since we operate independently."

"Plus, there's a few people on the acquisition team who would probably join us if they thought they had a chance at living a normal life," Maddie says, nodding her head. "Some are just there because of what it gets us. We have the best of everything: housing, food, no work other than training and the actual raids."

"Yeah, being a hired killer is an easy job," Clark says, voice laced with disgust.

"No, it's not," she says. "But some of us do it because it keeps us fed and alive. I decided to not die. I've done what I've had to do to live. I'm not proud of any of it. But I'm still alive, and now I can change some of what I've done. With your help, we can take back Prospect."

The back and forth with the brothers and Maddie continues for many minutes. In my opinion, they're legit in their desire to have us help them end the siege in Prospect. And I completely believe Maddie when she says they'll be coming after us. We already knew, though, which is why we're going on the offensive. We're so involved in the conversation, the opening of the door causes all of us sitting around the table to jump.

"Sorry I'm so late," Kelley says as she comes into the room. "We had an emergency at the clinic."

"Everything okay?" Clark asks.

"One of the children got stung by something, probably a spider or bee, and they had a reaction. It was fairly severe, but he'll be fine."

"A bee?" I ask.

She shrugs. "Or a spider. He was in the nursery when he started screaming." She steps to the table and says, "Hello, Jason."

"Mrs. Hudson. Did they ask you to be here to tell me about Olivia dying?"

"I'm so sorry for your loss," she says, stepping forward to give him an embrace.

When she releases him, he thanks her for her kindness, then turns to Evan. "Are we about done here so I can see my children? Or do you still think I'm a threat?"

"Jake, would you like to go get Tony and Lily?" Evan asks. "Now that we've had a good discussion and Kelley is here, I think it's time."

"I'll go too," I say, jumping up.

"Maybe tell them before you come in," Kelley says. "While a surprise sounds wonderful, it might not be."

Jake holds my hand as we walk the short distance to the dining room. After the scare we had with people walking up the road, we assume they've been given the all clear and regular school classes are in session. Regular isn't the right word. While we're getting ready for the attack on Prospect, only a few are currently teaching, causing lessons to be scaled down considerably. Mostly it's a babysitting service.

I let out a slow breath. "I'm so happy for Tony and Lily."

"Me too," Jake answers, giving my hand a squeeze. "It's a miracle for sure. And with this miracle, I'm praying for more."

We find Lily in the nursery. She quickly tells us about her friend Hunter and what happened. "It was so scary, Mommy. He screamed and then his entire face got big like this." She puffs her cheeks out. "Aunt Karen grabbed him and ran all the way to the clinic. Mrs. Pamela told us not to worry, but I still did."

I look to Karen, who gives a shrug. "Kelley stopped by a few minutes ago and said he'll be okay."

"We saw her," I say. "Quick thinking to get him there."

"It's been quite a day," she says. "I'm glad we got the all clear before Hunter's incident."

"We're going to take Lily with us," Jake says. "Are Tony and Malcolm upstairs?"

"Yes, Alina is with the older children."

Upstairs, Malcolm is less than happy when we tell him to stay while Tony and Lily go with us. Tony gives me a slight side eye as he asks, "Am I in trouble?"

"Not at all," I say, blinking to keep the tears away.

"Why do you look like you've been crying?" Lily asks.

"It's happy tears," I say, reaching for her hand. "Let's put on your jacket. You'll see."

Once we're outside and away from the other children, Jake says, "Do you want to sit on the deck for a minute?"

"I'd rather you just tell us and get it over with," Tony says, crossing his arms across his chest.

Jake lifts his head in my direction, indicating I should start.

"You know how we had the scare a little while ago about people coming up the road?" I ask. "You heard about that?"

"Yeah. But Aunt Karen and Mrs. Pamela said it was a false alarm," Lily answers.

"It was . . . sort of. There really were people walking up the road, but they aren't here to attack us."

Tony raises his eyebrows. "What does that have to do with us? With Lily and me?"

I give him a smile as tears again spring to my eyes.

"It's your dad," Jake says. "He was one of the people on the road."

"My dad?" Tony repeats, furrowing his brow.

"My first daddy is in heaven with my mommy," Lily says.

"Our dad's not dead?" Tony asks, his words coming in a rush. "He's here?"

I swallow hard as I nod. "He's here," I say in a squeaky voice. Tony starts to walk. I reach out and touch his arm. "I don't want you to be too surprised when you see him. He's lost some weight and looks a little scruffy. But he's so excited to see you."

"Does he remember me?" Lily asks, her faced scrunched up in thought.

"Yes, absolutely. And he loves you just as much now as ever before."

"Did you . . . does he know about our mom?" Tony asks in a shaky voice.

"He knows," Jake says. "Are you ready to see him?"

Tony lifts a shoulder and nods his head, then grabs his sister's arm. "Where is he?"

"He's in Deputy Clark's office."

"He's in the jail?" Lily asks as her eyes go wide. "Did he do something bad?"

"No way," Tony says. "Right?"

"Nothing bad at all," Jake says. "It was just the place they took your dad and his friends when they showed up so we could talk to them. Your mom—uh, Mollie said he's lost some weight, right? He looks different, so we had to make sure who he was so we could keep everyone safe. And we don't know his friends at all. When we left the office, they were in the locked rooms. I don't want you to be surprised."

"Our dad too?" Tony asks. "He's in the jail cells?"

"No, he was sitting at the table."

"Okay, let's go," Tony says as he starts to walk. Jake and I let them lead. Tony's still holding his sister's hand, guiding her. When we reach the door, he stops and looks at us. "I'm a . . . uh, I'm a little nervous."

"Do you want us to go first?" I ask.

"Yeah, maybe," he says as he steps aside.

"It's darker in the room than out here, so we'll pause for a moment after stepping in so our eyes can adjust," Jake says.

Inside the building, before my eyes have adjusted to let me see, I hear the scraping of a chair against the cement slab. "Tony? Lily?" Jason asks.

"Go ahead," Evan says quietly. "Go see your children."

"Dad?" Tony asks, as Jason takes a few steps toward him. "Dad!" he cries, then bounds across the room and jumps into Jason's waiting arms.

"Tony! You're so tall. Look at you!"

Lily, still standing next to Jake and me, whispers, "Are you sure he's my dad?"

I kneel on one knee and say, "I'm sure, sweetie. It's okay if you don't remember. You were almost a whole year younger when you saw him last."

"I kind of remember. It's just, when I close my eyes, he looks different."

"Lily's big too, Dad," Tony says, releasing Jason and motioning in our direction. "But sometimes she's a little shy."

Jason clears his throat, then says, "I understand. And Mrs. Hudson reminded me I look a lot different than the last time she saw me. Isn't that right, Lily?"

She gives a nod and steps close to me, holding on to my leg. "Are you really my dad?" she asks shyly. "Do you know when my birthday is?"

"I know when your birthday is and when Tony's is. And I know that when you were born, you had the biggest eyes ever."

Lily nods. "That's what my dad used to tell me. And then my dad would say— "

"I wondered if the rest of your body would ever catch up to your eyes. I think they did. Look how big you are."

She releases me and takes a few steps toward Jason and Tony. "That's what my dad said every time." She turns and looks at Jake and me. "Is it okay? Can I hug him?"

Not trusting my voice, I nod as Jake says, "I'm sure he'd like that."

She reaches her arms up toward him, letting him pick her up. After a few seconds, she says, "You should probably have a shower."

Jason gives a hearty, tear-laced laugh, before saying, "No doubt."

# Chapter 37

## *Saturday, Day 312*

## *Mollie*

"Do you think everything went okay with Sarah and the rest of them?" I whisper to Jake as I dress.

"I'm sure they're fine and where they're supposed to be," he answers quietly as he buttons his flannel shirt. It was snowing when we went to bed and cold in our room this morning, but it should warm up as the day goes on. Layers are smart this time of year. I already have my thermal long johns and undershirt on, having slept in them. With my lack of body fat, I find it much more difficult to keep warm than I did before.

Sliding into my insulated pants, I ask, "Do you think the new plan is a good one?"

With a shrug, he says, "Reggie Roberts seems to like it better, so that's something."

I put my finger to my lips as Malcolm squirms in his bed. We've moved to the first floor of the ski lodge, into a bunkroom set up for the home guard. Sissy and Andy share a bottom bunk, with Marc in the top. I was in a bottom bunk with Malcolm in the top, while Jake slept in a cot. Tonight, the children will move into the room Calley and Karen have been given. They'll all have camping cots or pads until this is over. Last night, because there are still people here leaving today, including Jake and me, people are sleeping wherever they can find a spot. We were fortunate to have a room as a family.

I step closer to Jake and whisper, "And you don't think Chase and Chance are setting us up?"

"I think we've taken precautions in case they are."

"Yeah, but are we taking *enough* precautions?"

"I don't know what else we can do. And more importantly, Evan, the security team, and the retired soldiers don't know what more we can do. They're the experts in this. You and me—we're just grunts." He gives me a wink.

I shake my head at him and then twist my back to relieve the ache. After the surprise appearance of Jason and the others, we had to rethink everything. Our foot soldiers, who were scheduled to leave at daylight the day after Jason and the Prospect people arrived, were pushed back until new plans were finalized and shared.

Reggie Roberts, who was very vocal about how the original plan would get everyone killed, including our children and elderly staying behind, finally said, "You know what? It might just work—provided you really *do* have the Prospect rebellion on your side and it's not a giant trap."

To help ensure it isn't a trap, we've kept the brothers, Maddie, and Joely separate. And we've also hidden our true numbers from them and shared only part of our plan—the part the rebellion is directly involved in. They don't even know we sent out two groups of foot soldiers.

One group includes Mike, his dad, several dozen other militia, and half of the security team. They left at noon two days ago, with our vehicles ferrying them down the road to a location where they'll then head east of Prospect and divide into two groups. One will stay at their eastern camp and the other will head south of town and set up there. Dax Cameron and another man are with them. Each will set up with one of the long-range rifles and a spotter, one east of town and the other south. A couple of others are also acting as overwatch, only with common hunting rifles, and will also have hidden locations.

Once our first group of foot soldiers were gone, we had a community meeting, which included the Prospect rebels. That's when the part of the plan we needed them to be involved in was hashed out. Chance and Chase both seemed to be rather disappointed at the size of our group, lamenting several times about how they expected our numbers to be larger.

Maddie kept reminding everyone that, while the town of Prospect still has around five thousand people—a huge loss of the original size of almost ten thousand—not everyone is loyal to Richard Majors. "It's not like they like him," she said. "He wasn't popular before the disasters started, and then when he killed Mayor Stringer and took over in such a violent manner, they definitely didn't like him. Most people are just trying to survive. They keep their head down and do what they're told while waiting for this nightmare to end."

"Exactly how do they think it's going to end?" Doris asked.

With a shrug, Maddie said, "There used to be talk of the governor stepping in, that he'd send the National Guard once he heard what happened in our town. When it didn't happen, people said maybe the president would help, but nothing happened there either. We've been on our own. And now most people are exhausted, hopeless, and just doing what they can to get through each day."

It sounds like they haven't heard the alerts the president and his people have put out. Do they not have a working radio? Or are Richard Majors and his team keeping things quiet? That'd make sense. If the townspeople thought help was on the way, he'd lose his ability to control by fear. As agreed, before bringing the rebels in to the meeting, we didn't share what we know about the president's announcements. If this is a trap, the less info they have, the better.

We spent hours going over the plan. Maddie said she was sure several people from the acquisition team would join the rebellion. It seems she thinks many, like her, hate what they do and are on the team only out of need for their own survival. The little bit I've heard about what they've done turns my stomach. Although Maddie insists she was only ever a guard and she knows what she did was wrong, I find myself being incredibly judgmental and not wanting her help or help from any of her raider friends.

"And your group on the road from Wesley is important," Maddie said, nodding earnestly. "Don't forget there's a bad element that overtook the town and is working in conjunction with Scott Majors. We've been on a raid with them, and they're scary."

"We have it covered," Evan said. "They won't get in."

"And remember, the town of Wesley will need to be . . . uh, what's the word?" Maddie asked, looking to Chance.

"Liberated?"

"Right. Shortly after Richard took over, many people from their town came to Prospect. The ones still in Wesley are essentially slaves. When I was there last month, I was surprised at the condition of the people. You'll need to free them after eliminating their captors."

"We understand," Evan said.

271

"And the bordello is on the road too," Chase said. "A lot of things need to happen concurrently. They need to be freed. Your people need to be ready for an attack from Wesley while they attack Prospect. I'm confident the rebellion will be able to somewhat neutralize the aggressors in Prospect, but we'll need to count on you to free the women and children being held in the bordello and to watch our backs from Wesley."

"It'll happen," Evan answered.

"We don't want to kill anyone we don't have to," Chase said, shaking his head. "While we know this—we know war is the only option—it's not what we want."

"It's not what we want either," Evan agreed. "We were living here peacefully. Our friends on the river too. But Majors and his henchmen brought war to us. There's no way they'll leave us alone."

"No," Maddie said. "They won't. And it can't keep going the way it is in Prospect, with them committing mass murder against not only those they raid but the elderly and infirm in our own town."

"We want people to have the opportunity to surrender," Chance said.

"It'll make things harder for our team," Leo said. "As we free the women in the bordello, we need surprise on our side. Asking them to surrender may not be possible."

"Understood," Chance said. "And we know the contingent from Wesley will come in with guns blazing. Just do what you can. If we massacre indiscriminately, we're no better than Richard and Scott Majors."

With a decent plan in place, the rest of our foot soldiers and security team left the next morning. Sarah is part of the group, along with Art, Ben, and Destiny. Some of them were driven down the mountain to a drop-off location to hike to their spots. The team Leo's leading, which Sarah and Destiny are a part of, will be the ones liberating the bordello and watching for the attack from Wesley. We only have a vague idea of how many guards are at the bordello, but at least we know the exact location, thanks to the brothers. They'll gather as much intel as they can before the attack and adjust as needed.

Art and Ben are part of the team launching a direct attack on Prospect in conjunction with the rebellion. Both teams are going to be in the thick of it and will have to trust Chance, Chase, and Maddie are being truthful.

Katie, Madison, Laurie, and Belinda also left so they can set up the triage area. Paul Cameron and two other men drove them using the teams, Paul's chuckwagon, and two open wagons. Paul is setting them up at a place he calls The Bowl, a hidden location on the land he owns outside of Prospect. He says it's far enough to not be found but close enough to get people to for treatment. The chuckwagon has been converted to use as a covered transport vehicle, removing most of the cooking items and installing benches.

The Prospect group doesn't know about our watchers, another security measure to try and keep the home guard safe. And our true home guard numbers have been hidden. As far as they know, it's only our extreme elderly, injured, and children staying behind. They don't know about the able-bodied or only mildly injured people, like Tim. We kept them out of the planning meeting. While the subterfuge feels wrong, it's also necessary. I want to believe what they say. And according to Kelley Hudson, they're being truthful. Even Reggie thinks they're on the up and up, but he also says we can't be too careful.

With our foot soldiers in place, today is the day. Jake, Angela, me, and the rest of the overwatch and sharpshooters are leaving. Chase, Chance, and Maddie will go with us, riding four-wheelers, horses, or the final team and wagon. Once we get close to Prospect, we'll camp overnight for our attack at dawn. The brothers and Maddie will go into Prospect to prepare the rebellion. With the different groups of rebels, Chase said they'll need the time to connect with everyone. That's the part we're risking—trusting they'll actually connect with people who want to defeat Richard Majors as opposed to running to him and his henchmen to serve us up on a silver platter. Just in case, the teams they don't know about are strategically stationed and ready to foil any traps—at least that's the plan.

"Is it time to get up, Grandmo?" Marc asks, rolling over to look at me.

"You can stay in bed if you want," I say. "Grandpa and I will be leaving soon, but Aunt Calley knows to come and get you for breakfast."

"Were you going to tell us goodbye?"

"We did last night so you could keep sleeping, remember?"

"Don't want to keep sleeping," Andy says. "Ready to get up. Want to go with you and Grandpa on the snowmobile."

"No snowmobile rides today, munchkin," Jake says. "Besides, where we're going, there won't be as much snow, so we're taking the quads."

"He likes the quad too," Marc says.

"We go on quad ride when you come back with my mommy?" Andy asks.

"Maybe so," Jake says.

"We should get up so we can go find Lily," Sissy says. "I don't like that she didn't sleep with us."

"I know it was a strange thing for you," I say. "You and Lily have been sharing a room for a while now. But now her dad is home, and it makes sense for her to stay with him. When we move back to the lodge, she'll share your room again."

"Only until we move back to the farm, right?" Marc asks. "Then we'll live in our trailer and Lily and Tony will live in your house?"

"I'm not sure," I answer. "We'll have to see what their dad wants to do."

"It makes me sad Lily isn't my aunt anymore," Sissy says. "It's fun having an aunt younger and shorter than me."

"She won't mind if you still call her Aunt Lily," Jake says. "I know you both had a lot of fun with it."

"I guess," she says with a huge sigh. "And if she's still going to call you Mom and Dad, then it's probably okay."

After Lily told Jason he needed a shower, she asked him if, even though he was home, she could still call Jake and I Mom and Dad. He didn't even hesitate before saying she absolutely could. When Lily introduced Jason to Sissy and her brothers, she said, "This is my first dad, but he said I can still have my second dad and new mommy, too, because they love me and he loves me. So now I have two dads, but only one mommy right now since my first mommy died. I'll see her again in heaven, though."

"Since everyone's awake, do you think we can get some breakfast?" Malcolm asks. It seems he's started a growth spurt. He's hungry and tired all the time. A growth spurt isn't an easy thing when we're on rations and busy from dawn to dusk. Even though the supply house is closed, where we usually get extra food for the children, Doris had things brought over to the lodge so there'd be snacks and extras for them. With so many of our people gone, they'll be okay on food.

On the flipside, there's no organized hunting crew to bring in fresh meat. The day before yesterday, Bryce Cameron got an elk. He hung it overnight and cut it up yesterday, giving them many days of meals. He, along with Alvin and a few others, will still hunt as needed. Plus, they'll be eating the sugar beets and other stored items.

Thankfully, the chickens are laying again, so they'll have plenty of eggs. And there's been a cow set aside to cull along with two goats and several rabbits. Leslie, who arrived a few months ago with Clarice and Ben, volunteered to snare wild rabbits. Clarice says Leslie became quite proficient at setting different types of snares and traps while they were traveling. There are several other youths in the community who have also been running snare and trap lines over the winter, giving good food options.

Clara Michaelson, Mick's wife, will be taking over care of the livestock in the corrals and the livestock shed. Art is usually in charge of the livestock shed, but he went with the foot soldiers.

"I know they said they'd have breakfast early for those of us leaving," I say. "We'll see if they have enough for you to have a little bit to tide you over until proper breakfast."

"You mean second breakfast?" Malcolm asks with a cheeky grin.

Jake shakes his head. "First, these dogs need to go out."

Hearing a phrase she knows, Penny gives a low whimper from her bed. Scooter bounces up, ready to go. Calley's going to have her hands full with the children and dogs.

Karen, who has taken over the main role of teacher since the death of her mom, Lois, a few months ago, won't be going on the raid either. It was decided she was a stable force for the children and her talents would be best used as part of the home guard. She'll even continue with classes to provide as much normalcy as possible. She's promised to help Calley with our brood and has also given her word to other worried parents that she'll be there for their children.

Upstairs on the main floor, the beds are all empty as people prepare to go. The aroma of fried meat is filling the room, causing my stomach to growl. My appetite is unpredictable these days, and Belinda would prefer I eat mostly chicken, rabbit, or eggs, so my reaction is a surprise.

"Hey, Mom," Angela says, holding Gavin on her hip. "I see your kids are up early too."

"Seems so," I say.

"Have you seen Calley yet?"

"No, but I didn't knock on her door either. She had trouble sleeping the night before, so I thought maybe it was best not to wake her."

"Okay, it's just— " She drops her shoulder, letting out a big whoosh of air. "I finally finished my letter, and I thought it'd be best for her to keep it. I was going to give it to Tim, but I didn't. He might read it, and that would embarrass me. I know Calley won't. Did you give her yours?"

I answer with a slight nod. Cole Gunderson suggested we all write letters to leave with a loved one, which are really more of a last will and testament. Sarah, Katie, and the others gave Calley theirs before they left. Even though we all talked and planned for the children, getting the letters was extremely hard on Calley. She got one from Mike first, since he left with the first group. That was bad, but then to get them from her sisters made it worse. Roy left his letter with Sheila.

Sheila has healed well enough, and the threat of infection isn't the concern it was before. Like everyone else, she's now living in the ski lodge, sharing a room with Kelley Hudson. With Katie, Laurie, Madison, and Belinda gone to act as medics in the field, only Kelley and June remain as our onsite medical team. June and her two children have a room next to Kelley and Sheila.

"Where is Tim?" I ask.

"He's at the jail. With Clark and his deputies now acting as militia, he was given that for his watch shift last night." Even though we're trusting the brothers and Maddie, they're still sleeping in the cells. Chase and Chance are in with Heath, while Maddie is with Joely. They all said they understood the need for it.

We offered to move Joely to the ski lodge, but she wanted to stay. I'm not sure how it will go when Maddie and the brothers leave and force Joely to stay behind. I haven't been around her other than when we were talking to Jason on the day they arrived, but Kelley has concerns about her attachment to the brothers and thinks she's likely to have a melt down when she realizes they're gone. The plan is to move her in with Kelley and Sheila. Hopefully it goes well.

With the excitement of leaving, the room quickly fills, not only with those of us going but with the families also.

"Mollie?" a gravelly female voice asks.

I turn to see Delores Lancaster standing too close to me. I don't have the energy for another round with her this morning. Pasting a phony smile on my face, I say, "Good morning, Delores."

She responds with her own forced smile. "May I speak with you privately?"

Angela raises her eyebrows at me. I give her a nod before saying, "Okay." Angela takes several steps away while Delores steps even closer.

"I've heard you're not feeling well but are still going on the raid."

I narrow my eyes. "I'm well enough to do my duty."

She waves a hand. "My husband, he had terrible pains in his back toward the end. All we could do was give him medicine for it. I, uh . . . I have a few I've kept back." She thrusts a small package toward me. "Here."

It's a seed packet: bachelor button flowers. "Okay?"

"There's three pills. OxyContin. It'll help keep the pain away so you can do what's needed. It's probably best to only take half at a time so you don't get loopy."

I give her a nod as my eyes fill. "Thank you, Delores. I'll return whatever's left over."

"No need. Just give them to Belinda, but don't tell her where you got them, okay?"

"Understood."

She gives me a genuine smile before turning and striding confidently across the room.

"Mom?" Angela says, moving next to me.

"Don't worry about it," I say, pocketing the seed package. "There's Calley," I motion to her as she crests the staircase, one hand holding her swollen belly to keep it from swaying with the motion.

Once Calley reaches us, she says, "It sure is hard to sleep with all the noise."

"I guess it would be," I answer with a smile. "Was last night better? Were you able to get comfortable?"

"Ugh, no. The bed is awful. I might make Malcolm sleep in it tonight and I'll take the floor. It couldn't be any worse."

"Your baby might not like that," Angela says.

"She couldn't hate it any more than she does the bed."

"She?" I ask, raising my eyebrows.

"Maybe," Calley shrugs. "It's about time for a girl, don't you think? Angela and Sarah both had boys."

"I don't think it works that way," Angela says. "Here." She thrusts her letter to Calley. "You're not going to need this, but here it is anyway."

Calley gives an exaggerated frown. "I really hate this."

"Yeah, we all do," Angela says.

Jason enters from the stairs across the room with Lily in his arms and Tony by his side. He raises his free hand in greeting. He'll be staying here as part of the home guard. Originally, he wanted to go along and be part of the attack team Sarah's on. Evan quashed that by saying he's never trained with the team. Physically, it makes more sense for him to stay here. Walking from North Dakota took a lot out of him. And his being here gives Jake and I peace of mind. If one or both of us don't return, we know his children—our children—will be well cared for.

I glance to Malcolm. He'll be well cared for too. Calley, Sarah, Katie, and Angela will see to it. I swallow a lump in my throat. My heart aches thinking of the danger my children face, with Sarah on the attack team and Angela by my side. Calley will be safe here, as long as we all do our jobs, and Katie should also be okay. But Sarah and Angela . . .

"Okay, folks," Evan says. "It seems we're all up and ready to go. Will someone retrieve our Prospect guests? Then we'll get to eating and head out. Alvin Caldwell, once they arrive, will you lead us in prayer?"

Normally, Chaplain Rick—who was killed in the sniper attack—or David Hammer would give the blessing. David is part of the watcher group and is already in place at their campsite. Bill Shane's security team is also gone, having been camping off and on since the attacks to keep an eye on the Prospect raiders. While I do have a general idea where the watcher camp is, Bill's team location isn't known to me, other than being close enough for them to be part of the direct attack on Prospect. We'll be meeting up with them later today.

Chase, his brother, and the girls come in the room followed by Tim. While they aren't cuffed and Tim doesn't have a weapon trained on them, it's obvious he's keeping a close eye. Did something happen while he was on watch that concerns him? Tim leads the Prospect people to Evan. They exchange a few quiet words, then Tim looks around the room. Seeing Angela and Gavin, he makes a beeline for them.

"Everything okay?" Angela asks in a quiet voice once he reaches her side.

"Yeah, I guess. The three of them were praying this morning. The girl was—I probably shouldn't have been listening."

"And?" I ask.

"And some of the stuff they've done—the team she was part of—makes me sick to my stomach."

"She talked about it while she was praying?" Angela asks.

He lifts his shoulders all the way to his ears. "She was begging for forgiveness, asking God for a chance to make it right. And it seems she was part of a harem or something."

I give a slight nod. She'd alluded to that.

"Anyway, when she was done, Chance reminded her she's a Christian and God's forgiven her sins. She needs to forgive herself. She told him she doesn't think she'll ever be able to forgive herself because the things she's done are too terrible. 'Sin is sin,' Chance said. 'While you might think your sins are too terrible, when you placed your faith in Jesus Christ for salvation, all of your sins were forgiven. When Jesus died on the cross, He died to pay the penalty for all of the sins of the entire world, yours included.' She started crying.

"Then Heath got involved in it and asked Chance to tell him more. Before I knew what was happening, Heath was praying and asking for Jesus to forgive his sins too. It was . . . it was overwhelming and wonderful. It makes me think we have it wrong, suspecting them of setting a trap. I think they're the real deal."

Realizing I'm in tears, I shake my head. Did any of us ever think of sharing the gospel with Heath? I know I didn't. Did Evan? He tried to get a dying man he didn't even know—someone complicit in the murder of his daughter—to accept Jesus' forgiveness before he died. But did any of us try and offer salvation to Heath? To Shannon or Roscoe?

# Chapter 38

## *Lucy*

I've heard nothing about Maddie. The day after she disappeared, her room was cleared of her personal belongings. The next day a new lady moved in. Charlotte is several years older than me and is, quite honestly, the most glamourous of us. She has amazing eyes and perfect lips and cheekbones. Her dark brown hair is wavy, and at one time she probably had what my mom would refer to as an hourglass figure. She's skinny now, but the bone structure is still evident. It still amazes me how Richard chooses such a variety of women.

Alyssa asked Mrs. Murphy about Maddie, but she quickly changed the subject, saying, "Sometimes there are things we must not know."

That garnered an eye roll from Alyssa, but she did drop it. Those first few days after Maddie left, I wondered about her and whether she made it out safely. At first I thought, if they caught her, she'd be brought back here. But when Charlotte so quickly arrived, I realized if they did catch her, she'd be disposed of quietly. They wouldn't want to draw attention to how someone who was an esteemed member of the acquisition team, and a personal favorite of the mayor's, could betray the town.

No. That wouldn't look good at all. It might even give credence to the terrible things the rebellion does. Not that I know what they're doing now. Living in the Bunn Mansion is like being in a different world. We're isolated and alone. We don't go out, and very few people come in. I must admit, I love it. I love the coziness and comfort of being here. The other women can be annoying, especially Alyssa and Star, but for the most part we really are becoming the family Richard wants.

I wonder if this new endeavor has been made public. Surely it would be. There's too many people living and working here for the town not to know—or at least have an idea—about what's going on. What do they think? Most of the town was incredibly supportive of the acquisition team, so being part of it was always something I could be proud of. When I was first promoted from sentry to acquisition, I held my head high. Sure, I know *how* I got on the team, but it was still a thing to be proud of. I'm not so sure this is the same.

Besides being extremely comfortable, our days are very structured. Just like on the acquisition team, we have daily fitness. Because of Maddie disappearing, we're restricted to the house and the grounds, but it's not an issue since Richard has an exercise instructor on staff. I didn't know her before, but she had a gym in town with weights, Zumba, spin class, yoga, Pilates, and probably more. A portion of the large freestanding garage—added to the house sometime after cars were commonplace but before the historical status, and not included on the tour—has been set up as an exercise space. Mrs. Murphy even joins us in the workouts.

They're much less intense than what I'm used to from Janet Kruse. These are almost fun, where Janet's sole goal was to make us miserable. The light exercise does make sense, considering none of the others are in the same physical condition I'm in. In my room, I'm still practicing the kicks, punches, and rolls I was working on with Lorita. I know there's no reason to now since I'll never go back to that life, but they're enjoyable and a way to add a little extra fitness into my routine.

In addition to the daily movement, we have classes. Yep, just like in school. Mrs. Murphy says it's imperative we're well read. While there is a library in the house, the books in it were all fakes for the museum tour. The town library was vandalized early in the attacks when Mayor Stringer was still in charge. Richard was able to have many of the books and items salvaged and put into storage. A good amount were brought to the library in the Bunn Mansion, and Mrs. Murphy brought much of her own personal collection.

We're reading and discussing *Canterbury Tales* by Chaucer. I'm not sure she could have picked a more boring book to start with. The copy she has is even written in Middle English and is not only dull but difficult to follow. Even the Bible Maddie left me is easier to understand than Chaucer. But we do it anyway, taking turns reading aloud and discussing.

Richard also had his collection of archived newspapers brought in at Mrs. Murphy's request. She insists knowing historical events will be beneficial. Personally, I find it hard to believe we'll really need any of this. Are they expecting aristocrats to visit? It's more likely the men will be scroungy and dirty looking, much like Jason Hatch. The way Richard talks, he thinks we're living in the English countryside in the early 1800s. I've read *Pride and Prejudice*, and I can guarantee none of the people I've encountered in these recent months remind me of Mr. Darcy—not even Richard when he's dressed in his finest.

Even though the education part is ridiculous, it's still much better than being under Janet's thumb. Mrs. Murphy never makes fun of me. And the few times I've seen Richard, at dinner or in passing, he's been kind and engaging. I'm beginning to believe I was right about him and Maddie was wrong. I think he genuinely wants the best for our town. Yes, he does love the fact he's in charge. And as he's said to me on more than one occasion, it's good to be king. But I don't think he's doing it to be cruel. He simply knows it's the way to save lives.

In my personal time, I've read a little more of the Bible. I know I shouldn't. The smartest thing to do would be to toss it in the woodstove, but I've decided it can be part of my education. If there really are well-educated men who visit, they'll likely have strong opinions on the Bible since it's known to be controversial.

Of course, I was always taught to never bring up religion or politics, so they'd have to start the conversation. Even though I don't believe it the way Maddie believes, I can certainly see the draw to the stories. Some of them are entertaining, much better than Chaucer. I've heard bits and pieces of the stories before, but to be able to read the entire thing gives me the full picture. Last night, I read about Moses and how he led his people out of Egypt and parted the Red Sea. I still think it's a bunch of hooey—who could move the ocean so people could walk through it? Even so, I enjoyed the story.

"Lucy?"

"Uh, yes?"

"You were a million miles away, dear. Is lunch not to your liking?"

"Oh. No, it's wonderful. I was just lost in thought."

Mrs. Murphy nods, but Star says, "Thought maybe you were getting shares from Red there." She points to Milena.

Since we've all moved in, Milena and Shelby have both improved. The *situation* isn't openly spoken of, but it seems both are on a small dose of something to keep them calm but not near the amount Milena was on when we first moved in. In those early days of living here, Milena was definitely drugged. Maybe Shelby too. But in her case, I think she'd just kind of snapped after being in the bordello. Now she's much more collected and seems to be adapting to living here. Sometimes she talks about her baby, Hannah, in a way that makes me think Scott and Major Lassiter's story of the baby being taken from her by the cult is untrue. When Mrs. Murphy hears her blabbering about the baby, she promptly redirects her.

The rest of the day passes as usual. As is our custom, we have dinner in the dining room with Richard joining us. He takes breakfast and lunch in his suite or is out on town business during those times, but dinner is, as he calls it, family time. We haven't had another decadent meal like we did the first night, but it's still highly organized and formal with the butler, whose name I finally learned after several days is Ramos, directing the rest of the staff as we're served. Mrs. Murphy continues to lead the conversation, often rehashing our lessons for the day.

"We have a special treat for you in the next few weeks," she says, nodding toward Richard. "Would you like to share with them, Mayor?"

With a bend of his neck, he says, "I'd like each of you to learn an instrument."

"An instrument?" Star asks. "Like the guitar?"

"Perhaps. But I was thinking something a little more ladylike. The piano would be good. Or the harp. I love the harp."

"Are there harps in Prospect?" I ask.

"Not to my knowledge, but it's something we're looking for. Our wonderful acquisition team seems to find the things we desire. And we'll also start dance lessons and horse riding."

"I already know how to dance and ride," Star says, while Alyssa nods.

"I'm sure you do, dear," Mrs. Murphy says. "But we'll be focusing on ballroom dancing and English riding as opposed to western."

"That's right," Richard says. "We're hoping you young ladies can bring some class back to the region."

I stifle the smile threatening to overtake me. English riding. He really does think we're living in a Jane Austin novel. Maybe it's the mansion. And Mrs. Murphy seems to be completely onboard with the foolishness. They can't really believe this, can they? Does Richard not remember our teams are preparing to go to battle against the cult his son says wants to wipe us out. Here he is talking about learning the harp, the waltz, and riding horses.

283

"Do you have English saddles?" Charlotte asks.

"Those we do have," Richard says with a smile. "It'll be wonderful. You'll all look amazing dressed in your finest riding clothes and on well-bred horses."

"Do you ride?" Star asks.

"Oh, no. Not me. But perhaps I'll learn alongside you. Yes, yes. That's what I'll do."

For the remainder of the meal, Richard prattles on excitedly about the new opportunities we'll have, his excitement urged on by the refilling of his wine glass. More than once he references how we'll be the ones leading Prospector County into a new age.

After dinner, we move to the library for more conversation and bourbon for Richard and anyone of us who wish it. I get a glass of wine with dinner each night, but I limit it to the one and pass on the liquor. With the dinner going so late, I'm tired enough as it is and don't need to add a depressant to my system. I cover my mouth to hide a yawn when there's a light knock on the door.

"Enter!" Richard calls out.

"Sir," Ramos says, "the general and three of his people are at the door."

"Show them in."

"He says he wishes to speak privately."

"Nonsense. Show them in."

"As you wish, sir."

I'm impressed with how Ramos has seemed to adapt the exact persona of the classic butler from television and books. He's a perfect fit for this mansion and how it likely was in the past. Undoubtedly, he's a big fake too. Just like Richard and the rest of us.

"Father," Scott Majors says, entering the library. Captain Murphy, Janet Kruse, and Major Lassiter are on his heels.

"Yes, Scott. What is it?" Richard asks without moving from his reclined position in his chair.

"I'd prefer we speak privately."

"Ramos relayed your message. What is it you want?"

Scott looks around the room, giving a shake of his head and a roll of his eyes before saying, "This is military business."

"Out with it," Richard says with a slight slur to his words.

"Fine. Whatever you want, *Mayor.*"

284

"That's right, Scott. It is whatever I want. In fact, I've been thinking and have decided it's time I do away with the title of mayor. I'm considering chancellor. Mayor Majors is a bit of a mouthful. Chancellor Majors has a nice ring to it."

Scott rolls his eyes and shakes his head. "Why not King Majors?"

Richard seems to consider it before saying, "Get on with it so we can get back to our evening."

With a clip to his words, Scott says, "There's something happening."

"And?"

"And Knight found one of the guys from the work crew sneaking around. He thought it might be one of the brothers who went missing with the Rivers girl."

"Was it? Did you find Maddie?" Richard asks, sitting upright.

"He lost him, but he did find a few others who were meeting in the little grocery store on the hill. Knight had one of his team members with him. He kept watch and sent for Lassiter. Fred made the wise decision to storm the building. Two are dead but one was captured and talked."

"Talked about what?"

"About being part of the resistance," Major Lassiter says, puffing his chest out.

"Really? Well done, Fred. Did he give you names?"

"He didn't. He insists he only knew the two he was with—and Chase Morgan. He's the brother of the boyfriend of the little tart that left you. He was the one who was meeting with them tonight, to tell them something big is happening and they should be ready."

I feel the blood leave my face at the mention of Chase's name. I knew he was trouble. But part of the rebellion? Was he responsible for killing Richard's wife?

"What's the *something big*?" Richard asks, leaning forward.

"We don't know," Janet says. "Fred killed him before we could get the details."

"It was an accident!" Major Lassiter cries. "How was I supposed to know he was such a wimp?"

Richard blinks several times before shaking his head. "You killed our only lead for stopping the rebels?"

"We don't need to worry about it, Dad," Scott says. "We now know of one of their meeting places, and we're searching for Chase Morgan."

"But you don't believe the three you killed are all of them, right?" The edge in Richard's voice makes me cringe.

"Not for a minute. We know there's more of them. And whatever big is happening, we'll stop it before it does."

"See that you do! Ladies, you're dismissed."

Scott and the others move away from the door while Mrs. Murphy hustles us out. The door isn't even fully closed when Richard loses all control and starts yelling at his officers. Some of the words he uses turn my ears red. A look of . . . what? Happiness? Passes between Milena and Shelby.

Maybe not happiness. Maybe knowing.

Once we're well into the hallway and away from the controversy, Mrs. Murphy says, "Let's gather in the upstairs sitting area. Make your way there. I'll be with you in a few minutes."

Standing by the upstairs window, Charlotte says in a whisper, "Some temper the mayor has—or chancellor, whatever he wants to be called. Is he like that often?"

"Not often," I answer as I step next to her. Solar lights along the fence line and trees light up the large backyard. This was another project ordered by Richard to improve our home. I love the way they look and never tire of seeing the nighttime view.

"I heard he was like that after the bombing of the hotel, but that's understandable with those animals killing his wife."

I give a nod. He was angry then. Angry to the point of belligerence. But Charlotte's right. His wife had just been murdered by the same rebels he's angry about now. It makes sense. And considering the damage the rebellion has done to the town in both death toll and property, his anger may be justified.

I read about that in the Bible too. God was so mad about what a town was doing, He wiped them out. And the lady who turned and looked back at the town was turned into stone . . . or was it salt? Something. There was even a guy swallowed by a whale who went to a town and preached against their wickedness. Maybe that's what's happening. The wickedness of the rebels is . . . is what? I shake my head. Chase is one of the rebels. He's as good as dead.

"Thank you for waiting for me, ladies," Mrs. Murphy says from the top of the stairs. "Please, let's all be seated."

Charlotte and I quickly take the chairs. Shelby and Milena are on the loveseat, both looking more alert than I've seen them to date. Star, Alyssa, and Rebecca look concerned.

"We have certain safeguards in place," Mrs. Murphy says.

"For what?" Star asks.

"In case something happens to the mansion like at the hotel."

Star narrows her eyes. "You'll have to give me a little more information. I'm new to this town."

"So am I," Rebecca says with a nod. "The hotel that's a partial pile of rubble? The man driving me in said there was an accident there."

Mrs. Murphy gives a slight nod. "Yes, this is true." She then goes into a brief explanation of the explosion, making sure to clarify the exact cause is unknown.

"But you think it was intentional?" Star asks. "And the mayor was the target?"

"I think nothing," Mrs. Murphy smiles. "But it's smart for us to have a plan in place to exit the building should the need arise."

"You want to have a fire drill?" Alyssa mocks.

"The maids' stairs for this wing are between Alyssa's and Charlotte's rooms. If you're unable to reach the main stairs, you should use the back stairs. As a last resort, go out either Milena's or Lucy's windows. A trellis is in that section of the house, which should aid you in getting out. Once outside, we'll have two gathering locations—one at the back of the property by the large tree with the bench, and the second at the beginning of the driveway where it meets the main road."

"Are we in danger?" I ask, wishing I wouldn't have been required to turn in my sidearm.

"Unlikely. I believe this is a rumor and nothing more. Now, are there any questions as to where we meet or how to exit the house?"

"You didn't really think they'd just leave us here, did you?" Milena asks with a sly smile. "The so-called rebels are the least of his worries."

"What if we're attacked?" Star asks. "Do you have a plan?"

"I do not believe we'll be attacked. Should it happen, should the house come under attack, you should get outside if you can safely do so. Otherwise . . . " She gives a slight lift of her shoulders. "Hide. Now let's call it a night. Tomorrow, we'll discuss what instruments you'd like to learn."

I'm in my pajamas and pulling the Bible from underneath my mattress when there's a light knock and the door immediately pops open. With the book fully exposed, I'm sure I look like a deer caught in headlights.

"I was hoping we could chat for a minute," Mrs. Murphy says.

"Uh, yes, of course." I nonchalantly place the Bible on my nightstand. Mrs. Murphy's eyes follow my movement. "Did you want to have a seat?" I motion to the chair and ottoman.

"Thank you." She sits carefully on the edge of the seat. "Dirk tells me you're trained in hand-to-hand combat."

I let out a laugh. "I'm familiar with it, but I'm not— " I shrug. "My skills aren't as good as many others on the team."

"But you're able to defend yourself?"

I slowly shake my head. "They'd have to be completely untrained or I'd need to be very lucky."

"Or blessed?" she lifts her head in the direction of the Bible.

"Oh, this? I . . . It's not mine. I found it in the room when I moved in."

"Is that so?"

"Yes. It was under my pillow on the first night."

"But you read it?"

"You're more than welcome to take it with you if this is a problem."

"There's no problem, Lucy. Tomorrow, I'd like you to teach the other ladies some self-defense. Charlotte is trained in Taekwondo, so she'll be sharing her knowledge too."

"It'd probably be best if she's the trainer."

"Perhaps. But what she knows isn't the same as what you know. Please remember, my duty is to keep all of you safe. That is my first obligation."

"Your first? I would think being loyal to Mayor Majors would be your first."

She raises her eyebrows at me. "Of course, dear. But you're my charges, and I won't let anyone—no matter their title or position— bring you harm." Mrs. Murphy stands to leave. "You're smart to keep the Bible tucked under your mattress. There's less hassle that way."

# Chapter 39

## *Sunday, Day 313*

## *Mollie*

Yesterday morning, Alvin prayed not only for the blessing of the food but for our mission, to do what is needed and to free the region from the evilness engulfing it. He also prayed God would touch us with His mighty hand and prevent as much bloodshed as possible. Few of us want to kill. We'll do what we must, but we'd prefer as many people live as possible. We know it's unlikely Richard, Scott, Fred Lassiter, and the true believers in their cause will surrender. And as overwatch, my job will be to take them out if necessary.

While I'd been hungry on those first whiffs of food, I was unable to eat much as nervousness overtook me. After saying goodbye to my family staying behind, we loaded into the few diesel vehicles that survived the EMP. Our fuel stores are running low, especially the gasoline—not that it matters much since the gas is going bad. The farmers knew to add fuel stabilizer to their tanks. Jake and I, plus several others who were storing fuel, did the same. But even with the stabilizer, we're on borrowed time. The gas without stabilizer added was used first, or at least we thought that was the case. A few weeks ago, when one of the generators was filled, it sputtered and wouldn't start.

That was before Aaron Ogden broke his leg, and as one of our resident mechanics, he was called in to figure out what was wrong with the genny. He opened the fuel tank and took a whiff, immediately suspecting the gas was bad based on the sour smell. He and his helpers drained the fuel out of the tank and the carburetor, disconnected all the lines, then once they were sure it was clean, put it back together. They got new fuel from a different tank, and it started right up.

The fuel they were using was from a drum and had been a compilation of several smaller containers scrounged up and put together into a larger one for ease of transport when we moved up the mountain back in September. It was believed all had been stabilized, but we must have made a mistake. Aaron thinks likely several of the containers were untreated and contained Ethanol, which has a shorter life than gas without Ethanol.

Aaron and his team checked the remaining fuel and decided the rest, minus the one drum, was okay, but we're now questioning how long it'll really last. Will it go bad before we run out? Stabilized gasoline is said to have a shelf life of one to three years. Two years is a huge difference. With untreated diesel, under proper storage, we can expect one year—longer if treated. The *longer* is again a question. Two or three years seems to be the main thought.

None of us really think we'll have fuel for much longer, either gasoline or diesel. But we do hope we'll have enough to plant our summer crops and move our things down the hill. Next winter, it's unlikely we'll have the use of generators, but that's a worry for another day. It's also a reminder that nothing lasts forever in this new world.

The bad gas won't be completely wasted. It's being used as part of our assault on Prospect. It won't work for starting combustion engines, but it'll still burn. The old fuel, along with a stash of alcohol and jars, will become infamous Molotov Cocktails made popular by the mafia and others throughout the years. We hope, after liberating Prospect and Wesley, we'll be able to acquire more fuel to use for our planting season, and maybe even for harvesting.

According to Maddie, Prospect has a limited supply of fuel, but the hoodlums in Wesley have a large stash. She doesn't know if it's been treated, and she seemed surprised that was even a thing, but she said those in Wesley seem to have little concern about burning fuel. That information gives us hope of an advantage. Ideally, Prospect will call for help and most of the Wesley criminals will respond in their vehicles, giving the opportunity to eliminate them at the same time.

The original plan was to take the snowmobiles with us, but it was decided the bare spots were too great. Instead, they're with the watchers, on the mountain where there's enough snow, so they can zip back to the lodge for an evac at the first sign of trouble. We have horses and quads with a couple of small utility trailers connected to them.

We also have another advantage we haven't shared with the Prospect group. Dusty Cameron and his family hid several ATVs, an ancient Jeep, and an old dump truck when they escaped last fall. On one of the recent scouting trips, Dax made a detour to check if they're still there. They are, and with some jury-rigging, he was able to get each of them started, giving us another mode of escape should we need to retreat in a hurry.

Angela, Jake, and I started to set up camp last night, as Evan went over the final plans with the brothers and Maddie.

"Make sure they wear the ties," Evan said, handing the brothers a backpack full of bright pink and purple napkins from our community collection. "They can wear them around their neck, arm, even their head—doesn't matter. Cut them in half if you don't have enough. But if we see anyone with a weapon or staging an assault without one of them on, I can't guarantee their safety."

"Understood," Chance said. "We'll make sure our people are wearing them. If we run out, we'll find something similar, okay?"

"Got to be really close to the same. Bright pink or purple is what we told the team yesterday, remember?"

"I'll take care of it."

"And keep the children and any noncombatants inside. We don't need them fouling things up."

"Right."

"We'll be waiting for your signal. You're sure you have what's needed to create an explosion."

"Absolutely. That won't be a problem. And your people know what to do from their end?" Chance asks.

"Zeb's an expert," Evan answers. Zeb Frost, owner of the ski lodge, had a small stash of explosive devices they used on the mountain for avalanche control. Or the proper thing to say would be *rarely* used. While he has them on hand, he hadn't had a need to release the mountainside for several years. He left with our second team and will be in place to create a diversion with his explosives while the rebels do the same.

Also, thanks to Lindsey Maverick and a care package she was given by her sergeant at the police force before she left California, we have several flashbangs and smoke grenades. They'll be used in the liberation of the bordello, but their existence was not shared with the Prospect group.

After a few more minutes of making sure the plans were in place, Chance, Chase, and Maddie left to rally their rebels and prepare for the predawn assault. After we were sure they were gone, we quickly repacked the minor unpacking we'd done and moved our camp. Better safe than sorry.

Our new location was well planned and already occupied by Bill Shane and two people from his scout team. After handshakes all around, Bill said, "So we've had some changes, huh?"

After the arrival of the Prospect group, a runner was sent with a note to Bill's squad, letting him know what was happening and the new plan, along with where to meet us. Although Bill knew the general idea of what we were now doing, the minor changes we made after the note was sent were relayed.

"If they can come through, it ought to work," Bill said, scratching at his beard.

"Yeah, *if*," Evan said. "If not, hopefully we have enough of a backup plan to live through this."

"That and God's blessing," Bill said.

Camping last night didn't leave me with the most refreshing sleep. I had a backpacker's cot instead of a mattress or bare ground like most of the others did, but the ache in my hips and back this morning is almost debilitating. The turmeric, ginger, and garlic, along with the willow bark tincture, seem to provide less and less relief. I suspect it won't be long until taking them is completely futile. I'd be lying if I didn't admit the thought of the excruciating pain scares me. And even more so, the thought of my husband and children witnessing it really bothers me. With our limited supply of medication, I have little hope of anything making me comfortable as the end approaches.

"You okay?" Angela asks as I wobble toward the trees for my morning business.

"Just stiff," I answer, thinking about the pills Delores gave me. A half might take the edge off the pain, but I can't risk it affecting my shooting.

"What about today? Being in the same position for too long—will you be able to move when we need to?"

"I will," I answer. After we arrived last night, Bill discussed the overwatch nests he and his men had arranged based on the info in the original note. Dusty Cameron and his spotter, a young man named Tanner, along with another overwatch and spotter pair, left last night to move to where they can see the housing development occupied by the acquisition team. Creek View Estates is on the eastern side of the town in an open area. Those shooters have a spot across the creek on a hillside and will be taking extremely long shots. Their main goal is to keep the group pinned down so no one is able to leave the development.

Bill and his two guys will move to a spot right outside of town so they can go in as part of the up close and personal attack, while the rest of us set up for our overwatch jobs. Bill did a great job finding our original spot, plus our backups. Sneaking in last night so we could familiarize ourselves with the plan, with the sun setting behind us to help hide our movement, wasn't difficult but did require some careful stepping as we used a game trail etched into the side of the mountain. To keep from being seen, he didn't take us to our first location. To access it, we'll need to walk along the narrow trail on the edge of the hillside completely in the open. From a hidden spot behind a rock outcropping, he pointed out where we'll need to go in the morning under the cover of darkness.

"Doesn't look very stable," Angela said as she pointed to a loose spot in the packed trail.

"It probably washed out a bit over the winter," Bill said. "At least there isn't snow on it. It's not slick."

The lack of snow here will be an advantage in some ways. When we were making ghillie suits, we made ones that'd blend into the stark background of this hillside along with ones for snow. Those of us on east-facing slopes are using the earth-based camouflage. Dax and his spotter took snowy ones since they'll be on a north slope where there's still plenty of snow patches.

The first location will give Angela and me a perfect view of our target: the Bunn Mansion where Richard Majors is now living and holding Milena and Shelby hostage. Our focus is the abundant backyard and especially the back and side doors. We'll be nice and close too, only about five hundred yards away.

While we do want to keep the bloodshed to a minimum, we've been given the go-ahead to take out Richard and Scott Majors plus his officers. The brothers had photos of both the Majors and a few others who are known to be loyal to their cause. Although some pictures weren't great, they were better than nothing. Someone from the resistance quickly found newspaper clippings, old school yearbooks, and photographs so we'd at least have an idea of who the bad guys are. And we already know what Major Fred Lassiter looks like since he lived among us for so long. Of course, then we just called him Deputy Fred and had no idea of the evil he was truly capable of. In addition to our known targets—anyone not wearing a pink or purple napkin or one of our militia arm bands—anyone shooting at us is also fair game.

Our second location still has an acceptable view of the backyard and side door but not the back door, and it's another hundred yards away. Unfortunately, getting to the second location will leave us exposed for a dozen yards as we traverse the hillside using the game trail. Angela will go first while I cover her. She'll cover me from behind a rock outcropping while I move. Then we're both well concealed while finishing the move to the next setup, a good twenty feet beyond the outcropping. The third location is hidden the entire way and will be an overwatch spot to finish the job. From there, we can move left or right as needed to hide our activity.

Evan and Jake have a similar setup to the south. Where I'm covering the backyard, they have the front. The rebellion will be targeting the Bunn Mansion and Creek View Estates, along with neutralizing any sentry who may be an issue. Chance assured us an inside man will help Milena, Shelby, and the rest of Majors's captive women escape before the assault.

After a cold breakfast under the cover of darkness, Bill and his men prepare to leave.

"You have your arm bands?" Evan asks. Last summer, everyone on the militia was given arm bands so we could differentiate who was in our group when in the middle of a battle. When Evan asks about Bill's, I pull mine out of my pocket and slide it up and over my jacket. Even though my camouflage will go on over my jacket, I want to wear the band because my blood type is written in permanent marker on the inside.

"Yep. All set. I made sure everyone on our team had them before we separated. You reminded your team leaders?"

"They'll make sure their units are wearing them. Friendly fire is something we're going to avoid."

When they've been gone long enough for wisps of light to start showing over the mountains to the east, Evan says, "Might as well get into position. Remember, the sun will be rising behind the town. You should be fine and not get too much of a glare, but you also won't have the protection of the sun behind you. They could locate you quicker than you expect. Be ready to move."

"How many shots do you think I'll have there?" I ask after putting on my backpack. Even though my backpack is a neutral brown, my camo suit will go over the top. It fits better that way and provides less of an outline.

"That's your closest location but not your most concealed. My guess is three to five. You'll know when it's time to move. Don't wait too long—you'll be exposed while you crossover to the next spot. Your second nest will be much more hidden but not as on-target. You'll know Richard Majors when you see him?"

I give a nod. "I studied the photos they had. Angela?"

"I'll know him. The others too."

Once each of us are dressed, Evan passes around a container of face paint, the kind Jake used for archery or goose hunting. We smear our faces to add to the concealment. "You have your radio?"

"I have it," Angela says. "One click go, three is abort."

"Affirmative. But one click will only happen if something goes wrong. Your main *go* is the rebels and Zeb lighting up the sky."

"Got it," I say.

"Let's move."

Jake pulls me into his arms. "I'll see you soon."

"See you soon. Be careful."

"You too." He pecks me on the lips, carefully avoiding my face paint, before stepping back and giving Angela a hug. After telling her to be safe and to watch out for me, he hugs me again. Angela and I start toward our side, while Evan and Jake go toward theirs. In the early morning light, I see Jake turn and look at me. I blow him a kiss, which he pantomimes catching and pressing against his heart. I smile as my eyes fill with tears.

Getting into position without the aid of light is a bit of a challenge. Getting to the rock outcropping we viewed our first location from last night is harrowing enough. The final thin trail along the hillside is nail biting.

"Be careful," I hiss, as Angela takes the lead. I hold my breath until she gets passed the washed-out area.

"No problem, Mom. Just stay close to the hillside."

Once we're passed the washout, I breathe a sigh of relief as we take the last little bit to our nest. We get comfortable and into position, then sit quietly waiting.

# Chapter 40

## *Lucy*

"Lucy. Lucy, wake up."

"What's happening?" I ask, sitting upright.

"Shh," Donna says, putting a finger to her lips. "The town is being liberated."

"Liberated?"

"That's right," a second voice says, stepping close.

"Maddie? What are you doing here?"

"Just what Donna said. We're taking our town back. Which side are you on?"

I blink in the dark, trying to get my eyes to focus. "What do you mean?"

"Put her in the bathroom," a man's voice says. "We'll deal with her later."

"Captain Murphy? What— " The rest of my words are cut off as a piece of tape goes over my mouth. I thrust out my arm to push away the culprit. Strong arms grab me, dragging me from the bed.

"Quietly," a female says in hushed tones.

Who all is in my room? And what exactly is going on? Liberating the town—traitors! I whip my head, looking for Captain Murphy. I mumble through the tape, trying to use my voice like Lorita taught me to, as I kick with my feet.

"She's strong," someone says, flipping me onto my stomach and yanking my arms behind my back.

"Don't hurt her!" Maddie says in an urgent whisper. There's a quick tearing sound from the duct tape and my hands are bound. I'm still kicking until someone sits on my legs, using the tape at my ankles. I buck a few times, attempting to get loose, to no avail.

"Lucy," Captain Murphy commands in a stern voice, "calm down so you don't hurt yourself."

I mumble what he can do with his orders as I'm lifted from the floor. The bathroom door squeaks when it's opened, and a man asks, "In the tub?"

"Might as well," Murphy answers as they plop me into the tub.

"Here," Maddie says, shoving a pillow behind my back. "I wish . . . it'd be great if we could know you're with us."

I nod vigorously, trying to communicate with my eyes, "*Untie me. I'll be with you.*"

"It shouldn't be long," she says. "Cut the head off the snake and everyone else becomes weak. There aren't too many true believers. Don't move around too much. You'll end up hurting yourself." Maddie turns to leave.

I make a humming noise to get her attention.

"You'll be okay, Lucy. Just wait here. You'll be safe."

"Did you tie the cloth to her?" Murphy asks.

"Oh! I forgot." She pulls a strip of fabric from her pocket, tying it around my right arm. "Don't take this off. It'll keep you alive. We'll be back for you." I hear the lock turn, then hear her say to whoever is in my room, "Are the rest of the women accounted for?"

"Everyone else is on board," Mrs. Murphy answers. *Mrs. Murphy too!* They're all a bunch of traitors.

"That's no surprise," Dirk says. "Other than Alyssa, we hand-picked the remaining women, knowing they'd support us."

I scrunch my forehead.

"Not exactly true," Mrs. Murphy says. "Milena and Shelby being kidnapped from their families secured their loyalty to the resistance. Him keeping them drugged has been of little help."

"They seem sober enough now," Maddie says.

"I've been weaning Milena from it since I arrived. He had her so doped up. But really, Dirk," his mom says, "I wish you would've told me about this long ago."

"We had to keep it quiet. You couldn't know or you'd be in danger."

"Even so, I could've talked to Lucy and made her understand. She's a good person . . . " Her voice fades away as they move away from the bathroom door.

They're part of the rebellion—Dirk, his mom, Maddie, even Donna. But how can that be? Dirk is the one who encouraged me to join Richard's crew when he first killed Mayor Stringer and took over the town. Was he faking his allegiance this entire time? Or did he reconsider? And what about all the raids we've done? He's been involved in them too.

I move my cheek to my shoulder, attempting to rub the tape off. *Was he involved in the raids?* I don't remember a time when he wasn't in charge of the perimeter. Maddie or I would often be stationed with him, watching to make sure no one escaped. But they rarely did.

I work at trying to remove the tape from my mouth and hands. While one corner has peeled up from my cheek, it doesn't seem to go any further. After working it for many minutes, I give up and lay back against the pillow, straining to listen for clues as to what is happening in the mansion. Where's Richard? Did they grab him from his room too? *Cut off the head of the snake.* That's what Maddie said. No chance they'll tie him up and stuff him in a bathtub. They'll kill him.

There's just enough light coming in the single bathroom window so I can make out the fixtures in the room. Suddenly, a distant boom shatters the silence. I sit up straight. That sounded like it came from The Estates. I'm leaning back on my pillow when the tub shudders and a loud percussion fills the air. The mansion seems to roll like a ship on the rough seas.

# Chapter 41

## *Mollie*

The sky is light, but the sun is still below the mountain when the far-off rumble of the first explosion reaches our ears.

"Ready, Mom?" Angela asks in a shaky voice as she puts the binoculars to her eyes. Her rifle is next to her, handy for when it's time to move or shoot.

With my heart pounding, I focus on my target. The scope has a special feature to brighten low-light situations. I'm watching Richard Majors's house when the side door and several windows blow apart.

"Wow," Angela says under her breath.

Wow indeed. In the next few seconds, everything goes crazy with explosions and shooting. Evan's rifle sounds once, causing Angela to jump.

"It was Evan," I say.

"Not someone shooting at us?"

"We're fine." I'm beginning to wonder if I'll have any targets of my own, and I'm praying I won't, when someone stumbles out the backdoor.

"No bandana," Angela says. "He's not a friendly."

I take the shot and watch him fall as I work the bolt to chamber another round. Two more are quickly behind him.

"More bad guys," she says.

My second shot is a miss. I take a deep breath and reposition on my target—a short man with a slight belly and receding hairline—for my final shot before we move. As he fills my scope, I realize it's Fred Lassiter. His mouth is open and he's moving his arm rapidly in the general direction of our hillside. I'm squeezing the trigger when the dirt beneath us flies up.

"Mom!" Angela says, her voice excited. "There's people coming around the house. They've found us. We need to move."

"Keep low and watch the loose spot," I say. "Once you're behind the cover, start firing and I'll move—just like we talked about."

"Okay," she says, her voice catching.

"Go," I say, as the men coming around the corner shoot again. They don't know exactly where we are; they're shooting based on where they *think* we are. When they see Angela, though, they'll know for sure.

I shift my aim to the group at the side of the house, choosing one with a rifle up to his shoulder, then squeeze the trigger. I have no idea if he went down when I reposition on the next man. He quickly steps back, finding cover. I locate a new target, who's also scrambling for cover, and shoot again. I take one more shot. This time, I'm able to see the successful results.

I hear Angela's rifle bark. Like me, she'll have six shots—five in the magazine and one in the chamber—before she needs to reload. While I have a second magazine and can make a quick switch, she only has the one. My goal is to reach her before she has to reload.

I grab my rifle with my left arm, tucking it close to my body, and take off as the men at the house resume shooting. There's plenty of light now to see the hazards. I'm steps away from the washed-out area when the ground disappears. Unable to stop my forward motion, I put out an arm for some sort of balance as my stomach drops.

I'm going down, and there's no way to stop it.

I let go of the rifle and pull both arms in close as I lean back, trying to turn the quickly disappearing game trail into a playground slide, hoping to ride it all the way to the bottom. I let out an involuntary *oomph* as the abrupt motion takes my breath away.

"Mom!" Angela's voice carries above the roar of war surrounding us.

My hope of an easy slide down the hill is gone as my left foot catches a rock, throwing me to one side and resulting in a plummet. Though I try not to, I scream out in pain. Another rock hooks my upper back. I see a flash of bright white followed by a warm feeling and searing pain.

When my motion stops, I'm staring straight up at the pink-tinged morning sky. My backpack is underneath me, putting me at an awkward angle. The pain now feels far away, almost like it was a dream. I blink several times and then turn my head toward Prospect. I'm in a gully at the base of the hillside and can't see anything, which means the shooters can't see me either. Even though I'm hidden from view, the shooting and other sounds are still evident.

I try to roll over, to make my way to my feet, but my body doesn't want to cooperate. My leg, which felt like it was on fire after hitting the rock, seems okay now and is without pain. The pain that coursed through me is also gone, leaving only a residual memory of how bad it was. I attempt a deep breath, which catches midway. The crushing I experienced over the winter is back, but it's substantially worse. An involuntary cough overtakes me as I gasp for breath.

"Great," I mutter as my world begins to spin.

# Chapter 42

## *Lucy*

The gunfire, explosions, and shouting have been going on for what feels like forever but is probably only minutes. I hate to think of the battle taking place outside of this bathroom. There's a good chance I owe Dirk, Maddie, Donna, Mrs. Murphy, and whoever else my life. Are they okay? Are the other women okay? What about Richard? A pang hits me as I think he may be dead.

*Cut off the head of the snake.*

Of course, Richard is the snake—him, Scott, Lassiter, and the other officers. Probably the entire acquisition team, too, people I've lived with for the past several months. I think of Lorita and the way she taught me to fight. Or *tried* to teach me. Is she fighting for her life against the rebels right now?

I take a deep breath. *What's that smell?*

With several short breaths, I sniff the air like a dog. The blasted tape across my mouth is messing with my sense of smell. But I think it's— my eyes go wide. Smoke. Of course. With all the explosions, it's to be expected . . . right? Yeah, sure. No need to worry about the fact I'm tied up in a locked room.

I concentrate on breathing normally. If the mansion is on fire, maybe the cast iron tub will give me some protection. I let out a snort. I'll die from the smoke long before the flames are an issue. The last few moments that I've been focusing on the possibility of a fire, I've failed to pay attention to the noise. The shooting seems to have lessened, and I haven't heard any explosions for several minutes.

I pay attention to the sounds. Someone's screaming. And there's crying nearby—maybe from a child. Someone's shouting what sounds like, *"Get on the ground!"* A single gunshot. A pistol. My nose is starting to burn. The smoke is getting stronger, closer. Time to find a way out of this death trap of a bathroom.

With my feet taped together, my movements are very fishlike. No. Make that mermaidlike. I move my torso to the edge of the tub. What was the shoulder roll thing Lorita tried to teach me? Can I do it from a cast iron tub onto a tile floor without busting my head wide open? Lorita made a big deal about protecting my head with my arms. My arms are tied behind my back. Maybe I can roll on my shoulder and get to my feet. I'm perched and ready to move when I hear the running of feet. The doorknob jiggles.

"Cover yourself! I'm coming in!" a man yells out.

*Cover myself?* My slow-acting brain realizes he's breaking the door in a fraction of a second before it happens. I'm still balanced in my awkward position and have only enough time to turn my head and lift my shoulder. There's a sharp pain and then a burn in my left bicep. I let out an audible gasp around the tape. Imbedded in my upper arm is a six-inch piece of the door sticking straight out. Six inches showing . . . how much is inside my arm? My pink pajama top is already sporting a stream of blood.

"We've got to get you out of here," Dirk says. "Ack, jeez. The door got you."

*"You think?"* I attempt to say around the duct tape, as smoke billows into the room behind him.

"It's too big for me to yank out. Hold on." He takes out a multitool. "I'll nip it off and we'll deal with it later." There's no time for me to protest as he uses the wire cutter part to trim the splinter so it's not hanging out as far. He's left enough to be able to remove it— provided he gets me out of here before the smoke overtakes both of us. He switches from the cutter to a knife and slits the tape around my legs. "Let's go," he says as he drags me out of the tub. The splinter in my arm burns like the approaching fire as he hefts me to my feet. We're already moving when he yanks the tape from my mouth.

"My arms?"

"When we're outside. I tried to get here quicker. Let's move."

"Where's the fire?"

"The mansion!"

"No! I mean, *where?*"

"West wing, both floors—Majors's quarters. The staircase is still clear."

As we step into the hallway, I say, "You sure?" Flames are visible in the sitting room.

"Change of plans," he says as we turn in the opposite direction. I struggle to keep up with his quick strides as he hustles us down the hallway. "Which door?"

"This one." I motion with my head to the door hiding the servants' staircase.

He reaches out and puts a hand on the door. I notice, like me, he's wearing a bright swatch of cloth around his arm. He shakes his head and lightly touches the knob. "No good. They're both hot."

"So? Let's just go."

He gives me a look. "Hot means fire. We need another way."

"Back to my room." I start to move. "There's a ladder out the window."

"A ladder?"

"Close enough."

The fire is at the opening of the hallway. I have little doubt the wall of the sitting room is gone, which means the fire is in Milena's room. My room's next to hers.

Dirk was smart to close the bedroom door when we left, but again he feels it. "I don't like this," he says. "It's warm to the touch."

"We're out of options!" The noise of the fire is filling the hallway.

He slowly opens the door. "Smoke but no flames. Let's go." Rushing to the window, he throws it open and looks out. "Oh, this is going to be fun," he mutters.

"Undo me."

Whipping out his knife, he quickly cuts the tape away. "You go first."

"No problem," I say, hiking my leg over the windowsill. My arm hurts and my feet are bare, but I'm getting out of this inferno.

"You'll need to hang and reach. The lattice is a good five feet below the window," Dirk says.

As I slowly lower myself, I keep my feet against the wall, letting my toes feel the way. "I can't find it!"

"You're almost there," he says.

With my injured arm screaming in pain, I'm not sure I have the strength to keep from falling. Suddenly, my feet connect with a wooden slat. "I'm on. Now . . . what should I do?"

"Hold on with your hands and go down another rung. Lean into the wall."

305

I make it down two more rungs. I'm hanging on to the window ledge with my fingertips when Dirk says, "The fire just broke through. I need to get out of here. Scoot over."

"Scoot over? Easy for you to say." I move to the right to give him room. He has one leg out when the window of Milena's room blows out. I'm far enough away to be uninjured, but the noise startles me and I momentarily lose my precarious grip on the ledge. Dirk doesn't even stop. He scurries over the ledge and is quickly balanced next to me, seeming to be much steadier. His additional height is an advantage.

"Use me as your ladder. Let go of the window and grab my arm. Go down another rung. Keep a hold of me."

"You're sure?"

"Go!" I do as he asks, making it all the way down him until I'm holding onto the top rung of the trellis. "Now quick. Get on the ground. I'm right behind you." The words are no sooner out of his mouth then the window of my room blows out, showering us in glass. Thankfully, I was looking down at the ground when it happened.

"You okay?" I ask.

"I'm okay. Go."

"I'm there," I say as I step onto the ground. A sharp pain shoots through my right foot, causing me to yell out.

"What happened?" he asks, dropping next to me.

"Bare feet. Glass."

He picks me up and starts running to the far eastern side of the house. We round the corner, and he skids to a stop.

"Well, Dirk, don't you look cozy?" Janet sneers, her pistol trained on us. "Not only a traitor to our town, but you're slumming around with the easiest girl in Prospect? What would the schoolboard say?"

Dirk carefully lowers me to the ground.

"Keep your hands away from your gun," she says, motioning with her pistol. She's close, only about ten feet away. Too close to miss. "You're about as unprepared as I'd expect." She uses the pistol as a pointer, aiming in my direction. "Pajamas. You couldn't even get dressed before going outside?"

I balance on my uncut foot and the big toe of the other.

"We need to go," Dirk says, his hands lifted away from his body in a surrender pose. "The fire's heading this way. The whole building is going to go up."

"Thank you, Captain Obvious. I always knew you couldn't be trusted. I told Richard—he's dead, you know."

"Richard's dead?" I say with a gasp. This shouldn't surprise me after the whole cut the head off the snake thing Maddie said, but the confirmation of his death hurts my heart.

"We took him alive," Dirk says. "He— "

"Like you care?" Janet says, waving the gun around like it's a glass of wine. "That redheaded little tart, she murdered him in cold blood. He didn't even have a weapon, and she went nuts. I saw her standing over his body. Her and the big blond bimbo," she sneers. "Pretty sure I winged at least one of them as they were running away. I sent Lorita after them to finish the job."

My heart lurches at my friend Lorita killing my friends Milena and Shelby. Wait. Are Milena and Shelby my friends? I admire the way they were pulling themselves together, and I did like Shelby when we lived in the same building. But with Lorita, there's a camaraderie, a bond knowing we're on the same team.

*The wrong team.* The voice makes me snap my head around in search of it.

Janet must have heard it too because she too swivels, looking around. "What are you doing?" she asks harshly. "Freak."

"I was just—didn't you hear that?" I ask, looking again for the voice.

"Janet," Dirk says calmly. "It's over now. It's time for our town to start healing. You've been a leader people look up to. That needn't change."

"Oh, they will," she answers. "Unlike you and this floozy, I've been loyal, and people will respect me. Me! With Richard and Knight dead—probably Scott too—and with that wuss Fred Lassiter running away like a scared little boy, I'll be the ranking officer. As soon as I get rid of you, *Captain* Murphy."

"Wait!" I cry as she raises her gun. "I wasn't part of this. They tied me up and put me in the bathroom."

Janet lets out a howl of laughter. "Of course they did. It doesn't surprise me a bit that you were completely useless. That's been you since I've known you, Lucy Fleming. Do you have any idea what a disappointment you were to your parents? Your mom especially. She had such high hopes for you, thought you'd make her proud. Ha! You were nothing but a failure from the get-go. The best thing to happen to her was getting out of this God-forsaken place and leaving you behind."

I stare at the ground, there's a silver-dollar-sized puddle of blood from my right foot. "I didn't betray him," I say quietly, lifting my eyes to meet Janet's. "They locked me up because they knew I wouldn't. His death is a huge loss to our town. Are you sure about General Majors? If he's still alive, we can . . . everything can go back to normal."

"Lucy," Dirk says with warning in his voice.

"No! I'm not a traitor! You did this, not me. Let me help you, Janet. Let me work with you."

"You're something, aren't you? Always looking out for yourself and willing to do whatever it takes."

"That's right," I say, straightening my shoulders. The pain from the splinter screams at me. I grit my teeth and take a breath. "I want to live, and I'll do whatever I must do."

Janet shakes her head. "I'm sure I'm going to regret this. And if it weren't for Lorita, who made a point of telling me she thinks you might be useful with a little more training, I'd put a bullet in your head right now."

"No, Lucy," Dirk says.

I shoot him the stink eye. "Thank you, Janet—Lieutenant Kruse."

"Don't be thanking me yet. Let me down and the bullet will become reality."

"You don't really think you'll be able to take back the town, do you?" Dirk asks.

"Not your concern. Get over here, Lucy." Janet motions to the spot next to her.

"What now, Janet?" Dirk sounds dejected as I take an unsteady step.

"Now I shoot you and we go on with things."

I'm about a yard from Janet with my uninjured foot planted firmly on the ground. My right foot, with at least one piece of glass sticking out of it, is behind me as I balance on my toes. In an instant, I raise my injured leg while pivoting on the ball of my stable foot and rotating. My kicking leg fully extends, as the top of my foot smacks Janet in the arm, sending her pistol sailing. I quickly retract my leg as I immediately go into a roll. I'm barely out of the way when a shot sounds, followed by a second. My roll puts me on my bottom. I crab crawl to the side of the house.

Janet is on the ground, her dead eyes staring into nothingness.

"Let's go," Dirk says, lifting me to standing. "I wish you would've given me some indication of what you were doing."

"Sorry," I say as we move. We're at the far corner of the house when the windows above and below blow out and the roof starts to go.

"No more time," he says as he breaks into a sprint with the mansion collapsing behind us.

# Chapter 43

## *Mollie*

"Mom?"

"Mm-hmm." I try to pull myself from my fog.

"You're alive! Thank you, God, thank you!"

"Mmm . . . " I answer as I open one eye.

Angela's tear-streaked face stares back at me. A bird sings in the distance.

"The attack?" I ask.

"Over, I guess. Shortly after you fell, several people wearing our napkins started to appear. I watched them as I reloaded. It was . . . " She lets out a sigh. "They didn't have much mercy—none, really." She shudders. "Richard Majors, at least I'm fairly certain it was him, was being walked away when he suddenly started fighting. Milena was there. She— "

"How long ago?"

"What?"

"When did it end? Did you hear from Jake?"

"Um . . . I lost the radio. I guess . . . " She lets out a small noise, something between a laugh and a cry. "It has a bullet hole in it."

"What?" I gasp. "Are you hurt?"

"I'm fine. The radio was on my hip. It's useless, but I'm fine."

"Praise God."

"I am—believe me, I am. And for finding you alive. I thought— " She makes the noise again.

"Help me up?"

"Are you kidding? Not with the way your ankle looks. We'll need a stretcher to get you out of here."

"My ankle?" I ask, crinkling my face. "It doesn't hurt."

"Really? It's— " She shakes her head. "It doesn't hurt at all?"

"It did, but not now. Are you sure it's over?"

"Yeah, I could see them—the rebels and a few of our people too, Cole Gunderson and Bill Shane plus a few others, including Art."

"Sarah? Leo?"

"No, but I wouldn't expect to. They're nowhere near the mansion or downtown."

"So we don't know if the Wesley people were stopped?"

"Oh! I just assumed they were." She shakes her head. "I don't know. I'm going to loop around and go back to where we camped. From there, I'll find Evan and Jake. They can use their radio to call for a medic. You're okay on your own?"

"What's wrong with my ankle?"

"Broken, and your foot is bent funny. Nothing is poking through the skin, but it's definitely broken."

"Okay. Anything else?"

"You've torn your ghillie suit. There's a cut on your arm. It's not bad, though—not even actively bleeding. And a cut along your cheek, which also stopped bleeding. Do you want a drink of water before I go? And are you comfortable with your backpack under you?"

"Backpack's fine—I can't even feel it. Water would be good. But you'll have to help me sit up."

"You can't feel the backpack?" Angela stares at me for a moment, then in a whisper says, "And you can't feel your leg? Can you move your leg? The not broken one?"

"I'm sure I can . . . see?"

"What'd you do?"

"I lifted my leg." I crinkle my forehead. As I say it, I wonder, *Did I lift it?* I know I thought of lifting it. "Didn't I?"

Angela turns to me, panic covering her face. "I don't want you to move, Mom. You might have—maybe something's wrong with your back? I'm going after Belinda. Don't move your head either."

"Okay," I whisper. "Can I have water before you go?"

"I'll help you, but I don't want you to move at all."

Angela takes out her water bottle. "Maybe with a spoon?" she asks. "That way you can just . . . not move." She pulls her spoon out of her pack. I notice she's shaking, causing her to spill the water as she tries to dribble it into the spoon.

"It's okay, Angela," I say. "Whatever happens, it's okay. I'm okay."

"What if your back's broken and you're paralyzed? Can you move your arms?"

"I'm wiggling my fingers," I say.

She looks at the hand nearest her and then the other hand. "Nothing's moving. Here." She gives me a spoonful of water and then several more. "Better?"

"Better."

"I'll be right back. Seriously, don't try and move. Not your hands, feet, anything. Just wait. Belinda will know what to do." She puts her hand on my cheek. "I'll be right back."

As she stands, a voice calls out, "Mollie? Angela?"

"It's Jake," I say.

Angela spins her head around. "Up there," she says, pointing toward where I tried to slide down the hill. "Jake! We're down here. Mom's hurt! We need Belinda!"

"Copy that," Evan replies. "I'll get a medic."

"I'll be right there," Jake says.

"Hurry, Evan!" Angela urges. "Jake, go around. You can't get down from there—not safely anyway."

I want to make some smart remark about how I tried to make a nice route down, but my wit seems to have left me. Angela's probably right. My broken leg doesn't hurt and the constant pains in my back and hips are gone. I close my eyes as I take a deep breath, which results in me coughing.

"Mom! Don't move."

"Trying. Not. To," I say as the coughing subsides. I felt that—the crushing on my chest is evident.

After many minutes, Jake calls out again. "Mollie?"

"We're here," Angela answers. A few seconds later, she says, "Jake, you need . . . you should sit on the other side by her head. She can't move."

"Can't move?"

"My back doesn't hurt," I say hopefully.

His Adam's apple bounces as he swallows. "No pain is good," he says quietly. "Can you feel me holding your hand?"

I close my eyes. "Not the sensation, but . . . I know you are. My heart knows."

"I just felt your hand move," he says with a smile.

"You did?" Angela asks. "Can you move the one on my side?" I lift my hand up from the dusty ground. "Yes! Okay. You bent your

312

wrist, that's good. But you should probably just hold still until Belinda gets here. That's probably best."

After a few minutes of quiet, I say, "Our radio is gone, but Angela thinks it's over."

"There are a few small skirmishes happening in town. The brothers were right. The rebellion did their part, and it seems many of the other people also joined in. Bill and Cole both checked in. Bill has Milena and Shelby with him."

"That's wonderful," I say.

He nods. "Leo's team got the hostages from the bordello, and as expected, the people from Wesley came roaring down the road. They stopped them—uh, cold."

"Sarah?" I ask.

Jake shakes his head. "Leo didn't say. I know they had a few losses, but he didn't give any names."

"But if Sarah would've been one, he would've said, right?" Angela asks.

Jake shakes his head again, this time combining it with a shrug. "I don't know. I don't know how any of our family is except Leo."

A tear runs out of my eye and into my ear as I worry about my daughter and the rest of our close-knit family.

"I saw Art," Angela says. "When I was still up top, after Mom fell and I was trying to take over as sniper for her."

I close my eyes, thinking about all that's happened this morning. "How long?" I ask.

"What do you mean?" Angela asks.

"How long did it take? What time is it?"

"Not too long," Jake answers. "From the first explosions to when we heard from Bill was about half an hour. We stayed in place until Cole, Leo, and the other team leaders checked in."

"I started moving as soon as the main shooting stopped," Angela says. "I watched you fall but couldn't do anything then."

"The klutz I am. I can't believe I fell where I'd been so adamant about being careful."

"It was the shooting. They shot when I was running. I felt the bullets hitting the dirt below me and above me. That must have been when they hit the radio."

"Your radio was hit?" Jake asks. "But you're not hurt?"

"Weird, huh?" she says.

313

"A miracle," I answer.

"The shooting is what took the hillside out," Angela says. "Not you being a klutz. I should've told you not to try it. I was shooting when I saw the dirt falling, but I didn't know it was completely gone. I'm sorry, Mom."

"You have nothing to be sorry for. Where's my rifle? Is it ruined?"

"It looks okay," Angela says. "But someone will need to make sure the scope isn't messed up."

"I'm going to . . . I just want to close my eyes for a minute."

"No, Mom. You need to stay awake. Keep talking to us until Belinda gets here."

While Jake and Angela try to keep me talking and alert, my eyes are closed and my mind drifts. A few times, I feel myself nodding off and one of them will say my name way too loud. While my body doesn't hurt, there's a pounding beginning behind my left eye and another at the base of my neck. A roaring headache is developing.

"Do you hear that?" Angela asks. "Sounds like one of the quads."

I'm trying to focus on the sound as Jake says, "I'm going to move to the edge, just in case it's not a friendly."

"I'll be ready," Angela says.

"Jake?" a voice calls out, causing me to open my eyes wide. The bright sunlight sears my eyes and does nothing to help the pounding in my head. I squeeze them shut.

"Here," Jake calls, while Angela says, "It's Belinda, Mom."

"Yes." My voice sounds weak.

It's a few minutes of Belinda calling and Jake answering before Angela says, "Right here, Belinda."

"Well, Mollie," Belinda says. "What are you up to now?"

"She can't move her legs," Angela blurts.

Belinda lets out a huge sigh.

"How's Katie?" I ask.

"Fine. She's still in The Bowl taking care of anyone who finds their way there or is brought in by one of the team. Madison, Laurie, and I go out to those who call for us."

"Do you happen to know anything about Sarah?" I ask. "Or Mike and his dad? Ben?"

"I haven't seen any of the men. Sarah's still at the bordello. Some of the women aren't in great shape. She's helping Leo triage until Madison can get there."

"You're sure?" I ask, my heart speeding up with excitement.

"That's what Leo said. Where do you hurt?"

"Headache. Bad one. Angela said she thinks my ankle is broken. It hurt when I came down the hill, but it's fine now."

"Can you feel me pressing on your leg?"

"Don't feel it."

"Mm-hmm," Belinda responds. After a few minutes, she has Jake help her get me in a cervical collar. "I'm going to splint your ankle and then we'll get going."

After she tends to my ankle, she does a quick check over the rest of me. "Looks like something might be wrong with your hip or pelvis too," she says.

"Really?" I ask. "That's not good."

"Nope. Still no pain?"

"Just my head. I . . . um, I have painkillers in my backpack."

"The turmeric?"

"Not that. OxyContin."

"Oh?"

"It's a long story. Could I have a half? My head might just explode when you move me."

Belinda and Jake carefully move me so they can get to the pack and also get me on the stretcher—not an actual stretcher but a roll-up game sled used for hauling elk out. Belinda gives me the half dose, then they secure me in the sled. I feel like a sausage the way they have me wrapped up.

Once I'm in and stable, Belinda says, "Had I known what we were dealing with, I would've brought one of our boards. As it is, we need to do our best not to jar her on the way out. Jake, you take her feet. Angela and I will get her shoulders. We want to keep her as straight as possible, which—well, it's not going to be fun getting her out of this gully."

"Should we wait until the pill takes affect?" Jake asks.

"We need to get her back," Belinda says. "We'll be as gentle as we can, Mollie."

When they lift me up, Angela says, "Mom, you don't weigh anything."

I can't see her face but do see Belinda's. She raises her eyebrows at me before saying, "Good thing or we'd never get her out of here."

My head's still pounding, and every so often I feel a pushing or tugging sensation, similar to the feeling of an epidural during childbirth. I can tell something's happening, but it's almost like it's happening to someone else and not me. When we're finally out of the gully, they gently set me on the ground.

"Put the gate of the trailer down," Belinda says. "I'll ride with her. Jake you drive the quad and Angela can ride pillion. Take it nice and slow and try not to hit any big bumps. How you doing, Mollie?"

"I don't hurt much," I say. "Even the headache's easing off. Guess the pill's starting to work. The crushing is back on my chest—an elephant's sitting there laughing at me."

"Okay. We'll get you to the medical tent and go from there."

We've barely started the bumpy trip when I feel the need to vomit. I let Belinda know and she quickly calls for Jake to stop while gently turning me to my side. Out of nowhere, she produces a small bag, holding it for me as I do what I need.

"Sorry, Mollie. I should've had you on your side when we started." She tells Jake to go ahead.

As we again start bumping along, I ask, "So I broke my back along with my ankle and hip?"

"The ankle is definitely broken. Your hip, maybe. But your back . . . I don't know for sure. You could just have some bruising and swelling, which will subside."

"Really? You believe that?"

"I don't know, Mollie."

"If it's broken, what can you do?" After several beats with no answer, I prompt, "Belinda?"

"Nothing. There's nothing I can do."

# Chapter 44

## *Lucy*

"Put me down," I demand.

"Let's put more distance between us and the mansion," Captain Murphy says.

"We're far enough. Put me down and tell me—is he really dead?"

We reach a large tree and he steps behind it, gently lowering me to the ground. "Let me take a look at your foot."

"Not until you tell me if Richard is dead."

He gives a shrug. "I have no reason to doubt what Janet said, but I don't know for certain."

Looking at my toes, I swallow the lump in my throat.

"Is this going to be a problem, Lucy?"

"In what way?"

"Look at me."

I shake my head as my tears begin to fall. He pulls me close as my sobs overtake me. Instead of berating me or telling me I'm stupid to be sad over Richard's death, he simply holds me and lets me cry.

After many minutes, I'm calm enough to croak out a question. "Why?"

"Why?" he repeats. "Are you asking why Richard died?"

"Why'd you do this?"

"What do you mean?"

"Turn on Richard and attack our town! Why would you do that?"

"He was killing us, Lucy. Can't you see? Can't you see what he was doing was wrong?"

"Wrong for who? We were saving lives! The things we did, they kept people alive."

He gives a slow shake of his head. "No, we were taking lives. Every time we went on a raid, we murdered people. And for what? So Scott Majors could commit mass murder in our town?"

317

I narrow my eyes. "You think the rumors of the . . . the mercy killings are true?"

"Mercy killings? They weren't killing people to be merciful. They're killing them because they believe they're a drain on society."

"Richard wouldn't do that."

"He knew about it. He gave Scott, Lassiter, and Doc Bohm free rein to do what they felt best regarding the elderly and handicapped—not even actual handicaps! It's a form of genocide."

I give him a hard look. "And you know this how?"

"I'm an officer, or was anyway."

"They told you?"

"They wanted me to be a part of it! When I refused . . . " He lets out a sigh. "I had several reprogramming appointments with Doc Bohm."

"Why did—all those months ago, you told me to join Richard. Why?"

"So you'd live! I thought . . . I didn't think it'd get to the point it has. But I should've known. History has a way of repeating itself."

"Now what?"

"Lucy? Lucy!" Maddie calls out, running toward me. "You're okay!"

She's opening her arms like she plans to crush me in a hug. I lift a hand to stop her. "I'm okay," I say gruffly. "No thanks to you. When you all locked me in the bathroom, did it occur to you that you were signing my death warrant?"

Maddie hangs her head for a moment before popping up and saying, "Jeez. Dramatic much?"

I purse my lips and give her a dirty look. "They killed him. I suppose you're happy."

"I'm not. I would've preferred us taking back the town without bloodshed."

"Sure you would've."

"It's true," Captain Murphy says. "While there were losses, we also have many who surrendered. Let's get you to the clinic for treatment." He stoops like he's going to pick me up again.

"I'll walk." I yank my upper body away from him.

"Really?" Maddie asks. "Your foot and arm . . . you should let him carry you."

I wave them both away and begin to hobble toward the old warehouse turned medical clinic. After only a few feet, with my injured foot aching and my noninjured bare foot catching a pebble, I let out a yelp. I drop my head. "Okay," I say quietly.

The medical clinic is barely controlled chaos. I'm directed to a chair. Dirk Murphy—I've decided I'm never referring to him as *Captain* again—deposits me to a standing position and then helps me sit.

"I'll be back to check on you later. Maddie, can you stay?"

"Planned on it," she says, giving me a smile.

I roll my eyes.

After Dirk leaves, I turn to Maddie. "How many of our friends did you murder?"

She makes a point of meeting my eyes. "While I don't know if I'm the one who fired the fatal shot, I did shoot at Lieutenant Knight."

"Humph."

"But I wouldn't consider him a friend. Would you?"

"Our real friends?"

"There were two men from the acquisition team also, Vie and Hays. We weren't friendly with them."

I shake my head. Vie and Hays were cruel. Both thought they were super soldiers, but neither had the skills Lorita and a few others do. Brutality and lack of conscience were their main assets. "How about Mae or Susie? You do remember the women we lived with for the past six months, right?"

"To my knowledge, the house was secured and they're still being held there. I don't think any of our roommates were killed or injured."

"But you don't know? And Lorita?"

Maddie drops her head. "I'm not sure. She and several others were pulled out of the Estate last night and given guard duty. I heard rumors—no, I don't think she made it."

"*She* was my friend. A true friend. Not someone like *you* who locked me in a room to die." My voice is raised enough people nearby turn to look. I glare at a lady who makes a *shushing* noise.

In a low voice, Maddie says, "The fire got away from us. We didn't know the explosives would be so . . . powerful."

"Really? You bombed the house and were surprised when it burned down? Look. I don't want you to wait with me. I don't even want to look at you or have anything to do with you—ever!"

"Lucy— "

"Go!"

This time my shout earns a reprimand from the triage nurse, who yells out, "No fighting in here."

"I'll, uh . . . I'll go now, but I'm coming back soon to make sure you're okay and to find you a place to stay tonight."

"Don't bother," I say, turning my body away from her.

# Chapter 45

## *Tuesday, Day 315*

## *Mollie*

The sound of crying wakes me. As the world comes into focus, I hear a soft voice making soothing sounds. "You're okay, Tate," she says quietly. "Give a big burp and you'll feel better."

"Does he have a bubble?" I ask.

"Sorry he woke you, Mom," Sarah says. "He fell asleep while I was feeding him, but then . . . "

"It's fine. I love hearing him."

"Let me put him in his basket and I'll get you a drink."

"Can you put him over here so I can see him?" I ask.

She moves into my line of vision and holds Tate out. His eyes are watery from his recent outburst. He wrinkles up his face to prepare for another wail.

"He's not happy, is he?"

Midmovement, his face relaxes and he makes a gurgling noise followed by a healthy belch.

"That should help," Sarah says with a small laugh.

"Is Mom awake?" Malcolm asks from the door to my bedroom. "Can I come in?"

"Of course," I answer. Although I can hear him, I can't yet see him. The original soft cervical collar Belinda put on me in the gully was replaced with a rigid neck brace—one of our salvaged items from an empty house in Bakerville. Now, I'm positioned so I'm on my right staring at the wall. A vast improvement from how I spent yesterday, bound to a skinny board using many lengths of fabric to further immobilize me for the trip from the medical tent in The Bowl back up the mountain.

They left me secured for several hours after we arrived, while my bedroom was rearranged to make my future care as easy as possible. Because of concern of skin breakdown, commonly called bed sores, I'm repositioned every couple of hours. What an ordeal it is!

"Here, squirt," Sarah says to Malcolm. "You hold Tate so I can get Mom a drink of water." Seconds later, she's sticking a straw in my mouth. I take a tentative sip, having learned too much too fast results in choking. Belinda says it's common in tetraplegia or quadriplegia—paralysis affecting all four limbs. We don't have a way to do x-rays or any in-depth medical studies, but there seems to be little doubt my fall resulted in me injuring my spinal cord, most likely my C6 or C7 vertebrae. I can lift my arms and even bend my elbows, though I can't really *feel* I'm doing it. Swallowing is a challenge, and I'm on a complete liquid diet. Breathing is always difficult, feeling like I can't get the air I need.

"Do you want me to read to you?" Malcolm asks. "Sarah said, when you woke up, it'd be my turn to sit with you and I should read."

"Would you like to read to me?" I ask.

"I will . . . or we could just talk."

"Talking is good too."

He scoots his chair close to my head so I can see him. "Tony and I are helping with the packing. Doris wants to get everything organized so we can move things back down to our houses. But we have to leave some things here. You know about that, right?"

"We'll take what we can," I say, happy to hear him talking of normal things. When we returned yesterday, he was almost inconsolable. With Belinda's help, Jake explained my injuries to Malcolm, Tony, Lily, and the grandchildren. They wanted the kids to be prepared before seeing me tied up to a board and unable to move. Yesterday was hard not only for Malcolm and the younger kids but for the older children too. Angela, Sarah, and Katie had almost twenty-four hours of knowing but were still teary eyed. Calley's first glimpse of me didn't go well. Like Malcolm, she was heartbroken, especially when it became clear I'll likely never walk or even be able to properly hold her soon-to-be-born baby.

"There was a huge talk—Dad said it was a debate—about all the hides we've collected over the winter," Malcolm says. "Someone said we should take them down with us and start working them during the summer. But someone else said we have way too much work to do over the summer and should've been working on them all winter."

"Right," I say with a laugh. "Because we didn't have enough work to do over winter."

"That's what Doris said! Anyway, they decided to hook up freezers to the solar systems and put most of the hides in the freezers to keep them, uh . . . "

"Frozen?" I offer.

"Yeah. Someone else said fresh. Frozen seems right, though. We'll leave most of them here and take only a couple down to work on. With the warmer weather, they'll rot fast if they don't get cured in time. And Mr. and Mrs. Frost, plus the others staying up here, will make sure the freezer ones stay frozen. They won't need much electricity since there will be so few people here, so the amount of solar power the freezers use won't be a problem."

"True. Good thinking."

"Yeah, then we'll move back here in the winter and we'll do more of them. Sarah says it'll be one of the jobs for the sewing crew. Unless, of course, things get better by then. We haven't heard any new announcements from the president, but Calley says it's only a matter of time. Do you think she's right?"

"I'm sure we'll know more soon."

"Did Dad tell you some people left this morning to start the planting?"

"I heard a little about it. Do you want to tell me more?"

"Mr. Sanchez says he'll be surprised if we get a beet crop before the fall, says he would've liked to have them in the ground two weeks ago. He and Mr. Michaelson, along with a couple of the Baker guys, all left and took about a dozen people with them to work the fields."

"That doesn't seem like enough people to do all the planting."

"Mr. Sanchez said the same thing! But they do have the tractor, or at least they think they do, the tractor Tate and Aaron got running last September before . . . " His voice trails off.

"Before Tate went missing?"

"I wish he would've come back, like how Tony's dad did. Sometimes, over the winter, I'd think maybe he and his dad found a warm place to stay and when the weather was better, they'd show up here."

"Many of us had the same hope."

"But it's not going to happen, is it?"

"Our God is a God of miracles, but . . . I just don't know, Malcolm."

I barely have the words out before Malcolm says how sad it makes him and then quickly switches gears to a new subject, this one about swords and how our novice blacksmith is taking some tips from Paul Cameron on knife making and thinks he could make swords.

I can't help but smile at my son's enthusiasm. Last summer, he attempted to convince our family militia—before the entire community banded together for security—swords would be a good idea as part of our self-defense. He proved his point when stopping an attack with a heavy plastic practice sword. Some might think Malcolm's fascination with swords is thanks to the apocalypse, but that's not the case. He had an interest in blades well before. A set of practice swords were his gift for his tenth birthday. It's been many months since he's had such an animated conversation about his interests. The threat of attack from Prospect hanging over us has put a shadow over our lives.

After much chatter, Malcolm asks if I'm getting tired.

"Some," I admit.

"Do you want me to read until you fall asleep? I could read softly so it doesn't keep you awake. Then I'll just sit quietly until my shift is over."

Because of the severity of my injuries, I need twenty-four-hour monitoring. After we arrived at The Bowl, where a tent had been set up for triage and a second tent for treatment, things didn't sound good for me. I wasn't sure I'd come home and be in my own bed. But I am home, and while it's not exactly my own bed, I'm immensely grateful. Our queen-sized bed was moved out and two twins moved in, but I'm still sharing a room with my beloved.

And I'm surrounded by my children and grandchildren.

Sarah showed up at The Bowl shortly after I did. Knowing she was okay allowed me to relax. Although Sarah and everyone in our family unit were fine, we lost two of our people in the raid and a few are missing. The losses were dreadful, but Richard Majors, his son Scott, and the other illegitimate leaders of Prospect were all brought to justice. A good portion of the acquisition team willingly surrendered and are now being held in the county jail.

While the bloodshed was kept to a minimum, the rebels still lost around a dozen people, and there were a couple of civilians murdered. The murderer was Fred Lassiter and an accomplice known as Doc Bohm. They were attempting to escape the town when the innocents got in the way. Where Deputy Fred and the Doc are now is unknown.

As much as I hate that killing Richard Majors and his followers was necessary, it gives us hope. It gives me hope my children may have a peaceful future.

Malcolm reads from *Treasure Island* as I drift off to sleep.

# Chapter 46

## *Lucy*

"Lucy, what are you doing here?" Chase asks, his blue eyes twinkling.

"I heard Lorita is one of the prisoners. I want to see her."

Maddie thought Lorita Ceballos was among the dead, but when I saw Mrs. Murphy helping in the medical clinic, she said Lorita was injured but alive. Lorita and the rest from the acquisition team who weren't part of the rebellion are being segregated and kept in the old jail. Mrs. Murphy implied it was for their safety, but I know better. They're prisoners.

I'd be one too if I were still living in The Estates at the time of the overthrow. The only reason I'm not being kept under lock and key is because I was wearing the stupid pink bandana when Dirk Murphy took me to the clinic, automatically designating me as a friendly. Sure. Whatever.

"Lorita?"

"Ceballos. She's—you can't have many female prisoners. Surely, you can figure out who she is."

He gives me a slow nod. "I haven't been in the cells. I'm just helping up front. Let me check with Doyle. Wait here."

Chase is gone several minutes before he comes back into the room, closing the door to the cells with a clank. "Okay. She's here. We have a room for visitation. Doyle's setting it up and will take her in there shortly. You'll be allowed fifteen minutes."

"You're so kind," I snap.

He gives me a smile. "I heard you were injured. You're doing well now? I noticed you had a bit of a limp when you walked in."

"I'm fine."

"Really? Fine?"

I smirk at him and then spin on my not hurt foot. Striding as best I can without a limp, I make my way to the hard plastic waiting room chairs.

I was sent away from the clinic with instructions to keep off my foot after the nurse removed several slivers of glass. The splinter in my arm came out easily, but both my arm and foot are susceptible to infection. When they released me from the clinic, I realized I had nowhere to go. The mansion was gone, and The Estates were under lockdown while everyone was processed and moved here. Mrs. Murphy said I should go next door to the old Rodeway Inn where they've set up temporary housing for anyone who lost theirs in the liberation.

The remaining members of the Bakerville community joined forces with the Prospect rebels to bring down Richard and his son. Scott, Lassiter, and most of the lieutenants were killed. And Janet Kruse who died before my eyes. Lieutenant Alvarez was part of the rebellion, as was Alyssa's brother and all of the new recruits who joined when he did.

Rumor is, Alvarez was responsible for bringing them in, with the sole purpose of a revolution. Another rumor is Alvarez had no idea Dirk Murphy was also part of the rebellion. Seems they had several different groups, each operating independently with only a couple of people knowing the leader of each group.

I'm not sure I believe this, but I heard Toad was one of those overseeing the entire operation.

I must admit, Toad overseeing anything is a surprise. I've always considered him to be unmotivated. While nice enough, he never really seemed to want much out of life. To think he had the ability to organize a town-wide rebellion with several groups independent of each other is remarkable. And unbelievable.

Also remarkable was the number of rebels killed: only around a dozen. And there were very few civilians killed or wounded. While the clinic was hopping when Murphy took me there, the stream of incoming injured quickly dwindled. So much so, one of our doctors was even able to go help the Bakerville group where they were triaging their wounded.

By the time I was treated, the ones still waiting to be seen were minorly injured and were almost all wearing the bright colored arm bands, indicating they were part of the resistance. Very few were regular town folk, and I saw no one from the acquisition team or sentries that I knew to be loyal to Richard. Or thought to be loyal. I never suspected Alvarez or Murphy to be anything but trustworthy and devoted to our town.

The door to the lockup area opens with a grating metallic creak. "We're ready," an unseen voice announces.

"C'mon, Lucy," Chase says.

Forgetting I'm supposed to show how tough I am, I limp to where Chase is holding the door. Doyle, a man I recognize as being in charge of garbage pickup, is waiting on the other side, a bored expression painting his face. He motions me to follow him. After only a dozen yards, he opens a windowed door. Lorita lifts her head, her face etched in sadness, and gives me a nod.

"You'll have fifteen minutes," Doyle says. "Stay on your own side of the table, and don't touch. I'll be watching."

"Well, la di da," Lorita says softly as soon as the door is shut. I move to my seat. As soon as I'm seated, she asks, "Why are you limping?"

"Glass. No big deal. Were you injured?"

She shakes her head. "Slightly, but I'm fine."

"I heard you were shot."

"No, I was shot before being tackled to the ground."

"How long will they keep you here?"

"I do not know. There's probably going to be a trial. Your friend Maddie visited me yesterday."

"She's not my friend."

Tilting her head, Lorita says, "I'm pretty sure she is. She kept you out of harm's way."

"She and Murphy bound me, locked me in a bathroom, and then set the building on fire."

"The building wasn't supposed to go up like it did. They thought the explosion would just create a disturbance—bring us out in the open so we could surrender."

"How do you know this?"

"Maddie told me."

"Yeah, well, she lies."

"I don't think so. She felt badly about me being here. She said it will maybe go better for me since I willingly gave up."

"Did you surrender?"

"Of course. Lieutenant Kruse sent me after the mayor's killers. They had him restrained, but he started fighting back. The women really had little choice."

328

"Ha. Milena hated Richard. Hated him before this ever started and hated him more when he— "

"When he planned to string her up at the gallows? Hate is understandable."

"He offered her a good life! A life of luxury."

"Did he? You think what you and her had to do was going to be easy?"

I lift a shoulder in response.

She gives me a nod. "When they ran to those helping with the uprising, I realized then it was over."

"And you just gave up."

"I told you before, I do what is needed to survive. Now things have changed. Majors is out and . . . someone else will be in. Someone who will lead in a different way. One who may not make our town as prosperous as Majors planned, but he may keep more people alive. Or more may die, I do not know. But I will make it clear I support the new regime."

"Yeah," I say. "Like we have a choice."

"There's always a choice. I heard about the choice you made to keep Captain Murphy alive."

"If I had to do it over again, I'm not sure I'd do the same. Janet could've led— "

"No, she couldn't. She wasn't a leader."

I shake my head. "Anyway, I just wanted to see how you are. If I can, um, be a character witness or something for you, I will."

"Thank you. When you see Captain Murphy, will you thank him for dropping off the reading material for me? Tell him I'm especially grateful for the Bible."

"He brought you a Bible?"

"Among other things."

"I didn't know you— "

"No. Not anymore. I grew up in a Christian home, reading the Bible and praying. Reading from scriptures now makes me wish I could return to that time."

"I doubt I'll see him, but if I do, I'll give him your thanks."

"Did you know the original colonies established by those on the Mayflower were to live in accordance with the Christian faith? That was one of the reasons my parents so badly wished to immigrate to the United States, because of the Christian heritage. They grew up Roman

Catholic but became Protestants when they were newly married. They thought it made sense to move here—uh, never mind, Lucy. Thanks so much for visiting me."

I give a nod as I stand to leave. "I read it too," I say as I step toward the door.

"The Bible?"

"Yeah. Maddie gave me one when I was, uh . . . "

"Yes. And are you a Christian?"

"No, of course not."

"Why do you say it like that?"

I turn to face her. "If I were to do that, wouldn't it be wrong? I mean, you know the things I've done. The things you've done. Maddie too. But she seems to think all she has to do is ask for forgiveness and, *poof,* she'll get it."

"I believe she is correct."

"How? We killed people. And Maddie and I . . . we . . . " I bug my eyes out at her, trying to convey what I don't want to say.

"Yes. I do remember some scriptures. One that sticks with me is, "For all have sinned and fall short of the glory of God." You think we in Prospect invented sin? No. Man has sinned from the time Adam and Eve were kicked out of the garden. God knows this. He hates the sin and wants us to stop and be holy. That's why He sent His son, Jesus, to earth. That's why Jesus died. He died as the ultimate sacrifice for our sinfulness. And when someone truly asks forgiveness, we get the Holy Spirit to help us so we stop sinning."

"But you . . . you still sin."

"Yes. For many years I lived a double life. I would tell my parents and my pastor what they wanted to hear, made them think I was a good little Christian girl. But all along, I knew in my heart I didn't believe. I was only pretending. My mama would often tell me, 'You can't get to heaven on my coattails.'"

"So she knew you were faking it?"

"She was very smart."

"If I see Murphy, I'll tell him you said thanks."

"Turn from your sin, Lucy. Acknowledge Jesus is the Son of God and ask Him to live in you—in your heart."

"And then what? Go to church every Sunday?"

"Maybe. You'll probably want to. You'll want to get to know Him better and let the Holy Spirit guide you."

"Doubtful. See you later." I knock on the window and the door immediately opens.

"Be back for you shortly," Doyle tells Lorita. When we're a couple of feet from the door, he says, "She's right."

"About what?"

"Accepting Christ as your Lord and Savior. If you ask and mean it, your sins will be forgiven."

"Did you listen to our entire conversation?"

"Uh, well, yeah. The speaker was on the entire time."

"Thanks for the privacy."

"This is a jail. There is no privacy."

"Humph."

"Anyway. There's twice daily service at Prospect Cowboy Church on Broadway."

"I'm not a cowboy."

"Being a cowboy isn't required. You just need to be open to learning about the Lord. Next service is at seven this evening."

"Not interested."

# Chapter 47

## *Mollie*

When I awaken, Kelley Hudson is in the room. I can't see her but hear her humming and recognize her tone.

"Kelley?" I say softly.

"Hey, Mollie. Just changing things around."

"Is my output okay?" I ask, regarding the urine bag. Even with our primitive medical items, I'm fortunate to have a line of intravenous fluids going in and a second line to take things out.

"It's what we expect," she answers.

"That's good," I say. While the liquid in and liquid out seems to be working as it should, there's much more involved with my needs— things we've only briefly discussed. And most of those things are unlikely to happen. If my medical issues were limited to sliding down the hillside and breaking my ankle, hip, and back, things might be different. But considering I was already ailing—believed to be terminal, even—there's only so much to be done for me. While the ankle fracture is obvious, and I'm in a cardboard splint to keep it stationary, the hip break is assumed and not being treated separately from the assumed fracture to my spine.

After Kelley finishes the medical stuff, she asks, "How's your pain?"

"No real pain. The headache is even getting better." In addition to the half dose of the narcotic I took before they carried me out of the gully, I had the other half later in the day and, at Belinda's insistence, a full pill before they trucked me home yesterday. I told Belinda to keep the final pill for someone else. I'm still on my regiment of willow bark tincture, turmeric, ginger, and garlic, which helps keep the headache down to a dull roar. Not feeling my hips and back, which were beginning to border on excruciating before my slide down the hillside, is truly a blessing.

"Any new feeling or sensations?"

"The skin on my left arm was tingling earlier, almost like a bug was walking on it. Sarah was in here. I had her check for spiders, but there wasn't anything there."

"That can happen with a SCI."

"SCI?"

"Spinal cord injury."

"Oh, yeah. I heard Belinda and the Prospect doctor talking about that. I just didn't put it together."

"It was good Dr. Brown was able to examine you. And good Jake was able to bring him to the triage tent for a consult. We're going to move you soon. Can I get you anything first?"

"Who's sitting with me next?"

"Calley was out there. I think it's her turn. I'm going to find Leo or someone to help me reposition you. I'll send Calley in to visit until we return."

"Jake's working on reloads in the armory. He could probably help."

"Good idea. I'll be back."

"Thanks, and uh . . . Kelley?"

"Yeah?"

"Thanks again for letting me be here. I know it's a hassle for you and the rest of the team to keep coming over."

She steps back into my view and gives me one of her beautiful smiles. "If it were one of us, this is what we'd want too, to be surrounded by our family and sleeping next to our husband."

"Not exactly next to," I say with a smile. "He scooted his twin bed over next to mine last night, so we're together but separate. That rascal did make a point of saying this morning how nice it was not having me hog the blankets. It seems, had he known separate beds with separate blankets would result in a warmer night of sleep, he would've done it years ago."

Kelley lets out a hearty laugh. "I hope he doesn't say anything to Phil. My husband is constantly complaining about me stealing the covers."

I let out a sigh. "He's being great about it. The children too. But I know . . . how long do you think it'll be?"

Her smile freezes as her eyes fill with tears. "There could be complications with the SCI. We don't know. You're having trouble breathing and swallowing. If things were normal, you'd be on oxygen and other intravenous solutions to give you more nourishment. And you'd be on antibiotics to help prevent the common kidney or urinary tract issues and we'd— "

"I know all this. I know you're doing what you can to keep me comfortable. And I know the sole issue isn't my paralysis but adding in what was already wrong with me. The cancer. How long?"

She shakes her head. "I don't know. Belinda and I discussed it before this. We told you. Just with the tumors and metastasis, or I should say what we believe to be cancer that has metastasized . . . we're only going off our clinical observations."

"Which is what you're doing with my fall too, right? Without x-rays or CAT scans or whatever, you're just going by what you see. And Dr. Brown agreed with Belinda's assessment."

"Yes, Belinda says he did. It's terribly obvious something is causing your paralysis—most likely a fracture. And it's also terribly obvious you have masses in your abdomen and other places. You've lost too much weight. You're having intense pain— "

"Not anymore."

"Yes, I do believe this may be a huge blessing. Your pain was going to become considerably more intense—unbearable even—and we wouldn't have any real way of controlling it."

"Jake prayed about this. Many times, he prayed and asked God to take my pain away. This is certainly not the way I thought God would answer, but . . ."

"His ways are always right," Kelley says. "And God's the one with the answer to your question too. We're going to do our best to give you as much quality of life as we can. How long that will be, I don't know."

"Do you think that quality of life could include wiping the tears out of my ear for me?"

"Definitely. And I'll help you blow your nose too."

Less than a minute after Kelley leaves, Calley comes in. "Hey, Mom." She scoots the chair close to me and plops down with a large sigh. "Man, it's good to sit down. Did Kelley tell you I had an appointment this morning? My baby's fine. I'm measuring right at thirty-six weeks."

"That's wonderful. How are you feeling?"

"Huge. Exhausted."

"Just a few more weeks."

"Katie offered to draw me."

"Like a maternity photo shoot?"

"Something like that. She's working on one now for Sarah, just doing it from memory. She says she wishes she would've thought of it when Sarah was still pregnant. At least for me she was able to take my picture with Malcolm's tablet, that way she doesn't have to get it done before I pop."

"It's brilliant. I so wish we would've thought of the tablet and using it sooner. I love that Katie is drawing too. Who knows when the photos could be developed? I love it."

"It's a good idea for sure. She's doing Sarah in colored pencil. I guess mine will be the same. She's going to sketch the children too, maybe at least one time per year until we can have actual pictures again."

"We should've thought of this before."

"Probably. But up until now, I don't think she was feeling creative, said she started thinking about it while she was camping down at the medical tent. She even started some rough drawings on scratch paper then. We should have her do you too."

"You think so, huh?" I ask with a laugh. "I'm not sure she'd be able to capture my best side right now."

"Not exactly the way you look today, but she can capture your . . . your essence. And your hair. I love the way your hair is now after you cut it short and stopped dying it. You should've done it years ago."

"Is that right? You think the grey suits me?"

She's silent for many minutes before saying, "I think you've become the woman God intended. And I hope someday to be like you."

"Oh, Calley," I say, lifting my wrist the small amount I'm able to, signaling I want her to come to me.

She takes my hand and steps into my view.

"You're amazing," I say. "The way you've acted through all of this, you're such a light in my life."

"Even those times I made fun of you and Jake?"

"You've made fun of us? Oh, you mean before all this happened?"

"Yeah. I never thought . . . Mom, I was sure you guys were just being paranoid all those times you said you were planning for an unknown future. It seemed so stupid then. But now . . . I know we lost Deanne, but if we would've stayed in Casper, I'm not sure any of us would've survived. And we wouldn't be having our baby."

"You and Mike made the choice to act. I know it was scary in those first few days when Mike was attacked. Fear is what— "

"Opened our eyes?"

"You're here now, and soon you'll be cradling your baby in your arms."

"You too, Mom. Maybe you'll get enough feeling and movement back to hold her."

I give a small smile. "Maybe so."

She lets out a sigh and returns to her chair. "Have you talked to Angela much?"

"Much?"

"Since you fell."

"She rode in the back of the truck with me while we were coming home. And she stayed with me the entire time they were getting this room set up for me. We talked, but—is something going on?"

"She blames herself, thinks it's her fault you fell."

I let out a scoff. "How could it be her fault?"

"Don't know. But she thinks it is."

"Is she scheduled to sit with me today?"

"Yes, later."

"I'll talk with her then."

Calley and I chat for several minutes before Kelley, Leo, and Jake arrive to reposition me.

# Chapter 48

## *Lucy*

Even though I told Doyle I'm not interested in going to his church, at six o'clock I start getting ready. At twenty before seven, I leave my hotel room. I arrive at the church, which has several missing windows now covered in cardboard, about five minutes before start time.

The line entering the building completely surprises me. Several people I recognize as workers are at the door greeting people and helping them find seats. As I get closer to the entrance, I start to feel completely out of place. Just as I swivel to leave, I hear someone call my name.

"Hey, I thought that was you," Toad says with a smile. "Are you alone? You can sit with me."

"I was going to head on home."

"C'mon. You walked all this way. Might as well stay and listen."

I bend my neck and let out a quiet sigh. Might as well. He says something to one of the doormen as we pass. "Do you work here?" I ask.

"Work? No. I just help. We're excited to be able to meet here again. For the last several months, we've been meeting in various places, trying to stay ahead of the— " He cuts off with an awkward smile.

"Christianity wasn't outlawed."

"Not officially. But after several of the town's pastors disappeared, we understood what was happening."

"What do you mean *disappeared?*"

"We'll sit here," he says, taking me to a seat near the back. Once we're seated, he leans close to me. "You didn't hear about the disappearances?"

I shake my head.

"It's true," he says. "At least half a dozen plus their wives and families—all pastors or associate pastors. The priest of the Catholic

337

church too. We thought Chaplain Rick too . . . you know, the hospital chaplain?"

"Yeah. I heard he left town."

"Turns out he did. But we thought he was the first. We found out yesterday he left the night Majors took over and was hiding out with the people from Bakerville. But he was killed earlier in the month when— " Toad again looks uncomfortable.

"When what?"

"They were attacked. He was among the dead."

"Attacked by whom?"

He gives me a long look.

"The scout team?" I ask in a whisper.

He gives a shrug. "Seems so."

"Why'd you do it, Toad?"

"Do what?"

"Go against Mayor Majors."

"It's getting ready to start," he says, giving me a smile. "Just enjoy it. We can talk later."

I let out a sigh and consider again how I don't belong here. Not in this building and not sitting next to Toad the Traitor.

As I make a move to leave, Toad gently touches my arm. "I'll answer all your questions after the service. Please stay."

I give a hesitant nod and stop my movement, but I don't exactly relax into my chair. I don't know the preacher, but he's someone I recognize from before the attacks. He starts with a prayer. I don't bother to bow my head or anything but choose to look around at the others gathered.

After a chorus of amens, a lady and a man go up front. She has a guitar, and he sings. They ask us to stand as they begin to play. The music is fine. Not concert quality, but not bad. You wouldn't know it's not a concert by the way the people around me, including Toad, are reacting—feet tapping, singing along; some people are even lifting their hands in the air and swaying along with the music.

They move from the snappy beat of the first song to a slightly slower song, which seems to really get people going. I listen to the words as the man sings about waiting on the Lord, and while he's waiting, he'll serve and worship. During this one, people are even crying and calling out amen.

When the song finishes, the preacher goes back up. He, too, is wiping his eyes. "Thank you, Nancy and Ian. It was beautiful as always. And such a perfect choice." He then turns to those in the chairs. "It's what we've all been doing. We've been waiting to be delivered from the difficulties of the last few months, from the fear of living under what was essentially an iron curtain. And while we were waiting, we were seeking ways we could continue to serve the Lord, ways we could bring those who were broken and without hope to Him. We knew He'd deliver us! We knew God would intervene and set us free!"

The entire room breaks out in applause, with people hugging and crying out how thankful they are. Is that what they thought? This preacher and people like Toad? Did they think they needed to be set free from Richard?

Hearing the preaching, watching the reactions, I realize things in Prospect were more than what I was seeing. The Prospect I was living in was extremely different than the Prospect these people lived in. And I feel like I missed out on something. I missed out on the trust and faith they relied on.

As the preacher continues, I'm reminded of the story I read about Moses. He listened to God and was able to lead the Israelites out of Egypt, giving them freedom from slavery. Moses had faith God would do the things He said. He listened as God spoke to him from a burning bush. If only it were that easy now. If God could speak to me and tell me what I'm supposed to do, that'd be helpful.

**I am.**

I turn to Toad to ask him what he said. His eyes are forward, completely focused on the preacher and everyone else. A feeling of comfort washes over me. My eyes fill as the words the pastor is saying seem to take on new meaning. I hear him, not only with my ears but with my heart, as he tells me God loves me. Jesus loves me.

Me—Lucy Fleming.

Even though I've done awful, terrible things, He loves me. And I can follow Jesus just like the fishermen in the early days of His ministry.

As the guitar begins to softly play, the preacher seems to look right at me as he says, "Can you see that you need Him? Can you see that you need Jesus?"

Toad leans close to me and whispers, "You okay?"

339

"I want to change. I want—no. I *need* what these people have. I think . . . I think I need Jesus. Will you tell me more?"

"Absolutely," he says. "I'd be honored, Lucy."

# Chapter 49

## *Mollie*

When I next open my eyes, the sun is no longer visible from my east-facing room. An oil lamp burns on the nightstand between the twin beds.

"You're awake?" Angela asks softly. "Do you need some water?" After she helps me drink, she asks, "Can I get you anything?"

"I don't think so. Was Kelley or Belinda in recently?"

"About fifteen minutes ago. Took a look at all your bags and tubes and said everything seems to be working as it should for the moment. Someone will reposition you after dinner."

"Where's Gavin?"

"Tim took him to dinner. They'll be here shortly."

"Did you eat?"

"Yeah, I got a plate from the kitchen. Rabbit stew tonight. I have some broth for you."

"Maybe in a bit. Anything exciting happening today?"

"They found another member of our militia. All the missing are now accounted for."

"How many dead?" I ask.

"Two more, giving us a total of four. The last two were found bound. They'd been . . . it seems they were tortured."

"Tortured? Why?"

"We don't know. Evan talked to one of the rebellion leaders, but they're at a loss too. It's . . . strange."

We're both silent for several minutes. Why would two of our people be captured and tortured? It makes zero sense.

"It's nice not having to gather firewood," Angela says. "I barely know what to do with myself with one less duty."

"Ah, but you got the new duty of sitting with me."

"Hardly a chore, Mom."

"Calley said you've been upset."

She's quiet for many moments before saying, "Calley has a big mouth."

"My injury is not your fault."

"Really? It feels like it is. I should've stopped you. I . . . I watched the hillside give way and did nothing."

"You watched and did nothing? You caught a glimpse of what was happening while you were shooting at Majors's henchmen—trying to keep them from killing me. That's hardly doing nothing."

"It wasn't enough," she says in a whisper.

I close my eyes as I try to collect my thoughts. I take a deep breath, causing a coughing fit. Angela quickly stands up close to me, trying to figure out how to help. She's just about to run for Belinda when it stops as suddenly as it started.

Once my breathing is regular, I say, "Remind me not to do that again."

"Does the coughing hurt?"

"Burns a bit. But mostly it's scary. I almost feel like I'm suffocating."

"Will it get better?"

I close my eyes while I consider her question.

"Mom?" she asks quietly.

"I'm still awake. I was just thinking. Who's around tonight? You kids and the spouses? Alvin and Dodie? And where's Jake?"

"Dinner. I think Katie is on overnight duty in the clinic. She starts at ten. She'll be taking care of you, too, you know."

"Yes. Can you see if you can get everyone gathered? I'd like to talk to all of you."

"What's this about, Mom?"

"Please?"

"Okay . . . " she says slowly. "When Tim arrives with Gavin, I'll have him round everyone up. Of course, most of them will probably show up when he does."

"Perfect, he can just gather the stragglers."

"Did you want to— "

"Wait until everyone's here, okay? It's easier for me if I just say it once."

"You're scaring me, Mom."

"Oh, honey. I can't— " I blink my eyes several times. "I'm going to share an answer to prayer. Would you read to me? From Psalms. Um, 107, I think."

She lets out a huff before grabbing the Bible from the nightstand. After a bit of flouncing and a loud sigh, both of which almost make me laugh, she starts to read. "Give thanks to the Lord, for He is good; His love endures forever." She pauses before asking, "Is this the right one?"

"I think so. Can you read a little more? I'll know for sure soon."

As she reads several more verses, I begin to think I've got the wrong spot. Then she says, "Then they cried out to the Lord in their trouble, and He delivered them from their distress."

"Yes! This is it. Keep going."

As she reads about the mighty power of God and His forgiveness, I'm struck with how utterly amazing our God is. The people cried out to the Lord in their trouble, and He brought them out of their distress. Just like He did for me. While I may not get the complete miracle I was praying for, the miracle of healing, I'm relieved of my distress— of my pain.

"Let them give thanks to the Lord for His unfailing love and His wonderful deeds for mankind."

"Amen," I say.

Angela stops reading. "Is that it? That's all you wanted to hear?"

"That part just . . . " I let out a sigh. "It means a lot to me."

"Keep reading?"

"Please."

She finishes the chapter and then I have her turn to Psalm 91, which we've been focusing on since early into the havoc. "Do you want to read it with me?" she asks.

"I still haven't learned the entire thing," I admit. "But I'll join where I can. Do you know it all by heart?"

She lets out a laugh. "No. But Tim does."

"Jake too."

"I know, I've heard them both reciting it," Angela says. "Funny, isn't it, how they've both really taken to the scriptures? And not just to say them for something to say, but to live them. I never . . . I never considered the need for a Godly man, a Godly marriage. Even though Tim and I both *said* we were Christians, we weren't like we are now. Now I truly feel God leading us. I knew we were both saved before, but we weren't spending time with God and getting to know Him. And we'd certainly never prayed together."

"Same," I say with a laugh. "Until a few years ago, when Jake and I hit rock bottom— "

"After Sharri and Kenny died?"

"Yes, after they died and we grew so far apart. I never thought we'd find our way back to each other. But God made a way."

"I never told you this, but . . . Tim and I, we weren't . . . we were talking about getting a divorce."

"You were? When?"

"When the attacks happened. He was working out of town so much, and I was just . . . just done. The week of the attacks, when he was home while they fixed his rig, I told him then. I told him I wanted to separate."

"Oh . . . I didn't know. I'm sorry."

"The attacks saved my marriage—that and me getting shot in the bottom." She lets out a hearty laugh. "He was really great to me while I was recovering. It was then he told me we were missing God in our marriage."

A rumble comes from the other room. "Speaking of your husband," I say. "Sounds like dinner's over."

"I'll have Tim gather everyone."

It takes about thirty minutes for everyone available to meet in my bedroom. While I wanted to bring Tony and Lily over, too, they're living with their dad in the ski lodge still. Jake suggested he could bring them, along with Jason, over after breakfast tomorrow. Leo's on guard duty, so he's also missing.

"Okay, Mom," Angela says. "You've had me freaking out for the last hour. What's going on?"

"There's something I haven't told you. I haven't told any of you— except Jake. He knows."

"About your injury?" Sarah asks.

"No . . . not exactly. I've been waiting until after we finished the attack on Prospect to tell you. You see— "

"About your sickness?" Malcolm asks.

"Shh," Calley says. "Don't interrupt."

"Malcolm's right," I say. "You all know I haven't been feeling well."

"But you were getting better," Calley says.

"She wasn't," Katie says. "Not really. Were you, Mom?"

"No, I wasn't. I'm not better."

"Right," Calley says, stepping close so her face is near mine. "Because of the fall. You're paralyzed, but lots of people . . . it's not that big of a deal, right? There's lots of people in wheelchairs. Or there used to be. Your back can heal, and you can— "

"Wait, Calley," Jake says, his voice full of compassion.

"The fall isn't my main issue. In fact, it probably did me a favor." I say the words in a rush. "My sickness, it's probably cancer."

There're a few gasps and someone, maybe Katie, makes a sobbing sound. Calley lifts her head and steps back. "But it won't be long until the hospital is functioning again, right? Then they can treat you."

"Maybe, if I had started treatment months ago. But now . . . no. It's spread. The cancer has spread to the point where Belinda and Kelley believe I'm terminal."

"No, Mom," Calley whispers. There's more crying, including Malcolm, who's within my view. Jake has his arm wrapped around his shoulders while Malcolm buries his head.

"Jake?" I say, my voice shaky.

He puts his free hand on my shoulder. "The back aches and weight loss, they were signs," Jake says in an equally wobbly tone. "The day after the sniper attack, Belinda told us. Told us she felt new masses and believes them to be on your mom's bones. Bone cancer. Even if she could have chemo or radiation tomorrow, it wouldn't help. It's too far advanced."

"What about the doctor in Prospect?" Angela asks. "Maybe he can do something."

I take a shallow breath so I don't choke, just enough to gather myself. "Belinda told him about all of it when he was seeing me. He agreed with her. And he agreed the only thing to be done is to keep me comfortable. Quite honestly, the injury is a blessing. The meds we have available would not be enough soon. The pain would be excruciating."

"You're dying?" Calley asks.

"I wish . . . I don't have some elaborate speech to give you about it," I say with a squeak to my voice. "Other than to say, our God is amazing. As my pain has been increasing, I've been praying for a miracle. The fall gave me that miracle. Not the way I wanted! But I don't hurt."

"I'm still praying for full healing," Jake clarifies.

"I've suspected Mom was sick," Katie says. "I even almost asked a few times. But there was always something going on. And as we've certainly learned over the last several months, death is a part of life. I'm just— " She takes a breath as tears threaten to overcome her. "I'm just so glad we have this time with you. And while I'm with Jake on praying for full healing, I'm also exceedingly grateful you aren't in pain."

"Mom had me read Psalm 107 earlier," Angela says. "It seemed an odd choice then, but I understand parts of it now."

"Will you read it to us?" Katie asks.

"Just a couple of verses." As Angela opens the Bible, there's much sniffing and nose blowing. She clears her throat and starts to read, then shakes her head when she's overcome with emotion.

"Let me," Alvin says, reaching for the Bible. In his strong voice, he says, "Then they cried out to the Lord in their trouble, and He brought them out of their distress. He stilled the storm to a whisper; the waves of the sea were hushed. They were glad when it grew calm, and He guided them to their desired haven. Let them give thanks to the Lord for His unfailing love and His wonderful deeds for mankind."

"Oh, that is good," Sarah says. "While I know the Bible tells us God answers prayer, as evidenced in this passage, it's still hard when it's not the answer we want. I want you to get well, Mom, to be fully whole, walking, and pain-free."

"But you also wanted Tate to come back," Malcolm says. "God took him too. And Keith, Lois, and Deanne."

"It's true," Sarah says. "Like Katie said, I'm glad we have this time with Mom. These last few months we've been able to live together on the mountain as a family. Some days have been terribly hard, but I'm very thankful for this time. And I know I'll see Tate again someday, thanks to his returning to Christ in those weeks before he went missing. Mom definitely has a miracle in being pain-free. But the biggest miracle for all of us happened over two-thousand years ago on the cross."

"And three days later when He rose again," Jake says. "The miracle isn't just Jesus' death but that He didn't stay dead. He died for our sins, but the resurrection fulfilled the prophecies and gave us the cornerstone of our faith. And gives us hope for when we die."

"And gives us eternal life," I say. "Surrounded by His glory."

346

# Chapter 50

## *Calley*

Mom told us she was dying on a Tuesday. It was one of the most painful days of my life. Especially realizing there was nothing we could do. I knew she was sick; we all did. But I still held out hope things would go back to normal—or we'd at least have better medical care—and she'd get well.

In the last few months, I could see how much weight she was losing. I had these little fantasies of spoon feeding her back to health. Part of me thought all she needed was a few good meals and to slow down, to stay in bed and just eat. After she fell, I still held out hope. She was definitely forced to stay in bed and recover then. But when she told us she was terminal and had been before she ever slid down that hillside, my world came crashing down.

Mike held me for hours as I cried. Having just lost his mom a few months before, he knew what I was feeling. At least for me I'd be able to say goodbye, to spend more time with her. His mom was taken in an instant with a bullet. At the same time, I'm not sure that wasn't easier. Knowing someone is dying, wasting away bit by bit and watching as it happens, is hard.

The day after Mom told us she was terminal, our community started moving off the mountain. The wagons and teams made moving home a slow process. In addition to the horses, the quads and trailers were also utilized, along with any gasoline-powered vehicles, loaded as full as possible for the trip down the hill. Jake's diesel and the others using the same fuel were allotted enough for two trips. We're leaving most things behind, taking only what's needed for the summer months. If things are still the same when winter approaches, we'll move back up to the resorts.

Mom, Doris, Aaron Ogden, me, and others unable to walk were transported down on the last trip. The able-bodied walked, leading the goats and sheep with them, camping overnight when they were about three-quarters of the way. Even Sarah walked while carrying Tate and helping the rest of her children. Of course, she had plenty of help from not only our family but the entire community to make sure they arrived safely. The cattle were taken a few days later, being driven by the horses in an old-fashioned cattle drive.

Also, on the final trip down, our dead from the winter were brought home, with one of the trucks dedicated as the hearse. The remains of those close to us were moved to Mom and Jake's icehouse until we all returned home and could dig the graves. Doris's daughter Lindsey was laid to rest next to her husband, Logan, who was killed last summer a few miles from Bakerville. Lois and Deanne were also buried. We had a nice service for them. Mom was even brought out, strapped to her board and gently placed on a camping cot. Jake was concerned about her being allowed to participate, but both Belinda and Mom said it didn't matter much.

Even though we had no remains to bury, Tate and Keith were included in the service. The hope they'd miraculously walk out of the mountains when spring arrived has faded. I think Sarah knew all along it was unlikely to happen, but she still held on to the small glimmer of possibility—held on for a miracle. I know Sarah put on a brave front of accepting Tate's death, but I'd often watch her as she'd stare out the window or when we'd be outside. She'd be looking for him. That stopped after the attack on Prospect, after Mom was so severely injured and a few from our community were killed. Now she seems to have resigned herself to the fact he's not coming back.

One day, I noticed a look pass between Jason Hatch and Sarah. I'm not saying there's something going on between them—both are still mourning the loss of their spouses—but there could be something. They'd make a good match. And in today's world, it makes sense for widowed parents to team up. Between them, they have six children. The smart thing to do would be to join forces.

The tiny house Jake bought on a whim in the early days of the attacks was left on the mountain, along with the big RV and camp trailer Leo purchased on one of their salvage trips. On Jake's first trip down the mountain, he brought Sarah's camp trailer, which had been loaned to another family to use over the winter. The family has decided to move into Prospect. After Majors was neutralized, the town has made huge advancements toward rebuilding. While Majors talked big about making Prospect a leader in the region, his ways of doing so weren't right. Now they have a chance to truly rebuild.

The ham radio was left on the mountain. The owner of the radio is among those staying behind and living on the mountain through the summer. They've promised to bring us any news about the nationwide rebuilding efforts as they hear them. With summer here, it's an easier hike or horse ride back and forth. The final broadcast we heard before coming home was the most promising to date. Denver is being rebuilt. They even have power in parts of it.

There was a call put out for people with specific skills to make their way there and help with the effort. We've lost a few of the single men and one family already. Jerry McCullough and Milena Maynard have also talked about going, but they're getting married first. Joining the ceremony will be Paul Cameron and Sally-Ann Hinkle—another double wedding. While Sally-Ann will never fully recover from the shooting that almost took her life, and did take the life of my mother-in-law Deanne, she's a fireball and isn't letting anything keep her from happiness.

Also brought down the mountain, towed by one of Phil Hudson's old pickups, was the tiny camp trailer of Aaron and Laurie Ogden's. Used as bachelor quarters over the winter, Laurie joked she'd never get the smell of feet out of it. Katie agreed, saying she didn't think it was a joke at all. With so many of the single men leaving to go to Denver and other families moving away, we won't need as much housing next year but can certainly use it now. We're full up on the homestead.

Like on the mountain, Jake set up twin beds in their bedroom. That was the easiest way to give Mom the care she needed. Belinda and TJ are living with us again, and also Madison, her baby Emma, Katie, and Laurie—four of the main people on the medical team, available to give Mom round-the-clock tending. Not that they did much. Belinda explained the concept of palliative care: keeping Mom comfortable.

Katie continued with her sketches. She drew the most amazing picture of Mom, one she found on the tablet. Malcolm had taken it when we were living at the dude ranch. She was sitting in a chair with a book in her hand, looking at the camera with a kind, questioning smile. She looked so beautiful, so at peace.

We were only home for a week when things started to go wrong with either the fall injury or the cancer. She still didn't have any pain.

But her body was shutting down, no longer able to use the nutrition the IV was giving. We'd take turns spooning broth or water into her, but it didn't help. She spent her time sleeping and was often confused when she was awake. It was hard to watch.

Belinda was sitting with her when she realized the end was close. When she called us in, I was surprised to see Mom more alert than she'd been in days. We were all there, with Jake holding one hand and Sarah holding the other. Belinda had me sit on the bed at her side. Angela, Katie, and Malcolm, along with Tony and Lily, were also right there, everyone sitting close and touching Mom, trying to show how much we loved her. Mike, Leo, Tim, Jason Hatch, and the rest living on our homestead were in the room but farther back.

I watched as a tear tracked down Mom's cheek. She smiled the sweetest smile I'd ever seen. Then she closed her eyes.

We buried her in our homestead cemetery. Jake asked that Mom be buried slightly away from the others so there will be space for him when he goes.

Today is the one-year mark since five planes were blown from the sky and our lives changed forever. David Hammer led a special memorial service commemorating the day. Mike and I didn't go to the short ceremony, but the rest of the family did. Everyone is much too busy with the daily chores to take too much time off.

The garden has now been in for several weeks, and the weeding takes a lot of time. There are new baby goats and lambs and lots of milk. Art and Jake are training the sheep on the milking stand. They started working with them before their lambs were born. The first-time moms seem to be doing okay with it. While the sheep aren't a dairy breed, they're giving enough to make the efforts worth it. And the lambs don't seem to be suffering with sharing. Sarah and Angela have even made soft sheep cheese.

I drop a kiss on my baby's head. Her soft hair tickles my nose. After a quick labor, she was born a month to the day after my mom died. Mike and I named her Mollie Deanne, in honor of our mothers.

Thank you for spending your time with the people of Bakerville! If you have five minutes, you'd make this writer very happy if you could write a short Amazon review.

I appreciate you!

Completing this series is bittersweet. And saying goodbye to Mollie forever wasn't easy. Perhaps one day we'll return to Bakerville and catch up with Jake and Mollie's children and grandchildren as they rebuild their little corner of Wyoming.

In the meantime, we'll join the group who left the mountain. The *Montana Mayhem* series follows Tamra, Rochelle, Leanne, Victoria, Kimba, and the rest as they strike on their own while searching for the desires of their heart.

Unfortunately, the road will not be easy, and sometimes the heart is hardened and deceitful. When things don't work out as they hoped, will they become stranded in the wilderness? Or will each be able to find their way home?

# Also by Millie Copper

### The Havoc in Wyoming Series
When a series of coordinated attacks devastate the United States, the people of Bakerville, Wyoming, must come together to survive. Unfortunately, not everyone has the town's best interest at heart. Some are striving for personal gain during the apocalypse.

### The Montana Mayhem Series
A group from Bakerville, Wyoming strikes out on their own while searching for the desires of their heart. Unfortunately, the road will not be easy, and sometimes the heart is hardened and deceitful. When things don't work out as they hoped, will they become stranded in the wilderness? Or will each be able to find their way home?

### The Dakota Destruction Series
After a series of coordinated attacks devastate the United States, Katie and Leo sacrifice everything to help their country. But some things aren't as they seem. Is it time to go home and start fresh, or can something good come out of this terrible situation?

### The Lights of the Collapse Series
As martial law descends and society crumbles, families must band together to survive, finding strength in their unity amidst the chaos. But with danger lurking around every corner and the very fabric of reality seeming to unravel, they discover that the greatest threats might be closer than they ever imagined.

### In The October Fall World
In the blink of an eye, an EMP changed everything for Lauren and her family. Now they are in a fight for survival, trying to keep their loved ones alive as society collapses around them. Their once peaceful town of Cody, Wyoming has turned into a powder keg. And with law enforcement a thing of the past, evil lurks around every corner.

## In The As The Light Dies World

Lisa Bentley thought having her daughter attacked and left for dead was the worst thing that could happen. She was wrong. She and her family lived an ideal life operating a bed and breakfast in the perfect Wyoming town. That world came crashing down when her daughter was attacked.

## Nonfiction Books

Millie has penned seven nonfiction, traditional food focused books, sharing how, with a little creativity, anyone can transition to a real foods diet without overwhelming their food budget. Many of her books also include preparedness and food storage tips.

Find these titles at MillieCopper.com

# Acknowledgments

Thanks to:

Ameryn Tucker, my editor, beta reader, and daughter wrapped in one. I had a story I wanted to tell, and Ameryn encouraged me and helped me bring it to life.

My youngest daughter, Kes, graphic artist extraordinaire, who pulled out the vision in my head and brought it to life to create the original cover. And to Dauntless Cover Design for the amazing current version.

Sheri at Light Hand Proofreading for not only looking for those pesky typos but also sharing in the creative process.

My husband, who gave me the time and space I needed to complete this dream and was very patient as I'd tell him the same plot ideas over and over and over.

Two more daughters and a young son, who willingly listen to me drone on and on about story lines and ideas while encouraging me to "keep going."

My amazing Beta Readers! Thanks to Ginger, Barbara, Dianna, and Tammy for your help in creating the final story. Your insights and abilities to see the things I miss are very much appreciated!

And to you, my readers, for spending your time with the people of Bakerville, Wyoming. If you have five minutes, you'd make this writer very happy if you could leave a review. I appreciate you!

# About the Author

Millie Copper, writer of Cozy Apocalyptic fiction and practical preparedness manuals, uses her homesteading, preparedness, and off-grid living experience as a guide to writing her 39 (and counting!) Christian Post-Apocalyptic fiction books, including the Amazon bestselling series Havoc in Wyoming.

Millie has penned nine nonfiction, traditional food focused books, sharing how, with a little creativity, anyone can transition to a real foods diet without overwhelming their food budget.

She has also authored hundreds of articles on her Homespun Oasis blog about traditional foods, alternative health, homesteading, and preparedness—many times all within the same piece.

Find Millie at www.MillieCopper.com
Facebook: www.facebook.com/MillieCopperAuthor/
Amazon: www.amazon.com/author/milliecopper
BookBub: https://www.bookbub.com/authors/millie-copper
Instagram: https://www.instagram.com/cozyapoc
YouTube: https://www.youtube.com/@MillieCopperWrites